"Stay here," he whispered, and reached beneath his tuxedo jacket to pull his gun from his holster. Armed, he headed toward her bedroom.

"Be careful," she whispered back, her sweet voice trembling with concern. For him?

Her words touched something inside Whit—something that he'd closed off years ago. The part of him that had yearned to have someone—anyone—give a damn about him. Of course she didn't really care, but those words distracted him enough that when he stepped inside the bedroom, the intruder got the drop on him. Before his eyes could even adjust to the darkness, something struck his head—knocking him down and knocking him out—leaving the princess at the mercy of the intruder...

D1098632

THE PRINCESS PREDICAMENT

BY
LISA CHILDS

...quin (UK) policy is to use papers that are natural, renewable and
...able products and made from wood grown in sustainable forests.
...g and manufacturing processes conform to the legal environme
...ations of the country of origin.

...d and bound in Spain
...ckprint CPI, Barcelona

First published in Great Britain 2013
by Mills & Boon, an imprint of Harlequin (UK) Limited,
Eton House, 18-24 Paradise Road, Richmond, Surrey TW9 1SR

© Lisa Childs 2013

ISBN: 978 0 263 90361 4
ebook ISBN: 978 1 472 00722 3

46-06

Harle[...] [...]
recycl[...] . The
loggin[...] ntal
regula[...]

Printe[...]
by Bla[...]

Bestselling, award-winning author **Lisa Childs** writes paranormal and contemporary romance for Mills & Boon. She lives in Michigan with her two daughters, a talkative Siamese and a long-haired Chihuahua who thinks she's a rottweiler. Lisa loves hearing from readers, who can contact her through her website, www.lisachilds.com, or snail-mail address, PO Box 139, Marne, MI 49435, USA.

To Tara Gavin and Melissa Jeglinski,
with deep appreciation for your professional expertise
and your warm friendship!

Chapter One

Six months earlier...

"I'm going to kill him! Let me in there!"

Whit Howell had been hired as the king's bodyguard to protect him from political threats and criminals—not from his own daughter. But as furious as Princess Gabriella St. Pierre was at the moment, she posed the greatest threat Whit had encountered yet during the ten weeks he'd been on the job.

"Your royal highness," he addressed her as protocol required even though they were alone in the hallway outside the door to the king's wing of the palace. "Your father has retired for the night and will not be disturbed."

"You damn well better believe he's going to be disturbed," she said, her usually soft, sweet voice rising to a nearly hysterical shout. "He'll be lucky to be alive when I'm done with him!" She rushed toward the double mahogany doors, but Whit stepped in front of them.

She slammed into him, her breasts flattening against his chest. With her stiletto heels on, her forehead came to his chin. Her hair—a thick golden brown, was falling over the tiara on her head and into her face and rubbing against his throat.

With her face flushed and caramel-brown eyes flashing with temper, she had never been more beautiful. He doubted she would graciously accept that compliment, though, so he bit his tongue to hold it back. Of course he had noticed she was attractive before but in the kind of untouchable, one-dimensional way that a model in a magazine was attractive. She hadn't seemed real then.

She certainly hadn't acted like any woman he'd ever known. Not only was she beautiful but also sweet and gracious—even to the people her father considered servants. She had seemed more fairy-tale fantasy than reality.

She was real now. And quite touchable. She put her hands on his arms and tried to shove him aside, so she could get through the doors to her father's rooms.

While she was tall, she was slender—with not enough muscle to budge him. She let out a low growl of frustration and then fisted her hands and started pounding on his chest. "Get out of my way! Get out of my way!"

Damn. If she raised her voice any louder, she was likely to disturb the king. And Whit couldn't lose this security job. Assignments like this had been hard to come by the past three years. So he stepped closer to her, using his body to gently push her back from the door. She kept swinging even as she stumbled. So he caught her around the waist and lifted her—up high to swing her over his shoulder. Then he touched a button on the two-way radio in his ear.

"Aaron?"

"Put me down!" Princess Gabriella screamed, pounding on his back now.

He crossed the wide hall, moving farther away from the tall wood doors to the king's wing. Then he touched the button again to call his partner. Former partner. They were no longer in the security business together. They had actually been hired separately to protect the king.

It was Aaron's night off, which he'd had to postpone until after the ball that had been held earlier that evening. But usually Aaron would still be on the job; the man was always on the job.

"Aaron? Timmer?"

Maybe his partner answered but Whit couldn't hear him over the princess's shouts. Her yelling had drawn some of the other palace guards to the hall outside the king's private quarters. Whit gestured at one of the men he'd personally hired, a man with whom he'd served in Afghanistan, like he had with Aaron Timmer. He could trust him to guard King St. Pierre while he deposited the princess in her private rooms.

"Stop! Put me down!" she ordered, her tone nearly as imperious as her father's.

There was none of the sweetness and graciousness Whit had seen in her the past couple of months that he'd been guarding the king. While she had always talked to him as she did to all the *help,* with him she had seemed especially shy and nervous—nothing like the woman currently pounding on his back. The sweet woman had attracted him; the angry woman exasperated and excited him.

As he carried her past the other guard, she implored the man, "Stop him!"

Like he trusted the guard, the guard trusted Whit,

a lot more than Aaron trusted him now. The guard let them pass.

"You creep!" she hurled insults as she pounded harder on his back. "You son of a bitch!" She added some even more inventive insults, using words he wouldn't have thought someone as privileged as she would even know. Then she ordered him, "Get your hands off me!"

She wriggled in his grasp, her breasts pushing against his back while her hip rubbed against his shoulder. She had curves in all the right places—curves that he wanted to touch…

But he shouldn't have been able to get his hands on her in the first place. Since the day, as an infant, she had been brought home to the palace, there had been threats to her safety. People had tried to kidnap her to ransom her for money or political influence from the king. To make sure that none of those abduction attempts were successful, she had been protected her entire life but never more so than now. Usually…

"Where the hell's *your* bodyguard?" he wondered aloud. Even though he hated the woman who protected the princess, he couldn't criticize how the former U.S. Marshal did her job. She went above and beyond to keep the young heiress safe; she had even had plastic surgery so that she looked exactly like Gabriella St. Pierre.

Could it be that they had switched places…

It made more sense that the woman he'd slung over his shoulder was the bodyguard than the princess… because the bodyguard rarely let the princess out of her sight. Unless she had secured her in her rooms and was now masquerading as her.

For what purpose?

To attack the king?

After the announcement her father had made at the ball that evening, the princess had more reason—a damn good reason—to want to hurt the man who had so hurt and humiliated her. Whit had done the right thing to not let her into the monarch's wing of rooms. Because if she really was the princess, he could understand why she was so pissed, and he wouldn't have blamed her had she wanted to kill her own father. But he couldn't let her—or her bodyguard—complete the task.

Which woman was she?

It mattered to him. He didn't want his pulse racing like crazy over the bodyguard. He didn't want his hands tingling with the need to touch her wriggling body. He had never been attracted to the former Marshal, and he didn't want to be.

Charlotte Green had already cost him too much. Just like every other woman he'd ever had contact with, she hadn't given a damn about him. Maybe she didn't really give a damn about the princess, either.

No guard stood sentry at the entrance to the princess's suite. He pushed open the unlocked door and strode down the hall to her private rooms and found no security there either. If the princess had been left in her wing of the palace, Charlotte Green had left her unprotected. No matter how much he despised her, he doubted she would have done that. But she wouldn't have let the royal heiress go running off on her own, either.

Sure, they were *inside* the palace. But that didn't mean they were safe, especially with guests from the ball spending the night in the palace. And even if they weren't, sometimes the greatest threats to one's life were the people closest to them. The princess had learned that tonight.

She must have also learned that yelling and struggling wasn't going to compel him to release her because she'd fallen silent and still. Her body was tense against his. And warm and soft…

And entirely distracting.

He needed to deposit her in her rooms and get the hell back to his post. Using his free hand, the one not holding tight to the back of her toned thigh, he opened the door to her sitting room. Painted a bright yellow, the room was sunny and completely different from her father's darkly paneled rooms. After going inside, he released her, and she moved, sliding down his body— every curve pressing against him. He bit back a groan as desire overwhelmed him, and he was the tense one now.

As her feet touched the floor, she stepped back, and then stumbled and fell against him. He caught her shoulders in his hands to steady her, and he realized she'd lost a shoe somewhere along the route to her room. She stood before him in only one stiletto slip-on sandal. She really was a fairy-tale princess; she was freaking Cinderella.

No, that wasn't right.

His mom had taken off early in his childhood, leaving him with a father who'd had little time to read him fairy tales. But Whit had picked up enough from movies and TV shows based on them to realize he'd gotten it wrong. If she was Cinderella, then she would be the bodyguard and not Gabriella.

"Who are you?" he asked.

Beneath the hair falling across her brow, lines of

confusion furrowed. Then she blinked brown eyes wide with innocence. Real or feigned?

"You know who I am," she haughtily replied.

"No one can really know who you are," he said, "but you."

She shivered, as if his words had touched a chord deep inside her. As if he'd touched her. And he realized that he held her yet and that his fingers almost absently stroked over the silky skin of her bare shoulders. Her gown was strapless and a rich gold hue only a couple shades darker than her honey-toned skin. She was so damn beautiful.

But beauty had never affected Whit before. He wasn't like his partner—his former partner. Aaron Timmer fell quickly and easily for every pretty face. Not Whit, though. He was a professional.

So he forced himself to let go of her shoulders and step back. And that was when he heard it. Her little shuddery gasp for breath as if she'd been holding hers, too—as if she'd been waiting for him to do something. Else. Like move closer and lower his head to hers…

But besides her gasp, he heard another noise—a low thud like someone bumping into something in the dark. Despite the brightly painted walls, the sitting room was dimly lit, but small enough that Whit would have noticed someone lurking in the shadows. However, a door off the room stood ajar, darkness from her bedroom spilling out with another soft thud.

Someone was already waiting to take Princess Gabriella to bed. But she gasped again—this time with fear—and he realized she'd heard the noise, too. And she wasn't expecting anyone to be inside her bedroom.

"Stay here," he whispered and reached beneath his

tuxedo jacket to pull his gun from his holster. Armed, he headed toward her bedroom.

"Be careful," she whispered back, her sweet voice trembling with concern. For him?

Her words touched something inside Whit— something that he'd closed off years ago—the part of him that had yearned to have someone—anyone—give a damn about him. Of course she didn't really care, but those words…

Distracted him enough that when he stepped inside the bedroom, the intruder got the drop on him. Before his eyes could even adjust to the darkness, something struck his head—knocking him down and knocking him out—leaving the princess at the mercy of the intruder…

BLOOD SEEPED INTO his blond hair, staining the short silky strands. Gabriella pressed her fingers to the wound, gauging the depth of it. Would it need stitches? Had he been hit hard enough for the injury to be fatal?

She moved her fingers to his throat. He had already loosened the collar of his silk shirt and undone his bow tie, which dangled along the pleats of the shirt. So she had easy access to the warm skin of his neck. At first his pulse was faint, but then it suddenly quickened.

She glanced at his face and found his dark eyes open and staring up into hers. How could he be so blond but have such dark, fathomless eyes? The man was a paradox—a mystery that had fascinated her since the day he'd walked into the palace to guard her father.

She had been able to think of little else but him. No matter where she'd been—fashion show or gallery opening or movie premiere—her mind had been on him—which had probably made her even more distracted and nervous every time the press had interviewed her.

She had been looking forward to tonight—to seeing him in a tuxedo. To blend in, all the security team had worn black tie. But she had seen only Whit, looking like every young woman's fantasy of Prince Charming. Then her father had made his horrible pronouncement and shattered all Gabriella's illusions of a fairy-tale happily-ever-after…

"You're alive?" she asked.

While he'd opened his eyes, he had yet to move—to even draw a breath. Of course he wasn't dead, but he must have been stunned. In shock? Concussed?

Finally he nodded, then winced and repeated her ridiculous question, "You're alive?"

Her lips twitched into a smile. "I'm fine."

"The intruder didn't take you," he said, as if surprised that she wasn't gone.

"No." She shuddered at the thought of being abducted, as she had nearly been so many times before…until the former U.S. Marshal had become her bodyguard a few years ago. As well as protecting her, the ex-Marshal had taught her how to defend herself. Fortunately Gabriella hadn't been put in that position tonight. But she wished she could have defended Whit and saved him from the blow he'd taken to the head.

"Who hit me?" he asked, "Charlotte?"

She chuckled at the thought of her bodyguard knocking him out in the dark. Charlotte would not have been so cowardly, as cowardly as Gabby had been when she'd allowed her father's pronouncement at the ball to stand instead of immediately speaking up. And when she had finally gathered her courage and her anger, this man had stopped her from talking to the king. She should have been angry with him. But she only felt relief when he had finally opened his eyes. The three minutes he'd been unconscious had seemed like a lifetime to Gabby.

"Charlotte?" he repeated but his tone was different now, as if he suspected that *she* might actually be her bodyguard.

That was nearly as ridiculous as Charlotte striking him. "It all happened so fast that I have no idea who it could be. After hitting you, he ran out the door. All I saw was that he was dressed in black pants and a black sweatshirt with the hood pulled tight around his face."

"It was a man?"

She nodded. "Tall and thin with no curves. But I suppose it could have been a woman." At all those fashion shows and movie premieres, she had met many tall, thin women. "But not Charlotte."

"No," he agreed, but tentatively, as if he debated taking her word for it.

"You don't trust me?" she asked, wondering if she should be offended or amused. Certainly it wasn't good to be thought a liar but that wasn't the issue for her.

Most people didn't consider her clever enough to be able to pull off any deception. The public believed she was an empty-headed heiress. They weren't being cruel or unfair. Because she was naturally shy and introverted, nerves got the better of her during interviews, and she usually babbled incoherently—earning the nickname of Princess Gabby.

"I'm not even sure who you are," he admitted, his

dark eyes narrowing with suspicion as he studied her face.

He really believed she might be Charlotte Green. Again she was flattered instead of offended. Most people might mistake the former U.S. Marshal for her— from a distance. Along with already having the same build and coloring, Charlotte had had plastic surgery so their faces looked alike, too. Except Charlotte had a beauty and wisdom that came with being six years older and so much more worldly than Gabriella. Her bodyguard was tough and independent while Gabby was anything but that.

Charlotte would not have been passed off tonight from one fiancé to another—publicly humiliated during the ball. What was worse was that the man who had traded Gabriella to the highest bidder like a brood mare at auction was her own father.

She expelled a ragged breath of frustration. "I wish I was Charlotte," she admitted. "Then I wouldn't be engaged to marry a stranger. I wouldn't have had people trying to kidnap me since I was a baby just so they could get to my father. No one would even care who I am."

"I would care," he said, with a charm of which she had not thought him capable.

She had thought him tough and cynical and dangerous and ridiculously handsome and sexy. She'd thought entirely too much of Whitaker Howell since he had stepped inside the palace ten weeks ago. She had also talked about him, asking the men he'd served with in Afghanistan to tell her about him. And the more she'd learned, the more fascinated and attracted she had become.

Now he was lying on her bedroom floor with her

straddling his hard, muscular body while she leaned over him. Her fingers were still in his hair. No longer probing the wound, she was just stroking the silky blond strands.

He must have become aware of their positions, too, because his hands clasped her waist—probably to lift her off. But before he could, she leaned closer. She had to know—and since he would probably never be this vulnerable again, she had only this chance—so she pressed her mouth to his to see how he would taste.

Like strong coffee and dark chocolate—like everything too rich and not good for her. Instead of pushing her away, his hands clutched her waist and pulled her closer. And he kissed her back.

No. He took over the kiss and devoured her—with his lips and his teeth and his tongue. He left her gasping for breath and begging for more. And instead of ignoring her, as he had earlier, he gave her more. He kissed her deeply, making love to her mouth—making her want him to make love to her body. She leaned closer, pushing her breasts against his chest.

He reached for the zipper at the back of her dress, his fingers fumbling with the tab before freezing on it. "We can't do this," he said, as if trying to convince himself. "I—I need to report the intruder—need to lock down the palace and grounds…"

She would have been offended that he thought of work instead of her…if she couldn't feel exactly how much he wanted her.

"We have guests staying overnight," she reminded him. "You can't disrupt the whole palace looking for what was probably a member of the paparazzi who passed himself off as either a guest or part of the catering staff. He was probably snooping in my rooms or waiting with a camera to get some compromising photos." And if he hadn't given himself away, he might have gotten some good shots—of her and Whit.

"I still need to report the breach of security," he insisted. "And I need to make sure you have protection. Where the hell is Charlotte?"

"I gave her the night off," she said.

"And she took it?" he asked, his brow furrowing with skepticism of her claim.

"She thought I'd be safe." Because Gabriella had sworn she wouldn't leave her rooms.

His dark eyes flashed with anger. "She thought wrong."

"I will be safe," she said softly, her voice quavering with nerves that had her body trembling, as well. "If you stay with me..." She drew in a deep breath and gathered all of her courage to add, "...all night..."

SHE AWOKE ALONE in the morning—her bed empty but for the note she found crumpled under her pillow. She had obviously slept on it.

Her fingers trembled as she unfolded the paper and silently read the ominous warning: "You will die before you will ever marry the prince..."

Whitaker Howell had not left her that note. So the intruder must have. He or she hadn't been just an opportunistic guest looking for a souvenir or a member of the paparazzi looking for a story. The intruder had broken into her rooms with the intent of leaving the threat. Or of carrying it out...with Gabriella's death.

Chapter Two

For six months Princess Gabriella St. Pierre had been missing—vanished from a hotel suite in Paris. A hotel suite that had become a gruesome crime scene where someone had died. For six months Whit Howell had been convinced *she* had been that someone. He had believed she was dead.

Just recently he'd learned that Gabby was alive and in hiding. Her life had been threatened. And instead of coming to him for protection, she had left the country. She hadn't trusted him or anyone else. But then maybe that had been the smart thing to do. Her doppelgänger bodyguard had been kidnapped in her place and held hostage for the past six months.

If Gabriella hadn't gone into hiding…

He shuddered at the thought of what might have happened to her. But then he shuddered at the thought of what still could have happened to her since no one had heard from her for six months.

Could someone have fulfilled the prophesy of that note? The man, who had accidentally abducted the bodyguard in Gabby's place, claimed that he hadn't written it. Given all the other crimes to which he'd confessed, it made no sense that he would deny writing a note. But if not him, then who? And had that person followed through on his threat?

Whit had to find Gabby. Now. He had to make sure she was safe. He knew where she'd gone after leaving the palace. Her destination was on the piece of paper he clutched so tightly in his hand that it had grown damp and fragile.

"Sir, are you all right?" a stewardess asked as she paused in the aisle and leaned over his seat.

He nodded, dismissing her concern.

She leaned closer and adjusted the air vent over him. "You look awfully warm, sir. We'll be landing soon, but it may take a while to get to the gate."

"I'll be fine," he assured her. Because he would be closer to Gabriella—or at least closer to where she had been last. But after the woman moved down the aisle, he reached up to brush away the sweat beading on his forehead. And he grimaced over moving his injured shoulder.

He had been shot—a through-and-through, so the bullet had damaged no arteries or muscles. But now he was beginning to worry that the wound could be getting infected. And where he was going, there was unlikely to be any medical assistance.

He didn't care about his own discomfort though. He cared only about finding Gabriella and making damn sure she was alive and safe. And if he found her, he had to be strong and healthy enough to keep her safe.

Because it was probable that whoever had threatened her was still out there. Like everyone else, her stalker had probably thought her dead these past six months. But once they learned she was alive, they would be more determined than ever to carry out their threat.

"SHE'S ALIVE."

Gabriella St. Pierre expelled a breath of relief at the news Lydia Green shared the moment the older woman had burst through the door. For six months Gabby had been holding her breath, waiting for a message from her bodyguard. Actually she'd been waiting for the woman to come for her.

Especially in the beginning. She hadn't realized how pampered her life had been until she'd stayed here. The floor beneath her feet was dirt, the roof over her head thatch. A bird that had made it through her screenless window fluttered in a corner of the one room that had been her home for the past six months.

Once she had stopped waiting for Charlotte to come for her, she had gotten used to the primitive conditions. She had actually been happy here and relaxed in a way that she had never been at the palace. And it wasn't just because she had been out of the public eye but because she had been out from under her father's watchful eye, as well.

And beyond his control.

She had also been something she had never been before: useful. For the past six months she had been teaching children at the orphanage/school Lydia Green had built in a third-world country so remote and poor that no other charity or government had yet acknowledged it. But she had learned far more than she'd taught. She realized now that there was much more to being charitable than writing checks.

Lydia Green had given her life and her youth to helping those less fortunate. She'd grown up as a missionary, like her parents, traveling from third-world country to third-world country. After her parents had died, she could have chosen another life. She could have married and had a family. But Lydia had put aside whatever wants and needs she might have had and focused instead on others. She had become a missionary, too, and the only family she had left was a niece.

Charlotte. The women looked eerily similar. Lydia had the same caramel-brown eyes, but her hair was white rather than brown even though she was still in her fifties.

"Charlotte called?" The first day Gabriella had arrived, somewhere between the airport and the orphanage, she had lost the untraceable cell phone her bodyguard had given her. But it probably wouldn't have come in as far into the jungle as the orphanage was.

Lydia expelled her own breath of relief over finally hearing from her niece and nodded. "The connection was very bad, so I couldn't understand much of what Charlotte was saying…"

The orphanage landline wasn't much better than the cell phone. There was rarely a dial tone—the lines either damaged by falling trees, the oppressive humidity or rebel fighting.

"Did she tell you where she's been and why she hasn't contacted us?" Not knowing had driven Gabriella nearly crazy so that she had begun to suspect the worst—that Charlotte was dead. Or almost as bad, that Charlotte had betrayed her.

Lydia closed her eyes, as if trying to remember or perhaps to forget, and her brow furrowed. "I—I think she said she'd been kidnapped…"

"Kidnapped?" Gabby gasped the word as fear clutched at her. That would explain why they hadn't heard from the former U.S. Marshal. "Where? When?"

"It happened in Paris."

Gabriella's breath caught with a gasp. "Paris?"

She was the one who was supposed to have gone to Paris; that was what anyone who'd seen them would have believed. Whoever had abducted Charlotte had really meant to kidnap Gabby. She shuddered in reaction and in remembrance of all the kidnapping attempts she had escaped during her twenty-four years of life. If not for the bodyguards her father had hired to protect her, she probably would not have survived her childhood.

"Is she all right?"

"Yes, yes," Lydia replied anxiously, "and she said that the kidnapper has been caught."

"So I can leave..." Gabby should have been relieved; months ago she would have been ecstatic. But since then she had learned so much about herself. So much she had yet to deal with...

"She said for you to wait."

"She's coming here?" Nerves fluttered in Gabby's stomach. She was relieved Charlotte was all right, but she wasn't ready to see her.

Or anyone else...

"She's sending someone to get you," Lydia replied, with obvious disappointment that she would not see her niece.

Gabriella was to be picked up and delivered like a package—not a person. Until she'd met Lydia and the children at the orphanage, no one had ever treated Gabriella like a person. Pride stung, she shook her head and said, "That won't be necessary."

"You're going to stay?" Lydia asked hopefully.

"I would love to," she answered honestly. Here she

was needed not for *what* she was but *who* she was. She loved teaching the children. "But I can't..."

She had no idea who was coming for her, but she wasn't going to wait around to find out. Given her luck, it would probably be Whit, and he was the very last person she wanted to see. Now. And maybe ever again...

Lydia nodded, but that disappointment was back on her face, tugging her lips into a slight frown. "I understand that you have a life you need to get back to..."

Her existence in St. Pierre had never been her life; it had never been *her* choice. But that was only part of the reason she didn't plan on going back.

"But I would love to have you here," Lydia said, her voice trembling slightly, "with me..."

They had only begun to get to know each other. If they had met sooner, Gabriella's life would have been so different—so much better.

Tears burning her eyes, Gabriella moved across the small room to embrace the older woman. "Thank you..."

Lydia Green was the first person in her life who had ever been completely honest with her.

"Thank you," she said, clutching Gabriella close. "You are amazing with the kids. They all love you so much." She eased back and reached between them to touch Gabby's protruding belly. "You're going to make a wonderful mother."

The baby fluttered inside Gabriella, as if in agreement or maybe argument with the older woman's words. Was she going to make a wonderful mother? She hadn't had an example of one to emulate. Her throat choked now with tears, she could barely murmur another, "Thank you…"

She didn't want to leave, but she couldn't stay. "Can I get a ride to the bus stop in town?"

She needed a Jeep to take her to a bus and the bus to take her to a plane. It wasn't a fast trip to get anywhere in this country while the person coming for her would probably be using the royal jet and private ground transportation. She needed to move quickly.

"You really should wait for whoever Charlotte is sending for you," Lydia gently insisted. "This is a dangerous country."

Sadness clutched at her and she nodded. That was why they had so many orphans living in the dorms. The compound consisted of classroom huts and living quarters. If disease hadn't taken their parents, violence had.

"I've been safe here," she reminded Lydia.

"At the school," the woman agreed, "because the people here respect and appreciate that we're helping the children. But once you leave here…"

"I'll be fine," she assured her although she wasn't entirely certain she believed that herself.

"You have a bodyguard for a reason. Because of who you are, you're always in danger." Lydia was too busy and the country too remote for her to be up on current affairs, so Charlotte must have told her all about Gabby's life.

Gabriella glanced down at her swollen belly. Her bare feet peeped out beneath it, her toes stained with dirt from the floor. "No one will recognize me."

Not if they saw her now. She bore only a faint resemblance to the pampered princess who'd walked runways and red carpets.

But she wasn't only physically different.

She didn't need anyone to protect her anymore—especially since she really couldn't trust anyone but herself. *She* had to protect her life and the life she was carrying inside her.

A WALL OF HEAT hit Whit when he stepped from the airport. Calling the cement block building with the metal roof an airport seemed a gross exaggeration, though. He stood on the dirt road outside, choking on the dust and the exhaust fumes from the passing vehicles. Cars. Jeeps. Motorbikes. A bus pulled up near the building, and people disembarked.

A pregnant woman caught his attention. She wore a floppy straw hat and big sunglasses, looking more Hollywood than third world. But her jeans were dirt-stained as was the worn blouse she wore with the buttons stretched taut over her swollen belly.

It couldn't be Gabby.

Hell, she was *pregnant;* it couldn't be Gabby…

His cell vibrated in his pocket, drawing his attention from the woman. He grabbed it up with a gruff, "Howell here."

"Are you there?" Charlotte Green asked, her voice cracking with anxiety. "Have you found her yet?"

"The plane just landed," he replied.

He had only glanced at his phone when he'd turned it back on, but he suspected all the calls he'd missed and the voice mails he had yet to retrieve had been from the princess's very worried bodyguard.

"But Whit—"

"Give me a few minutes," he told her. "You're not even sure she's still here."

Wherever the hell *here* was; from his years as a U.S. Marine, he was well traveled but Whit had never even heard of this country before. Calling it a country was like calling that primitive building an airport—a gross exaggeration.

"I finally reached my aunt Lydia this morning," Charlotte said. "She confirmed that Gabby is still at the orphanage."

He exhaled a breath of relief. She was alive. And not lost. "That's good."

Nobody had kidnapped the princess as they had her bodyguard. Gabby was right where Charlotte had sent her six months ago. Why hadn't she answered the woman's previous calls then?

"She's all right?"

"No." Static crackled in the line, distorting whatever else Charlotte might have said.

He stopped walking, so that he didn't lose the call entirely. Reception was probably best closest to the airport, so he took a few steps back into the throng of people.

"What's wrong?" Whit asked, the anxiety all his now. "Has she been hurt?"

"Yeah…"

And he realized it wasn't static in the line but Charlotte Green's voice breaking with sobs. He had never heard the tough former U.S. Marshal cry before—not even when armed gunmen had been trying to kill them all. His heart slammed into his ribs as panic rushed through him. "Oh, my God…"

It had to be bad.

Not Gabriella…

She was the sweetest, most innocent person he'd ever met. Or at least she had been…

"Charlotte!" He needed her to pull it together and tell him what the hell had happened to the princess. In a country as primitive as this, it could have been anything. Disease. A rebel forces attack. "What's wrong?"

"It's my fault," she murmured, sobs choking her voice. "It's all my fault. I should have told her. I should have prepared her…"

"What?" he fired the question at her. "What should you have told her? What should you have prepared her for?"

The phone clanged and then a male voice spoke in his ear, "Whit, are you there?"

"Aaron?" He wasn't surprised that his fellow bodyguard was with Charlotte. Since Aaron Timmer had found her after her six-month disappearance, the man had pretty much refused to leave her side. "What's going on?"

"Don't worry about that," his fellow royal bodyguard advised. "It's just personal stuff between Charlotte and Princess Gabriella."

When the princess and her bodyguard had disappeared, Whit and Aaron had launched an extensive search to find them. Aaron had reached out for leads to their whereabouts. Whit had done the same, but he'd also dug deeply into their lives and discovered all their secrets, hoping that those revelations might lead him to them. So now he knew things about Princess Gabriella that she had yet to learn herself.

Or had she finally uncovered the truth? She must have and that was why Charlotte was so upset; she was probably full of guilt and regret. He recognized those emotions because he knew them too well himself.

"Damn it!" If that was the case, Gabby had to feel so betrayed. He added a few more curses.

"Whit," Aaron interrupted his tirade. "Just find Gabriella and bring her home to St. Pierre Island. We'll meet you there. The royal jet is about to land at the palace."

"The king is still with you?" The monarch was really their responsibility, one that both men had shirked in favor of protecting the women instead. King Rafael St. Pierre hadn't seemed to mind.

"He's secure. Everything's fine here," Aaron assured Whit. "What about there?"

"I just got off the plane." The third one. It had taken three planes—with not a single one of them as luxurious as the royal jet—over the course of three days to bring him to this remote corner of the world. And it would take a bus and a Jeep to get him to the orphanage deep in the jungle where the princess had been hiding for the past six months. "I haven't had a chance to locate Gabby and assess the situation."

Shots rang out. And he dropped low to the ground while he assessed this new situation. Who the hell was firing? And at whom? Him?

Nobody knew he'd been heading here but Charlotte and Aaron. Not that long ago he would have been suspicious; he would have considered that they might have set him up for an ambush. But the three of them had been through too much together recently. And if they'd wanted him dead, they wouldn't have had to go to this much trouble to end his life. They could have just let him bleed out from the bullet wound to his shoulder.

But the shots weren't being fired at him. They weren't that close, nowhere near the dirt street where Whit stood yet. But the shots were loud because they echoed off metal. Someone was firing inside the airport. His hand shook as he lifted the cell to his ear again.

Aaron was shouting his name. "What the hell's going on? Are those shots?"

"I'm going to check it out," he said as he headed toward the building—shoving through the wave of people running from it.

"You need to get Gabriella," Aaron shouted but still Whit could barely hear him over the shrieks and screams of the fleeing people.

Whit flashed back to that woman getting off the bus and heading inside the airport. "Gabby! Is Gabby pregnant?"

"Yes—according to Charlotte's aunt."

It was hardly something the woman would have lied about. But how? But when? And whom?

"She's probably six months along," Aaron added.

Realization dawned on Whit, overwhelming him with too many emotions to sort through let alone deal with.

Oh, God...

"That's Gabby..." Inside the airport where shots were being fired.

He shoved the phone in his pocket and reached for his gun before he remembered that he didn't have one on him. He hadn't been able to get one on the first plane he'd boarded in Michigan and hadn't had time to find one here.

Would he be able to save her? Or was he already too late?

Chapter Three

As disguises went, the hat and the glasses were weak. But it had fooled Whitaker Howell. He had barely glanced at her when she'd disembarked from the crowded bus. Of course he had seemed distracted, as he'd been reaching for his phone while moving quickly through the crowd milling from and to the airport.

She'd had to fight the urge to gawk at him. He had looked so infuriatingly handsome and sexy in a black T-shirt and jeans. But the sense of betrayal and resentment and anger overwhelmed her attraction for him. She didn't want to see Whit Howell much less be attracted to him any longer.

When she'd glimpsed him through the window, she'd thought about staying put in her seat. But since he was probably the one who'd been sent to retrieve her, he would have boarded the bus for the return trip and she would have been trapped.

When Charlotte had become her bodyguard three years ago, that was one of the first self-defense lessons she had taught Gabriella. Avoid confined places with limited exits. And given her girth, the exits on the bus had definitely been limited for her since it wasn't likely she'd been able to squeeze her belly out one of those tiny windows. So she had gotten off the bus and hurried toward the airport.

That was another of Charlotte's lessons. Stay in crowded, public places. So Gabriella had breathed a sigh of relief when she'd walked into the busy airport. She needed to buy a ticket for the first leg of the long journey ahead of her. She still had most of the cash Charlotte had given her to travel. She hadn't needed it at the orphanage. Even though she was using cash, she would still have to present identification. She fumbled inside her overstuffed carry-on bag for the fake ID that Charlotte had provided along with the cash.

She couldn't even remember the name under which she'd traveled. Brigitte? Beverly? As she searched her bag for the wallet, she stumbled and collided with a body. A beefy hand closed around her arm—probably to steady her.

"I'm sorry," she apologized. She glanced up with a smile, but when she met the gaze of the man who'd grabbed her, her smile froze.

It wasn't Whit. He had probably already boarded the bus on its return trip to the orphanage. She didn't know this man, but from the look on his deeply tanned face, he knew her—or at least he knew of her. Most people thought her life a fairy tale; she had always considered it more a cartoon—and if that were the case, this man would have dollar signs instead of pupils in his eyes.

"Excuse me," she said and tried to pull free of the man's grasp.

But he held on to her so tightly that he pinched the muscles in her arm. "You will come with me," he told her, his voice thick with a heavy accent.

She was thousands of miles from home, but it had

come to her. First Whit and now this man, who sounded as though he was either from St. Pierre Island or close to it, probably from one of the neighboring islands to which her father had promised her. Well, he'd promised her to their princes, but she would belong to the island, too. Like a possession—that was how her father treated her.

And it was how this man obviously intended to treat her. She glared at him, which, since she'd taken off her sunglasses in the dimly lit building, should have been intimidating. Charlotte hadn't had to teach her that glare—the one that made a person unapproachable. Gabriella had learned that glare at an early age—from her mother, or the woman she'd always thought was her mother.

The man, however, was not intimidated, or at least not intimidated enough to release her.

So she pulled harder, fighting his grip on her arm.

"Let me go!" she demanded, the imperious tone borrowed from her father this time. No one had ever dared refuse one of *his* commands, no matter how very much she had wanted to.

The first time he'd offered her as a fiancée she'd been too young and sheltered to understand that arranged marriages were archaic and humiliating. She'd also been friends with her first fiancé—she and Prince Linus had grown up together—spending all her holidays home from boarding school with him.

But the night of the ball her father had broken that engagement and promised her to another man, a prince who'd already been engaged to one of Gabriella's cousins. So her father had actually broken two engagements that night. He hadn't cared about the people—not that he'd ever considered her a person—he'd cared only about the politics, about using her to link St. Pierre to another, more affluent country.

The man moved, tugging Gabriella along with him. He pulled her through people—toward one of the wide open doors that led to the airstrip in the back and the private planes. The planes for which a person didn't need a ticket or even a flight manifest in this country…

And if Gabriella got on that plane, she would probably never get off again. Or at least she would never be free again. Panic overwhelmed her, pressing on her lungs so that she couldn't draw a deep breath.

Don't panic.

Charlotte was undoubtedly still thousands of miles away, but it was her voice in Gabriella's ear, speaking with authority and confidence. And hopefully, in this case, the truth for once.

Gabriella exhaled a shaky breath and then dragged in a deep one, filling and expanding her lungs with air. It was stale and heavy with the humidity and the odor of sweaty bodies and jet fuel and cigarette smoke. There was no airport security to help her. She had to take care of herself.

Assess the situation.

Despite the lies, Charlotte had helped her. Perhaps she had even considered her lies helping Gabriella, protecting her. But Charlotte had known there would be times like this when she wouldn't be there, so she had taught Gabby how to protect herself.

The man wasn't much taller than she was. But he was heavier—much heavier even with the extra pounds she was carrying in her belly. Most of his extra weight was muscle. He had no neck but had a broad back and shoulders. And at the small of his back, there was a big bulge. He had definitely come in on a private plane and from some airport with about the same level of security as this one. None.

Choose the most effective mode of protection.

Charlotte had been trained to fight and shoot and had years of experience doing both. She had taught Gabby some simple but *effective* moves. But Gabriella's experience using those methods had been in simulated fights with Charlotte, whom she hadn't wanted to hurt. Then.

A sob caught in her lungs. She didn't want to hurt her now, either. Or avoid her like she'd initially thought. She wanted to see Charlotte and talk to her, give her a chance to explain her actions and her reason for keeping so many secrets. But Gabriella couldn't do that if she didn't get the chance—if she wound up held hostage or worse.

And by effective, I mean violent...

Charlotte Green had lived a violent life, and she possessed the scars to prove it. Both physical and emotional.

Gabby only had the emotional scars until now.

She wouldn't be able to use her simulated fight moves to fend off this muscular man—probably not even if she wasn't six months pregnant. But because she was six months pregnant, she couldn't risk the baby getting hurt.

So instead she reached for the gun and pulled it from beneath the man's sweat-dampened shirt. The weapon was heavier than she remembered. She hadn't held one in the past six months. But before that she'd held one several times. With both hands, using one to hold and balance the gun while she focused on flicking off the safety and pulling the trigger with the other.

But the man held one of her hands. When he felt her grab the gun, he jerked her around and reached for the gun. So she fumbled with it quickly, sliding the safety and squeezing the trigger.

Because she hadn't wanted to hit anyone else in the crowded airport, she'd aimed the barrel up and fired the bullet into the metal ceiling. Birds, living in the rafters, flew into a frenzy. And so did the people as the bullet ricocheted back into the cement. She breathed a sigh of relief that it struck no one. But the cement chipped, kicking up pieces of it with dust.

The man jumped, as if he'd felt the whiz of the bullet near his foot. And he lurched back. When he did, he released her arm. Now she had two hands, which she used to steady the gun and aim the barrel—this time at the man's chest.

People screamed and ran toward the exits. They thought she was dangerous. The man didn't seem to share their sentiment because he stepped forward again, advancing on her.

"I will shoot!" she warned him.

He chuckled. Then, his voice full of condescension, said, "You are a princess. What do you know of shooting guns?"

"More than enough to kill you…" Like the simulated fights, she hadn't shot a weapon with the intent of hurting anyone…except for all the targets she had killed. She was good at head shots. Even better at the heart-kill shot.

Of course those targets hadn't been moving. And the man was—advancing on her with no regard for the weapon. He was mad, too, his eyes dark with rage. If he got his hands on her again, he wasn't just going to kidnap her. He was going to hurt her. And hurting her would hurt her unborn child.

So when he lunged toward her, she fired again.

ANOTHER SHOT RANG out. But it didn't echo off metal as the earlier shot had. It was muffled—as if it had struck something. Or someone...

Gabriella...

Whit held back the shout that burned his lungs. Yelling her name might only put her in danger—if she wasn't already—or increase the danger if she was. Maybe that hadn't been Gabby he'd glimpsed getting off the bus. Maybe she was still back at the orphanage. If she'd known someone was coming for her, wouldn't she have stayed and waited?

Or maybe she hadn't wanted to be found. If the shooting involved her, she had been found, but the wrong person had done the finding. The person who'd written that threatening note?

Whit shoved through the screaming people who were nearly stampeding in their haste to escape the building. There was no sign of the pregnant woman he'd glimpsed getting off the bus. She wasn't with the others running away.

And then he saw her and realized that she was the one they were all running from—she was the one with the gun. She gripped it in both hands.

As Whit neared her, he noticed the blood spattered on her face, and his heart slammed into his ribs with fear for her safety.

"Gabby," he spoke softly, so as to not startle her, but she still jumped and swung toward him with her body and with the barrel of her gun.

He barely glanced at it, focusing instead on her face—on her incredibly beautiful face but for those droplets of blood.

Anxiously he asked, "Are you hurt?"

A groan—low and pain-filled—cut through the clamor of running people. Gabriella's lips had parted, but she was not the one who uttered the sound. Whit lowered his gaze to the man who had dropped to his knees in front of Gabby. The burly man clutched his shoulder and blood oozed between his fingers.

Whit flinched, his own shoulder wound stinging in reaction. "What the hell's going on?"

Gabby took one hand from the gun to tug down the brim of her hat—as if her weak disguise could fool him twice.

The man took advantage of her distraction and looser grip and reached for the gun. But he could only grab at it with one hand, as his other arm hung limply from his bleeding shoulder. He had the element of surprise though and snapped it free of her grasp.

She lunged back for it, her swollen belly on the same level as the barrel of the gun. But Whit moved faster than she did and stepped between them. Before the man could move his finger to the trigger of the gun, Whit slammed his fist into the wounded man's jaw. The guy's eyes rolled back into his head as his consciousness fled, and he fell back onto the cement floor of the airport, blood pooling beneath his gunshot wound.

Whit's shoulder ached from delivering the knock-out punch, and he growled a curse. But his pain was nothing in comparison to the fear overwhelming him. He'd only just learned where Gabby was and he'd nearly lost her again.

Maybe forever this time—if the man had managed to pull the trigger before Whit had knocked him out.

"What the hell were you thinking?" he shouted the question at Princess Gabriella.

His fear wasn't for himself but for her, and he hadn't felt an emotion that intense since the night before she disappeared. The night she'd begged him to stay with her. At first he'd thought she'd only wanted protection but then he'd realized that she'd wanted more.

She'd wanted him. But then the next morning she'd left him without a backward glance. So he'd probably just been her way of rebelling against her father's attempts to control her life. That was what that night had been about, but what about today?

"I—I was defending myself," she stammered in a strangely hoarse tone, as if she'd lost her voice or was trying to disguise it. She ducked down and reached for the gun that had dropped to the floor with the man.

But Whit beat her to the weapon, clutching it tightly in his fist. "No more shooting for you, Princess."

"I'm not a princess—"

"Save it," he said. "I damn well know who you are." He had no idea why she was denying her identity to him, though. But that wasn't his most pressing concern at the moment.

He leaned over to check the man for a pulse. He was alive, just unconscious. And that might not last long. "Who is this? And why did you shoot him?"

"He tried to kidnap me," she said, apparently willing to admit that much even though she wouldn't admit to who she was. "So I grabbed his gun."

Whit uttered a low whistle of appreciation. Even without a weapon, the guy would have been intimidating, yet she'd managed to disarm him, too. Maybe she wasn't Princess Gabriella. "How do you know he was going to kidnap you?"

"He tried to drag me out there," she gestured toward the big open doors in one of the metal walls, "to a plane."

As Whit glanced up to follow the direction she pointed, he noticed men—about four of them—rushing in from the airfield. They must have heard the shots, too. And they were armed.

"We have to get the hell out of here," he said.

Or the man's friends were liable to finish what he'd started—abducting Gabriella. And Whit with his shoulder wound and his borrowed gun were hardly going to be enough protection to save her.

She must have seen the men, too, because she was already turning and moving toward the street. Whit kept between her and the men. But they saw the guy on the ground, and they saw the gun in Whit's hand.

And they began to fire.

"WHAT'S WRONG?" Charlotte asked anxiously. "What did Whit say?"

It wasn't so much what he'd said as what Aaron had overheard when he'd been on the phone with his friend. But Charlotte was already worried about Princess Gabriella; he didn't want to upset her any more.

She settled onto the airplane seat across from him. After her trip to the restroom, her eyes were dry and clear. She'd composed herself. But how much would it take for her to break again?

She'd already been through so much—kidnapped

and held hostage for six months. And she was pregnant, too, with his baby.

Aaron's heart filled with pride and love. But fear still gripped him. He wasn't like Whit; he couldn't hide his emotions. Whit usually hid them so well that Aaron had often doubted the man was even capable of feeling. But he'd heard it in his voice—his fear for Princess Gabriella's safety—once he'd realized she was also where the shooting was.

"I know something's wrong," Charlotte persisted, but she pitched her voice low and glanced toward the back of the jet where the king had retired to his private room. "Tell me."

Aaron uttered a ragged sigh of resignation and admitted, "I heard shots…"

Charlotte's eyes widened. "Someone was shooting at Whit? He wouldn't have had time to get a gun yet. He won't be able to defend himself."

On more than one occasion, Aaron had seen Whit defend himself without a gun. But he hadn't been injured then. "Whit wasn't the one getting shot at."

She gasped. "Gabby? Was it Gabby?"

"I don't know," he said. But from the way Whit had reacted to the news that the princess was pregnant, too, he was pretty sure that it was her. "It's a dangerous country. It could have been rebel gunfire. It could have been anything…"

"Call him back!" She reached across the space between them and grabbed for the cell phone he'd shoved in his shirt pocket.

But Aaron caught her hand in his and entwined their fingers. "He won't answer," he told her. "He needs to focus on what's happening. And there's nothing we can do from here anyway."

That was why he hadn't wanted to tell her. She would want to help, and that wasn't possible from so many miles away. That feeling of helplessness overwhelmed Aaron, reminding him of the way he'd felt when Charlotte had been missing. He'd been convinced that she was out there, somewhere, but he hadn't been able to find her.

Now Whit needed help—Whit, who'd so often stepped in to save him—and Aaron was too far away to come to his aid.

Panic had tears welling in her eyes. "We can have the pilot change course—"

"We're almost to St. Pierre," Aaron pointed out. "We'll be landing soon."

Panic raised her voice a couple of octaves. "Once we drop off the king, we can leave again—"

"No," he said. "There's a doctor meeting us at the palace. You need to be checked out." Even after he'd rescued her from where she'd been held hostage, she'd been through a lot.

She shook her head, tumbling those long tresses of golden brown hair around her shoulders. "I need to protect Gabby."

He knew it wasn't just because she was the princess's bodyguard. But he had to remind her, "You need to take care of our baby first."

"We shouldn't have let Whit go alone," she said. "He's hurt too badly to protect her."

"We hadn't thought she would need protecting," Aaron reminded his fiancée.

"We did," Charlotte insisted, squeezing his fingers

in her distress. "Six months ago someone left her that note threatening her life. That's why I sent her into hiding." And set herself up as a decoy for the princess. Her plan had worked. Too well.

"But nobody knows where she is." Or the paparazzi would have found her, no matter where she'd been. And there would have been photographs of Princess Gabriella on every magazine and news show, as there had always been.

"If those shots were being fired at her," Charlotte said, her beautiful face tense with fear, "then someone must have figured it out."

"How?" he asked. "Nobody but you and I and Whit know where she is."

She glanced to the back of the plane. "After I talked to my aunt and confirmed that Gabby was actually still with her at the orphanage, I told the king. I thought he had a right to know."

"Was he furious?" Aaron asked. Charlotte had done much more than just violating protocol as a royal bodyguard.

"He called St. Pierre and sent out another plane with a security team as Whit's backup." She drew in a deep breath, as if trying to soothe herself. "They should be there within a few hours."

Aaron had heard the shots. He wasn't reassured. In fact he was disheartened. He had wasted so many years being mad at Whit for something that hadn't been the man's fault. Had he repaired his friendship only to lose his friend?

If Princess Gabriella had been involved in the shooting, then Whit would have stepped in and done whatever was necessary to try to save her life—including giving up his own.

By the time the security team made it to where Whit and Gabriella were, they would probably be too late to help. With Whit injured and unarmed, it was probably already too late.

Chapter Four

Gabby pressed her palms and splayed her fingers across her belly, as if her hands alone could protect her baby from the bullets that began to fly around the airport—ricocheting off the metal roof and cement floor. She wanted to help Whit, but she had no weapon—nothing to save him. So she ran.

He returned fire as he hurried with her to the entrance. Keeping his body between her and the men, he used himself as a human shield. She would have been moved—if she hadn't known that it was bodyguard protocol to put themselves between their subject and any potential threat.

These men weren't potentially a threat; they were definitely a threat. To Whit more than to her. They probably wouldn't want to risk fatally injuring her—if they intended to kidnap her. It was hard to collect a ransom on a dead hostage. But if they'd been hired by whoever had left her that letter, then she was in as much danger as Whit was.

Maybe more.

She ran out of the building, but the street was as deserted now as the airport was. All the people had scattered and left. It was no safer out here than it had been in the deserted metal building.

But she had Whit. He'd stayed with her, his hand on her arm—urging her forward—away from the danger. But the danger followed them. Shots continued to ring out. Whit's gun clicked with the telltale sound of an empty magazine. He cursed.

Panic slammed through Gabby. The men chasing them were not about to run out of bullets—not with all the guns they had. Should she and Whit stop and lift their arms in surrender and hope they were not killed? Before she could ask Whit, he made the decision for them.

He lifted her off the ground and ran toward the street. Gabby didn't wriggle and try to fight free as she had six months ago. Instead of pounding on him, she clutched at him, so that he wouldn't drop her. He leaned and ducked down, as if dodging bullets.

Gabriella felt the air stir as the shots whizzed past. But with the way he was holding her—she wouldn't feel the bullets. They would have to pass through Whit's body before hitting hers. Again, it was bodyguard protocol, but she couldn't help being impressed, touched and horrified that he might get killed protecting her.

He ran into the street, narrowly avoiding a collision with a Jeep. The vehicle screeched to a halt, and Whit jerked open the passenger door and jumped inside. He deposited her in the passenger seat and forced his way into the driver's seat, pushing the driver out of the door.

The man scrambled to his feet and cursed at him. Then he ducked low and ran when the gunmen rushed up behind him, firing wildly at the vehicle. Whit slammed his foot on the gas, accelerating with such force that Gabriella's back pressed into the seat. She grabbed for the seat belt, but there wasn't one.

"Hang on tight," Whit advised.

She stretched out her arms and braced her hands on the dash, so that she wouldn't slam into it and hurt the baby. "Please, hurry," she pleaded. "Hurry—before they catch up to us."

"Where the hell am I going?" he asked. "Which way to the orphanage?"

Panic shot through her, shortening her breath as she thought of the danger. "No. No. We can't—we can't risk leading these men back to the orphanage." Those children had already lost so much to violence; she wouldn't let them get caught in the cross fire and lose their lives, too.

"I'll make sure we're not followed," Whit assured her. "But we have to hurry."

She hesitated. She'd been uncertain that she could trust anyone again, let alone him. But this wasn't her heart she was risking. It was so much more important than that. Whit was good at his job. Charlotte wouldn't have had the king hire him if he and Aaron hadn't been good bodyguards. So she gave him directions, leading him deeper and deeper into the jungle.

The Jeep bounced along the rutted trails, barely passing between the trees and the other foliage that threatened the paths. Gabby left one hand on the dash and reached for the roll bars over her head with the other, holding tight, so that she didn't risk an injury to her unborn child. She also kept turning around to check the back window and make certain that they had not been followed.

"No one's behind us," Whit assured her with a glance at the rearview mirror. "I've been watching."

She uttered a breath of relief that they wouldn't be leading danger back to the orphanage. At the speed that Whit was driving, they arrived in record time at the complex of huts and larger wood-and-thatch buildings that comprised the orphanage.

"This is it," she said with a surge of pride and happiness, which was the polar opposite from the way she'd felt when she'd first seen the complex six months ago. When she'd accepted that it was really where Charlotte had sent her, her heart had been heavy with dread and her pulse quick with panic. "We're here."

Whit stepped on the brake but didn't put the transmission into Park. Instead he peered through the dust-smeared windshield at the collection of crude outbuildings that made up the orphanage complex.

"This is it?" he echoed her words but his deep voice was full of skepticism.

"This is it," she confirmed. Now that she knew how hard it was to build in the jungle, she was even more impressed with what Lydia had achieved—and with what Gabriella had helped her manage during her stay. "Pull around the back of that hut. That's mine."

He followed her direction, parking the Jeep where she pointed. But before she could open her door, he reached across her. His hand splayed over her belly. He leaned close, so close that she felt his breath warm her face when he asked, "Is this mine?"

She shivered at his closeness and the intensity in his dark eyes. But she couldn't meet his gaze and lie to him. So she glanced down and noticed the blood that trickled down his arm. And she gasped in shock and horror. "You were shot!"

Perhaps it had only been his duty as a royal bodyguard, perhaps it had been his concern for the child he suspected might be his—but he'd taken a bullet that had been meant for her. And after being hit, he'd driven the Jeep over tough terrain to get them to safety.

"We need to get you inside," she said, fighting back her panic and concern. During her time at the orphanage, she'd learned to not let the children see her anxiety when they were hurt because it only upset and hurt them more. "And I'll have Lydia call for the doctor."

She opened the door and slipped out from under his hand. Then she hurried around to the driver's side and opened his door.

In addition to the blood trailing down his arm and turning the shoulder of his shirt an even darker black with wetness, he had sweat beading on his brow and upper lip. It was hot and humid in the jungle. But she'd heard the other guards talking about Whit's deployments to the Middle East—usually because she had asked them to tell her about the blond bodyguard— and they had always said how he had never perspired— not in the heat—not under pressure.

Was he hurt that bad?

She lifted his arm and slid beneath it, in order to help him from the driver's seat. But he didn't lean on her. With a short grunt of pain, he unfolded himself from beneath the wheel and stepped out of the Jeep to stand beside her. Close beside her, his tense body nearly touching hers. He leaned down, so that their gazes met and locked.

"I don't need a doctor," he said, dismissing her concern. "I need the truth."

She had given up denying her identity to him. She'd only been able to fool him once, but he obviously had no doubt about who she was now. So what did he mean? "The truth about what?"

His throat moved, rippling, as if he swallowed hard. And after clearing his throat, he asked, "Is that baby you're carrying mine?"

The baby shifted inside her, kicking at her belly, as if he, too, wanted to know the answer. She placed her palms over her stomach again, protectively. And because she felt so protective, she wasn't willing to share her baby with anyone.

Not even the baby's father.

Whit moved to lift his arms—probably to grab her and maybe shake the truth out of her—but the movement had his handsome face contorting with a grimace of pain. And a groan slipped from between his gritted teeth.

"Doctor first," she insisted. "Then we'll talk…"

Maybe by the time she had Lydia summon the doctor from the clinic in the more populated town close by, she would have figured out if she was going to tell Whit the truth.

WHIT GLANCED DOWN at the dirt floor beneath his feet and peered up at the thatched roof. The hut was primitive and small. There was only enough space for the double bed that stood in the middle of the room, enshrouded in a canopy of mosquito netting. He sat on the edge of that bed, so he had a clear view out the window and the doorway. To make sure no one had followed them from the airport.

There was no screen or glass in the window; it was just a hole to the jungle. There was no door either—just the threshold through which Gabby passed as she returned from wherever she'd gone to summon a doctor.

Her bodyguard had sent her here to keep her safe? Anger at Charlotte Green coursed through him. Any animal—two-legged or four-legged—from the jungle could have come inside and dragged her off never to be seen again. After he had learned all the secrets about Gabriella St. Pierre, he'd begun to question Charlotte's motives. Now he questioned them again.

"This is where you've been staying?" he asked, still shocked that the princess of St. Pierre would have spent one night in such primitive conditions let alone six months.

Gabby glanced around the tiny hut, and her lips curved into a wistful smile. "Yes…"

Not only had she stayed here but she seemed to have actually enjoyed it.

"I'm sorry I was gone so long," she said, "but Lydia was with a class. My class, actually." Her smile widened. "And the children were so thrilled that I came back…"

"You've been teaching here?"

"Yes, it's a school as well as an orphanage." She peered through that hole in the wall as if checking the jungle for threats. "Are you certain that no one followed us?"

"They would have been here already," he pointed out. Because they would have had to follow them directly from the airport in order to find this place. But he looked out the window, too. "You're safe."

"It's not me I'm worried about…" Her palms slid over her belly, as if protecting or comforting the child within. "Those kids have already been through so much…"

When he had first met Princess St. Pierre, he had been impressed that someone as privileged and probably pampered as she must have been seemed to actually care about people. She had showed genuine interest in the lives of the palace staff. But here she had taken that interest to a whole other level, sacrificing her own comfort to care for others. She wasn't just a princess; she was a saint.

He had nothing to offer a princess; he had even less to offer a saint. All he could give Princess Gabriella St. Pierre was his protection. He stared at her belly. Unless he'd already given her something else…

He opened his mouth to ask again the question that had been burning in his mind since the minute he had realized the pregnant woman from the bus was Princess Gabriella. Was that baby his?

But before he could ask, she hurriedly said, "The doctor should be here soon. The clinic is just a mile away."

"I don't need a doctor."

"You've been shot," she said, moving her hands from her belly to his arm.

Blood still trickled slowly from the old wound in his shoulder, over his biceps, down his forearm, over his wrist to drip off his fingertips onto the dirt floor.

"Yes, I was shot," he admitted with a wince of pain as he remembered the burn of the bullet ripping through his flesh. "But not today."

Her brow furrowed in confusion. "But you're bleeding…"

He shrugged and then winced again as pain radiated throughout his shoulder and his fingers tingled in reaction. "The wound must have reopened."

"When you carried me…"

Despite the men chasing them, firing shots at them, he had enjoyed carrying her. He had savored her slight weight in his arms, the heat of her body pressed against his, her hands clutching at him—holding him close. It had reminded him of that night—that night he had taken on the responsibility of guarding her.

But he hadn't really protected her…not if that child was his. He groaned.

"You are hurting," she said and commanded him, "Take off your shirt." But she didn't wait for him to obey her royal order. She lifted his T-shirt, her fingers grazing his abdomen and then his chest as she pulled the damp fabric over his head. Expelled in a gasp, her breath whispered across his skin.

Despite the oppressive heat, he nearly shivered in reaction to her touch. For six interminable, miserable months he'd thought she was dead. He had thought he would never see her again. That he would never touch her…

Was she real? She was so beautiful that he doubted it, as he had the first time he'd met her. She couldn't be real. Maybe he had been shot again, and this time he'd died and found an angel. He snorted in derision of his ridiculous thought. As if he would ever make it to heaven…

"This wound isn't very old," she observed, her teeth nibbling at her bottom lip with concern. "When were you shot?"

"Five or six days ago…" He couldn't remember

exactly; everything had happened so quickly and then it had taken him so many days and flights to reach her. Maybe he should have waited for one of the royal jets to be available. But the king had needed to return to St. Pierre so he had taken his, and Whit hadn't wanted to wait for one to come in from St. Pierre. He hadn't wanted to wait another minute to see Gabriella and make sure she was safe. He had never imagined he'd find the Princess of St. Pierre like this…

Literally barefoot and pregnant.

"You should be in the hospital," she admonished him, as she rose up on tiptoe and inspected his wound.

"I saw a doctor already," he assured her. "I'm all stitched up. I'm fine." So they could talk. And maybe he would have insisted on it already if he wasn't worried about what she would tell him. Several years ago he had sworn he would never become a father. Or a husband. He'd had no intention of ever attempting a long-term relationship.

"You were shot!" she snapped at him, temper flashing in her eyes. "How did that happen?"

He shrugged and then cursed as the movement jostled his wounded shoulder, sending pain radiating down his arm until his fingers tingled.

Damn it…

He shouldn't be the one to tell her any of this. He was only supposed to retrieve her from her hiding spot and bring her back to the opulent palace on St. Pierre Island. Then her father and her bodyguard could explain everything…

The king and the others had probably landed on St. Pierre by now, so they could send the royal jet here. And Whit could bring her home where she belonged—with her family and her fiancé. He grabbed his cell phone from the front pocket of his jeans, but the screen was illuminated with a disheartening message. No service.

"That's not going to work," she informed him. "You're not stalling…"

"Stalling?" he scoffed. "I'm trying to call the palace."

Her breath caught, and her eyes widened with panic.

And he realized something. "You weren't in that airport to take a flight home."

"Home?" she repeated.

"The country of which you're the princess," he reminded her. "Where you grew up, where you live…"

"I grew up in a boarding school," she said. "And I've been living here."

At another boarding school/orphanage. Was that how she'd felt growing up? Like an orphan? Or was that feeling new because of what she might have learned about herself and all those secrets he'd uncovered?

"You know what I mean," he said. "You weren't heading back to St. Pierre." She'd been running again. And that was probably why she had worn the disguise and tried to deny her identity to him. She hadn't wanted him to bring her back to St. Pierre.

Instead of denying his claim, she changed the subject. "Tell me why you were shot," she urged him. "I know Charlotte was kidnapped. The telephone connection was bad but Lydia understood that much."

And knowing that, she hadn't intended to go back to St. Pierre? Charlotte's concern that Gabby was upset with her might have been warranted.

"I know Charlotte's safe now," Gabriella said, as if she'd read his mind.

Or his expression, which would have been odd given

that everyone—even those to whom he'd been closest—always claimed that he had a poker face, that they could never tell what he was thinking or feeling. Or if he even felt anything.

"The kidnapper was caught," she continued. "Did you get shot rescuing Charlotte from him?"

"Aaron rescued her," he said. Because his fellow royal bodyguard was madly in love with Charlotte. "I got shot when we went back to where she'd been held captive and tried to discover who was behind the kidnapping."

She drew in a quick, sharp breath. "But he was caught, right?"

He nodded, wishing again that he'd been part of the takedown. But he'd been knocked out cold from the painkillers the doctor who'd stitched up his gunshot wound had given him.

"Who was it?" she asked, her eyes wide with fear. She must have figured out that she—not Charlotte—had been the kidnapper's intended hostage.

He drew in a deep breath, hoping to distract her. He was only responsible for her safety, not a debriefing. "We need to get back to St. Pierre, and the others can explain everything."

Anger flashed in her eyes again, and she narrowed them. "If you're not going to tell me what I want to know, why should I tell you?"

Debriefing wasn't part of his job, but he hadn't made any promises to lie to her. Only to keep her safe. "The kidnapper was Prince Linus Demetrios."

She gasped at the name of her ex-fiancé. "No. Linus wouldn't have shot you. He would never hurt anyone. He's not capable…"

As sheltered as her life had been, she had no idea of what desperate men were capable. He hoped she never found out.

"He actually wasn't responsible for my gunshot wound," Whit admitted. "But he was responsible for Charlotte's kidnapping."

"He thought she was me?" she asked, her voice cracking with emotion and those dark eyes filling with guilt.

He didn't want to tell her, didn't want to make her feel worse. But he wouldn't lie to her, as everyone else had. So he just nodded.

"But why would Linus want to kidnap me?"

"He didn't want to lose you," Whit said. While he didn't appreciate the man's methods, he understood his reasoning.

"How was kidnapping me going to keep me?" she asked. "Did he intend to never let me go? To hold me captive forever?"

Whit sighed and figured he might as well explain the man's twisted plan as best he understood it. "He intended to get you pregnant, so he would have a claim to St. Pierre through an heir."

Hurt flashed across her face. "Of course he didn't really want me. He wanted my country." Her eyes widened with shock. "Did he…hurt Charlotte?"

"No. He was going to go about it artificially, but she was already pregnant—"

"Charlotte's pregnant, too?"

"Yes," he said. "With Aaron's baby."

Her pain and indignation forgotten, she smiled. "That's wonderful. And the baby is all right despite her being abducted?"

"Fine," he assured her. "She's fine. You can see for yourself soon enough."

She shook her head. "No…"

Was she refusing to return or was she denying something else entirely? "What do you mean?"

"That plan couldn't have been Linus's alone. He wasn't that clever or that conniving," she said. "But his father…"

"His father?" At the ball, he'd been warned to be especially vigilant of King Demetrios after Gabby's father made his announcement changing her engagement. The man had been enraged, but he hadn't spoken a word, just left in a blind fury.

"King Demetrios was determined to join his country to St. Pierre," she explained. "He could have masterminded the whole plot."

And if that plot had been thwarted, would he have stepped in again with the help of the man who tried grabbing Gabby in the airport? Maybe his son's arrest hadn't stopped his machinations.

"Is everything all right?" a woman's voice—as soft and sweet as Gabby's—asked.

Whit turned toward the doorway, toward the woman who, except for having white hair instead of golden brown, looked exactly like Gabby. He glanced from her to the princess and back—just in confirmation of what he already knew.

And seeing the look of understanding and betrayal on Gabriella's face, she realized that he'd known. And anger chased away her guilt.

THE SENSE OF betrayal overwhelmed Gabriella. She'd told herself that Whit wouldn't have known—that he might not have been keeping secrets like everyone else in her life had. But when he'd looked from her to Lydia and back, he hadn't been surprised by their uncanny resemblance.

He'd known that they were related. He'd known that Charlotte Green was more than Gabby's bodyguard; she was her sister, too—an illegitimate princess.

But then so was Gabby. Just like the baby she carried was an illegitimate royal. She pressed her palms over her belly as the baby shifted inside her, kicking so hard that Gabby's stomach moved. Her sister was also pregnant, her baby probably conceived the same night that Gabby's had been.

Gabriella was happy for her, but she didn't want to be with her. Not yet. Six months hadn't been long enough for her to come to terms with how she had been betrayed—by her father. By her sister…

She hadn't thought of Charlotte as just her bodyguard; she'd considered her a friend. She'd been such a fool…

Whit had gone with Lydia back to her office, so that he could use the landline phone—so that he could call for the royal jet to take her back to St. Pierre. He'd saved her from a kidnapper only to kidnap her himself—to take her somewhere she didn't want to be.

She glanced out through that open window to where he'd parked the Jeep. The keys dangled from the ignition. During the past six months, she'd learned to drive a manual transmission.

She grabbed up her backpack from the bed and headed out to the Jeep. It would take a while for Whit to get his call through, and even longer for him and whoever he called to understand what each other was saying. By the time he finished with his call, she would be almost back to the airport.

Authorities must have been called. Someone would have reported the shooting and Whit stealing the Jeep. With the local police swarming the airport, nobody would try to kidnap her again. She would probably be safer there than here with Whit.

But her hand trembled with nerves as she lifted the handle and pulled open the door. She stepped up into the Jeep and slid beneath the wheel. But before she could swing the door shut behind herself, a strong hand jerked it from her grasp.

She didn't look to confirm her fear of being abducted. But that hand couldn't belong to Whit. He couldn't have returned to the hut yet.

Had the men actually followed them but stayed out of sight until they'd found her—alone and vulnerable?

Chapter Five

Whit had left her alone and vulnerable. Some damn bodyguard he was.

And when he had stepped inside her hut and found it empty, he'd felt every bit as sick as he had when he'd seen that trashed hotel suite in Paris. The walls had been riddled with bullets, the rug and hardwood floor saturated with blood. He'd thought her dead then.

He didn't think her dead now. He thought her pissed off. So he wasn't surprised to find her trying to take off in the Jeep.

But she was surprised to see him. Her lips parted in a gasp when he stopped the door from closing. Then he reached for her.

She slapped at his hand and then turned, kicking out with her leg. Her foot connected squarely with his kneecap, which caused his knee to buckle and nearly give beneath his weight.

"Damn it!" he cursed her. And Charlotte. Her bodyguard had taught her some self-defense moves—in addition to teaching her how to shoot.

If the guy in the airport hadn't been trying to abduct her, Whit might have felt sorry for him taking the bullet in his shoulder. He knew too well how that felt. His throbbed with pain, but he ignored the discomfort as he tugged her from the vehicle. "Where the hell do you think you're going?"

"Whit?" She finally focused on him, her eyes widening with surprise. She stopped fighting and allowed him to guide her back inside the hut. "I thought you were calling St. Pierre."

St. Pierre. Not home.

Whit could relate. He'd never really had any place he had called home. After his mom had left, he and his dad had moved around a lot—his dad following the seasonal work of construction. Then Whit had joined the marines, going from base to base, deployment to deployment. And becoming a bodyguard had brought Whit into other people's homes without ever giving him a chance to make one of his own.

"Your aunt is making the call for me," he said. He had asked her to the moment he'd realized he shouldn't have left Gabby alone—because of her safety both physically and emotionally.

"You know who she is." Her usually sweet soft voice was sharp with resentment, and her eyes darkened with anger. "You were just like everyone else keeping secrets from me and using me."

Not only was she angry, she was in pain, too. He reached for her, trying to close his arms around her to offer comfort and assurance. "I didn't—"

But she jerked away from him, as if unable to bear his touch. But then she touched him, pressing her palms against his chest to push him back.

"How could you…" her voice cracked with emotion "…how could you be with me that night and not tell me what you knew?"

If anyone had used anyone that night, she had used him—probably to get back at her father for humiliating her at the ball. She must have figured having his daughter sleep with the hired help would shame the king.

"I didn't know, that night, that you and Charlotte were related," he said. But he should have noticed the resemblance sooner since he'd known the U.S. Marshal before her plastic surgery; the surgeon hadn't had to change much to make her Gabby's virtual twin.

She stared at him, her eyes still narrowed with skepticism. She probably thought he should have known, too.

He continued, "I didn't find out until after you'd disappeared." And remembering his anguish over that, his temperature rose and his blood pumped faster and harder in his veins. She'd let him and her father and her fiancé believe she was dead. She was hardly the saint he'd painted her to be. "How could you?"

"How could I what?" she asked, her brow furrowing with confusion.

Images of that hotel suite flashed through his mind again, bringing back all those feelings of fear and loss and…

"How could you just take off?" he asked. And leave everyone behind worried sick about her.

"I had a threat," she replied. "That person who hit you over the head that night left something under my pillow."

"A letter threatening your life," Whit said. If she hadn't distracted him from doing his job that evening, he would have been the one to find the note. Or if he'd followed his instincts and locked down the palace, he might have found the person who'd left the threat. "I know."

"Then you must know why I disappeared," she said, as if he were an idiot unable to grasp a simple concept. "I was in danger."

"Still are." His gut tightened with dread at the thought of that man pointing the gun at her and her unborn baby.

She shook her head. "The kidnapper was caught."

"Then who were those men at the airport?" he asked. "They sure as hell looked dangerous to me. Then again I didn't get a good look at them—I was too busy dodging the bullets they were firing at us."

"They probably thought we'd killed their friend," she said, making excuses for the men. "I shot him, and you knocked him out."

Whit nodded. "Yes, because he was threatening your life—just like the person who'd left the note. So you are definitely still in danger."

She shrugged, apparently unconcerned. "The man who grabbed me was an opportunist. He recognized me, saw that I was unprotected and tried to take advantage of the situation."

"Why was he here?" Why? Had he followed Whit right to her? And if he'd followed him from the place Charlotte Green had been held captive in Michigan, then he could have followed him to the orphanage.

"This country is a war zone full of rebels and mercenaries," Gabriella said.

"Then why the hell would your bodyguard send you here?" Maybe his doubts about Charlotte's motives had been right. Maybe she hadn't been trying to protect Princess Gabriella when she'd had plastic surgery to look just like her; maybe she had been trying to take her place as the legitimate heir to the country of St. Pierre and the fortune of the king.

But Charlotte had seemed to genuinely care about her assignment. About her *sister.* Then he realized the answer to his own question. "She couldn't tell you. The king had sworn her to secrecy with the threat of firing her if she told you the truth."

Gabriella gasped and then blinked furiously as tears pooled in her eyes. "My father wouldn't allow her to tell me?"

He had begun to appreciate Charlotte Green when she'd saved his life four or five days ago. But he really appreciated her now, for finding a way around the king's royal decree. "So she showed you. She had to know that once you met her aunt you would figure it out."

Charlotte had found a way around the king, but with the way she'd handled the situation, Gabriella had been alone when she'd learned the truth. Even though Lydia was related to her, she was a stranger. There had been no one there for Gabby who could have held her, who could have comforted her.

His arms ached, not from the gunshot wound, but with the need to hold her, to have been the one who comforted her when her world had turned on its axis. And when everything that she had believed to be true had become a lie.

She expelled a shaky breath. "I figured out that my father, that *my family,*" her voice cracked as emotion overwhelmed her, "has made a fool of me my entire life."

He reached for her again, and this time she didn't fight him off. Instead she wrapped her arms around his shoulders and clung to him. And his arms, which had ached to hold her, embraced her.

He ignored the twinge of pain in his shoulder. He ignored everything but how warm and soft she was and how perfect she felt.

Then, even as close as they were, there was a movement between them. The baby shifted in her stomach, kicking him as he or she kicked Gabby. While it was only a gentle movement, Whit felt the kick more violently than he had the princess's when she'd tried to fight him off at the Jeep.

This baby inside her could possibly be his. He could be a father?

GABBY FELT HIM tense, so she pulled back—embarrassed that she had clung to him. More embarrassed that she'd wanted to keep clinging to him. She had missed him, missed his touch—his strength. That night he'd guarded her he had made her feel safer than she'd ever felt. He'd made her feel *more* than she had ever felt.

Even now, her tumultuous emotions were all mixed up about him. She had to remind herself that, like that night, he was just doing his job. She meant nothing more to him than a paycheck from her father. She'd realized that when she'd woken alone the next morning and even more so when she'd left for Paris and he hadn't tried to stop her.

She'd felt like such a fool for throwing herself at a man who really hadn't wanted her. And then she had come here…and discovered exactly how big a fool she'd been.

"I could never figure out why my mother—the queen— hated me so much," she admitted.

The woman had never shown Gabby an ounce of affection or approval. On her deathbed, she had even refused to see Gabriella—not wanting hers to be the last face she ever saw. She had never been able to tolerate even looking at Gabby. That was why she'd sent her off to boarding schools when she'd been scarcely more than a toddler.

"But she wasn't really my mother," Gabriella said. She had actually been relieved to learn that; it had explained so much. It wasn't just that she was so unlovable her own mother hadn't been able to love her. The queen hadn't been her mother. But then her biological mother hadn't loved her either since she'd so easily given up her baby.

"The queen couldn't have any children," she continued. He undoubtedly already knew this, but she needed to say it aloud—needed to bring the secrets to light since she had been left in the dark too long. "So the king had his mistress give him another baby—one he intended to claim and make the queen pretend was hers. Unlike Charlotte, whom he never claimed."

"He has now," Whit said, as if it mattered.

The king had denied the paternity of his eldest for thirty years. And for twenty-four years he'd denied Gabby a relationship with her sister and her aunt. Gabriella would never be able to forgive him that—let alone having traded her from one fiancé to another like livestock. But, as things had turned out, he had been right to break her engagement to Prince Linus. Despite her friendship with him, he hadn't been the man she'd thought he was.

Even if he hadn't masterminded the kidnapping plot, he had gone along with it. He'd put Charlotte's life and the life of Gabby's future niece or nephew at risk. But he hadn't done it out of love. He'd done it so he could make a claim on her country.

Nobody in her life had actually been the person she'd thought he or she was.

As if on cue, Lydia Green stepped through the doorway and entered the hut. Her gaze went immediately to Gabby, as if surprised to find her still there and emotionally intact.

Gabby was surprised, too. But then if Whit hadn't caught her, she might have been halfway to the airport by now.

"Did the call go through?" Whit asked.

Gabby held her breath, hoping that it hadn't. She didn't want the royal jet being sent for her—because she knew there was only one place that jet would bring her. Back to St. Pierre.

But Lydia nodded. Her gaze still on Gabby, her eyes filled with regret. She knew this wasn't what Gabriella wanted. She was the first one who actually cared what Gabby wanted.

"When are they going to send the royal jet?" Whit asked.

Her aunt still wouldn't look at him, continuing to stare at Gabby—much as she had the first time Gabriella had shown up at the orphanage. When her sister had signed off her parental rights to her youngest child, Lydia had thought she would never see the baby again. She had been elated when she'd realized who Gabriella really was.

Gabby had been devastated. Her biological mother had basically sold her. Unlike Lydia who'd followed her parents into missionary work, Bonita Green had resented never having material possessions. She'd spent her life conning people out of theirs until one of those marks had cut her life short.

Gabby would never have the chance to meet the woman—not that she ever would have wanted to. The queen and a former con artist were her only maternal examples. Gabby rubbed her belly, silently apologizing to her baby. It wasn't really a question of if she would screw up; it was more a question of how badly.

"Are they going to send it?" Whit anxiously prodded Lydia for a reply.

Her aunt continued to focus on Gabby. "They already sent it—several hours ago actually. It should be here soon."

She obviously wondered if Gabby still wanted to go. Gabby had actually never intended to go back there. But she wasn't going to put Lydia in the awkward position that Charlotte had when she'd sent Gabby here. So she nodded her acceptance and forced a smile.

Her aunt released a soft sigh, but Gabby couldn't tell if it was of relief or disappointment.

"Before you leave for the airport, come say goodbye," Lydia said, "again."

"We will," Whit answered for them both.

Once her aunt had gone, Gabby admonished him, "You shouldn't have spoken for me."

His jaw tensed; perhaps he clenched his teeth in response to her imperious tone. But he didn't apologize or argue. He only headed for the doorway, as if she were going to blindly follow him.

"I'm not leaving," she explained. She had no intention of going where she couldn't trust anyone.

THE WOMAN INFURIATED him. From the moment he'd met her, he hadn't been able to figure her out. She was unlike anyone else he'd ever known. "If you're not leaving, why the hell did I just stop you from taking off in the Jeep?"

"I was trying to get away from you," she said dispassionately, as if her words weren't like a knife plunged in his back.

"Why?"

"Because I can't trust you," she said—again so matter-of-factly that it was obvious she had never considered trusting him at all.

But before he could defend himself, she continued, "I can't trust anyone on St. Pierre. That's why I'm not going back."

He understood her reasons. But he had a job to do—protect her. And after the close call at the airport, he wasn't convinced he could do that alone. Especially not here. He had a gun but no bullets, a shoulder throbbing with pain and a possible infection. "You can't stay here."

She let out a wistful sigh. "I know."

She'd been leaving earlier, and in a disguise, because everyone knew where she was now. He couldn't blame her for wanting to stay hidden.

"Where were you going?" he asked again.

She chuckled but without humor. "You really are just like everyone else," she mused. "You think I'm an idiot. But you shouldn't believe my image. It's a lie just like the rest of my life has been."

He'd already learned that for himself.

She lifted her chin with stubbornness and pride. "I'm not telling you where I'm going."

"Fine," he said. "I'll tell *you*. You're going with me."

Back to St. Pierre? Could he bring her back there? To the family who'd lied to her? To the stranger she didn't want to marry?

His stomach churned with revulsion over the thought of her marrying anyone, of her lying in anyone else's bed, in anyone else's arms…

He forced away the repugnance and the twinges of jealousy. He had no right to either. Unless…

"We are leaving," he continued. "As soon as you tell me who the father of your baby is."

She flinched, as if he'd slapped her. Or insulted her. Because she'd often been photographed with movie stars and athletes, the media had painted her as a promiscuous princess. But he had intimately learned exactly how wrong they had been about her—as wrong as when they'd claimed she was ditzy.

She was neither.

"You've been working for my father too long," she said. From the disdain in her voice, the comment was obviously more complaint than compliment. "You're beginning to act just like him."

He winced now, definitely offended. Fortunately he had only been hired to protect the man, not to like him. King St. Pierre was tough to like. He was a difficult man. Period.

"Since I do work for your father, I need to carry out his orders," Whit replied, choosing to ignore the insult and focus on what was more important. "He wants you safely back in St. Pierre."

She snorted—a sound he would have thought her entirely too ladylike to make. Wouldn't some princess etiquette class in one of those fancy boarding schools she'd attended have polished the ability to snort right out of her?

She lifted her chin again, looking every bit the royal ruler despite her dirty jeans and blouse. "You're crazy to think I will be safe in St. Pierre."

He might have agreed with her if he hadn't just re-established his friendship with Aaron. He trusted that man with his life and hers. "You'll be safer there than you are here where you were just nearly abducted and shot at…"

She might have been right about it being a crime of opportunity. Maybe it was just a dangerous country with dangerous men. Maybe he hadn't been followed straight to her…

"That can happen in St. Pierre, too," she pointed out.

"I will make sure it doesn't happen," he said. "I will protect you." And with Aaron and Charlotte helping, he had a good possibility of actually keeping her safe.

"You will protect me from kidnappers and killers," she agreed—again with that damn calmness that infuriated him. "But will you protect me from my father?"

He couldn't say that her father wouldn't hurt her—because he already had. With his lies. With his manipulations…

Maybe she had learned some of her father's moves because she had veered the conversation away from what he wanted to know. She'd stalled him long enough. Maybe it was her form of payback for having had to wait twenty-four years before she'd learned the truth.

"Gabby," he began, about to urge her to stop the cycle of secrets now.

But the roar of a Jeep engine drew his attention to the

doorway. If he'd missed a tail from the airport, he had lost his ability to do his job properly—then he couldn't protect the princess.

But there was only one man in the Jeep. Both the man and the vehicle must have been familiar to the kids because they came out of nowhere to greet him, dancing around his feet like puppies as he hopped out of the vehicle. The kids hadn't greeted him and Gabby like that. Maybe they'd been in class. Or maybe they had been taught to never approach a strange vehicle or a strange man. This man wasn't unfamiliar to them.

Despite the black medical bag clutched in his hand, he looked too young to be a doctor.

Whit should have cancelled the house call Lydia had arranged; he didn't need a doctor. He needed the truth from the princess; he needed to know the paternity of her baby.

"Gabriella," the man said. With the familiarity of a frequent visitor, he stepped through the hut doorway without knocking and waiting for her permission to enter. "I am sorry I took so long getting away from the clinic."

She offered this man the smile she used to give Whit when they'd first met. It was a smile full of warmth and welcome and beauty. Whit wondered if she would ever smile that way at him again.

"Dominic, it's fine," she assured the doctor, her concern for Whit's injury obviously long forgotten. "I know how busy you are."

The guy answered her smile with a wide grin. Not only was he young but good-looking, too, since women seemed to like that whole tall and dark thing. Or at least that was what he'd witnessed with the women who'd gone for Aaron Timmer over the years. As easily as his partner had fallen for women, they had responded to him, too.

This guy also had charm. His grin widened as he took Gabby's hand in his with a familiarity and possessiveness that had Whit gritting his teeth. "If you had been the patient, I would have dropped everything..."

For her. Not for Whit. The doctor had clearly fallen for the princess.

Maybe Whit had been wrong to assume the child she carried was his. Maybe her baby belonged to this man.

Whit should have been relieved that he might not be the father. But his heart dropped with regret. And then possessiveness gripped him.

He did not want Princess Gabriella or the baby she carried belonging to any man but him.

Chapter Six

"The doctor gave me a clean bill of health."

Aaron Timmer grinned at the news. He was apparently as relieved as she was that their baby was all right. But Charlotte wasn't worried only about the baby she carried. She was worried about the baby sister she'd failed to protect as she'd sworn she would.

"I'm clear to travel," she said. "Clear to do my job."

Aaron shook his head. "You don't have a job anymore," he reminded her. "The king doesn't want you working for him."

King St. Pierre claimed that he wanted Charlotte as a daughter now, not as an employee. But she worried that he'd dismissed her because he no longer trusted her to safeguard the princess—not after she had already failed. Charlotte had spent six months in captivity and during that time all kinds of unimaginable horrors could have happened to Gabriella—since she'd been left completely unprotected.

"She's pregnant, too," Charlotte said, as with awe, she remembered her aunt's words the first time they had talked. The phone connection hadn't been good, but she'd not misinterpreted that.

Aaron sighed. "Did you tell your father that news?"

Charlotte tensed—not used to thinking of the king as her father even though she'd known for a few years now. Gabby had just discovered her real parentage. So she was dealing with all those conflicting emotions while she was going to become a mother herself.

"I haven't told him yet," Charlotte admitted. "I'm concerned…"

"About how he will react?"

The king had never treated Gabby with the respect she deserved. He'd never treated her like what she was—an independent, modern woman. "He already arranged for her to marry another man."

"You don't think the baby she's carrying is Prince Tonio Malamatos's?" Aaron asked, referring to Gabby's fiancé.

The prince had been waiting at the palace when they arrived. As soon as the king had notified him that the princess had been found, he had come from his country with an entourage that included his ex-fiancée. When Charlotte had stepped off the plane, he'd mistaken her for Gabby and tried to embrace her. She shuddered as she remembered the man's clammy hands touching her arms, of his pasty cheek trying to press against hers.

Gabby never would have let that man touch her. Charlotte shook her head. "And neither do you. You know who the father is."

He expelled a ragged sigh. "Whit. If they'd been involved before she disappeared, it would explain why he was acting so strangely when you and Gabby went missing." Aaron had admitted that he'd been suspicious his old partner had been involved in their disappearances. "And why he was so anxious to bring her back once you told him where she was."

"I knew she had a crush on him," Charlotte admitted. "But I hadn't thought Whit would ever act on her vulnerability to him."

"Neither did I," Aaron admitted. "He's always been the professional, unemotional one."

Charlotte smiled as she thought of her sister. "Gabby has a way of getting to a person, of stealing her way into your heart."

But that hadn't worked with their real mother or with the queen. The person actually had to have a heart for Gabby to work her way inside. From everything Charlotte had heard about him, Whitaker Howell didn't have a heart either. But he had acted very worried about Gabriella and her safety.

Charlotte was also anxious about her sister. "I hope she's had access to medical care. And that she's not in need of it now."

"She's fine," Aaron said, referring back to Charlotte's most recent conversation with her aunt, who had called the palace at Whit's request. "Whit rescued her at the airport."

Charlotte breathed a soft sigh of relief. Whit had saved her. Just because he'd been doing his job? Or because he cared about Gabby?

In order to board the royal jet and return to St. Pierre, they would have to go back to the airport. And what if the gunmen were waiting there to try to grab Princess Gabriella again?

"We still should be there, too," Charlotte insisted. While the doctor had cleared her for flight and work, he'd cautioned her to take it easy. She'd been restrained to a bed for the past six months, so she'd lost some of her strength and stamina.

"The other jet has already taken off," Aaron said. "They're hours ahead of us and may have already landed."

"But they're not you and me," she pointed out. "And I'm not sure if Whit should trust anyone but you and me." Not with his life and certainly not with Gabby's.

Aaron snorted. "That shouldn't be a problem since Whit rarely trusts anyone."

"That's what's kept him alive for the past thirty years," Charlotte pointed out. But the problem was that he was traveling with a woman who trusted everyone, who always saw the good in people no matter what they'd done. Gabby would forgive Charlotte— eventually. But she wouldn't be able to do that unless Whit could keep her alive.

SIX MONTHS AGO Whit had been willing to let her marry another man, but today he had barely let the doctor speak to her before he'd ushered Dominic Delgado back to his Jeep. Dominic was an irrepressible flirt. Was Whit jealous?

Hope fluttered in her heart—and in her belly as the baby kicked with excitement. Could Whit care enough to feel jealousy?

He strode back through the doorway. "We have to leave now. The royal jet may have already landed."

So he hadn't been jealous at all. Just impatient to carry out his orders to bring her back to St. Pierre and her father. Disappointment quelled her flash of hope. But then she didn't want him to be jealous of her. Because if Prince Linus had been acting of his own accord and not his father's, then it must have been his jealousy that had cost Charlotte six months of her life.

She doubted he'd acted alone, though, because she doubted he'd cared enough to be jealous of her.

"You really want to bring me back to St. Pierre?" she asked. And her disappointment grew.

She had been right to leave him six months ago. Despite that night they'd shared, he hadn't cared anything for her—not enough to stop her from leaving. Not enough to stop her from marrying another man.

"You need to go back to St. Pierre," he stubbornly insisted. A muscle in his lean cheek, beneath the couple of days' worth of stubble and above his tightly clenched jaw, twitched.

"Why?" she asked. Nobody on St. Pierre genuinely cared for her—at least not enough to have ever been honest with her. "So my father can force me to marry Prince Tonio Malamatos?"

"That is not the reason why the king wants you home," Whit said.

She wasn't foolish enough to entertain any flutters of hope this time. Her question was more rhetorical than curious; despite the secrets he'd kept, she still knew her father well. Too well. "So he's broken that engagement for me, too?"

Good thing her question had been rhetorical because he didn't answer it. That muscle just twitched in his cheek again.

"Maybe Prince Tonio took my disappearance as a rejection and resumed his engagement to my cousin?" Actually Honora Del Cachon wasn't her cousin since Gabby wasn't really the queen's daughter. Like the queen, Honora had never liked Gabby, either. The night of the ball—when she'd been publicly humiliated—instead of blaming the king, Honora had glared at

Gabby with such hatred that she shuddered even now, remembering it. "They could actually be married by now." And she fervently hoped that they were.

Whit shook his head. "Prince Malamatos refused to break your engagement until he had proof that you were dead."

"He waited for me?" she asked. Unlike Prince Linus, he didn't even know her. They had only met a few times over her lifetime, and had rarely spoken more than a couple of words to each other. So his loyalty wasn't personal.

Was her country that important to him?

Whit jerked his chin up and down in a rough nod. And for a second she wondered if he'd read her mind. But he probably only meant that the prince had waited for her.

"So he still intends to marry me when I return?" Panic rushed up on her now, so that she struggled to draw a deep breath. "And my father will expect me to obey his royal command and marry the prince."

"You can talk to him this time," Whit said, "instead of running away."

His words stung her pride. "You think I ran away six months ago?"

He gave a sharp nod. "I know that's what you did."

"I was threatened," she reminded him. Physically and emotionally. "And Charlotte thought I would be safer here." From both threats.

"Charlotte thought wrong."

"I was safe for six months," she said. And happy, despite feeling like a fool for giving her love to a man without a heart and for believing her family's lies. "I was safe until you came here."

He flinched but didn't deny that he might be responsible for the danger she'd stumbled into at the airport. "You're not safe anymore," he said. "We need to leave."

Distress attacked her again, making her heart race and her stomach flip. "You don't care about me." She'd realized that long ago but it still hurt to know she'd given him so much and he'd given her so little.

She touched her belly. Actually he'd given her much more than he'd realized.

"Gabby," he said, his breath expelling in a ragged sigh of exasperation. Then he lifted his arms and reached for her, as if he intended to offer her comfort or reassurance.

But she held up a hand between them, holding him off. "And that's fine. I don't care that you don't care what'll happen to me on St. Pierre. But what about your baby? Don't you worry what will happen to him?"

There. She'd done it—she'd told him the truth. He was about to be a father.

But why would he care since he obviously didn't spare a thought for the baby's mother? She would try not to take it personally; perhaps Whit Howell cared about nothing and no one.

ALL THE BLOOD rushed from Whit's head, leaving him dizzy while heat rushed to his face. Sweat beaded on his brow. He brushed it away with a shaky hand. Maybe he should have let the doctor examine him, so he could have known for sure that he wasn't on the verge of having a stroke.

His heart raced, pounding fast and hard. And his lungs were too constricted for him to draw a deep breath. He had been in some of the most dangerous places and situations in the world, but he'd never felt such panic and fear before.

"Are you all right?" Gabby asked. Moments ago she'd pushed him away, but now she reached for him, her small hands grasping his forearms.

He nodded. But it was a lie. He wasn't all right. He was about to become a father—one of several things he'd sworn he would never be: a father, a husband, a besotted lover...

By leaving them, his mother had destroyed his father, sinking him deeper into the bottle, so that he hadn't been able to hold a job. Three years ago, when Whit had lost a job and struggled to get another, he'd felt like he was becoming his old man. And he had become more determined than ever to not even risk it. That was why he'd put up with the king and his asinine royal commands—because he hadn't wanted to lose another job. But now he risked losing so much more than just a job.

"Are you sure?" he asked.

She jerked her hands off his arms as if his skin had burned her. Maybe it had. He felt like his face was on fire. And he still couldn't draw a deep breath.

But then she lifted her face toward his, and her big brown eyes were bright with indignation. "You know there was only you..."

His muscles tensed like they had that night when he'd realized she was a virgin, that despite all the media reports to the contrary, she had never been promiscuous. She had never been with another man before. Whit had tried to pull back, had tried to stop, but they'd both been too overcome with passion. And she'd urged him to take her—to take her innocence.

He'd done it because he'd wanted her so much and because he had really believed she'd wanted him. But the next morning when he'd returned to his room to change his clothes so that no one would realize that he'd spent the night with her, she had packed up and booked her flight to Paris. And he'd realized that he'd probably just been an act of rebellion for her, that she'd used him as revenge against her father.

"I know that I was the only one before you disappeared." He heard the Jeep's engine droning in the distance. "But you've been here six months…" Close to a man who had obviously fallen for her.

She lifted her hand, as if she intended to slap him, but then she drew in a breath and her control. And instead of touching him, she pressed her palm to her belly. "I am six months along. I was already pregnant when I came here."

He waited for more, waited for her to assure him that she'd slept with no other man but him. She offered no such assurances about her love life.

She only assured him, "This baby is yours."

But only the baby. She was not his. And she would never be.

If he brought her back to St. Pierre, her father might very well do as she feared; he might force her into marrying a strange prince. It was King St. Pierre's country, his rules. And he sure as hell wasn't going to let his princess become involved with a bodyguard.

"Where were you going?" he asked.

She blinked and then narrowed her eyes in confusion. "Six months ago?"

"No. Today," he clarified. "At the airport. If you had time to buy a ticket, where were you going to go?"

"The United States."

She'd be safer there than St. Pierre.

"Any state in particular?" he wondered.

She pressed her lips together, as if refusing to answer him. Obviously she still intended to give him the slip, and she didn't want to make it easy for him to find her again.

"I'm not letting you out of my sight," he said. Especially not after what had happened at the airport. She could have been kidnapped or killed. And if he took his eyes off her for a moment, she would try to lose him again—leaving herself and their baby vulnerable.

Their baby?

He waited for the panic to surge back, but he could still breathe. His heart was beating—strong and steady—instead of the frantic pace it had when he'd first realized her baby was really his.

"Then why does it matter where I was going?" she asked with a slight shrug.

He fought an internal battle between following the rules and following his gut, between betraying friends and betraying her. His shoulder throbbed, as if his struggle had been physical as well as emotional. Or maybe it was infected. He really should have let Dr. Dominic examine it. But he ignored the pain and mimicked her shrug. "Because I want to know where we're going when we get to the airport."

She gasped in surprise over his admission. "You're not taking me to St. Pierre?"

He couldn't. Even before she'd told him the baby was his, he doubted he could have brought her back to the people who'd betrayed her—who'd manipulated and lied to her for her entire life. She deserved better than that.

She also deserved better than him.

Maybe he should leave her here with the doctor and Lydia—people who were able to love and already loved her. That would be the right thing to do, but Whit rarely did what was right. Because even if it was right, it wasn't safe to leave her in a country where a man had already tried to abduct her and had nearly shot at her.

"No," he replied. "But we can't stay here, either."

"Because everyone knows where we are," she said, as if she'd read his mind again. But she continued to stare up at him, as if debating whether or not to trust him.

After discovering how many people had lied to her and for how long, she shouldn't trust anyone. Ever. Again.

He could figure out another place for them to go. During his years in the service, he had traveled so much that he had discovered some places where a man could hide. But a pregnant princess?

"I was going to Michigan," she said.

"Michigan? How did you know that's where Charlotte was held for six months?" Had she already forgiven her sister and wanted to check on her?

Her brow furrowed with confusion. "I didn't. Where in Michigan was she held?"

"At a private psychiatric hospital called Serenity House." He nearly shuddered as he remembered the place that had been Charlotte's prison for six months and had nearly been where Whit had breathed his last.

She flinched with obvious regret and embarrassment. "I told Linus about Serenity House."

"How did you know about it?" he asked. She was

inquisitive by nature; his men had told him that she'd often asked them about him. But he hadn't realized how knowledgeable she was.

"Someone told me about it," she replied, evasively avoiding his gaze.

Nothing had been less serene than a pregnant woman being held captive there for six months, restrained to a bed. It was also where Whit had been shot and would have been killed had it not been for Charlotte. He owed her his life. Could he keep her sister from her?

"Who did you talk to?" he asked, more worried than curious.

She shrugged. "Just somebody who lives near there."

"Did you meet her through Charlotte?"

She nodded. "Charlotte met her while she was still a U.S. Marshal. I think it was on her last assignment that they met."

And Whit's last assignment as Aaron's partner before they dissolved their business and their friendship. "Josie Jessup?"

Gabby shook her head. "That's not her name."

"It probably isn't now," he said. "But I bet it sure as hell was. I know who she is. And I've always known where she was in northern Michigan—not that damn far from Serenity House."

He had betrayed Aaron to make sure that Josie stayed safe, when he'd helped Charlotte fake his and Aaron's former client's death to put her in witness relocation. So to make sure she was safe, he'd found out where the U.S. Marshal had hidden her.

Gabby nipped at her bottom lip and then nodded. "Charlotte called her JJ."

"Charlotte shouldn't have told you anything about

her." A man had been killed trying to find out where the woman, heiress to a media mogul's empire, was hiding. Whit had been forced to kill the man in order to save Aaron's life and Josie's. His shoulder throbbed just thinking about the danger her knowledge put Gabriella in.

"Why the hell would Charlotte tell you where she is?" he asked. "Nobody should know." Maybe that was why the man at the airport had tried to grab Gabby—not because of who she was but of what she might know. It was information that someone had already killed for—information over which Whit had nearly died. Before he'd killed the man, the man had had gunmen try to kill him and Aaron. That was when Whit had taken the hit to the shoulder.

"She trusts her," Gabby explained. "And if anything happened to Charlotte, she trusted JJ and me to help each other."

While he'd been protecting her over three years ago, Whit had figured out that Josie Jessup was a smart, resourceful woman. What he hadn't realized was how smart and resourceful Gabriella St. Pierre was.

"We can't go there," he said.

"Of course not now," she agreed. "Charlotte would look for me there. That would have been a stupid place to hide." She shook her head, apparently disgusted with herself for considering it.

Gabby had yet to realize how intelligent and capable she was. She must have read and believed too much of what was printed about her. Whit knew, intimately, how wrong the media had always been about her.

"If Charlotte was still missing, you would have been smart to go to Josie," he admitted.

With the former U.S. Marshal's help, Josie had learned how to disappear. And maybe that was what Gabby needed to do—not just for six months but for the rest of her life. It might be the only way she would escape her father's archaic insistence on ruling her life like he ruled his country—as a sole dictatorship.

"Why didn't you go to Josie earlier?" he asked, wondering why she hadn't the minute she'd discovered Charlotte had been keeping secrets from her.

Gabby glanced around that primitive hut. "I didn't want to leave here."

It obviously wasn't the conditions that had made her want to stay. So it was either the orphans, her aunt or Dr. Dominic. He hoped like hell it wasn't the doctor.

WHAT DID HE think about becoming a father?

Gabriella kept studying Whit's handsome face, but he revealed nothing of his feelings—after the initial shock. Maybe he was still in shock. But that could have been from the gunshot wound more than over what she'd told him.

"You really should have had Dominic examine you," she admonished him.

Whit shook his head. "I don't need a doctor. I need to get you out of here. Did you have all your stuff packed up?"

She nodded. Everything she needed was in her big backpack-style bag. She could no longer wear anything she'd brought with her six months ago. The clothes either didn't fit or hadn't stood up to the elements or how hard she had worked.

"Then we need to go," he said, heading toward the doorway.

But Gabriella stayed where she was, standing next to the bed, fingering the edge of the mosquito netting. "Can I really trust that you're not going to bring me back to St. Pierre?"

She had debated with herself before telling him about Michigan. While Charlotte hadn't trusted her with the secret that affected her own life, she had told her all about Josie Jessup and how Whit helping her relocate the woman had ruined his friendship with Aaron. So she knew he was very familiar with Josie's situation. Gabriella had no intention of putting JJ in danger. She'd only wanted to put herself and her unborn baby somewhere safe.

But apparently Michigan wasn't safe, either. But at least in Michigan, no one would make her marry someone she didn't know, let alone love.

He uttered a ragged sigh. "I'd like to think that you're wrong about your father—that he won't force you to marry Prince Malamatos…"

"You don't know my father like I do," she said.

After what she'd learned about her biological mother, she had to accept that she didn't know her father very well, either. Not that she didn't believe he would have cheated on the queen but she didn't believe he would have fallen for a con artist. Then again he hadn't fallen for the woman or he wouldn't have stayed with the queen. Or would he—just for the sake of propriety? Hell, the only thing she knew for certain was that nothing mattered to him as much as his country—certainly not either of his daughters.

Whit nodded his head in agreement. "That's why I can't risk it."

"Why do you care if I'm forced to marry the prince?" she asked.

He clenched his jaw again, so tightly that he had that muscle twitching in his cheek.

"Don't worry," she said. "I know you haven't suddenly developed feelings for me." When he had so obviously not given a damn about her before now. "I know it must be because of the baby."

"I don't want another man claiming *my* child," Whit said, his voice gruff.

"So *you're* claiming your child?" she asked.

His chest lifted, pushing against his black T-shirt, as he drew in a deep breath. Then he nodded. "I believe you—that the baby's mine."

"But that doesn't mean you have to claim him," she pointed out, especially since he'd reacted to the news as if she'd shot him.

His already dark eyes darkened more with anger and pride. "You think I could walk away and pretend I don't have a child growing inside you?"

"So if I wasn't carrying your baby, you could walk away?" She needed to know that—needed to face the fact that it didn't matter that they were having a child together. They had no future together.

"I didn't say that."

"You didn't have to," she said. She grabbed up her bag from the bed and headed toward the doorway.

But he caught her arm, turning her back toward him.

"What?" she asked. "I thought you were in such a hurry to leave that you couldn't even take a minute for the doctor to examine you."

"Forget the damn doctor!" he snapped.

"I think you mean that." Literally. That he wanted

her to forget about Dominic. Did he think she'd been involved with the flirt?

"I spent six months thinking about you," he said, almost reluctantly as if the admission had been tortured from him, "thinking that you were dead and blaming myself for letting you go to Paris." His anger turned to anguish and guilt that twisted his handsome face into a grimace. "So, no, I couldn't walk away—even if you weren't carrying my baby."

Now the guilt was all hers. When she'd gone into hiding, she hadn't thought that anyone would miss her. Least of all Whitaker Howell.

"I'm sorry," she said. "I never meant for you to feel responsible."

Whit groaned, as if he were in pain. But was it physical or emotional? "I don't like feeling responsible. I don't like feeling...*anything*." He tugged her closer. "You make me feel all kinds of emotions I don't want to feel."

"I'm sorry," she said again, in a breathy whisper as attraction stole away her breath.

He was so close, with such an intense look of desire in his dark eyes. Then he was even closer, as he lowered his head to hers. His lips skimmed across hers, gently, only to return with hunger and passion.

Gabby reeled with the force of emotions so intense that her head grew light and dizzy. She clutched at his shoulders, holding tightly to him as her world spun out of control.

Six months had passed but she wanted him as desperately as she had the night of the ball, the night they'd conceived their child. Maybe she wanted him even more because now she knew what to expect.

Ecstasy.

But he tensed and stepped back from her. There was no desire on his face anymore—just shock and horror.

Then she heard it, too—the sound of engines, revving loudly as vehicles sped toward the compound. It wasn't just the doctor returning. There was more than one vehicle—more than one man.

They had waited too long. They'd been found, and if it were the gunmen from the airport coming, they had put the lives of everyone in the compound at risk.

Chapter Seven

Whit cursed. How had he let himself get so distracted? He would like to blame his gunshot wound. But he knew the real reason was Gabriella and all those feelings she made him feel that he didn't want to.

Like guilt. It pummeled him.

"If the guys from the airport found us, we can't let them hurt the children," Gabby said as she rushed toward that open doorway.

Whit stepped in front of her so she wouldn't run outside. "I won't."

She shook her head. "You can't protect them against all those men. I'll just let them take me. It's the only way to keep everyone safe."

She was serious—and more self-sacrificing than anyone he'd ever met. If he survived this, he might personally track down every paparazzi who'd called her a spoiled princess. A shallow ditz. They had no idea who Gabriella St. Pierre really was.

Whit wrapped his arm around her and rushed her toward the Jeep. He turned the key in the ignition and shifted into Drive. "We'll lead them away from here."

It was the only way to keep the children safe. They

wouldn't destroy the compound looking for them—if they saw them leave.

"Hang on tight," he ordered her. If only the damn vehicle had seat belts...

And if only the road between the compound and town was more than a narrow path cut through the jungle...

He'd barely made it down that path when there had been no other vehicles on it. He really had no room to pass the Jeep and truck that were barreling down the track toward the compound. But he barreled ahead, and metal scraped metal, the driver's side of the Jeep scraping along the pickup.

Men filled the truck, inside the cab and standing in the box with long guns slung over their shoulders.

"Get down!" he shouted at Gabby.

"No!" she yelled back—even as bullets pinged against the metal of Whit's side of the vehicle. "They need to see me so that they know I'm not at the orphanage!"

As if to prove her point, she lifted her head higher and peered around him. And the windshield exploded as a bullet struck the glass. It continued into the rearview mirror, cracked the plastic and shattered the mirror.

"Get down!" he shouted again. But instead of waiting for her to comply, he reached across the console and pushed her lower.

Then he focused again on the road—just as a Jeep steered straight toward them. He clutched the wheel in tight fists, holding his own vehicle steady on the trail. And he trusted that the guy driving the other vehicle would give in to impulse—the impulse to jerk the wheel at the last moment.

Whit resisted his impulse even when Gabby lifted

her head and screamed. But he didn't turn away. Metal ground against metal again, but the impact was lessened as the other driver twisted his wheel and turned the tires. Whit pressed hard on the accelerator, careening past, as the other vehicle bounced off trees and rolled back onto the trail—on its roof.

Shots rang out, continuing to break glass and glance off metal. Whit wouldn't have looked back even if the rearview mirror hadn't been broken. He kept speeding along the winding trail, widening the distance between him and the men who would have grabbed Gabby had they not escaped in time.

And, because his feelings for her had distracted him, they nearly hadn't escaped. For her sake, he could not succumb to emotion again.

GABBY COULDN'T STOP looking back—at the men who stood on the trail firing at them. And at the compound beyond the men. "Are you sure they won't go to the orphanage?"

"They saw you," he reminded her. "They know you're not there."

"But they might go to the compound," she said, her stomach churning with worry. "They might question Lydia to find out where we're going."

Whit snorted derisively. "They know damn well where we're going."

"The airport?"

"We have no other option," he pointed out. "We can't stay here."

"So once they get the Jeep moved and it is no longer blocking the trail, they'll come after us?" She had to know, had to make certain...

Whit nodded.

She exhaled a breath of relief. "So they won't go back to the compound." That was her most pressing concern—making sure the others were safe from the threat against her.

"Like I said, they know where we're going," Whit repeated. "Once they get that Jeep out of the way, they're going to be hurrying to catch up with us—not going back."

And Lydia would have heard the shots and the vehicles; she would have taken the children to the hiding place they'd built into the ground beneath the floors of one of the schoolrooms. They would be safe.

She wasn't so certain about Whit and her and their unborn child. While they'd lost the men—temporarily— he was driving so fast that it was possible they would crash, too, just as the men had.

"They want you," he continued. "You're the one the king will pay for..."

The king had already done it once—when he'd bought her mother's parental rights. It was no wonder so many others had tried to kidnap her over the years. They knew her father would pay their ransom.

But that was back when she had been blindly obedient. Now that she'd hidden from her father for six months, now that she'd become pregnant with the baby of a man who had nothing to offer him politically or monetarily...would he pay for her release? Or was she completely useless to him?

Whit's brow furrowed as he stared through the shattered windshield. "But if they wanted him to pay a ransom, why did they shoot so closely to you? Why risk it...?"

Her skin tingled with foreboding—the same way it had when she had found that crumpled letter under her pillow six months ago. Maybe they didn't want to kidnap her. Maybe they wanted to kill her as that note had threatened.

She braced one hand against the dashboard again and wrapped her other around the roll bar in the roof. She implored him, "Please, hurry."

Not that she needed to urge him to speed; he was probably already traveling too fast on dangerously curved, narrow roads.

"I'll protect you," he assured her.

She believed he meant it, but she wasn't necessarily convinced that he could. "I thought you were going to kill me when that vehicle was heading straight toward us…" And he hadn't backed down.

That was what his men had said about him; that he had never retreated from a fight—in battle or in the barracks. When he and Aaron Timmer had taken over as royal bodyguards, they had brought in their own men as backup. And she had quizzed all those men about their blond superior.

"I had it under control," he said. "You shouldn't have been scared."

She was afraid but not for herself; she was concerned for the child she carried.

And she was scared for the safety of the baby's father, as well.

She should not have trusted him. Whit had had no right to make her promises or offer her assurances that he had no idea if he would be able to carry out.

But he hated that her usually honey-toned complexion

had gone pale with fear, her voice trembling with it. Her earlier scream echoed yet inside his head.

He didn't want her scared but he wanted her hurt even less. He had to protect her.

How? By taking her back to St. Pierre? He'd also promised that he wouldn't do that. But did he have a choice?

His shoulder was throbbing. His gun was out of bullets. He needed backup—backup he could trust: Aaron or Charlotte or any of the ex-military security guards he'd brought on board at the palace.

What had those armed men wanted with her? Were they working for Prince Linus's dad, or whoever the corrupt U.S. Marshal had been working for who had tried to find out where Josie was?

Were they intent on carrying out a kidnapping for ransom or a murder for hire?

Finally they neared the airport, and he slowed down to pull the Jeep off the road. Gabby reached across the console and grasped his arm. "Where are we going?"

Whit needed backup. But he didn't want her at the mercy of her father's royal commands. "We'll figure it out when we get inside. We're getting on whatever plane is taking off first."

He didn't give a damn where it was going. He just needed to get them the hell out of this place. After the earlier shooting, the airport should have been swarming with police. But he noticed no marked cars. No yellow caution tape…

Why hadn't the police come? Had they been called? Was there even a police force or military presence in this primitive country?

Gabby had a question of her own. "What about the royal jet?"

"We're not getting on it."

But the moment they stepped from the Jeep, men surrounded them. They weren't dressed in police or military uniforms but expensive suits. And like the men who'd stormed the compound, these guys, with jackets bulging over shoulder holsters, were armed.

And vaguely familiar. They had been royal body-guards. But he and Aaron had relegated them to perimeter palace guards when they'd taken over as co-heads of security for the king.

"Hey, Bruno. Cosmo," he awkwardly greeted the couple of guys whose names he hoped he correctly remembered. These men had been loyal to the king and to the former head of security, Zeke Rogers. Whit hadn't trusted that they would be as loyal to him and Aaron. It had actually been his call to move them out of the palace. Did they know that? Did they hold a grudge because of it?

"You kept us waiting," the one named Bruno re-marked, his beady eyes narrowed even more with sus-picion—especially as he studied the princess.

Did he suspect she was an imposter? Charlotte?

Or was he just as stunned as Whit had been to find her not only alive but pregnant?

"You should have given up on us and returned to St. Pierre," Whit advised them.

But no matter that Zeke was no longer their boss, they would remain loyal to the king and their country—probably out of respect and fear.

"We have orders," Cosmo added.

"Plans have changed," Whit said with the tone he

used for giving orders in the field and on the job. And for the past several months, he had been giving these men their orders. To guard the gates of the palace. "It's too dangerous to take the princess back to St. Pierre."

Bruno pushed back his jacket and showed the Glock he carried inside the holster. "We have protection."

Whit didn't, and a strong foreboding warned him that he needed it. These men weren't acting like they did on St. Pierre. They weren't acting like he was their superior anymore. Had he been demoted? Zeke had been temporarily reinstated when he'd followed Aaron to Michigan to rescue Charlotte. But that reinstatement was only to have been temporary.

"Did you not hear me?" he asked, in his best no-nonsense boss tone. "I said that plans have changed. We are not going back to St. Pierre."

"We don't have to listen to you anymore," Cosmo said. "We take our orders from someone else now."

Damn. He had been demoted. Or fired.

They had protection, obviously. But he felt like he was the one who needed it now. Could he bluff them into thinking the gun he carried was loaded yet?

As Cosmo grabbed it from him, he realized it was too late. He shouldn't have trusted these men; he shouldn't have trusted anyone—just like Gabriella shouldn't have trusted him.

He couldn't keep any of his promises to her.

AARON'S HEART POUNDED slowly and heavily with dread. "Who did you send as Whit's backup?" he asked the king.

Rafael St. Pierre sat behind his desk in the darkly paneled den in his private wing of the palace. The past six months had added lines to the man's face and liberal streaks of gray to his thick hair. St. Pierre shrugged shoulders that had once been broad enough to carry the weight of his country, but in recent months they had begun to stoop with a burden too heavy—concern for his daughters' lives and safety. "I do not know the names of the men who went."

Neither did Aaron. And that worried him. "The men that Whit and I brought on are all still here in St. Pierre. They were told that Whit did not want them as backup."

"Then that is why they were not sent," the king replied.

Aaron shook his head. "Whit didn't know you were sending that jet after him. If he had known, he would have requested the men that he and I brought on to the security team."

"Are you certain?" the king asked. "I do not believe Whitaker Howell is as loyal as you believe he is."

Just a week ago, Aaron would have agreed with the king. He'd thought Whit had betrayed him when he'd let Aaron believe that they had failed to protect their last client. Whit had actually helped Charlotte, in her previous position as a U.S. Marshal, fake the woman's death and relocate her. Neither of them had thought Aaron would be able to stand the client's dad's suffering as he mourned her; they'd worried that Aaron would give up the secret.

Maybe they had been right to worry. Because the secret he had now was on his lips, threatening to slip out. The king should be warned that Princess Gabriella was pregnant.

"If Whitaker Howell was loyal, he would not have gotten my daughter pregnant while she's engaged to another man!" the king shouted, anger exploding with his fist slamming against his desk.

Aaron didn't have much room to talk; he had gotten the king's other daughter pregnant. Charlotte hadn't been engaged, though.

"How—how did you hear that?" Aaron wondered. Charlotte hadn't told her father yet, and Aaron had managed to keep the secret until now. "Who—who told you?"

"A man who is actually loyal to me," King St. Pierre replied. Coldly.

He obviously wasn't too happy that Aaron had claimed Charlotte—as his fiancée—before the king had even claimed her as his illegitimate daughter and heir.

Aaron's head began to pound as realization dawned. "This isn't good…"

"No, it's not," the king agreed. "I trusted you and your partner. I believed the recommendations that Charlotte had given you both as exemplary chiefs of security. Yet you two were barely on the job a couple of months before my daughters both went missing."

"They were not hired to protect me and Gabby," Charlotte said as she joined them in the king's den. The guard at the door would have not dared to deny her admittance—even if it wasn't now common knowledge that she, too, was royalty, she could have easily overpowered the man.

She was that good. And Aaron was so proud that she was his.

"You're supposed to be resting," Aaron reminded her. For six months he had been so worried about her, but finding her hadn't changed his concern for her. If anything, given what she had endured and the baby she was carrying, he worried more.

She shook her head. "I spent nearly six months in bed. That's more rest than I can handle and retain my sanity."

The king rose from his chair, all concern now. "But you've been through a horrible ordeal—"

"That was not Aaron and Whit's fault," she said. "They were hired to protect *you*. I was supposed to protect Gabby and myself." Her voice cracked with fear and regret. "I am the one who failed."

Aaron reached for her, sliding his arm around her shoulders. She was the strongest woman he'd ever met—physically and emotionally. But she was hurting now—for her sister.

"What's not good?" she asked him.

And, just as they had all thought of him, Aaron couldn't lie. "Somehow King St. Pierre learned that Gabriella's pregnant."

She shook her head. "That's not possible. I didn't learn that until after I talked to Aunt Lydia, and I haven't told anyone but you."

"And I only told Whit," he assured her. "But the man who was shooting at her—he would have realized she was pregnant..."

The king slammed his fist into his desk again. "Are you saying that members of my own security team are trying to kill my daughter?"

Charlotte cursed with the vulgarity of a sailor rather than a princess. But then she had only just been identified as royalty. "This is why I wanted you to hire Whit and Aaron," she said. "Because all of your other security staff were mercenaries."

The king shrugged. "What is wrong with that? They are ex-soldiers, like Aaron and Whit."

"Mercenaries are not ex-soldiers," Aaron said. Because no one was ever really an ex-soldier. "They are still fighting but only now instead of fighting for their country or their honor, they fight for money."

"So they are easily bought," Charlotte explained. "And they are only loyal to the person who's paying them the most."

The king cursed now and dropped back into his chair as if he weighed far more than he did. His burden of concern and guilt was back—maybe even heavier than before.

"We need to call Whit," Charlotte said, "and warn him."

Aaron shook his head and lifted the phone he'd had clamped in his hand. "I've been trying. I can't get a call through to him."

"Call Lydia at the orphanage," Charlotte said. "Maybe they're still there."

"She won't pick up, either," Aaron said.

Both of the royals sucked in little gasps of air and fear.

"But remember the reception is bad down there," Aaron said, trying to offer them both comfort and hope even as his own heart continued to beat slowly and heavily with dread. "It doesn't mean that anything has happened."

Yet.

Would Whit realize before it was too late that the men who'd been sent as his backup were actually his greatest threat?

Chapter Eight

Gabby's heart pounded fast with fear—faster than it had even when Whit had been playing chicken with that other vehicle.

He was playing chicken again—resisting the armed men as they tried directing them through the airport toward the waiting plane. They pushed at him—with the gun barrel, and their hands, shoving him forward. He flinched as one of them slammed his palm into his shoulder.

Gabby bit her lip, so she wouldn't cry out with pain for him. He had already been hurting from earlier, and these men were using that weakness—exploiting his pain. She was too familiar with that cruel treatment—from the queen and her father.

"You kept us waiting long enough," Bruno remarked bitterly. "We have to go."

Gabby needed to leave now, too. With the men focused on Whit, she might have been able to escape. She could try to run back to the Jeep. And take it where? Leaving Whit behind?

Before she could make the decision, she was grabbed. A strong hand wrapped tightly around her arm, the pudgy fingers pinching her flesh. This time she cried out loud, more in surprise and protest than fear, though.

"Let her go!" Whit yelled, his voice so loud it went hoarse. He began to fight. Forgetting or ignoring his injury, he swung his fist into one man's jaw—knocking him out as easily as he had the one she'd shot earlier that day.

He had saved her then. But there were too many of them for him to be able to save her now. A gun barrel was pressed tight to his back, between his shoulder blades.

It was almost as if Gabby could feel it, too. The bite of steel, the fear of taking a breath since it might be her last. Or Whit's last. She didn't want him to move, but he continued to struggle.

"Don't," she whispered, imploring him with her eyes to stop fighting. These men had claimed they no longer took orders from Whit. Had her father fired him? Or were they actually working for someone else?

"I will shoot you," Cosmo warned him.

"Is that one of your orders?" Whit asked. "Did the king tell you to shoot me?"

Gabby took that breath now—in a gasp of shock. She had long ago realized that her father was not the nicest man. He was selfish and manipulative. But was he a killer? Would he have Whit murdered?

She wouldn't put it past him—if he'd learned that his bodyguard had impregnated his daughter and potentially foiled his plans for a royal merger. He would never approve of her being with a man who offered *him* nothing—no money or political influence.

"Stop!" she said, shouting even though she barely

raised her voice. Instead she used her father's imperious tone—the one with which he issued commands that no one dared to disobey.

And the men actually stopped pushing them forward—toward that damn plane. It was a royal jet sitting on the primitive tarmac, but it wasn't her father's personal, far more luxurious jet. So he had not made the trip to retrieve her himself. Had he missed her at all the past six months?

"As Princess of St. Pierre, I am ordering you to release Mr. Howell," she commanded. Relieved that she had kept her nerves and adrenaline from cracking her voice, she expelled a soft sigh.

Whit jerked free of Cosmo while two other men helped up the one he'd knocked to the ground. Bruno groaned, too disoriented to avenge himself on the man who'd struck him. Taking advantage of Bruno's weakness, Whit reached for the man's weapon.

But before he could grab it, a shot was fired—into the ceiling, like she had fired earlier. The bullet ricocheted off the metal and sent people running for safety, screaming.

Gabriella covered her stomach with her palms even though she knew her hands weren't enough to protect her child. She had to use her brains instead.

"Stop!" she yelled again. This time her voice did crack—with a show of weakness and fear. And men like these, men like her father, always took advantage of fear and weakness to assume control.

But perhaps she was the only one who'd noticed her vulnerability because the men again paused in their scuffle. Even Whit this time…as if he was afraid she might be caught in the crossfire or the ricochet if more bullets were fired.

"I will not be using the royal jet today," she imperiously told them, "so you need to take it back to St. Pierre."

The other men turned toward Cosmo, as if to verify her claim. He shook his head. "We have orders that supersede yours, Your Majesty."

Damn her father! The king was the only one whose orders would supersede the orders of the princess of St. Pierre. Was he so desperate to force her into marriage with a stranger that he would risk her safety? That he would authorize the violent treatment of Whit?

Her stomach lurched, and so did her baby, with the fear that her father had learned of her pregnancy. And his anger had overwhelmed whatever capacity he'd had for human kindness.

With a quick glance at his watch, Cosmo said, "We need to board the plane now."

Her father must have been keeping them to a tight timetable. And if she kept them waiting any longer, they would get more impatient and probably violent.

For fear that Whit or someone else might be struck if more shots were fired in the airport, she allowed herself to be ushered outside to the waiting plane. Whit fell into step beside her, occasionally lurching ahead of her as one of the men pushed him.

She wanted to yell again, but he gave a barely perceptible shake of his head. He must have already decided not to fight her father's orders. He had decided the same thing six months ago when he'd waved her off to meet with a designer for the gown in which she would marry another man. Even though she hadn't really gone to meet that designer and she'd had no intention of buying a wedding gown, Whit had not known that. He just hadn't cared…

She'd been foolish to think that he ever might be jealous of her. It didn't matter to him that she was carrying his child. That had not changed the fact that he had no feelings for her—despite what he'd said back at the hut about her making him feel.

And that kiss…

Her lips still tingled with the sensation of his mouth pressed to hers. And that kiss brought back memories of how they'd made their baby—of how those kisses had led to caresses and making love.

No. She'd been the only one making love. She was beginning to think, as those who knew Whitaker Howell best had warned her, that he wasn't capable of feeling anything. They had been referring to his seeming inability to feel fear no matter how dangerous the situation. But if a man couldn't feel fear, then he probably couldn't feel love, either. She should have realized that then, but she'd been so hopeful and naive.

What a difference six months had made in her life. Back then she'd been a silly girl building foolish fantasies around a man who would never be hers. Who would probably never be anybody's…

And now she was a woman about to become a mother, being forced to return to a life she'd never wanted and over which she had no control. Her father was a difficult and selfish man, but was he really so intent on getting his own way that he would risk Whit's life and hers?

At the bottom of the steps up into the plane, she hesitated. If she ran now, would they shoot her? Or just chase her down and force her onto the plane?

And what would become of Whit if he tried to help her? Would he even try?

W‌HIT'S GUTS TWISTED into a tight knot of anger and frustration as he stared down into Gabriella's beautiful face. Her skin was pale, her eyes wide and dark with fear. She stared up at him expectantly, as if waiting for him to save her.

He had to help her. He shouldn't have made those promises—to protect her and to not bring her back to St. Pierre, but he had. And he needed to figure out how to keep them.

But he was outgunned and outmanned. And if he struggled again, the men might leave him behind—alive or dead.

And then Gabriella would be alone with them.

He lifted his chin to break free of the hold of her gaze. And he turned away from her, heading up the stairs first. He wanted to be aboard—needed to get on that damn flight with her. He couldn't let her go back to St. Pierre alone.

He glanced over his shoulder. A couple of the men flanked her, each grabbing an arm to guide her—hell, to nearly lift her—up the stairs to the plane. He clamped his arms to his sides, so that he wouldn't reach back—so that he wouldn't pull her from their grasp. They better not be squeezing her arms, better not be pinching or bruising her.

He hated them touching her. Hated more that they might be hurting her.

He turned away to step through the door to the plane. As he was shoved down the aisle, he passed a man already sprawled in one of the seats. The guy's shoulder was bandaged, and his arm was in a sling. A big bruise was turning from red to purple along his swollen jaw.

This was the man who had tried to abduct Gabby earlier—when she'd been alone. He must have arrived at the airport the same time Whit had. Hell, maybe he'd even beaten him there. Gabby had figured that the man being there was just a coincidence—that he had seen her alone and unprotected and decided to take advantage of the opportunity. Whit didn't believe in coincidence. He'd figured the man might have followed him from Michigan.

But what if this man had already known where Whit was going? Where Gabby was?

The guy was obviously affiliated with the top guards from the previous royal security regime. As an independent security contractor or a mercenary? He could have been working for anyone. The person who'd left her the threatening note. Or Prince Linus's father. Or whoever wanted to find Gabby's new friend, JJ…

Behind him he heard Gabby's gasp as she, too, recognized the man. Then her gasp turned to a moan. Whit whirled back just in time to see her crumple into a heap in the aisle. He tried to rush toward her, but the guys holding him pushed him down into a seat.

"Princess!" yelled one of the men, as if his shout would bring her back around.

But she wasn't unconscious. Instead she was clutching her stomach. "I'm going to be sick," she warned them. "I need to use the bathroom."

Cosmo helped her to her feet. Then he guided her down the aisle toward the restroom in the back. As she passed Whit, he fisted his hand at his side, so that he wouldn't reach for her. But he didn't need to touch her to assure himself she was all right.

She shot him a pointed glance. She knew they were in danger, and she was working on a way to get herself and their child the hell out of it. The media couldn't have been more wrong about her.

But no matter how smart she was, she was six months pregnant and as outnumbered and weaponless as he was. Whit had to help her and not just because it was his duty. And not just because it was his baby she carried...

"I need to call the king," he said, slowly reaching for his phone. But his fingers no more than closed around it before one of the men knocked it from his hand. As soon as it hit the aisle, the man slammed his foot down onto it. "I need to tell him that the princess is too sick to travel."

As if on cue—and maybe his words had been exactly that—retching sounds drifted down the aisle from the restroom. This wasn't the king's royal jet; this was another in the fleet, used more for cargo than for passengers. The seats were not as luxurious nor the bathroom as large. She had to be uncomfortable in the tiny space. Hopefully she wasn't really sick; hopefully she was just faking in order to keep the plane on the ground.

"She is too far along in her pregnancy to fly," Whit said, as he stood up. "We can't take off."

"We have orders," Cosmo said. He moved away from the bathroom door—as if unable to tolerate the noises Gabriella was making inside the tiny room. He walked up to Whit, clasped his wounded shoulder and shoved him back down into the seat. "We're taking off..."

Whit ignored the pain coursing down his arm and fisted his tingling fingers. "You can't—"

They weren't listening to him or Gabby. One of the men sealed the outside door shut and then knocked on the cockpit door.

"...now," Cosmo finished with a triumphant grin. "We're taking off *now*."

"If the king knew she was sick," Whit persisted, "he wouldn't want her flying."

The engines fired up, causing the plane to vibrate. Then it moved as it began to taxi down the runway. "You can't take off now!" Whit shouted. "She's not even buckled in."

She would be tossed around in that tiny space—with no seat belt and nothing to protect her and her baby from getting hurt. It would be even worse than her ride in the Jeep because it would be thousands of feet in the air with the risk of turbulence.

He tried to rise up again, but another man shoved him into the seat. Whit couldn't reach her—couldn't help her.

Cosmo snorted. "If she's going to get sick, better she be sick in there than out here." He shuddered, and his throat moved, as if he were struggling with sickness of his own.

"She could be hurt," Whit said. "The king will not approve of that."

Emotionally hurting his daughter hadn't bothered the king. But when the man had seen that trashed hotel suite in Paris and he'd thought she might be physically hurt, Rafael St. Pierre had been distraught. He hadn't feigned his worry for her during the six months she'd been missing.

"So what's he going to do?" Cosmo asked. "Fire us again?"

"He didn't fire you," Whit replied. "You were just reassigned." But maybe he shouldn't remind them that he was the one responsible for their demotion. Then again, maybe goading them would make them rethink their loyalty to the king. "You were assigned to the same job a trained guard dog can do."

As a fist slammed into his jaw, he regretted his words. Bruno shook his hand and cursed. Then he grabbed at the seats around him as the plane's tires lifted from the airstrip.

Whit's back pressed against the seat they'd pushed him into, but he tried to stand up again. He had to get to Gabby—had to make sure she was all right. "If she gets hurt, the king might do more than fire you. He wouldn't have ordered his own daughter harmed!"

"No, he wouldn't have," Cosmo agreed. "You keep making the mistake of assuming our orders are coming from the king."

Oh, God! The royal security force had been compromised and the royal jet hijacked.

Whit doubted he had to worry about their bringing them back to St. Pierre. He had to worry about their bringing them anywhere.

Alive.

GABRIELLA'S HEART POUNDED fast and furiously, and it wasn't just because she was a somewhat nervous flyer. She had her hands braced against opposite walls of the tiny bathroom. And her ear pressed to the door, she heard everything being said between the men.

They weren't acting on her father's orders. She

figured that might have been the case when she'd boarded and recognized the man she had shot. The fact that he'd already been aboard the plane meant that he was working with the men from her father's old security team. And she doubted her father would have approved that man nearly shooting her. Because he would have if not for Whit knocking him out.

She had suspected then how much danger she and Whit and their baby were in. So she had feigned the fainting and sickness to get away from them.

Having her suspicions confirmed actually produced a flash of relief before panic overwhelmed her. These men didn't work for her father.

So who did they work for?

The person who'd left that note threatening her life? Or Linus's father, determined to carry out his creepy plot? Or were they working for themselves, having come up with their own retirement plan: ransom?

If that was their plan, they might let her live—at least until they got money from her father. But what about Whit? They had no reason to keep him alive.

She had been waiting for the royal bodyguard to help her. But he was the one who needed her help. She had only just realized that when she heard him goad the men.

"You can't fire those guns on a plane. One stray bullet and you could bring it down."

Were they already going to execute him?

She eased open the door slightly and peered through the crack. Whit was in the aisle, pushing against the men standing between him and the cockpit.

"Then we'll make sure all of them hit you," Bruno

replied, lifting his weapon to point the barrel right at Whit's chest.

The men were so focused on him that they didn't notice as Gabby eased out the door. She stepped into the aisle and snuck toward the back of the plane—to the cargo hold.

Assess the situation...

Charlotte's words echoed inside Gabby's head. Her former bodyguard had used this very scenario as an example in order to teach Gabriella how to protect herself during a plane hijacking.

Gabby remembered giggling at the time, totally amused that her bodyguard had been so paranoid that she'd thought something that farfetched could happen aboard the St. Pierre royal jet. But now that the scenario had become a reality, Gabriella was frantically trying to recall the advice Charlotte had offered. She wanted that voice inside her head, but all she could hear was Whit's.

"Bullets have a tendency to go right through me," he cockily replied and rolled his wounded shoulder as if to prove his point.

Damn him and his macho bravado...

If he got the renegade guards to fire, he would not only die but he would risk the whole plane going down. Gabby needed to find a parachute. Because sometimes the most effective mode of self-preservation was escape...

She pushed open the door to the cargo hold, hoping she would find at least a parachute—hopefully more. But as she slipped into the hold, a commotion erupted inside the plane. Flesh connected with flesh as men threw punches and kicks.

Gabby flinched with every grunt and groan—as if

the blows were hitting her. And inside her belly, the baby flipped and kicked. Whit wasn't the only fighter. Gabby could fight, too, and not just how Charlotte had taught her. She could fight now as a mother fighting to protect her child.

And her child's father.

She only hoped she found something to help Whit before it was too late and the men had already killed him.

Chapter Nine

Pain radiated from Whit's shoulder throughout his body—to every place a blow had connected. But he had landed more blows than he'd received. He had even knocked out a couple of the men.

But then Bruno lifted his gun again, this time swinging the handle toward Whit's head. He ducked and the blow glanced off his wounded shoulder.

He groaned so loudly that his throat burned from the force of it. Pain coursed through him, but rage followed it, chasing away the pain. Blind with anger, Whit reached out and jerked the weapon from Bruno's beefy hand.

Before he could slide his finger onto the trigger, barrels pointed at him and triggers cocked with ominous clicks.

"Drop it!" Cosmo ordered.

Whit shook his head. "You're not the one giving orders here. Who is?"

"You're not going to find out," Cosmo said. "You're going to be dead long before we land."

Even though he'd grabbed a weapon, there were still too many fighting him. He might not make it off this plane, but he had to know about Gabby. "What about the princess? Does the person giving orders want her alive or dead?"

"What does it matter to you?" Cosmo asked. His eyes narrowed and he nodded. "Ever since you started at the palace, she was always asking everybody about you and following you around, mooning over you. So is that baby she's carrying yours?"

Whit clenched his jaw, grinding his teeth together with frustration that he couldn't claim his baby. Doing so might risk the child's safety and Gabby's. The last man who had thought he'd kidnapped her, but had abducted Charlotte instead, had wanted to get her pregnant with his own child. Even though Prince Linus was in custody, he was still a wealthy man; he or his father could have paid these guys to abduct the right woman this time.

Cosmo took Whit's silence as affirmation and shook his head in mock sympathy. "Too bad you'll never get to see it being born."

Because they were going to kill Whit or because they were going to kill Gabby, too?

"Shoot the damn gun!" The order echoed inside the cabin, but it was a female voice that uttered it. A sweet, strong voice—Gabby's. She stood near the entrance to the cargo hold.

When he'd heard her stop her fake retching, he'd figured she was going to sneak out of the bathroom soon. So he'd provided a distraction for her. That was why he'd started swinging despite being outmatched. He had wanted to distract the other men, so they wouldn't notice her. Apparently she'd gone from the bathroom to the cargo hold. Looking for an escape or a weapon?

"Whit," she said, making it clear her order was for him, "trust me—shoot the gun!"

"What the hell?" Cosmo whirled toward her with his gun drawn.

And Whit couldn't trust that the other man wouldn't fire. So he did. He lifted his gun and fired a bullet through the roof of the cabin.

The other men cursed as the plane dropped, losing altitude fast. Whit leapt over them, heading toward Gabby. He had fired the gun because he'd figured out her plan; he only hoped it wouldn't get them killed.

"You TRUSTED me," she said, surprised that he had actually fired. And afraid that he had. She swung a parachute pack toward him.

But the plane lurched and Whit nearly missed it. And he narrowly missed the hands reaching for him as he grabbed up the pack and ran into the cargo hold with her. He shoved the door shut and jammed something against it. "There better be another way out," he said. "And fast…"

She pointed toward the parachute and turned her back toward him to show she'd already put on hers. His hands caught the straps, pulling them tight, as he double-checked all the lines and cords.

"Are you sure parachuting will be safe for the baby?" he asked.

"Getting shot will be a hell of a lot less safe," she pointed out, as the men fired now, shooting their guns into the hold.

Whit pulled his pack on and adjusted the straps, pulling them taut. His shoulder wound was again oozing blood, which trickled down his arm in rivulets. The parachute straps were going to stress the wound even more. She should have considered that, should have thought of something else. But he agreed, "We have no other option now."

"Is the plane going down?" she asked, as it continued to lose altitude.

"Probably crash landing. We have to get out soon." He hurried over to the luggage door to the outside and struggled with its latch. "I think I can get it open..."

She hadn't thought out any of her plan. Maybe Whit shouldn't have trusted her. Maybe he shouldn't have fired. But if he hadn't, he would probably already be dead. While she hadn't been with him these past six months, at least he had been alive. At least she'd had hope that he might one day become the man her naive heart had believed he was. But if he was dead...

Then Gabby had no hope.

"Come here." He held out his hand. "We have to be ready to jump when I open this luggage hatch."

She'd faked getting sick earlier but her stomach lurched now, threatening to revolt for real. She hadn't thought this plan out well—hadn't considered all the consequences. She had parachuted before—with Charlotte, who had set up a scenario eerily similar to this so that Gabby would be prepared if her plane were ever hijacked.

Gabriella had loved the freedom of parachuting, the weightlessness of floating on air. But she hadn't been pregnant then. She'd had no one else to worry about except herself.

The door to the cabin vibrated as if one of the men were kicking it or slamming his shoulder into it.

"We have to do this now," Whit said. "We're dead for sure if we don't."

And possibly dead if they did...

He opened the door to the outside, causing the plane to buck as if they were trying to ride a crazed bull. Whit grabbed her hand and tugged her out with him—sending them both hurtling through air.

If only there had been time to tell him...

Tell him what?

That she loved him? Six months ago she'd thought she was falling for him, but she hadn't even known him. She'd been attracted to his masculine beauty and his aura of strength and mystery. And the fact that he hadn't seemed to give a damn about anything or anyone...

She'd wished she could have been like that—that the queen's rejections and cruelty hadn't mattered to her. But she'd thought the woman was her mother, so she'd been devastated and desperate to please—so desperate that she'd let her father bully her.

And she'd let people lie to her—because she'd felt the secrets and hadn't probed deeper. She hadn't demanded the truth because she'd been afraid to hear it. She hadn't thought herself strong enough to handle it.

But she was a hell of a lot stronger than she'd realized. She was strong enough to jump out of a crashing plane.

But she wasn't strong enough to tell Whit that she had nearly fallen for him...before she'd begun to fall with him...

All she could do was hold tightly to his hand and hope she didn't lose him—hope that she didn't lose her baby or her life.

HE WAS LOSING her. His arms ached, his shoulder burning, as he struggled against the straps, tugging off the chutes before they pulled them both under water. Part of the chute, the part they'd slipped on with the straps, was a life jacket. But it was thin and barely enough to keep them above the surface of the choppy water. They had landed in the ocean—with no land in sight.

And only God knew what waiting, beneath the surface, to devour them…

After the struggle on the plane, his wound had reopened. Was his blood baiting the water? Maybe he should leave her before he drew sharks to them. He tried to peer beneath the surface but the setting sun reflected off the water, blinding him. Making the water look as if it were all blood…

"Gabby!"

She squeezed his fingers. She had been clinging to his hand since they'd leaped out of the dropping plane. "I'm here…" But she sounded sleepy, groggy, as if she were so exhausted that she was about to pass out.

Whit recognized the signs in her voice because he felt them in his own body. He pushed his legs to kick, to keep them above the waves that kept lifting them only to drop them again. Water slapped his face, as if trying to keep him awake. He needed that because the life jacket wasn't enough to keep his head above water, but only enough to keep them from dropping to the bottom of the sea. It would make their bodies easier to find when they were dead…

"Are you all right?" he asked.

"Yes," she replied.

"And the baby?"

She smiled. "He's fine. Kicking as if he's trying to swim, too."

"He? You keep calling the baby a boy," he realized. "Do you know…?"

She shook her head now, her wet hair slapping across the surface of the sea. "I don't know for certain. It's just a feeling I have."

A gut instinct. Whit understood that, but unfortunately the gut instinct he had now was bad. If only he'd had more time before they'd jumped, he could have tried to find supplies to take along. But he might have lost them anyway, like he had the gun he'd shoved into the back of his jeans. It had fallen out when they'd hit the water and sunk like a rock.

"I can't believe," she said, "that we survived…"

His gut tightened with dread as he worried that she spoke too soon. "We survived the plane crash," he agreed.

But would they survive a night in the sea?

"Did it crash?" she asked, leaning back to stare up at the sky. It was nearly black now, the last of the light glowing on the surface of the water. There were no lights in the sky.

"Not near us…" He had worried that it might go down as they were jumping and take them both out as it crashed. While he and Gabby had been drifting on air, he'd caught glimpses of the plane as it spiraled forward and downward. With its speed, it had gone a good distance ahead of where they landed in the water.

But given the waves and tides, some of the wreckage could drift back toward them.

"But you think it crashed?" she persisted. Maybe she was so concerned because she needed a distraction, or needed to make sure that the men weren't going to come after them again. But knowing her, she was probably worried about the well-being of the men who would have killed them with no hesitation or remorse.

"I don't know." And truthfully he didn't. He'd been in worse situations and had had pilots pull up the throttle and safely land the aircraft. "I don't know who the pilot was. The king's pilot could have handled the changes in cabin pressure. He could have kept it in the air and landed somewhere." But he knew it hadn't been that pilot, or the plane wouldn't have been waiting at the airport as long as the men had complained they'd been waiting.

She expelled a breath of relief. "Yes, they might be okay, then…"

She really was too good—too perfect—to be real. He must have conjured her up from those old, half-forgotten fairy tales. He wasn't as perfect as she was. Hell, he wasn't even close to perfect or forgiving or caring. So he had to ask for clarification, "You're worried about men who would have had no qualms over killing us?"

He tensed as he glimpsed something dark in the water, moving just beneath the surface. Beneath them. Had the sharks begun to circle? They, too, would have no qualms over killing them.

"When I told you to shoot," she said, in a voice hoarse with remembered panic and with regret and probably dehydration, too, "I—I didn't realize that the plane might crash…"

"It doesn't matter if it did," Whit said. "You were in danger." And still was, with no land in sight, and the waves getting rougher. Their bodies bobbed as the waves lifted and then dropped them—almost as if the water toyed with them, giving them hope only to dash it away. He held more tightly to her hand, his own going numb with cold and the effort to keep hanging on. "You had to save yourself."

"I—I don't know for certain that they would have killed me," she said, her teeth chattering slightly.

With the sun no longer warming the water, it had quickly gone cold. Flesh-numbingly cold.

"You think they only intended to kidnap you?" They hadn't seemed concerned enough about her safety, and they knew the king well enough to know that he would have paid no money without proof of life.

"I don't know what they intended to do with me," she said with a shaky sigh. "But I do know what they intended to do with you. They were definitely going to kill you, Whit."

He shivered but not just with the cold. He'd had close scrapes over the years, probably more than his share even for a marine and a bodyguard. But he'd always managed to figure his own way out. Until now…

"So you weren't worried about yourself," he said. "You were worried about me." He wasn't used to people worrying about him. His mother certainly hadn't when she'd packed up her stuff and left him with his father. Back when they'd been friends and partners Aaron had worried, but then Aaron worried about everyone.

"They had no reason to keep you alive," she said, "and more reasons to want you dead."

"With a bum shoulder and no weapon, I didn't pose much of a threat to them," he pointed out.

She chuckled. "But you're Whitaker Howell. You're a legend for the feats you've pulled off in battle, for the people you've protected as a bodyguard. They would see you as quite the threat."

"Or quite the pain in the ass," he said. "And it probably didn't help that I brought in my own men to take their jobs when Aaron and I were hired as co-chiefs of royal security."

She must have shaken her head because a wet piece of her hair slapped against his arm. Her hair and her skin was so cold. He wanted to put his arms around her and warm her up. But then he risked them both slipping under water.

"So you parachuted out of a plane to save me," he mused. "And here I was the one who promised to protect you." A promise he was still struggling to keep, as he tried to keep them both afloat.

Water splashed her face, and she sucked in a breath and coughed. And as she panicked, her head slipped beneath the choppy surface. Whit panicked, too, but he didn't let go of her hand. And with his other arm, his injured arm, he dragged her back up. She sputtered and coughed again, expelling salty water from her constricted lungs.

"Are you all right?" he asked.

"Y-yes," she stammered. "And you are my protector."

With the right resources, he was a damn good bodyguard. He could protect anyone from armed gunmen, from bombs, from fires...

But he had no idea the threats that lurked beneath the surface of the water. And no way of protecting her from them. Or from the water itself as it chilled their skin and blood, threatening hypothermia.

He'd been told it was a peaceful death. It was how his father had gone, too drunk to get the key in the door—he'd died on his front porch during the dead of winter—while Whit had been in the sweltering heat in a desert on the other side of the world. He wasn't going out like his old man. "We need to stay awake," he said. "We need to stay alert..."

"To what?"

He wouldn't tell her his fear that there was something circling them. He focused instead on offering her hope. "If the plane did go down, someone would have noticed it on radar. They might send out boats or helicopters to search for survivors."

Given that he'd seen no sign of land when they'd dropped into the sea, a search party was their only chance.

"You think help's coming?" she asked.

"Yes, if not strangers—then Aaron and Charlotte will send someone or come themselves."

"But how will they know where to look for us?" she asked. "How will they know to look for us—that we're still alive?"

"Aaron will know," Whit said. "Just like he knew that Charlotte was alive." But that was because he loved the woman, because he had a bond with her. Or it was because the man always looked for the best in a situation.

Whit should have known that Gabriella was alive the past six months. But he'd never been as hopeful or optimistic as Aaron. He always expected the worst; there was less risk of getting disappointed that way.

"He loves her?" Gabby asked.

"Yes."

She fell silent, just floating in the dark. So he prodded her, "We need to keep talking..."

"About—about what?"

He chuckled. "Your nickname is Gabby. You can't think of anything to talk about?"

"I—I only chatter when I'm nervous."

If there was ever a time to be nervous, it was now—adrift at sea at night. "Tell me about the orphans," he said.

She wasn't gabby. She was eloquent, as she told him beautiful stories of the children's triumph over all the tragedies of their lives. She talked until her teeth chattered too much for her to get the words out. "Your turn," she told him.

"I'd rather hear you…" And he would. He loved the sound of her voice, the way it slipped into his ear and into his heart.

"If you want to distract me from how cold I am," she said, "I'm better at listening." Something else about her the paparazzi had gotten completely wrong.

"You're going to make a great mom," he said. If he could keep her and their baby alive…

She sniffled, either from the cold or from emotion. "I don't know about that. I didn't exactly have a loving mother growing up. Or biologically. What kind of mother gives up her baby for money?"

"At least she had a reason," he said. And he talked. He told her about his mom and his dad. Maybe he told her the stories to warn her that he wouldn't be a good husband or father. Or maybe he just told her to keep her awake.

But her grasp on his hand loosened, and her fingers slipped free of his. He couldn't lose her now—he couldn't lose her and the child she carried. Since he was a kid, he had sworn he would never have a family—that he wouldn't put himself through the risk of disappointment and pain.

But now his greater fear was that he was going to lose the chance at having one. Even if a search party was dispatched, the wreckage of the plane was nowhere near them. They would probably be presumed dead. And soon that might be true…

THE KING'S DEN WAS FULL of people now. Because she was so beloved, nearly every member of the household staff had gathered to hear word of Gabriella's well-being. Her fiancé was also there, along with his ex-fiancée, who claimed she had come out of friendship to him and relation to Gabby. She was the queen's cousin, which made her no relation to Gabby. But Charlotte wasn't about to explain that situation—or even talk to her.

Nor was she going to talk to the father and brother of Gabby's ex-fiancé, who claimed they had also come out of concern. She was surprised they'd had the audacity to show, after what Prince Linus Demetrios had done. But maybe they wanted to watch King St. Pierre suffer, as they were bound to suffer with the prince in prison now. They probably blamed the whole thing on the king, for breaking that engagement in the first place.

Charlotte suspected that he was blaming himself, too. Even with all the people gathered around, he looked so alone, removed from the others as he sat behind his ornate desk on a chair that was too modern to resemble a throne. But it was still one regardless of the design.

The man was used to being in control—not just of his own life but of every life in St. Pierre. He was helpless now. Charlotte's heart shifted, as if opening slightly to him. He had made mistakes. So many mistakes…

But so had she.

Would Gabby ever forgive either of them? Or had she died hating them both?

A man strode into the den, and all the chatter in the room ceased. All heads turned to him, as if he were the king about to make a royal decree.

But Charlotte knew him best, so she knew what he was going to say before he even opened his mouth. The anguish and hopelessness was in his blue eyes, dimming the brightness that Charlotte loved so much. The regret was in the tight line of his mouth, and the anger and frustration in the hard set of his strong jaw.

Guilt attacked her first. It was all her fault—her stupid plan that had put them all at risk. But even before the plan, she had hurt Aaron. She'd cost him his friendship with the man who'd been as close to him as a brother. While she'd spent the past three years getting to know her sister, he had lost those three years of friendship; he and Whit had been estranged. Because of her…

They had only just repaired that friendship to lose it again. Forever, this time…

Aaron cleared his throat, as if choking back emotion. But it was clear and steady as he spoke, "The plane went down. A search party went out to the wreckage, but there were no survivors."

Now the grief hit her. Hard. Grabbing her heart and squeezing it in a tight fist.

"She's dead," a woman's voice murmured into the eerie silence after Aaron's pronouncement.

"We don't know that," he corrected her. "Her body wasn't found."

"But you said no survivors…" The woman was Honora Del Cachon, the ex-fiancée of Prince Malamatos.

"From the wreckage of the plane," Aaron said. He looked at Charlotte now, his gaze holding hers. His eyes had brightened again—not as much as they usually were when he looked at her. But he wasn't entirely without hope. "But I'm not sure Princess Gabriella went down with the plane."

"Why not?" Charlotte asked the question now. She had to know if he was only trying to make her feel better or if she had a real reason to hope.

"Because Whit's body wasn't found either…"

She wanted to be as optimistic as the man she loved. But she wasn't like him and Gabriella—who always found the good in everything. She was more like Whitaker Howell, more realist than idealist. "But if they parachuted out before the plane crashed…"

She had an idea of where it had gone down because she'd been with Aaron and the king when they'd been told it had gone off radar. Aaron had gone out to the area where it had crashed, to look for survivors and verify that it had been one of the royal jets. She'd wanted to go along, but he'd insisted she stay behind—probably because he'd worried that she might lose the baby if she had proof that her sister was dead.

That was probably why he was offering false hope now. She couldn't take it.

"…they landed in the middle of the sea," she said, "with no land in sight. No help…"

The only boats to pass through the area, where they would have had to jump to escape before the plane crashed, were drug runners, arms dealers and other pirates.

"And they would have been in the water all night," she added. "With as cold as it gets when the sun goes down, there is no way they could have survived."

She hated that the brightness dimmed again in her fiancé's eyes. But she couldn't cling to a lie. She had to face the reality that her sister and Whit were gone.

Forever...

Chapter Ten

"Stop!" she ordered him. "Put me down."

But Whit ignored her protest and tightened his arms around her. The waves slapped at his legs as he fought his way from the surf to the beach. He staggered onto the sand.

"I can walk," she said, but she wasn't certain if she spoke the truth. After hours in the water, her legs were so heavy and weak that they had folded beneath her when she'd tried to stand in the shallows.

That was when Whit had grabbed her up his arms, arms that had strained against the waves to swim them to shore. Land. They had reached land.

Or was it just a mirage on the endless water? Or a dream? She had nearly fallen asleep several times. Her life jacket had been fairly useless, so her head would have slipped beneath the surface if not for Whit holding her above water.

How had he stayed so strong? So alert? Amazed by the man's power, she stared up into his handsome face.

Despite the cold they'd endured all night, sweat beaded on his forehead and above his tense mouth. His arms shook from exertion. He was more than exhausted. He was wounded, blood streaking down his arm from his shoulder. It was a miracle the blood hadn't drawn sharks to attack them.

"Put me down," she ordered again.

He stumbled as his feet sank in the sand, but he didn't drop her. That promise he'd made to protect her was one he obviously intended to keep—no matter what it cost him. His health. His strength. His life.

He trudged across the sand, which gave way to a slate patio and stairs leading up from the beach to a glass-and-stone house perched on a hill high above the water. "This island is inhabited," he said.

When they'd first noticed it, it had seemed little more than a clump of trees in the distance. As they'd swum toward it, the island had gotten bigger but not much. It was just a small stretch of sand, a rocky cliff and a clump of trees. They'd worried that it would be uninhabited. But maybe this was just a tiny peninsula of a bigger island.

"You're not going to carry me up all those steps." Gabby fought harder, so that she finally wriggled free of his grasp and slid down his body. Her legs, numb with cold and exhaustion, trembled and threatened to cave again before finally holding her weight.

Fortunately there was a railing beside the stairs, which Gabby climbed like a rope to help her to the top of the steep hill. She gasped at the view at the summit. It was just the hill and the house and the beach below that. The other side dropped off even more steeply to rocks and water. It was no peninsula of a larger island or continent.

"This is someone's private retreat," she said as Whit joined her at the top.

He was battered and bruised from his battle with the

men aboard the plane. And his skin was flushed either from the sun or with a fever.

After those interminable hours in the darkness, she welcomed the warmth of the sun. But maybe the shock of going from the frigid water to the sunlight was too much for Whit. Could his body handle any more trauma?

He nodded. "There's a helicopter pad over there." He gestured with a jerk of his chin as if his arms were too tired to lift.

She followed his gesture to where the trees had been cleared on the other side of the hill from the house. "No helicopter. So nobody's home?"

Whit walked around—or more accurately— staggered and peered between the trees down all sides of the hill. "There's a dock on this side of the island." This time he managed to point but not with the arm of which the shoulder was wounded. "But no boat."

Panic struck Gabby. She'd been so hopeful that this place would prove their salvation. But with no means of escaping if someone were to follow them here, they were trapped.

"So there's nothing but the house?" she asked.

IT WAS ONE hell of a house. Nowhere near as grand as the palace, of course, but Whit preferred its simple lines. Made of glass and stone, it became part of the landscape, bringing the outside in as sunshine poured through the windows, warming the slate floor beneath their feet.

The door hadn't been locked. There would have been no point—probably nobody knew where the place was but the owner. Maybe that was a good thing; maybe a bad thing…

It depended on who owned the place and for what reason he required such seclusion. This part of the world wasn't known for its tourism, more for its guns and drugs and lawlessness.

Whit had checked every room to make sure the place was empty before he'd left Gabby inside alone. Even though he'd only been gone minutes, he expected to find her asleep when he stepped back inside, but she was in the kitchen, flitting around like a bedraggled butterfly.

"You got the power on," she said with a sigh of relief. "There must be a generator?"

He nodded as he took a seat on one of the stools at the granite kitchen island. Like the rest of the house, the kitchen was all slate and glass. "And enough gas to keep it running for a while."

"There's a lot of food, too," she said. "Dry goods and canned fruit and vegetables and juices. We'll have enough to eat until someone finds us."

Whit nodded, hoping that the right people would find them and not the ones they'd just jumped out of a plane to escape. Or worse yet, the person who had given those men their orders. And what exactly had those orders been? To kidnap the princess? Or kill her?

"Nobody will look for us here," she said, as if she'd read his mind and wanted to set it at ease. "They probably think we're dead."

"Maybe they're right." His head pounded and his shoulder throbbed. And his stomach rumbled with a hunger more intense than he ever remembered, even when he'd been a kid and his dad had forgotten to buy groceries. Or he'd spent the money on liquor instead of food. "I feel like hell."

She pushed a plate of food at him. She'd done something with canned chicken and pineapple, and as he ate it, he became certain he wasn't dead. Because this felt too much like heaven, with her as an angel, and he'd never imagined he'd wind up *there*.

As soon as he finished eating, she was at his side, helping him up from the stool. His legs shook from the effort. God, he was so damned tired. He'd never been so tired—not even during his first deployment with those bombs exploding all night every night...

"You need to rest," she said, guiding him down the hall toward the bedrooms.

He shook his head. "I have to keep watch. Make certain no one takes us by surprise..."

She chuckled and assured him, "We'll hear them coming..."

He listened and could hear nothing but the waves crashing against the shore below. He never wanted to hear water again—never wanted to be near it—not after all those endless hours they'd spent drifting in it.

"Go to sleep," she said, gently pushing him down onto the bed.

He caught her hand, needing to keep track of her. He couldn't lose her again—not like he had six months ago—when he'd thought he'd lost her forever—not like when she'd slipped away from him at sea.

"Don't go," he said. "Don't leave..."

The words brought him back to his childhood—to what he'd said when his mother had packed her bags and walked out with them—leaving him behind. She hadn't paid any attention to what he'd said, to what he'd wanted or needed.

But Gabby settled onto the bed beside him. And her cool hand stroked across his brow. "You're so hot. I wish Dominic was here."

Jealousy flashed through him that she wanted another man…when he wanted only her.

"You need a doctor," she said.

He shook his head. "No. I only need you…"

I ONLY NEED *you*.

He'd been delirious with a fever when he'd said those words. He probably hadn't even known who she was. But still she couldn't get that line out of her head. And when she slept…she dreamed it was true.

That he really needed her. That he loved her as she had never been loved. Now she was back to being the young girl weaving foolish fantasies.

It was time to wake up. The sun was beating hard through the windows, warming the room and her body. She squinted even before she opened her eyes. But the sun wasn't shining in her face.

A shadow covered her—the broad-shouldered shadow of a man. Backlit by sunshine, she couldn't see more than the shadow at first. So she screamed.

He leaned back, and the sun bathed his face and glinted in his golden hair. "It's all right," he said. "You're safe. It's just me."

Then she wasn't safe at all. Not emotionally. He'd gotten to her again—gotten into her heart. The night they'd spent on the water, endlessly talking, she'd learned more about him than any of his friends could have told her. She wondered if even Aaron knew exactly how Whit had grown up. Alone.

He had probably thought they were going to die. That had to be the reason why he'd told her all that he had. All his pain and disappointments…

Or he'd hoped that if they lived, she would know better than to expect a happily-ever-after from him. He didn't believe they existed. And with good reason.

She shouldn't believe in them, either. But even though she hadn't experienced them personally, she'd seen them—when she'd visited boarding school friends who had found happiness with men who loved them.

But maybe Whit couldn't love—because he didn't know how. And she wasn't certain that was something that could be taught. No one had taught her to love, but it hadn't stopped her from falling for this man. With resignation and wonder, she murmured, "It's just you…"

His lips twitched into a slight grin at her remark. His hair was damp and water glistened on his bare shoulders and chest.

"You took a shower," she said, around the lump of desire that had risen up to choke her. A droplet trickled down his chest, and she had to fight to resist the urge to lick it away.

"I needed to—to wake up," he said. "Looks like you did, too. Your hair's still damp." He put his hand in it, running his fingers through her hair—which was probably still tangled despite her efforts to comb through the thick mess.

Grateful for the generator running the pump, she'd taken a shower and put her clothes in the mini–washing machine she'd found. But she hadn't found any clothes to wear while she slept. So the only thing between her and him was a thin sheet and the towel draped low around his lean hips.

"How long was I asleep?" he asked. "Days?"

He touched his jaw—which was clean-shaven now. He must have found a razor because when she'd checked on him last he'd had a lot of dark blond beard growing on his jaw. Even asleep, he'd been tense—his jaw clenched. "Weeks?"

She had lost track of time, thinking of him. Dreaming of him. But since her hair was still damp, she hadn't been asleep that long.

"A day and a half," she said. "And you probably still need more rest."

"No." He shook his head and leaned close again. His dark eyes were intense as he met her gaze. "That's not what I need."

Her pulse started racing, her blood pumping fast and hard through her veins. She had to ask, "What do you need?"

"You," he said. "Only you…"

She must have been sleeping yet—caught so deeply in the dream that it felt real. Like his lips skimming across hers, she could feel the warm soft brush. And then his tongue slid inside her mouth—in and out. Her skin tingled with desire and then with his touch, as his hands skimmed over her naked shoulders. He moved his lips across her cheek, to her neck.

She shivered now.

"Are you cold?" he asked.

She shook her head. Her skin was catching fire with the intensity of the passion she felt for him. That desire chased away the last chill from their night in the cold sea. "No…"

He kissed one of her shoulders and then her collarbone and the slope of her breast. Then he pushed down the sheet, skimming his hands over her breasts. But he stopped with his palms on her belly. "Can we do this?" he asked.

"We jumped out of an airplane," she reminded him. And during the whole parachute trip down to the water, the baby had kicked—as if with excitement. He was probably already as fearless as his father. Panic flickered at the thought, at how she would have to worry about him, like she worried about Whit.

"I doubt a doctor would have recommended that." Whit tensed, his eyes widening with shock.

"Are you all right?" she asked. "Are you hurt?"

She knew he had needed more rest and a doctor to examine his wound. But it looked better now, the edges of skin melding together around the puckered hole where the bullet had entered his body.

"I—I'm fine," he said. "And so's he. He's kicking." He stared down at her belly, obviously awed that there was life inside her. "He feels strong."

She smiled at the fatherly pride he was already showing. "He is."

"You really think the baby's a boy?" he asked, almost hopefully.

Did all men want sons? She knew her father certainly had. Perhaps that was why he hadn't claimed Charlotte because she hadn't been the male heir he'd really wanted. And then by the time Gabriella had come along, he'd wanted an heir so desperately that he'd taken what he'd gotten despite his disappointment. Now he intended to barter her for a man, for a son-in-law, to help him rule his country.

No matter how much she had fallen for Whit, her father would never approve him as her husband. He had no family. No country. Nothing her father could take in trade. Gabriella only wanted one thing—from both men. Love.

If she couldn't get it for herself, perhaps she could for her child. "I don't know for certain he's a boy. The orphanage had no access to an ultrasound to prove it."

"What about other prenatal care?" he asked.

"Dominic took care of me."

That muscle twitched in his cheek again. "You should have found me, should have told me, and given me the chance to take care of you."

"I didn't know that you'd want to," she admitted. "In fact I was pretty convinced that you wouldn't want to."

He uttered a ragged sigh. "If you had asked me if I wanted to become a father, I would have told you no."

She flinched as his brutal honesty struck her hard. "I'm sorry…"

"But now that it's going to happen," he said, "I'll deal with it. I'll figure out how to be a good parent."

"Figure out?"

He shrugged. "I told you—that night on the water—I didn't have good examples."

"I know," she murmured. The stories had been more about warning her than sharing with her.

"My mom took off when I was little," he reminded her, "and my dad cared more about drinking than raising a kid."

As it had when he had first told her about his upbringing, sympathy for him clutched her heart. "I'm sorry…"

"You didn't have any better examples," he reminded her—again with the brutal honesty. "Aren't you scared?"

"Terrified," she admitted.

"You don't need to be," he assured her, stroking a fingertip along her cheek. "You will be a wonderful mother."

He had told her that before—on the water. And she hadn't asked then what she should have. "How do you know?"

"Because you care about people," he said. "You're not selfish..."

"Like my father?" Would she be as controlling with her kid as he'd been with her?

"He wasn't responsible for those men on the plane," Whit said in his defense. "They weren't following *his* orders."

So he wasn't a monster, just a bully. "I know," she said. "That's why I figured out we needed to jump."

"You took a huge risk..."

Her heart flipped with fear even just remembering. So many things could have gone wrong.

"Take a risk on me," he said, lowering his head to hers. He kissed her again—with passion and desire.

He had to be real. This couldn't be a dream. But what did Whit want her to take a risk on? Loving him?

It was too late. She'd already fallen in love with him. Six months ago. And so many things had gone wrong...

Except for conceiving their child. And except for making love with him. That hadn't felt wrong. That had felt as right as what he was doing to her now.

He made love to her mouth and then he made love to her body, kissing every inch of her. He teased her breasts with his tongue, tracing a nipple with his tongue before tugging the taut point between his lips.

She cried out as pressure built inside her body. She arched her hips up, silently begging for the release she knew he could give her. And he teased her with his fingers, sliding them gently in and out of her. Then he pressed his finger against the point where the pressure had built. And she came, screaming his name.

He moved away, dropping onto the mattress next to her. Sweat beaded on his brow and his upper lip, and the muscle twitched in his cheek.

"Are you all right?" she asked, concern chasing away the pleasure afterglow.

He groaned. "I will be. I just need a minute."

His body betrayed him. He'd lost his towel, so she saw the evidence of his desire.

"Make love to me," she urged him.

"I don't want to hurt you," he said, and he pressed a hand to her stomach. "Or him…"

"We're fine," she assured him. But she wasn't completely fine because the pressure was building again. "But I need you. I need to feel you inside me." And because she was afraid that he would hold back, she took the initiative.

She straddled his lean hips and eased herself down onto his pulsing erection. She moaned as he sank deeper and deeper.

He clutched her hips and lifted her up. But instead of pulling her off, he slid her back down. Up and down. He thrust inside her. And as he thrust, he arched up from the mattress. He kissed her, imitating with his tongue what he was doing to her body.

The intensity of the pressure built and built…until

he reached between them. He pushed against her with his thumb, and she came again.

He thrust once more and uttered a guttural groan, as he filled her with his pleasure.

Tears stung her eyes from the intimacy of their joined bodies and mutual ecstasy. Her heart swelled with emotion, with love. She had never felt anything as intense until she'd felt her baby's first little flutter of movement.

She loved Whit with the same intensity that she loved their baby. And she wanted to share that love with him.

But when she opened her mouth to speak, he pressed his fingers against her lips. "Listen," he said.

And she waited for him to speak, hoping that he was going to declare his feelings. Hoping that he loved her, too.

But he said nothing. Instead he cocked his head and narrowed his eyes. Then he asked, "Do you hear that?"

"What?"

"I think it's a helicopter."

"You think the owner is coming back?" Heat rushed to her face over the embarrassment of the homeowner finding them naked in his bed.

"I hope so," Whit said, but his body had tensed again. And that muscle was twitching in his cheek.

"But you don't think it is?"

He shrugged. "It could be. But my gut's telling me that it's not."

"You think they found us?" She had almost hoped they would believe she was dead again and not look for her.

"I think we're about to find out."

Chapter Eleven

Earlier, when he'd awakened from his long sleep, Whit had checked out the house again. Instead of just searching rooms, he'd searched every drawer and cupboard. And he'd found something the owner had left behind that he'd worried might prove useful.

A Glock.

He pressed it into Gabby's hand. "You take this," he insisted. "And stay out of sight."

They had dressed quickly, in clothes that were still damp from the washer, and Whit had retrieved the gun, before they'd slipped out of one of the many sliding doors of the house. That first day, he had found a little storm shelter close to the outbuilding that held the generator. But the cavelike hole was so small that they both barely fit inside its stone walls. That didn't matter, though, since Whit wasn't staying. He moved toward the cement steps that led back to the trapdoor like entrance.

Gabby clutched at his arm with fingers that trembled. "Don't leave."

"You'll be safe here," he assured her.

"Then you will be, too," she said. "Stay here. Stay out of sight with me."

He shook his head. "That might be help arriving on

that helicopter." It had probably already landed, but the generator was too close to the shelter and too loud for them to hear over the droning engine. "It could be Aaron and Charlotte."

He doubted it, though. If the plane had crashed, there probably would have been no survivors—no one to share the news that they'd parachuted out. But before the plane had gone down, one of them might have called his boss—the one really giving the orders. That person might be aware that they'd gotten off before the crash.

And he might have launched a search party to make sure they hadn't—or wouldn't—survive.

"I'll go with you," Gabby said, anxious to see her sister now. How like Gabby it was to have already forgiven Charlotte for the secrets she'd kept…

"We don't know for sure who it is," he pointed out. Even if it was the homeowner, Whit wanted to meet him alone first and gauge the person's trustworthiness before he revealed the princess of St. Pierre. "So I need to check it out first."

"Then take the gun with you," she said, pressing the Glock back into his hand, "in case it isn't help arriving."

"If it isn't, you may need the gun," he said. "It didn't take me long to find the shelter—they could find it, too." He intended to cover that door in the ground, though, with branches and leaves.

"You'll need the gun more than I will, then," she argued, "since you'll be encountering them first."

The woman was infuriating and beautiful and generous and loving. And Whit should tell her all those things. He had wanted to tell her earlier. Those words and so many others had been on the tip of his tongue, but then he'd heard the helicopter in the distance. And he had known that this was neither the time nor the place for him to share his feelings.

And if that wasn't help arriving, there may never be a time and place for him to tell her that he was falling in love with her.

"You need the gun," he said, "to protect yourself and our baby."

She drew in a shuddery breath and finally stopped trying to push the gun on him. He knew that she wouldn't have kept it for herself, but she wanted to protect their baby.

So did Whit. He would make sure that she wouldn't need to use that gun. He would protect her and their baby no matter the cost—even if he had to give up his life for theirs.

GABBY FLINCHED AS the baby kicked her ribs—hard. He was kicking her, too, like she was kicking herself for keeping the gun. She should have insisted Whit take it with him. She shouldn't have let him leave the shelter with no protection.

Maybe she should sneak out and see who had arrived, see if Whit would need the gun. She climbed the stairs toward the trapdoor, and standing beneath it, she listened intently. But all she could hear was the generator and the sound of her own furiously beating heart.

The baby kicked again, and she pressed her free hand against her belly—trying to soothe him even as her own nerves frayed. If she really was safe where she was, why hadn't Whit taken the gun?

Could she risk her child's life to save his father?

Whit would never forgive her if she ignored his

wishes and risked her own safety and their baby's. But perhaps even being where she was would endanger them. If someone found them, inside the shelter, they would be trapped. She could get off a few shots, might hit one or two of them. But what if there were more than a couple of them?

No. She couldn't stay in the shelter. It wouldn't be safe if she were to be discovered hiding in the cavelike hole because there was only one way out—through the trapdoor. She tried to lift it now, but it was heavy.

She managed to raise it an inch and dirt and grass rushed in through the narrow space. Choking on dust, she dropped it back down. Whit had covered it, had tried to camouflage it.

His friends claimed that his instincts were legendary and had saved more than one life during their deployments. For him to hide her as he had, his instincts must have been telling him that it wasn't help arriving.

They'd jumped out of a plane that had probably crashed. Why would anyone suspect they lived? Charlotte and Aaron were too realistic to believe in miracles. The only person who might know they'd survived was the one who'd hired the men, if the pilot or one of them had called him before the crash.

And if it was one of them, then Whit was disposable. He was only in the way of whatever plan that person had for her. Kidnapping or killing…

Whit, no doubt, had a plan to protect her and their baby. Like covering the hole to the shelter so no one would find her. But she worried that in order to carry out his plan he would have to sacrifice too much.

Perhaps his life…

WHIT HAD WALKED BACK through the living-room slider before passing through the house to the front door. That way, hopefully, the person wouldn't realize he had been outside.

He drew in a deep breath and opened it to a man he wasn't surprised to see. The guy was bald with heavy black brows and more scars than Whit and far fewer morals. Zeke Rogers had accepted his demotion with even less grace than the other men. He had to be the one who'd been giving them orders—since that had been his job before Whit and Aaron had taken it from him.

Whit was glad that he'd given Gabby the gun because Zeke was smart. He would find her eventually—unless Whit could outsmart him.

"You're like a cat with nine lives, huh?" Zeke remarked almost idly. He obviously wasn't surprised to see Whit either, or to find him alive and on this island. "You just keep coming back from the dead."

"I haven't died once," Whit corrected him. Yet. He had a feeling this man intended to change that.

"I heard about the bullet you took in Michigan," Zeke said. "That's why the king had me resume my duties at the palace, as his royal guard."

"We agreed that would be best," Whit admitted, "while Aaron and I concentrated our efforts on finding Charlotte and Princess Gabriella. But Charlotte has been found." And Aaron should have resumed his duties as chief of security, dismissing Zeke again.

"The princess has been, too," Zeke claimed.

Whit's stomach muscles tightened as if he'd taken a blow. But he resisted the urge to glance toward the shelter and make sure Gabby wasn't being dragged from her hiding place. Zeke could have other men searching the island. One of them could have found her.

But she was a fighter. He doubted she would have been taken without firing at least one shot, which he would have heard even over the drone of the generator engine.

Denying Zeke's claim, Whit shook his head. "She's gone..."

"The king sent you to retrieve her from Charlotte's aunt's orphanage." The man had obviously been briefed—either by the king or by someone else. "You had her. You two were on the royal jet together before it went down."

"It went down?"

Zeke nodded, but his face displayed no emotion. He didn't give a damn that men he'd worked with had probably lost their lives. Probably while they'd been trying to carry out his orders...

"Were there any survivors?" Whit wondered.

Zeke shook his head now. "Just you and the princess."

So he had been in contact with the men on the plane—obviously right up until the moment it went down. "Why would you think that?" Whit asked, trying to get the man to make the admission. Not that it mattered if he confessed...

Whit was convinced Zeke Rogers wasn't there to help him or Gabby.

"Well, obviously you're alive."

Whit nodded. "Obviously."

"You and the princess parachuted out of the plane."

There was no point in denying what Zeke had apparently been told. "That's true."

"You weren't easy to track down," Zeke said, resentment flashing in his beady eyes. "I had to talk to some parachuting experts and some experts on ocean currents to figure out where the hell you might have washed up."

Whit had a feeling the man had been hoping to find bodies rather than survivors. "It really was nice of you to go to all the trouble to rescue me."

"I'm not here to rescue you," the man ominously corrected him.

Whit lifted his arms, ignoring the twinge in his shoulder, and gestured around the empty house. "Well, I'm the only one here."

Zeke chuckled. "Where are you hiding the princess?"

Whit forced a ragged sigh of regret and resignation. "She didn't make it."

"She wasn't on that plane when it went down," Zeke insisted. "She parachuted off with you."

"Yes, but that was much too dangerous in her condition. There were complications…" He paused, as if choked up.

"With her pregnancy?" Zeke asked.

He was too superstitious to lie about that, not wanting to tempt fate. So he just shook his head. "She was weak and the water was just too damn cold. We were in the sea overnight." He shuddered, for real, as he remembered the frigid water and how it had numbed his muscles and burned his skin. How the hell had they survived?

He shuddered again. "She didn't make it…"

Zeke narrowed his eyes. His voice terse with skepticism, he asked, "You just let her die?"

"I couldn't do anything to help her." He really hadn't. She'd fought for herself and for their child.

Zeke snorted, derisively. "So you're not the hero everyone thinks you are."

Whit shrugged. "I never claimed I was a hero."

"You haven't needed to—all those men you hired that you served with—they make the claims for you. That's why the king made you his right-hand man." Along with the resentment, there was hatred.

"You'll probably get that job back now," Whit said, "since I failed to protect what matters most to the king." No matter how callously he'd treated his daughter, the man did love her. He had been so genuinely distraught over her disappearance that he had to care. And as Whit had learned for himself, the woman was damn hard not to love. He'd fought his feelings, but it was one of the first battles he'd ever lost.

"I thought she mattered to you, too," Zeke remarked.

"Why would you think that?"

"Heard she was following you around like a puppy before she disappeared," he said. And now there was jealousy. He was too old for Gabby. But hell, at thirty, with the life he'd lived, so was Whit. "And nobody missed the way you looked at her, too."

"She's a beautiful woman."

Zeke arched one of those creepily bushy brows.

"Was," he corrected himself, silently cursing the slip. "She was a beautiful woman."

"She was pregnant, too," Zeke said.

"Did you have a bug on that plane?" he wondered. The men wouldn't have had much time to tell him everything. But the first man, the one Gabby had shot, would have had time to inform him of the princess's pregnancy.

"I'm just thorough," Zeke said. "I believe in doing a job well."

Whit couldn't argue with him. While Zeke had protected the king, the monarch had not been harmed. But Charlotte hadn't trusted the former mercenary. She had suspected that his loyalty was for sale to the highest bidder, and that if someone paid him more than the king, that Zeke Rogers would do whatever they wanted. The man had no morals, no principles and no conscience. Obviously Charlotte had been right.

"Maybe you should have been sent to retrieve the princess then," Whit said.

"I have been," Zeke retorted. "Now."

The skin on the nape of Whit's neck tingled with foreboding. "It's too bad that you're too late."

"It would be if I actually believed you." The man pushed past Whit and strode purposely through the house, searching every room.

Feigning shock and offense, he asked, "You don't take me at my word?"

Zeke snorted in reply and just continued to search.

Whit followed, breathing a sigh of relief that he'd stripped the bed in the room in which he'd awakened. It didn't look as though anyone had slept in it. It didn't look as though anyone had slept in Gabby's bed, either. The sheets were tangled and damp.

But Zeke didn't seem to notice. He checked under the bed and the closet and continued through the house.

"Satisfied?" Whit asked. "She's not here."

"I won't believe Princess Gabby is gone," Zeke replied, "until I see her dead body." And if her body wasn't dead, did he intend to make it that way?

"You're not going to find it in the house." Whit

managed to furrow his brow with feigned confusion. "I've been checking the beach…"

"Waiting for her to wash up?"

He flinched at the agonizing thought.

"Give up trying to sell me on this line of bullshit, Howell," Zeke said. "There's no way in hell you lost her in the ocean."

He nearly had—when her hand had slipped out of his. But he'd caught her before she'd slipped beneath the water.

"We didn't land near each other," Whit lied. "By the time I swam toward where she'd landed, the chute lines had pulled her under. She was gone…"

Zeke pulled his gun from the holster beneath his jacket. "You better hope you're telling the truth, Howell, because if I find her…"

"You're going to kill her?"

Those bushy brows arched in question. "Why would that matter to you—if she's really already dead?"

"Just didn't think the king would order his daughter killed," Whit said. "So who are you working for now?" He knew Zeke didn't intend to let him live, so he might actually tell him the truth.

"Someone who wants the princess to never return to St. Pierre."

"Who?" Whit persisted.

Zeke taunted him, "If she's really dead, what does it matter?"

Whit couldn't say it—couldn't bring himself to utter the lie. Before today he had never been superstitious, but he couldn't risk it now—that saying she was dead wouldn't somehow make it come true.

"I want to know who you're working for," Whit persisted.

"Why?" Zeke asked. "It's not like you're going to need a job anytime soon."

Whit shrugged. "You don't know that. The king is not going to be happy with me for not bringing the princess home."

"The king won't fire you," Zeke assured him. "Because he won't need to. I'll fire you for him." And he lifted the gun and pulled the trigger.

Chapter Twelve

The sound of the gunshot echoed off the hilltop. Gabby felt the vibration of it in the sliding door against which she leaned, trying to see inside. But Whit had pulled the drapes across it, blinding her to what was going on inside the house.

Who had gotten off the helicopter? And had Whit just calmly let them inside the house to shoot him?

Her heart pounded furiously and so loudly she could hear it ringing in her ears. Or was that just the echo of the shot yet?

The wind picked up, whipping her hair around her face. And she realized what the noise really was: the sound of another helicopter.

Was it backup for the first? More of the men from the plane?

She clutched the gun she held. Should she storm inside the house? Or should she run to the helicopter in the hopes that it might actually be someone to help? Her head pounded with indecision and fear. Her instincts had her wanting to storm inside the house—wanting to protect Whit.

So she followed her instincts and pushed open the patio door. She listened but heard no voices, no sound above the pounding of the helicopter blades as it approached that small pad on the other side of the house. She drew in a deep breath and lifted the gun before stepping inside.

Glass crunched beneath her feet as she crept across the living room. The coffee table top had shattered, leaving only the brass frame. And that had been twisted. Chairs had toppled onto the slate flooring.

There had been a struggle. But there was no body left behind to tell her who had won or who had lost. Where was Whit? And with whom had he struggled?

He had rested for a day, but he hadn't completely recovered from their overnight in the sea or his gunshot wound. As she studied the mess, she noticed the dark liquid spattered across the glass fragments and the slate. She crouched down, as far as her burgeoning belly allowed, and reached a trembling finger toward the spill. Then she lifted her hand and analyzed the stain smeared across her fingertip. A bright red stain.

Had Whit's wound re-opened or did he have a new one?

Tears stung her eyes. Tears of regret and guilt and anguish. She shouldn't have waited so long before coming out of the shelter. She should have followed him right back inside the house. What kind of mother was she going to be for her baby if she'd done nothing while his father had been harmed?

Where was Whit? How badly was he hurt?

She wasn't just concerned that her baby might have lost her father. She was concerned that she might have lost the man she loved…and before she'd even had a chance to tell him how she felt.

WHIT HAD HAD to get Zeke outside—because he'd noticed the shadow outside the slider. And he'd known that Gabby had been too worried to stay where he'd put her. She'd been worried about him—when she should have been more concerned about herself and their child.

She'd done the same thing at the orphanage—making sure the men had seen her, so that they would leave her aunt and the kids alone. She had used herself as bait to lure the danger away from the others.

She cared so much about everyone…but herself.

"It took two of you to replace one of me," Zeke taunted him as he pushed Whit forward with the barrel of the gun buried between his shoulder blades. "You really think you alone are any match for me?"

"Are *you* alone?" Whit asked. He had seen no other men with the guard. And Zeke had been a helicopter pilot when he'd served his country and later when he'd served whatever country had paid him the most.

Zeke snorted. "More alone than you are. Where is she?"

"I told you. She's dead." He hated saying it; hated how the words felt in his mouth. Bitter and sickening. And he hoped like hell his superstition wouldn't be proved a reality. Ever.

"The next time I shoot, it won't be a coffee table," Zeke warned him. "And the only one who's going to be dead is you."

Whit chuckled and reminded Zeke, "But you're the one who's bleeding."

When the guard had shot the coffee table, Whit had struck him hard—trying to knock him out. But the man had an iron jaw. All Whit had done was broken his skin and drawn blood.

And rage.

Zeke had swung the gun toward Whit then. But he'd kept him from firing by saying that her body had washed up on the beach. And so he'd drawn Zeke outside to the steepest edge of the hilltop.

The wind picked up, and the pounding of helicopter blades alerted them to the arrival of another aircraft. Backup for Zeke?

But all his men must have been gone because he lifted his gun and aimed it at the helicopter. As it flew over them, Whit recognized the royal seal of St. Pierre. Maybe Aaron was inside—maybe he and Charlotte had figured out Zeke's duplicity and followed him here.

Zeke must have come to the same conclusion because he squeezed the trigger, getting off one shot before Whit struck him. Instead of swinging toward the man's iron jaw, though, he slammed his fist into Zeke's arm—with enough force to knock the weapon for his grasp.

The Glock flew from the man's hand, dropping over the cliff. While Zeke turned toward where it had fallen, Whit pushed—sending the man tumbling over the side.

But Zeke's arms thrashed. And as he reached out, he caught Whit's shoulder and pulled him over the edge, too. He felt the weightlessness that he had when he and Gabby had jumped from the plane. But this time he had no parachute strapped to his back—nothing to break his fall on the rocks.

AARON'S HEART LURCHED as the helicopter took the hit. His gaze flew to the pilot, who grappled with the controls as the aircraft shuddered and shook. "This is why I wanted you to stay at the palace," he told his fiancée.

"And let you take on Zeke Rogers alone?" Charlotte asked, shaking her head at the thought.

"I would have brought some of the men Whit and I trust," he said.

She passed over the island, struggling to bring the helicopter under control again. Over open water, the engine sputtered once. Twice.

"We can't trust anyone," she said. "But each other…"

He trusted her. He trusted that if anyone could save them right now—it was her.

But what about Whit? Were they already too late to save him and Princess Gabriella? Were they on this island—as the parachuting and ocean current experts had told first Zeke and then them?

Or had they been lost at sea as Charlotte had been so convinced? She wouldn't let herself hope. Instead she'd been intent on tracking down who was responsible for the attempted kidnapping that had gone so very wrong…

And when they'd gotten on Zeke's trail, it had led them here. To this private island getaway. Or rather, hideaway, given that the man who owned it had used questionable methods accruing the wealth to acquire the island.

He could have been the one shooting at them. Whit wouldn't have been. He would have recognized the royal seal and waited to see who landed. Then he might have started firing if he'd realized Zeke Rogers had sold himself to a higher bidder.

Why had it taken the king so long to realize that Charlotte had been right not to trust the man? Why had he?

It was a mistake that had cost him. He'd aged another

ten years with the realization that he had been the one who'd put his daughter at risk. Not Charlotte. Not Whit.

And what about Whit?

No bodyguard had ever taken an assignment as literally as Whit. He would do whatever was necessary to protect a client—even give up his own life for theirs. Aaron suspected that was never truer than now, with Princess Gabriella carrying Whit's child. The guy had always claimed that he would never get married, never be a father. Aaron didn't know his reasons why, but he doubted one of them had been death.

A dead man couldn't become a husband or father...

Aaron should have married Charlotte before they'd ever left Michigan. He shouldn't have let him talk her into making sure Gabby was safe first.

"That's definitely the helicopter Zeke took," Charlotte said. The royal seal was on the bottom of it but it was the same royal blue and bright magenta of the one she flew. Or tried to fly.

The engine sputtered again. They needed to land. But Zeke had planted his helicopter in the center of the small cement pad. The island wasn't big enough to have a clearing where they could land. There was only the house and then the hill dropped steeply off to the rocky beach below.

He trusted Charlotte. But there was only so much she could do. The helicopter was going down whether or not she found a place to land safely.

GABBY'S THROAT BURNED yet from the scream she'd uttered when she had watched the two men tumble over the cliff on the other side of the helicopter pad. She'd checked out the island earlier—when Whit was asleep.

She knew this side had no stairs leading to a beach. It had no sand—only jagged rocks from the top of the hill to the water below.

Dread kept her legs locked in place—unable to move forward, to run toward the edge of that cliff. She had a horrible feeling that she knew what she would see when she looked over the edge.

Like a bird of prey, the helicopter circled back again. It was the colors of her country. But that offered Gabriella more fear than comfort. The only one she could trust who worked for St. Pierre was Whit.

And he was gone.

The helicopter engine sputtered. The metal screeched, trees scraping it, as the helicopter made its crash landing. It landed in a tiny clearing behind her, between her and the house. Leaving her an unobstructed view of that cliff.

She kept watching it. But Whit didn't pull himself up it. Neither did the man he'd pushed over the side. No one came back up.

Finally she forced herself to move toward where they had fallen. But her legs trembled so badly that she had no balance. She stumbled and pitched forward. To protect her baby, she put out her hands—and dropped the gun Whit had left her for protection into the thick grass.

Behind her the helicopter engine whined down to silence. It was eerily silent. So quiet that she heard the footsteps on the grass.

Panic overwhelmed her, sending her scrambling for the gun. She delved her hands into the grass. But it was so thick and long that she couldn't find the weapon.

She had nothing to protect her. No gun. No Whit.

Tears of loss and fear and frustration stung her eyes, so that they watered. And her throat filled with emotion. She couldn't even scream.

But what did it matter? Who would hear her? Anyone who cared was gone.

Strong hands grasped her arms and pulled her to her feet. She drew in a shuddery breath, trying to summon the strength and courage to fight.

Whit might have been gone. But she still had her baby. She had to fight for him—to protect him and herself from whoever had come for her.

So when she turned, she lifted her leg and kicked out with her all might—hoping to knock her attacker's legs from beneath him—hoping to knock him off balance enough that she could escape.

But there was more than one.

Chapter Thirteen

Aaron caught Charlotte, stopping her fall. Gabby gasped in shock over seeing her sister and realizing that she'd nearly knocked down the woman—the very pregnant woman.

"Oh, my God!" she exclaimed. "Are you all right?"

Charlotte nodded. "Are you?"

The tears she'd momentarily blinked away rushed back, filling her eyes and her throat, so she barely got out her, "Yes."

It had been Charlotte and Aaron on the helicopter. Charlotte and Aaron who had nearly crashed. She'd nearly lost them, too.

"Where's Whit?" Aaron asked anxiously, his blue eyes bright with fear for his friend's safety.

Hysteria threatened, but Gabby pushed it back to reply, "Whit's gone…"

"Where's Whit?" Aaron asked, glancing around the small area. "Did Zeke take him somewhere?"

Zeke Rogers. That was who had landed in the first helicopter. That was who had fired those shots. That was whom Whit had been fighting when he went over.

"Come quick," Gabby ordered. She hadn't believed

help would come, but it had. So maybe she needed to believe again—in Whit. To hope...

"They were fighting," she said, gesturing ahead of her at the cliff as she struggled to run through the tall grass, "and they fell."

She ran but Aaron wasn't pregnant, so he was faster. He beat the women to the cliff, stopping only at the edge. His jaw clenched as he stared over the side.

When Gabby rushed up, he turned around and stopped her with his arms on her shoulders. "Don't look!"

That had been her first instinct, too, not to look when she was so certain of what she would find. Utter despair and loss. But she hadn't thought there would be help, either. She hadn't really believed that anyone would ever find her and Whit. So she had to look. Had to know for certain...

She tugged free of Aaron's grasp and looked around him. Her gaze was immediately drawn to the edge of the water below, to the body so busted up on the rocks so that it looked like a broken marionette.

"That's not Whit," she said with horror. It couldn't be Whit. He couldn't be gone.

But they wouldn't be able to confirm or disprove the identity of the body because waves tugged at it, pulling it from the rocks to disappear into the ocean.

She screamed.

WHIT'S ARMS BURNED with his effort to hang on, his hands wrapped around a rock jutting from the cliff. The rock was damp, and his grip began to slip. He didn't want to wind up like Zeke, who'd crashed onto the rocks below. His eyes had been wide open, staring up at Whit in death. But now he was gone.

And Whit heard Gabby's scream. It chilled his blood with fear—for her safety more than his.

"Gabby!" he yelled back. "I'm coming. I'm coming!"

He wouldn't leave her—not like this. Not any way. As one hand slipped off a wet rock, he lurched up, reached out blindly with his free arm and somehow managed to clasp another rock while not letting go of the one he held. The rough edges cut into his palm, and his shoulder strained with the movement. But he didn't care. His own discomfort was nothing in comparison to the fear and anguish he'd just heard in Gabby's scream.

She screamed again—his name. But now her voice was full of hope and relief. "Whit!"

He stared up at the hilltop and found her leaning over the edge. A rock beneath her foot slipped loose and tumbled down the cliff. And she slipped, too.

"Gabby!"

But strong hands grasped her arms and pulled her back. He couldn't see her—couldn't see who had her or if she was really safe.

"Gabby!"

Now someone else stood on the edge, staring down. "Son of a bitch," a deep voice shouted. "What the hell…"

"Aaron!" Relief that Gabby was safe flooded Whit. His friend would protect her, like Whit had tried, with his life if necessary.

"How the hell am I supposed to reach you?" Aaron asked with frustration, as if he were trying to figure out a particularly vexing puzzle.

Whit's grip, on one rock, slipped again. But once again he held tight with the hand that had a hold on

a rock and swung his free arm. He managed to catch
the edge of another rock—higher up. "I'm coming," he
assured them.

Aaron must have taken him at his word because
he disappeared from sight. Disappointment and panic
flashed through Whit. They had only just regained their
friendship and their trust. So he suffered a moment's
doubt—wondering if his old friend was really going
to help him.

That panic had him swinging his arm again, trying
to reach a higher rock. But his fingertips slipped off,
and his arm swung back—nearly making him lose the
grip he had with his other hand. He kicked out, trying
to find a toe hold.

And beneath him the waves crashed against the
rocks, as if getting ready to carry his broken body out
to sea, too.

But he wasn't giving up. Not yet. Not ever. He swung
his arm toward the wall of rocks again—trying to catch
hold. And his fingers touched something else—rough
fibers. A rope dangled over the edge.

"Grab it!" Aaron shouted.

Whit grasped the rope in a tight fist. But he didn't
let go of the rock with his other hand. And finally he
got a hold with his foot.

"I got you," Aaron said. "I can pull you up."

Maybe he could. While not as big as Whit, Aaron
was a strong guy. But still Whit couldn't completely
give up control or trust. Instead of just holding on and
letting Aaron pull him up, he used the rope as a railing
to make the climb himself.

He was climbing up to Gabby—to make sure she
was safe. Even though Zeke was gone, it wasn't over.

If Zeke had been working for someone, that person could hire another mercenary to finish the job. But even if they figured out whom Zeke had been working for, Gabby would always be in danger; her life and her safety always at risk because of who she was. Princess Gabriella St. Pierre.

And he was just a royal bodyguard…with nothing to offer her but his protection. And he hadn't done a very damn good job of protecting her yet.

She would be safer with Charlotte. And happier with a prince. So when he stepped foot on the topside of the hill, he resisted the urge to grab her up in his arms and hold her close. And when she reached for him, he caught her hands and stopped her from embracing him. Because if he gave in to temptation and hugged her, he would never let her go again.

"Are you all right?" she asked, her beautiful face stained with tears she'd shed over him.

She was too good for him. Too good for anyone…

"What the hell happened?" Aaron asked.

Whit nodded. "I'm fine. It was Zeke who hit the rocks."

Charlotte nodded. "We figured it was Zeke."

"Acting out of revenge," Aaron said, "for us getting him fired."

Whit shook his head. "It was about money."

"Was he going to kidnap me to get my father to pay him a ransom?" Gabby asked. She tugged her hands free of Whit's, as if self-conscious that she'd reached for him and he'd held her off. She slid her palms over her stomach, as if to soothe their baby.

He could walk away from her—to keep her safe. But could he walk away from his son? Hell, the child—heir to a country—would probably be in even more danger than Gabriella had been.

"I think it was about money," Whit agreed. "But I think someone was paying him…"

Gabby flinched, as if in pain. And he couldn't add to that—couldn't tell her what Zeke had been paid to do: kill her.

"You're not feeling well," he said.

She glanced up at his face, as if dazed. And she began to tremble. "I'm fine," she said. But she had to be lying.

"Aaron, get them back to St. Pierre," he ordered.

"What about you?" Aaron asked. "Aren't you coming with us?"

"I need to clean up around here—make sure Zeke was alone." And that the man was dead. He intended to go down to the beach below.

And Charlotte and Aaron must have read his intentions. "Aaron can stay with you. I'll take her," the former U.S. Marshal said. "We have a pilot with us."

"But your helicopter was hit."

"The bullet did no structural damage."

"Is the pilot someone we can trust?" Whit asked. Before they could answer, he shook his head. "You better fly them, Aaron." Because somewhere out there, someone still wanted Gabriella dead.

"I'm the one who flew us here," Charlotte said. And then she was the one who'd landed the helicopter after it had been hit. "I've had my pilot's license for years."

"Of course you have," Gabby murmured—with a flash of bitterness.

And Whit remembered that the women had unfinished business between them. Charlotte had kept secrets from Gabby that she'd had no right to keep even though she'd had her reasons. Maybe sending the two of them off alone together wasn't the greatest idea.

"So let's go," Gabby said, and she left him without a backward glance—as if she'd dismissed him after he'd done his job. Was that all he was to her? An employee? While she walked away, Charlotte and Aaron embraced—as if the thought of spending just mere hours apart was intolerable to them.

"Be safe," Aaron implored his fiancée.

"Always."

"I love you."

"I love you more," she said and pressed a hand to her own swollen belly. "Because I love you for the both of us." With another quick kiss for her baby's father, she followed Gabby to the helicopter pad.

Both men stood until the helicopter lifted off and flew away—its engine loud and strong and its course straight.

"No smart remarks?" Aaron asked.

"About what?" He knew, though. He'd teased Aaron in the past about his public displays of affection. The man always fell easily and hard. But he'd never fallen as hard as he had for Charlotte Green, and those feelings were so much stronger because they were reciprocated. Whit couldn't tease him about that—not when he was envious as hell of what his friend had found.

Aaron narrowed his eyes, which were an eerie pale blue, and studied Whit's face. "Are you really okay? You didn't hit your head when you went over the cliff?"

Whit shook his head. "There are steps over here leading down. We need to check down there—"

"He's gone," Aaron said. "There's no way he survived

that fall." He shuddered. "I can't believe that you did— that you caught yourself. You are so damn lucky—like a cat with nine lives."

Whit nearly shuddered, too, at Aaron making the same comparison the mercenary had.

"But knowing you like I do, you probably used up the last of those nine lives today," Aaron continued. "So we shouldn't risk going down that cliff."

"Maybe Zeke lost his phone," Like he'd lost his life, on the rocks, "when he fell. If we can find that and figure out who he was talking to, maybe we can figure out who hired him."

"You think Gabby's still in danger?" Aaron asked, with a glance toward the sky—obviously concerned about both women. But the helicopter was long gone.

"I know she is." And even after they found whoever had hired Zeke, she would still be in danger—still have people trying to kidnap her for her father's fortune.

"What else do you know about her?" Aaron asked. "Who the father of her baby is?" The question was obviously rhetorical; his friend was pretty damn sure it was his.

Whit clenched his jaw.

And Aaron whistled. "I can't believe it—after everything you've said about never getting married—"

"That hasn't changed," Whit said. There was no way in hell a princess would ever consider marrying him. And even if she did take the chance on him, her father would never approve their marriage.

"And the fact that we have a job to do hasn't changed, either," he continued. "We need to protect her."

"From whom, do you think?" Aaron asked.

Whit shrugged. "I don't know. We thought it might

be Prince Linus's father. She doesn't think her ex-fiancé could have concocted that elaborate a plot on his own."

Aaron gasped. "King Demetrios and his younger son are at the palace. They said they were concerned about her. Why would they want to hurt the princess?"

Whit shook his head. He couldn't fathom why anyone would want to hurt Gabby. "I don't know if they're involved. All we know for certain is that someone wanted her to *never* return to St. Pierre."

And Gabriella was already on her way…

"I DON'T NEED to ask who the father of your baby is," Charlotte remarked, once she and Gabby walked into their private suite of rooms in the palace.

They hadn't talked at all on the helicopter. Gabby hadn't been ready to deal with the woman she now knew was her sister. Nor had she been able to deal with her disappointment over how Whit had treated her. It was like their making love had been just her dreaming.

Because he had acted like it had never happened. He had acted like they had never been intimate enough to have conceived the child she carried. His child.

"You don't?" Gabriella wondered. Because Whit had certainly not betrayed their relationship. But Charlotte had always been able to read her—even while she, herself, had been keeping so much from Gabby.

"You love Whit," Charlotte said, her voice soft with sympathy. From the way he'd acted, she had undoubtedly been able to tell that Gabby's feelings were not reciprocated. "You were falling for him six months ago, but now you love him."

Gabriella shrugged. It didn't matter how she felt

since her feelings were not returned. He'd asked her to take a risk on him…

A risk that he would figure out how to love? That risk had obviously not paid off.

"I don't need to ask who the father of your baby is, either," Gabby said, her heart warming as she studied Charlotte's face—so like her own except for the happiness that illuminated it from within—making her breathtakingly beautiful.

"I got pregnant the night of the ball," Charlotte said, pressing her palms to her belly as Gabby always did. "The same night I assume you must have since we both left the next day." Her light of happiness dimmed. "I'm sorry. I'm sorry that my plan went so wrong."

"You were the one who was kidnapped," Gabby reminded her. "I'm sorry…"

Charlotte shook her head. "It wasn't your fault. None of it was. Aaron found me." The light inside her brightened again. "He rescued me."

"He loves you."

Charlotte smiled. "Yes. He asked me to marry him, and I accepted. I love him."

Gabby flinched with jealousy and then was angry with herself for being so petty as to envy someone else's happiness.

Charlotte reached out, pulling Gabriella into a close embrace—or as close as their pregnant bellies allowed. "And I love you," Charlotte said. "That's why I couldn't tell you that I'm your sister. I couldn't tell you about our mother."

"But you knew how the queen hated me," Gabby said, pulling free of her. "You knew how that bothered me." Even after the woman had died. "You could have told me she wasn't really my mother."

Charlotte shook her head. "If I told you the truth, I would have been fired. It killed me to keep it from you, but it was better to keep the secrets and keep you safe."

Whit had been right about her reasons. Tears stung Gabby's eyes. "You—you wanted to tell me?"

Charlotte nodded, and the gesture had tears spilling from her eyes to trail down her face. "As soon as I found out I had a sister, I wanted a relationship with you. That's why, when I found the letter in the things my mom left behind when she died, I quit the U.S. Marshals."

"I thought you quit because of what happened with Josie and Aaron and Whit."

Charlotte had had Whit help her fake Josie's death so that she could relocate her. Making Whit keep the secret from Aaron had destroyed their business partnership and their friendship.

"Making Whit keep that secret…" Charlotte let out a shuddery breath. "I understood what it cost him…when I had to keep secrets from you."

"It won't cost you what it cost Whit," Gabby assured her. "You won't lose me." She hugged Charlotte tightly. So tightly that their babies kicked in unison.

Charlotte laughed. "They're already getting to know each other."

"They're going to be close," Gabby said.

"And so are we now that we have no secrets." Charlotte squeezed her. "Thank you for forgiving me."

"It wasn't your fault," Gabby said. "It was his…" Her stomach churned as she thought of him and how little he'd really thought of her.

"He apologized to me," Charlotte said. "He wants to treat me as a daughter now. Not an employee. Aaron will continue to work for him and protect us all."

What about Whit? But only Whit could answer that.

"He wants to make up the past to me," Charlotte said. "And I'm going to stay here and give him the chance."

Her sister was more forgiving than she was.

"He wants to see you," Charlotte said.

To control and manipulate her, no doubt.

She shook her head, wanting to put off the moment when she had to face her father, and all his disappointment. "I need to get ready first."

"Sure, clean up."

She didn't need a shower. She needed to gather all her courage and resentment and tell her father that she was not one of his loyal subjects. She was his daughter, and he was finally going to treat her and her wishes with respect.

"Don't keep him waiting too long," Charlotte said. "He's been through a lot these past six months. Thinking you were dead…" Her voice cracked with emotion as she added, "…and that I was dead, really changed him."

"He's not going to fire you over my finding out that you're my sister?"

Charlotte shook her head. "No. He acknowledged me as his daughter."

Maybe that was because he was about to disown Gabriella for letting him worry for six months and for getting pregnant with the baby of a man who wasn't royalty—except for being a royal bodyguard.

Whit had risked his own life to protect Gabby. But before she could romanticize his actions, she had to remind herself that he'd only been doing his job. She meant nothing to him.

"I'm glad I'm not the only princess now," Gabriella said. "But be careful that he doesn't try to run your life as he has mine."

"Talk to him," Charlotte urged.

Was it possible to talk to someone who had never listened to her? She nodded, acknowledging that she had to at least try.

Charlotte smiled as she headed for the door. "I'll let him know that you'll be meeting with him soon."

As soon as she could gather her courage and control her anger over all the secrets he'd kept from her. To splash some water on her face, Gabby stepped into her bathroom and gasped in shock.

Scrawled across her mirror in scarlet red lipstick was a note even more ominous than the letter left under her pillow. "You should have stayed dead!"

Chapter Fourteen

"I want to see her now!" Prince Tonio Malamatos commanded Whit as he paced the front salon of the palace. It was the most public parlor, the one farthest from the royal quarters and the royals.

Whit's head was still pounding from his struggle with Zeke Rogers. But he wasn't above fighting another man, and this tall thin man would be easily beaten. If only Whit had that right...

Gabby carrying his child wasn't enough—not when she was still engaged to this man. An engagement he apparently had every intention of seeing through to his wedding day—even though his ex-fiancée had arrived at the palace with him. Damn Aaron for hurrying off to find Charlotte as soon as they arrived, leaving Whit alone to deal with this royal pain in the ass.

He wasn't the only one demanding to see her. King Demetrios had also requested an audience with her, to extend his apologies for the behavior of his son, and, Whit suspected, to introduce her to his other son. The young man followed his father like a puppy, like the ex-fiancée followed Prince Malamatos. Whit had had other men follow them back to their rooms. Men he trusted stood guard to make sure they wouldn't leave their rooms undetected.

"She needs to rest and recover," Whit told the prince. "She's been through a lot."

King Demetrios had accepted that excuse the first time Whit had offered it, and he and his son had retired to the guest rooms King St. Pierre had offered them. Prince Malamatos was much more stubborn.

"Whose fault is that?" the woman asked, her tone as waspish as her thin face. Honora Del Cachon, with her pale face framed with thin, dark hair, was a brittle and bitter woman—some distant relative of the queen. The queen had already been dead when Whit started working for the king, so he'd never met her. But meeting this woman gave him some indication of what Gabby had dealt with, and how she'd grown up with disapproval and resentment and cruelty.

Whit was hurting too much and too tired to worry about protocol. Hell, he didn't remember what she was anyways—a princess? A duchess? He figured she was just a royal bitch. "I could give you a list of names of men who were trying to hurt her."

But still one name eluded him. He and Aaron had found nothing of Zeke's—not even his body. While they'd been searching the island, they had had the guards they trusted searching Zeke's apartment. They had found nothing there to indicate who had hired him—if anyone even had. There had been nothing to link him to anyone else. Maybe he had been acting on his own—out of vengeance.

"You are not going to take any responsibility for the princess's condition?" the woman demanded, her tone as imperious as the king's.

She was not a queen; Whit knew that much about her. Obviously she did not realize that herself. And how the hell did she know that Gabby was pregnant?

Aaron had said that only he, Charlotte and, *damn it,* the king knew.

"What do you mean?" he asked her.

"Are you not a royal guard?" the woman said. "Is it not your duty to protect her?"

"I am her fiancé," Prince Malamatos declared. "I will protect her from now on."

"She's been hiding for six months," the woman said, turning now on the man to whom she'd been engaged. "She does not want to marry you."

"She was frightened," the prince stubbornly defended Gabriella. "I will hire many royal guards, men who can be trusted, and she will feel safe in my palace."

"She is pregnant," the woman said, betraying that she did know a secret.

Prince Malamatos didn't react to her news; obviously it wasn't news to him. Who had already told him? This woman or Zeke Rogers?

"How do you know?" Whit asked her.

The woman's shoulders lifted in slight shrug. "I saw her and the one who looks just like her as they arrived," the woman explained. She leaned closer to Whit, as if ashamed that she was about to gossip. "They are both the king's daughters, you know. The queen, my dear cousin, revealed to me on her deathbed that they are both his children by a former mistress. He bought her Gabriella like one would buy a doll or a puppy."

The prince betrayed no surprise. Obviously he already knew that, too.

"Why are you really here?" he found himself asking the man. Did he want to marry Gabby or punish her for betraying him during their engagement? St. Pierre wasn't that far away in geography or culture from the places that practiced honor killings. Was Prince Malamatos's country such a place?

"That's impertinent of you," the prince replied. "But as I told you, I want to see my fiancée. I want to set a date for our wedding."

"You still want to marry her?" the woman asked. "Even though she is pregnant with another man's child." From the arch glance she cast at Whit, it was apparent she knew which man.

The prince shrugged. "To merge my country with the resources of St. Pierre, I will claim the royal bastard as my own. After all, I will be marrying a royal bastard."

Whit wasn't tired enough to ignore what the man said. Or maybe he was too tired to summon the control it would have taken him to ignore that comment. For he swung and smashed his fist into the prince's weak jaw.

The man crumpled to the ground, the woman screaming and hovering over him.

"Whit!" Aaron yelled as he walked back into the salon. "What the hell!"

"Did you hear what he said about the princess?" Whit demanded.

"It was all true," the woman replied. "You are a barbarian."

He was a man in love. But all he could offer Gabriella was his protection, of her life and her reputation…

"The king wants to see you," Aaron told Whit.

Whit's stomach knotted with dread at the look on his friend's face. He couldn't meet his gaze. Obviously the king was furious with him. Someone must have told him about the baby.

"He's going to fire you for your impudence," the woman said.

If he was going to get fired for it, he might as well tell the king exactly what he thought of him and the way he'd treated the sweetest woman Whit had ever known. He stormed past Aaron, heading toward the king's private rooms.

GABBY ROSE UP on tiptoe and tried to scrub at the mirror with a tissue. She scrubbed so hard that the mirror actually cracked from the pressure she applied—and probably from age, as well. It was an antique with a gilded frame.

Perhaps she should have called Charlotte back and shown her the message on the mirror. But Gabriella had chosen to ignore it—at first. She'd showered and changed into a gown. Since it was evening, formal dress was protocol even if there hadn't been guests in the palace. Fortunately she'd found a dress with an empire waist and a skirt billowy enough for her pregnant belly. Wearing a tiara was also protocol, so she'd turned to the mirror in order to see where to pin the diamond-encrusted jewelry into her hair.

And she hadn't been able to ignore the message any longer. Because the shower steam had smeared the lipstick and sent it running down the glass in rivulets, Gabby couldn't see beyond it.

And she wasn't certain she wanted Charlotte to see it. The last time she'd shown her a threat, her bodyguard had whisked her away and they'd both disappeared for six months. Gabby wouldn't have minded going back to the orphanage, but she couldn't now that people knew she'd been there.

Was there any place for her to be safe? She thought of Whit's arms, wrapped tight around her, her head on his chest with his heart beating strong and steady beneath her ear. She would be safe with him—only with him.

The door creaked open, and she lifted her gaze to the mirror to see who'd come up behind her. Her heart filled with hope that it was Whit—that he was back and had come to see her the moment they had landed.

It was probably Charlotte though, prodding her because she'd kept the king waiting too long. Keeping him waiting was never wise. But then she peered around the lipstick blocking the image in the mirror and realized that he would probably be waiting longer.

"Hello, Honora…" She turned to greet the woman holding a gun on her.

"You are not surprised to see me."

She gestured behind herself at the mirror. "I figured out that was your shade. It certainly isn't mine."

"Of course not," Honora snapped. "You wouldn't wear something so stylish."

"I was thinking…" Garish. But it wasn't wise to provoke the lunatic holding a gun on her. "…exactly that."

"You've always envied me," Honora said.

"I have…" Given her very little thought over the years. The queen's cousin had always been unpleasant to Gabby—even when they were children.

"You've always wanted what I have."

A nasty disposition? Dissatisfaction with everything in life? Hardly.

"That's why," Honora continued, "you had your father arrange your engagement to my fiancé. You have to have everything I have."

For years Gabriella had just thought her cousin was nasty; she hadn't realized that the woman was actually delusional and paranoid and possibly mentally ill. "I'm sorry…"

"You should be—you will be—for trying to ruin my life!" Honora raised the gun so that the barrel pointed at Gabby's heart.

"I'm sorry that my father manipulated all of us," Gabby said. "It was him. Not me. I didn't ask him to break my engagement to Prince Linus."

"You would have married that psychopath?"

She shouldn't throw stones, but Gabby wasn't about to offer her that advice. "I had no idea my father was going to arrange an engagement with Prince Malamatos."

"Of course you did," Honora scoffed. "Of course you put him up to it. And of course your father will give you whatever you want. He has spoiled you rotten, just as my cousin the queen complained."

Gabriella snorted in disgust. "The queen constantly complained."

"Do you blame her?" Honora asked, obviously outraged on her dead relative's behalf. "She was forced to raise her husband's bastard as her own. That was cruel."

No, how the queen had treated Gabriella had been cruel. She hadn't cared that she'd been an innocent child, unaware of her parents' duplicity.

"As cruel as it will be if you were to try to force Tonio to raise your bastard as his own."

"I wouldn't do that," Gabriella insisted.

"You won't have to," Honora said. "Tonio is an honorable man. He intends to claim your bastard, which is more than I can say for that barbarian that actually fathered your kid."

"Barbarian?"

"The American," she said, her lip nearly curling with disdain. "The golden-haired one. I can understand why you would bed him…" She gave a lusty sigh. "But you should have been more careful than to become pregnant with his child. But then, of course, your father was careless too when he got his mistress pregnant with first your sister and then you."

Apparently Gabriella had been the only one not privy to the secrets of her family. She pressed her palms to her belly in which her child moved restlessly. "I don't regret this baby."

"I regret you," Honora said. "I wished you had never been born. So I will fix that now." Her finger twitched along the trigger.

"You don't want to kill me," Gabby bluffed. "You just don't want me to marry Prince Tonio. And since I have no intention of doing that, there is no reason to hurt me." Or her child.

Honora chuckled bitterly. "You would be a fool to break that engagement. Not only is he a handsome, powerful man but he is the only one who'd be willing to marry a woman carrying someone else's bastard."

"I don't want to marry anyone," Gabby insisted. She wanted to punch this woman in the face for the horrible name she kept calling her baby. She drew in a deep breath and reminded herself that Honora was sick.

"You're lying!"

She expelled the shuddery breath she'd just drawn. "Yes. I am."

The gun trembled in Honora's hand. "I knew you were lying. I knew you wanted Tonio—because he's mine!"

"He is yours—all yours," Gabby assured the deranged woman. "I don't want to marry *him*. But I do want to marry someone."

The woman stared at her through eyes narrowed with skepticism and faint curiosity. "Who do you want to marry?"

Gabby stroked her hands over her belly, and she couldn't stop her lips from curving into a wistful smile. "The father of my baby."

But Whit marrying her was about as likely as Gabriella being able to talk Honora out of shooting her. She had to try…getting through to Honora. She'd given up on Whit. He'd faced death dangling from a cliff, and even that close scrape hadn't lowered his guard enough for him to let his feelings out. Maybe he really didn't have any feelings—for her or anyone else.

"THAT BARBARIAN?" Honora scoffed. "He has nothing to offer you."

Whit couldn't argue with her—even if he dared let his presence be known to either woman.

He had been on his way to see Gabriella and say goodbye when he'd noticed that royal bitch slipping into Gabby's private rooms. His first thought had been to turn around and leave without saying goodbye. But then he'd noticed the glint of light off the metal object Honora gripped in her hand.

A knife? A gun?

She wasn't sneaking into Gabby's room for girl talk. For revenge for her broken engagement? Was she the one who'd paid Zeke to make sure Gabriella never returned to St. Pierre?

He slipped into the room behind her. But before he

could grab her, she'd pulled the gun. If only it had been a knife…

He could have pulled his trigger and killed her before she got close to Gabby. But with the gun, even if he shot her, she might reflexively pull the trigger. She might kill Gabby—or the baby—even as she was dying.

"Whitaker Howell," Gabriella saying his name drew his attention back to her, "is twice the man that Tonio Malamatos is. I don't want your prince, Honora."

The woman gasped in shock and horror. "Do you really expect me to believe that you would prefer a bodyguard over a man who will soon rule his own country and, according to the deal he made with your father, this country, as well?"

If Malamatos thought King St. Pierre was about to step down as ruler of the country named for him, he had gravely misunderstood their deal. Or was that just the reason he'd given his crazy fiancée for breaking their engagement?

Maybe old Tonio had been afraid of telling the woman the truth—that he just didn't want to marry her. Whit opened his mouth to draw the woman's attention to him and away from Gabriella.

But then Gabby was speaking again. "Whit Howell is a hero," she said. "He was a hero during his deployments with the U.S. Marines, and he was a hero protecting his clients. And he saved my life more than once."

"Zeke Rogers assured me that no one would," Honora said. "I paid him a lot of money to make sure you would never return to St. Pierre."

"He died trying to do the job you hired him to do," Gabby said—with apparent sympathy for a man who'd intended to kill her.

How could she be that selfless? That good? Especially given how no one had ever given her the love and concern that she freely offered to everyone else. She was just innately good. More people like her were needed in the world—not fewer.

Honora shrugged off any responsibility. "Your barbarian killed him."

Zeke's death had been an accident. Whit had wanted him alive, so that he would be able to tell them who had hired him. But he'd pushed him too hard...

"Whit is not a barbarian," Gabriella said. "He's a good man."

How could she say that about him? How could she see in him what he had only seen in her?

"You really are in love with a bodyguard," Honora remarked as if horrified.

"Yes," Gabriella said—as if proud of the declaration.

Could she actually love him?

No. She was probably just trying to convince the crazy lady that she was no threat to her relationship with the prince. Gabriella St. Pierre was far smarter than anyone had given her credit for being—including this jilted fiancée.

"Then you're stupider than people think," the woman replied. "Your father will never approve. In fact he just fired the man."

Gabby gasped now. "He fired Whit?"

The woman uttered a cackle of pure glee. "Guess he didn't approve of the hired help getting his daughter pregnant."

King St. Pierre hadn't actually explained his reasons for terminating Whit's employment. He'd just bellowed that he was done here and had only hours to leave the palace and St. Pierre.

Honora was probably right that the man had wanted better for his daughter than a bodyguard. And he wasn't wrong. Her other fiancés had been able to offer her palaces and countries. Whit didn't even have a home to call his own.

Never had...

That was why he hadn't argued with King St. Pierre. He'd only nodded in acceptance and walked out. He'd figured it was for the best—for Gabriella and for their baby.

Whit couldn't give them what the prince could. But he could give them what the prince couldn't: his protection. He lifted his gun.

But he had to get Gabriella's attention to let her know that she would need to get out of the way when bullets started flying. She needed to drop to the marble floor or jump into the marble tub. He had to make sure that neither she nor their baby was hit.

But Honora was still talking, still taunting Gabby with knowledge she must have gained from spreading money around to servants or from listening at doors herself. "And Howell packed his bags and left without ever bothering to come say goodbye."

"That's not true," he corrected the woman. "I came to say goodbye. But you first, Honora..." Hoping that the woman turned toward him, with her weapon, his finger twitched on the trigger.

He had to make this shot count. Had to kill her before she killed Gabby. And he had to make damn sure he didn't miss and kill the woman he loved himself.

Chapter Fifteen

"Stop!" Gabriella yelled but not at the woman who held the gun on her. "Don't shoot her!"

She had only just noticed Whit when, with his gun drawn, he'd stepped through her bathroom doorway. So she had no idea how long he had been standing there.

Long enough to realize that Honora was mentally ill?

Long enough to learn that Gabriella was hopelessly in love with him?

Whit held his fire—probably out of instinct more than his actually caring what she'd said. "You tell me to shoot on an airplane but not in your bathroom. Afraid I'll break the mirror and get seven years of bad luck?"

The mirror was already broken—the bad luck all hers. Or maybe not.

Honora swung toward him with her gun drawn.

"Don't shoot him, either," Gabriella said. "You don't want to kill him."

"Because you love him?"

"Yes," Gabriella said. "And because he's an amazing shot. He will kill you, and then you will never have a future with Prince Tonio."

"I have no future with him now!" Honora trembled

with rage. But instead of firing at Whit, she turned back to Gabby. "Because of you!"

Gabby shook her head—as a signal for Whit, and Charlotte and Aaron who'd snuck into the room behind him, not to shoot Honora. "I don't want to marry your fiancé," she reiterated. "The only man I will ever marry is the man I love."

And that was what she had intended to tell her father when she met with him. Now she may never get the chance to talk to him.

"All I want is to marry the man I love," Honora said. The facade on her thin face cracked like the mirror behind Gabriella. "But he doesn't love me…" She lifted the gun again, but this time she pressed the barrel of it to her own temple.

"Don't!" Gabriella said. "Don't do it!"

Honora's finger trembled against the trigger as her whole body shook. "Why not? I have nothing to live for."

"What you feel isn't real love—real love is reciprocated."

Gabby needed to remind herself of that—that what she felt for Whit wasn't real. It wasn't what Aaron and Charlotte had. She may have gotten pregnant the same night Charlotte had, but that was all their situations had in common.

While the woman appeared to contemplate Gabby's declaration, she was distracted enough that Whit reached out and snapped the gun out of her hand.

"Noooo…" Honora cried, and she crumpled into a ball on the floor.

Gabriella reached out and touched her hair; it was as

brittle as the woman herself. "You'll be okay," she said. "We'll get you some help. It'll get better."

"I'm sorry," she said, her voice breaking with sobs. "So sorry…"

"Get her help," Gabby told the others.

"I'm not leaving you alone with her," Whit said, stepping closer as if he intended to step between them.

But Honora was no threat. With her arms wrapped tight around herself, she was barely holding herself together.

Outwardly Gabriella probably appeared calm. But inside, she was shaking as badly as her would-be killer. She realized she'd taken a risk in not letting Whit just shoot the woman. But too many people had already died. She hadn't wanted anyone else to lose their life.

And although she and her baby had escaped harm, she was shaken at how close a call she'd had.

"I'll stay while you get help," Charlotte offered. "I'll make sure they're both okay." She looked at Gabby as if she knew that nerves and emotions swirled tempestuously beneath the surface. And she knew that Gabby needed Whit gone so that she wouldn't fall apart and fall at his feet, begging him to love her back.

"You need to talk to the king anyway," Aaron told Whit.

Had Honora been telling the truth? Had he been fired? And was he going to just leave without saying whatever he must have come here to say to her?

He walked out without a backward glance. And Gabriella's heart cracked like the mirror.

"I FIRED YOU," King St. Pierre reminded Whit of their conversation only an hour ago. "Then I told Aaron to make sure you had left my property. Instead he found you saving my daughter's life."

"She saved her own life." Because if he'd shot Honora as he nearly had, she might have fired, too. And if a bullet had struck Gabby or the baby…

The king's brow furrowed, as if he tried to fathom how the princess could have protected herself. "Did she use the maneuvers her sister taught her?"

So he really was claiming his oldest as his daughter, too, now.

"No, Gabby used her innate talent—the one no one taught her," Whit said and with a pointed stare at the king added, "and the one no one managed to destroy."

Anger flashed in Rafael St. Pierre's dark eyes. "What do you mean?"

"No matter how cruel your wife was to her or how disinterested you were, she never grew bitter or selfish," Whit said, amazed at the strength that had taken Gabriella, even as a child, to remain true to herself. "She stayed sweet and caring, and it was those qualities that saved her life. She talked Honora out of hurting her and out of hurting herself."

The king sucked in a breath of surprise. "Gabriella did that—on her own?"

Whit nodded. "Despite my interference, she calmed Honora down." He flinched as he remembered how the woman had reacted to his presence. Maybe if he'd stayed quiet, if he'd trusted Gabby to take care of herself, she would have reached the woman even sooner.

The king uttered a heavy sigh of regret. "Are you sure it was Honora who paid Zeke Rogers to kill Gabriella?"

"She confessed to all of it." Actually she had bragged

about it, but he suspected now that that bravado was part of her illness.

Gabby had been right to save her. The woman could be helped, and he knew his sweet princess would make sure she got help.

The king stared at Whit. "You may need to testify to what you heard."

He nodded. "Fine." He wanted the woman put someplace where she couldn't hurt herself or anyone else again.

"So you will need to remain on St. Pierre until her trial."

"I thought you wanted me out of your country," Whit reminded him now.

"Perhaps I reacted before I had time to understand the situation."

The fact that Whit had gotten his daughter pregnant while she was engaged to another man, a man who was now really free and ready to commit to someone else—was that the situation the king had needed time to understand?

Whit needed more time because he still didn't understand it, had no idea why Gabriella would even look at him much less let him touch her. Make love to her…

He had nothing to offer her. Nothing like her other fiancés. But maybe he had something…

Maybe he had the one thing no one else had ever given her…

"You have my permission to explain yourself," the king said, as if issuing a royal decree.

"You're not the one I need to explain myself to,"

Whit said, only just realizing himself what he had to say and to whom.

The king's face flushed with fury as he slammed his fist onto his desk. "If you intend to continue in my employ, you will damn well answer to me."

The fist pounding didn't intimidate Whit in the least. In fact it amused him how a grown man could act so like a spoiled child. "You already fired me."

"That was precipitous of me. If you explain yourself, I will reinstate you," the king said, offering another royal decree.

And Whit chose to ignore this one, too. "I'm not going to tell you what you want to hear," he said, "so you might as well fire me again. Or still."

"Young man—"

"You know what—it doesn't matter if you've fired me or not," he said. "I can't work for you any longer. I quit."

"What the hell are you doing?" Aaron asked the minute Whit slammed open the door and stalked into the hall. He must have nearly knocked his old friend over with the door, for Aaron had jumped back. "You can't just walk away from this job."

"I can't work for him." It didn't matter what King St. Pierre thought of Whit and what he had to offer his daughter. It mattered more to Whit what the king had never offered Gabby—his love or respect. And he couldn't work for a man so stupid and cruel.

"Why not?" Aaron asked. "You two are awfully alike. And I do mean awfully."

If he wasn't so damn tired—physically and emotionally—Whit might have swung his fist into the other man's face for uttering such an insult. "I am nothing like that man."

"You're both stubborn and selfish and think you're always right and you appoint yourself to decide what's right for other people."

Whit flinched at the anger and resentment in his friend's voice. Aaron might as well have physically struck him because the hit was that direct. And probably that accurate.

Maybe he'd been a fool to think that Aaron could ever forgive him, that their friendship could ever be repaired after Whit had betrayed him.

"I thought you were done being mad at me."

"I am," Aaron said. "But if you leave here, *she* will never get over being mad at you."

"Gabriella?" Whit chuckled. "She just forgave the woman who tried to have her killed."

"Honora may have threatened her, but she never really hurt her," Aaron explained. "You've hurt her. I saw it on that cliff—when you wouldn't let her hug you. And I saw it in her rooms when you turned and walked away—like you're walking now."

He was actually tempted to run as he headed toward his room in the employee's wing. This time he would finally pack up his things. There was nothing for him here.

"I can't believe you're being so stupid," Aaron said, following him like a dog nipping at his heels. "You already know how hard it was to find a job like this but you just willingly gave it up."

"There are other jobs," he said. "Hell, I could re-enlist if I can't find anything else."

Aaron sucked in a breath of shock. "You'd go back to active duty?"

"Why not?"

"I can give you two reasons—Gabby and your baby," Aaron said. "You might be able to find another job, but you'll never find another woman who loves you like she does."

He had never found anyone who loved him at all— let alone like Gabby had claimed to love him. "She was just saying those things to Honora," he insisted, "to make the woman think she was no threat. To make her think she has no intention of marrying Prince Malamatos."

"You think she does intend to marry him?" Aaron asked.

He shrugged. "As his ex-fiancée said, the man's quite a catch. A real prince of a guy."

"She's crazy," Aaron reminded him, "and so are you if you walk away from a woman like Gabriella."

"You've thought me crazy before," Whit said with a shrug, as if his friend's opinion didn't matter. But it mattered a lot—especially that Aaron believed she loved him.

But then Aaron had never been the best judge of character—because, like Gabby, he always saw the best in everyone. Even Whit.

Conversely, Whit always saw the worst in every-one—even himself. Except for Gabby—because there was only good in her.

And if he was the man she and Aaron thought he was, he would walk away and give her a chance at the life she deserved—that she had been born to live.

"YOU FIRED the man who saved my life!" Gabby accused her father the moment she stepped inside his rooms.

His shoulders drooping, he sat behind the desk in his darkly paneled den. His hands cradled his head, as if he had a headache or was trying hard to figure something out. Veins popped on the back of his hands and stood out on his forehead. He looked stressed and weary, as if he'd aged years in the six months she and Charlotte had been gone.

Despite her anger and resentment with him, affection warmed her heart. No matter how he had treated her and those she cared about, he was her father and she loved him. She nearly opened her mouth to tell him so, but then he lifted his gaze.

Instead of looking at her face, he looked at her belly—at the child she carried. And she thought she glimpsed disappointment on his face.

That was all she had ever done with him and the queen. Disappoint them.

"Whitaker Howell quit," her father corrected her.

She shook her head. "I heard that you fired him."

"Perhaps," he admitted with a slight nod of acquiescence, "but then I gave him the chance to stay, and he chose to leave."

Of course he chose to leave. Now that she was safe, he had no reason to stay. He had done his job. And that was all she must have been to him.

She blew out a ragged breath of pain and regret that he hadn't tried to stay, that he hadn't at least tried to love her and their baby.

Take a risk on me...

She had risked everything—her heart, her future, her baby's future. And she'd lost him.

"But Prince Malamatos is here," the king continued. "He refuses to leave until he sees you and makes certain you have survived your ordeal."

"Ordeal?" she asked. "I hope you're talking about recent events and not the six most useful and productive months of my life."

"At the orphanage?" he asked, with a brow raised in skepticism. "I can't believe Charlotte sent you there to hide."

"I'm glad she did," Gabby said. "Otherwise I might have never learned the truth."

The king's mouth drew into a tight line of disapproval. Had he never intended to tell her the truth?

"I was referring to the country she sent you to," he clarified, "and how dangerous it is."

"Yet I was in no danger until everyone learned where I was." And then because she had to know, she asked him, "Would you have ever told me?"

"About your mother?" he asked and then uttered a heavy sigh. "I promised the queen that I would never…"

Because then Gabriella might have realized that it hadn't been her fault the woman hadn't loved her… The woman had been cruel right up until the end. "After she died, you could have told me."

He sighed again. "But your biological mother had already died, so there seemed no point in dredging up ancient history."

And probably his embarrassment over his affair with a con artist.

"No point in my getting to know my sister and my aunt?" Perhaps he hadn't wanted her to get to know and emulate two of the strongest women she had ever met— because then she wouldn't blindly obey him. His efforts to keep her ignorant had been futile. It didn't matter how short a time Gabriella had known them; she was still going to emulate them. He was done controlling her life.

"We will discuss this another time," the king imperiously announced—which meant that he never intended to discuss it.

Because he had been wrong and would not admit it. And he compounded that arrogance when he continued, "You have kept your fiancé waiting long enough."

She shook her head. "Prince Malamatos is not my fiancé. He's yours. You chose him. You can marry him. I'm not."

"Gabriella!" The king shot up from his chair, anger turning his face a mottled red. "You are impudent."

"No," she said. "But I should have been before now. I should have made it clear to you that while you rule this country, you do not rule my life. I will make my own decisions from now on."

He pointed to her belly. "Being a single mother is what you choose?"

No. But she couldn't force the baby's father to love her. Too weary to deal with her father, she turned toward the door.

"Prince Malamatos will claim the baby."

"Like the queen claimed me?" she asked. "I won't take the risk of his treating my baby the way I was." She wanted to give this child two parents who loved him. And Honora had already shared Tonio's opinion of Gabby's baby; it was an inconvenience but he would adjust to include it in his plan of ruling two countries.

"You need to talk to your fiancé," he persisted, "and let him discuss your future."

Another man telling her what to do? Disrespecting what she wanted?

She shook her head. "No one talked to me about this engagement. You didn't. Tonio didn't. I don't even know the man. Why would I even consider marrying him?"

"You have always been so naive and idealistic, Gabriella, believing in fairy tales of love and happily-ever-after," her father said with a snort of disdain. "That is why I have had to make your decisions for you."

She turned back to him and met his gaze and decided to share with him the real struggle between them. "I want to hate you, Father."

He sucked in a breath, as if she had struck him in the stomach. Or perhaps the heart…

"But I can't," she assured him. "I feel too sorry for you."

Pride lifted his chin. "You feel sorry for *me?*"

She gave him a slight smile, one full of pity for all he had missed experiencing. "Because you have never been in love."

"What makes you think that?" he asked, but he didn't rush to deny her allegation either.

"Because if you had ever felt love—true love—yourself," she explained, "you would not try to force me to marry someone I don't love…"

He studied her face as if he were truly seeing her, as if he had really heard what she'd told him. Perhaps it was a first for them. Then he cleared his throat and asked, "You love Whitaker Howell?"

"Yes."

He dropped heavily back into his chair. "He did not stay," he said, as if warning her. "He did not fight for your hand in marriage."

She flinched as if he'd struck her now. And he had aimed directly for her heart. "It doesn't matter whether he stays or goes." It did not change the fact that she loved him. That her heart would belong to him and no other—certainly not any fiancé her father found her.

The king chuckled. "You were never able to lie. I could always tell whenever you tried to be less than truthful with me."

"If only I had been able to tell the same," she murmured. It would have saved her from all the years she'd spent in the dark, oblivious to all his secrets and lies.

He heard her. His skin flushed again. But he ignored her comment and continued, "You are lying now. Whether Whitaker Howell stays or leaves, it matters to you. Greatly."

She shrugged. "But *I* don't matter to him. Even you said that he wouldn't fight for me."

"He fought for you," the king reminded her. "He fought to save your life. He fought to find you these past six months."

"He was just doing his job," she told him, as she'd kept telling herself.

The king shook his head. "Not just his job. He cannot say enough good things about your caring and your selflessness."

"He can't?" Hope flickered, warming her heart.

The king grinned and nodded. "He loves you."

Gabby's head pounded with confusion. "Then why would he leave?"

"Because you are a princess and he is a bodyguard. He thinks he has nothing to offer you." The king's brief grin faded. "And he's right."

"If he loves me," she corrected her father, "he has *everything* to offer me." Because love was all she had ever wanted...

She turned toward the door. But her father made a sound, something akin to a sniffle, that had her turning back to him. He lifted his gaze to hers, and his eyes were wet with emotion. "I have loved you," he said, as if he'd read her mind, "I have always loved you."

She had waited her entire life for her father to declare his feelings for her. But suddenly how he felt didn't matter so much to her anymore. "I have always loved you, too," she said. It was why she had always tried so hard to please him. But now she wanted to please herself. So she headed for the door.

"He's probably already gone," her father warned her.

Probably. But she would not be deterred now. "Then I will find him."

"It took us six months to find you," he said. "It'll take you much longer to find Whitaker Howell if he doesn't want to be found."

Chapter Sixteen

"Stop!"

The shout reverberated off the walls of the corridor leading away from the wing of employees' rooms. Just as he had earlier, Whit automatically obeyed. He froze in place, his suitcase clutched in his hand.

"That's the second time today that you've told me to stop," he said, turning toward her.

Gabriella's eyes were bright with anger—an anger so intense that she trembled with it. She wasn't the only angry one.

He kept flashing back to what had happened with Honora, and in his head, it ended differently—it ended badly, with Gabriella bleeding on the floor. "You could have gotten yourself killed the first time."

"She wasn't going to hurt me," Gabby insisted.

He dropped the suitcase, so he could reach out and shake some sense into her. But he only closed his hands around her bare shoulders. Then he had to fight the urge to pull her closer. And never let her go…

But first he had to deal with other emotions—with the helplessness and fear that had raged through him when he'd stood in the doorway watching that madwoman threaten the mother of his unborn baby—the woman he loved.

"She hired Zeke and those other men to kill you," he reminded her. "She didn't intend to just hurt you—she intended to kill you!"

"She intended for them to kill me," she agreed—maddeningly. "Them—not her. She isn't capable of personally killing someone—it made it real for her. And she realized that it was wrong."

He tightened his grip on her shoulders, tempted again to shake her. She was so sweet and innocent, so hopeful that there was goodness in everyone. "Murder is wrong no matter if you do it yourself or hire someone else to do it for you."

"She's not well," Gabby defended the woman who'd nearly killed her.

"And neither are you," he said, "for taking the risk you did with yourself and our baby."

"Our baby?" she asked, her eyes widening with shock. "You're claiming him now?"

He narrowed his eyes at her. "I already have. I never doubted that he was mine."

She narrowed her eyes back at him. "Not for a moment? Not even when you met Dr. Dominic?"

"I hate that guy," he admitted, barely resisting the urge to grind his teeth with the jealousy that shot through him. He had never been jealous before—had never cared enough to be jealous of anyone else.

Her lips curved into a slight smile. "Of course," she agreed. "He moved to a third-world country to offer his services free to take care of orphaned children. He's a horrible, horrible person."

A grin tugged at Whit's lips, but he fought it. He

knew how ridiculous he was being. "Yes, a horrible person."

"And ugly, too," Gabby said, her brown eyes warming and twinkling as she teased him back.

His heart pounded harder with excitement; the woman attracted him more strongly than any other woman ever had.

"I'm glad you see that, too," he said.

"I always thought he was hideous," she said with a girlish giggle.

"A regular Dr. Jekyll and Mr. Hyde," Whit added.

Her amused smile faded. "No. That would be you."

He chuckled at the illogical insult. "How's that?"

"One minute you're this sweet, funny guy and the next you're acting like my father," she accused him, "bossing me around and unilaterally making decisions that affect both of us."

"What decisions have I made?" he asked. She and Aaron had both really read him wrong. But then it wasn't their fault when he'd been afraid to make himself clear before now.

She pointed a trembling finger at the suitcase. "You decided to quit. To just take off and leave me and your baby behind without another thought."

He chuckled at how wrong she was. "You're more like your father than I am," he argued. "You're the one who keeps shouting out orders at me."

"Is that why you quit?" she asked. "You're sick of getting bossed around?"

Aaron had already told him he was a damn fool for quitting. But Whit didn't want to do this as her father's bodyguard—as a member of the staff or even as the baby's father.

"By your father, yes," Whit agreed. "But I think I'm getting used to your bossing me around."

He slid his hands from her shoulders, down her bare arms to grasp her hands. Once their fingers were entwined, he dropped to his knees. "And just so you know…I could never not think about you. For the past six months every thought I had was about you."

She sucked in a sharp breath, pulled her hands free of his, and touched her belly.

"Are you okay?" he asked. "You're not having contractions or anything?"

She bit her lip.

He pressed his hands over hers on their baby. "Gabby, are you all right?"

She nodded. "I just…" Her voice cracked with the tears that pooled in her eyes. "I can't believe this… I thought you were leaving. Or that you might already be gone. And I didn't know if I could find you…if my father was right and you didn't want to be found…"

She was chattering as nervously as she did for reporters until Whit reached up and pressed a finger across her lips. "Shhh…"

She stared down at him, her eyes so wide with fear and hopefulness.

"I had no intention of leaving without you," he said, still on his knees. "I know you never wanted to come back here. That's why I quit. I didn't want to force you to live where you've never been happy."

Now the tears fell with such intensity she trembled as uncontrollably as she had when they'd been freezing in the sea. "I will be happy wherever you are."

"So you'll marry me?"

She threw her arms around his neck and clung to him, too choked with sobs to answer him.

Was she saying yes? Or sorry? He couldn't understand her. "Gabriella?"

She loved him; he knew it. But was love enough to overcome their differences?

"You haven't answered me," Whit said, his voice gruff with impatience as he closed the door to her suite behind them.

"I will answer your question," she said, "after you answer mine."

"What question can you have?" he asked. "I thought my proposing said everything."

Of course he did. He was a man. He didn't understand that she needed more of an explanation. That she needed more...

"Why did you propose?" she asked, her heart beating frantically with equal parts hope and dread. "You haven't told me yet *why* you proposed." But she had a horrible suspicion she knew the reason, that she carried it in her belly.

His brow furrowed with confusion. "I thought my reason was obvious."

She touched her belly. The baby moved restlessly inside her. "I hope it isn't..."

His mouth dropped open with shock, and then his jaw tightened and a muscle twitched in his cheek. He was obviously offended and angry. "You think the only reason I want to marry you is because you're pregnant?"

That was her fear—that he only wanted her for what she was—the mother of his child—and not for who she was.

Too choked with fear to answer him, she simply nodded.

He chuckled. "You and I are quite the pair, aren't we?"

"What do you mean?"

"I would have told you how I felt earlier," he said, "but I didn't think you could love me."

Shock and sympathy for the pain that flashed across his handsome face had her gasping. "Why not?"

His broad shoulders lifted and dropped in a heavy shrug. "I didn't think I had anything to offer you."

"Didn't you hear what I told Honora about you?" she asked, pretty certain that he had been there at least long enough to have overheard some of what she'd told the deranged woman. "About all the reasons I love you?"

He nodded. "I heard, but I thought you were lying— that you were tricking her into thinking that you didn't want her fiancé."

"You thought it was all a ploy? Everything I said to her?" Was it that he thought that little of himself or that much of her? "You think I'm that smart?"

"I know you're that smart," he said. "And you're loving and caring and forgiving. You're so damn beautiful inside and out that I couldn't even believe you were real. I thought you were just some fairy-tale princess until that night…"

Her face got hot with embarrassment. She had been unbelievably bold that night. He had tried to be all business—just a royal bodyguard. But she had undressed in front of him…

"I'm talking about earlier that night," he said, as if he'd read her mind. Maybe he had noticed that all her skin had flushed with desire and her pulse was leaping in her throat. "About when you got so angry you actually pounded on me."

She laughed. "You like abuse?"

"I like everything about you. Your sweetness and your fire. Your patience and your passion…"

"Like?" she asked. "I need more to say yes." She needed love.

"I love you with all my heart," he said. "That's the only reason I want to marry you." He laid his hand on her belly. "This baby is just a bonus—like the prize in a box of Cracker Jack."

"Cracker Jack?"

"I forget that you're not American," he said. "Cracker Jacks are—"

"I know what Cracker Jacks are." She wrinkled her nose at his less than romantic compliment. "Sticky popcorn."

"Sweet." He leaned down and brushed his mouth across hers. "And I love sweets…"

"And I love you," she said. She lifted his hand from her stomach to her arm and then she squeezed his fingers together. "Pinch me to prove this isn't just a dream."

He moved his hand from her arm to her butt and pinched.

She squealed—with shock and delight. Then she reached around and pinched his butt.

He laughed out loud. "I can't believe this is real, either," he said. "You make me happier than I thought it was possible to feel. You make me *feel*."

And so many people had warned her that he couldn't—that the man didn't have a heart. But as his arms closed around her, she laid her head on his chest and heard his heart beating strong and fast. For her…

His hands cupped her face and tipped it up for his kiss. His lips brushed across hers. But then he deepened the kiss. His tongue slid inside her mouth, tasting and teasing her.

Gabby didn't want to be teased anymore. She wanted to make love to the man she loved. So she unbuttoned his shirt and unclasped his belt. Whit helped her discard his clothes. Then he reached for her and the zipper at the back of her gown. He fumbled with the tab before tugging it down. Her dress slid down her body—leaving her naked but for a bra that barely covered her full breasts and a thin strip of satin.

He did away with her underwear, too, and then— despite her extra weight, he easily lifted and carried her to the bed. "You are even more beautiful now than you were that night," he said, his hands stroking over her more generous curves.

"I'm huge," she said, pursing her lips into a pout.

He kissed her mouth. "You're beautiful." He kissed her cheek. "Breathtaking…" He kissed her neck.

She moaned as desire quickened her pulse so that it raced. And her skin tingled.

"You're beautiful," she said.

With his shock of blond hair and dark eyes, he was beautiful—and strong with muscles rippling in his arms and chest. And his back.

She dug her fingers in, clutching him close. "I am so in love with you." She had fallen for him at first sight and then she had fallen harder and deeper the more she'd gotten to know him. "You are an amazing man."

He touched her intimately, stroking her until she

writhed beneath him. Pressure wound tightly inside her, making her body beg for release.

He lowered his head and kissed her breasts, tugging one nipple between his lips. He nipped gently at it.

And she came, screaming his name.

The man gave her pleasure so easily—so generously. She pushed him back onto the mattress and reciprocated. Her lips moved from his mouth, down his throat, over his chest. And lower. She loved him with her mouth, until he tangled his fingers in her hair and gently pulled her away.

"You're killing me," he said, his chest rising and falling as he struggled to catch his breath. "I can't take any more."

"You're going to have to get used to it," she warned him. Because she intended to spend the rest of her life loving him.

Whit couldn't believe how happy he was—how happy Gabriella made him. He wrapped his arms around her, holding her close as he rolled her onto her back.

She arched her hips. "Make love to me," she said, bossing him again.

And he loved it.

He groaned, his arms shaking as he braced himself on the bed and gently pushed himself inside her. But she tensed and gripped his shoulders.

"Stop!"

Sweat beaded on his upper lip, as he struggled for control. It reminded him of that night they had first made love—when he had discovered that she had never made love to another man before him. She hadn't told him to stop that night, though. She'd begged him to continue—to make love to her. And then she'd moved beneath him, taking him deep inside her.

"Why do I have to stop now?" he asked, gritting his teeth with the effort to control his desires. "Is the baby all right?"

"The baby is fine," she assured him. "But you shouldn't be."

"I'm damn well not fine," he said. "I want to make love to my fiancée."

"I am not your fiancée yet. I didn't answer your question," she reminded him. "I asked you why you asked. But I never answered you."

He tensed. "You told me you loved me, too." But she had never told him yes.

"But I haven't accepted."

"Why not?" Had she changed her mind? Did she think that love wasn't enough to overcome their different upbringings?

"I didn't have the chance yet," she said with a teasing smile.

The woman infuriated him and fascinated and captivated him.

"So what is your answer to my proposal?" he asked. "Will you marry me?"

"Of course I will marry you," she said, as if he'd been silly to worry. "I can't wait to be your wife."

He breathed a ragged sigh of relief. "And I can't wait to be your husband."

"Now," she said, "make love to your fiancée."

He chuckled. "You are getting really comfortable bossing me around."

She smiled. "Do you mind?"

He thrust gently inside her. "We want the same things," he said.

"Each other…" She moaned and arched, taking him deep inside her, as she raked her nails lightly down his back. She met his every thrust, moving in perfect rhythm with him.

She came, her body squeezing him tightly as pleasure rippled through her. And her pleasure begot his. The pressure that had built inside him exploded as he came.

"Gabriella!" His throat burned from shouting her name. He dropped onto his back next to her and wrapped his arm around her, holding her close to his side. "Now that I've made love to my fiancée, I can't wait to make love to my wife. We need to get married as soon as possible."

Then he needed to find a job and a house—someplace safe enough for him to protect a princess and a royal heir.

"I want to get married here," she said.

He sighed, hating that he was already unable to give her what she wanted. "I don't think your father will agree to that."

"I think he will," she said, "and I think he'd like you back working for him."

"I don't care what he wants," Whit said. After the way he'd treated his daughter, the man deserved little consideration for his feelings. But then Whit remembered how much the man had emotionally and physically suffered the past six months. "I care what you want. And you don't want to live here. You didn't even want to come back here."

"I didn't want to come back and marry a strange prince," she explained. "But I don't mind living here.

No matter how much time I spent in boarding schools growing up, this was still my home."

"I never had a real home," he admitted.

"You do," she said. "With me and our baby."

"We're a family," he said. "But we need a home—one where I can keep you both safe."

"I think that home should be here," she said, "with Aaron and Charlotte and even my father..." She looked up at him, as if she held her breath waiting for his decision.

He could keep his wife and child safe here—especially with Aaron and Charlotte's help. "Are you sure this is what you want?"

She smiled. "Our baby growing up with Aaron and Charlotte's?"

"They're staying here?"

"Charlotte wants to get to know the king as her father. He asked her to stay—not as employee but as his daughter. I want to live with my sister. I want my baby to know his aunt and cousin."

She painted a pretty picture for Whit—not just of a home but of an extended family, as well.

"They say it takes a village to raise a child," he remarked.

"We have a country."

He grinned. "We have more than I ever believed I would have...because of you."

"We have happily-ever-after," she said. "Like a real fairy tale."

"And I have my real fairy-tale princess."

It was a dream—one he never would have dared to dream—but it came true anyway. And his happy present and future made him think of his past and someone who'd had to give up her home and her family or lose her life.

He hoped she'd found a new home. A new family and the happiness he had.

CHARLOTTE WAS HAPPY—happier than she'd thought possible as she lay in her fiancé's arms, listening to his heart beat strong and steady beneath her cheek.

But one thing marred her happiness and kept her from sleeping peacefully...

A man had killed trying to find out where a witness was. Like Zeke Rogers, he'd been paid. They had found out who'd hired Zeke, but she had yet to find out who had hired her former partner to locate Josie Jessup.

No one but she, Aaron, Whit and Gabriella knew where JJ was. But it worried her that someone else out there knew the woman was alive and was determined to find her. And Charlotte didn't even dare try to contact Josie to warn her. Because whoever wanted to find her knew that Charlotte was the one who'd hidden her. They were undoubtedly waiting for her to lead them right to Josie.

And only the devil knew what they intended to do when they found her. Kill her?

* * * * *

She'd spoken to the boy, and her soft voice had hit him like a blow to the stomach.

While he might not have recognized her body or face, he could not mistake that voice as hers; her voice had haunted him, too. Before he could recover, he turned his attention to the child, and reeled from another blow. With his curly black hair and dark green eyes, the child was even more recognizable than the woman. He looked exactly like the few childhood photos of Brendan that his stepmother hadn't managed to *accidentally* destroy.

He didn't even remember closing the distance between them, didn't remember reaching for her. But he held her, his hand wrapped tightly around her delicate wrist.

She lifted her face to him, and he saw it now— in the almond shape and silvery green color of her eyes. What he didn't recognize was the fear that widened those eyes and stole the color from her face.

"Josie…?"

ROYAL RESCUE

BY
LISA CHILDS

MILLS
BOON

First published in Great Britain 2013
by Mills & Boon, an imprint of Harlequin (UK) Limited,
Eton House, 18-24 Paradise Road, Richmond, Surrey TW9 1SR

© Lisa Childs 2013

ISBN: 978 0 263 90361 4
ebook ISBN: 978 1 472 00723 0

46-0613

Harlequin (UK) policy is to use papers that are natural, renewable and recyclable products and made from wood grown in sustainable forests. The logging and manufacturing processes conform to the legal environmental regulations of the country of origin.

Printed and bound in Spain
by Blackprint CPI, Barcelona

To Philip Tyson for proving to me that heroes really do exist! Thank you for being my white knight!

Chapter One

Goose bumps of dread rising on her arms, Josie Jessup slipped into a pew in the back of church. She hated funerals, hated saying goodbye to anyone but most especially to someone who had died too soon. And so senselessly and violently—shot down just as his adult life was beginning.

The small church, with its brilliantly colored stained-glass windows, was filled with her former student's family and friends. Some of them nodded in polite acknowledgment; others glared at her. They probably blamed her for the career he had pursued, the career that had cost him his life. At the local community college where she taught journalism courses, she had recognized the kid's talent. She had even recommended he cover the story that had killed him, because it had been killing her that she couldn't cover it herself.

But she couldn't risk anyone recognizing her. Even though her appearance had changed, her writing style hadn't. If she had written the story, certain people would have recognized it as hers no matter whom the byline claimed had authored it. And Josie couldn't risk anyone realizing that she wasn't really dead.

That was her other reason for hating funerals—

because it reminded her of her own, of having to say goodbye to everyone she loved. She actually hadn't attended her funeral; her ashes hadn't been in the urn as everyone else had believed. But still she'd had to say goodbye to the only life she'd known in order to begin a new life under a new identity.

But apparently she wasn't making any better choices in this life than she had in her last, since innocent people were still getting hurt. She hadn't pulled the trigger and ended this young man's promising life. But she blamed herself nearly as much as some of these people blamed her. If only she hadn't mentioned her suspicions regarding the private psychiatric hospital and the things that were rumored to take place there…

The gnawing pangs of guilt were all too familiar to her. The first story she'd covered, back in college, had also cost a young man his life. But then she'd had someone to assure her that it wasn't her fault. Now she had no one to offer her assurances or comfort.

Chatter from the people in front of her drifted back. "Since Michael was hoping to sell the Serenity House story to one of Jessup Media's news outlets, I heard Stanley Jessup might attend the funeral."

Josie's breath caught with hope and panic. She wanted to see him. But she couldn't risk his *seeing* her. For his own protection, her father had to go on believing that his only child was dead.

"Not anymore," the other person responded. "He's in the hospital. They don't even know if he'll make it."

Josie leaned forward, ready to demand to know what had happened to her father. But before she could, the other person had already asked.

"He was attacked," the gossiper replied. "Someone tried to kill him."

Had all the sacrifices she'd made been for naught? Had her father been attacked because of her? And if so, then she'd done nothing to protect him except deprive him of what mattered most to him. She had already been guilt-ridden. Now that guilt intensified, overwhelming her.

If her father didn't make it, he would die never knowing the truth. She couldn't let that happen.

"JESSUP...HOSPITALIZED in critical condition..."

The breaking news announcement drew Brendan O'Hannigan's attention to the television mounted over the polished oak-and-brass bar of O'Hannigan's Tavern. At 9:00 a.m. it was too early for the establishment to be open to the public, but it was already doing business. Another kind of business than serving drinks or sandwiches. A dangerous kind of business that required his entire focus and control.

But Brendan ignored the men with whom he was meeting to listen to the rest of the report: "Nearly four years ago, media mogul Stanley Jessup's daughter died in a house explosion that authorities ruled arson. Despite her father's substantial resources, Josie Jessup's murder has never been solved."

"Josie Jessup?" one of the men repeated her name and then tapped the table in front of Brendan. "Weren't you dating her at one time?"

Another of the men snorted. "A reporter? Brendan would never date a reporter."

He cleared his throat, fighting back all the emotions just the sound of her name evoked. And it had been more than three years....

Wasn't it supposed to get easier? Weren't his memories of her supposed to fade? He shouldn't be able to see her as clearly as if she stood before him now, her pale green eyes sparkling and her long red hair flowing around her shoulders. Brendan could even hear her laughter tinkling in his ear.

"At the time I didn't know she was a reporter," he answered honestly, even though these were men he shouldn't trust with the truth. Hell, he shouldn't trust these men with anything.

He leaned back against the booth, and its stiff vinyl pushed the barrel of his gun into the small of his back. The bite of metal reassured him. It was just one of the many weapons he carried. That reassured him more.

The first man who'd spoken nodded and confirmed, "It wasn't common knowledge that the girl wanted to work for her father. All her life she had seemed more intent on spending his money, living the life of an American princess."

An American princess. That was exactly what Josie had been. Rich and spoiled, going after what she wanted no matter who might get hurt. She had hurt others—with the stories Brendan had discovered that she'd written under a pseudonym. Her exposés had started before she'd even graduated with her degree in journalism.

Brendan should have dug deeper until he'd learned the truth about her before getting involved with her. But the woman had pursued him and had been damn hard to resist. At least he had learned the truth about her before she'd managed to learn the truth about him. Somehow she must have discovered enough information to have gotten herself killed, though.

The news report continued: "The death of his daughter nearly destroyed Jessup, but the billionaire used his work to overcome his loss, much as he did when his wife died twenty years ago. The late Mrs. Jessup was European royalty."

"So she was a real princess," Brendan murmured, correcting himself.

"She was also a reporter," the other man said, his focus on Brendan, his dark eyes narrowed with suspicion.

It had taken Brendan four years to gain the small amount of trust and acceptance that he had from these men. He had been a stranger to them when he'd taken over the business he'd inherited from his late father. And these men didn't trust strangers.

Hell, they didn't trust anyone.

The man asked, "When did you learn that?"

Learn that Josie Jessup had betrayed him? That she'd just been using him to get another exposé for her father's media outlets?

Anger coursed through him and he clenched his jaw. His eyes must have also telegraphed that rage, for the men across the booth from him leaned back now as if trying to get away. Or to reassure themselves that they were armed, too.

"I found out Josie Jessup was a reporter," Brendan said, "right before she died."

IT'S TOO GREAT a risk... She hadn't been able to reach her handler, the former U.S. marshal who had faked Josie's death and relocated her. But she didn't need to speak to Charlotte Green to know what she would have told her. *It's too great a risk...*

After nearly being killed for real almost four years ago, Josie knew how much danger she would be in were anyone to discover that she was still alive. She hadn't tried to call Charlotte again. She'd had no intention of listening to her anyway.

Josie stood outside her father's private hospital room, one hand pressed against the door. Coming here was indeed a risk, but the greater risk was that her father would die without her seeing him again.

Without him seeing her again. And…

Her hand that was not pressed against the door held another hand. Pudgy little fingers wriggled in her grasp. "Mommy, what we doin' here?"

Josie didn't have to ask herself that question. She knew that, no matter what the risk, she needed to be here. She needed to introduce her father to his grandson. "We're here to see your grandpa," she said.

"Grampa?" The three-year-old's little brow furrowed in confusion. He had probably heard the word before but never in reference to any relation of his. It had always been only the two of them. "I have a grampa?"

"Yes," Josie said. "But he lives far away so we didn't get to see him before now."

"Far away," he agreed with a nod and a yawn. He had slept through most of the long drive from northwestern Michigan to Chicago; his soft snoring had kept her awake and amused. His bright red curls were matted from his booster seat, and there was a trace of drool that had run from the corner of his mouth across his freckled cheek.

CJ glanced nervously around the wide corridor as if just now realizing where he was. He hadn't awakened until the elevator ride up to her father's floor. Then with protests that he wasn't a baby but a big boy now, he had wriggled out of her arms. "Does Grampa live here?"

"No," she said. "This is a hospital."

The little boy shuddered in revulsion. His low pain threshold for immunizations had given him a deep aversion to all things medical. He lowered his already soft voice to a fearful whisper. "Is—is Grampa sick?"

She whispered, too, so that nobody overheard them. A few hospital workers, men dressed in scrubs, lingered outside a room a few doors down from her father's. "He's hurt."

So where were the police or the security guards? Why was no one protecting him?

Because nobody cared about her father the way she did. Because she had been declared dead, he had no other next of kin. And as powerful and intimidating a man as he was, he had no genuine friends, either. His durable power of attorney was probably held by his lawyer. She'd claimed to be from his office when she'd called to find out her father's room number.

"Did he falled off his bike?" CJ asked.

"Something like that." She couldn't tell her son what had really happened, that her father had been assaulted in the parking garage of his condominium complex. Usually the security was very high there. No one got through the gate unless they lived in the building. Not only was it supposed to be safe, but it was his home. Yet someone had attacked him, striking him with something—a baseball bat or a pipe. His broken arm and bruised shoulder might not hurt him so badly if the assault hadn't also brought on a heart attack.

Would her showing up here as if from the dead bring on another one? Maybe that inner voice of hers, which sounded a hell of a lot like Charlotte's even though she hadn't talked to the woman, was right. The risk was too great.

"We shoulda brought him ice cream," CJ said. "Ice cream makes you feel all better."

Every time he had been brave for his shots she had rewarded him with ice cream. Always shy and nervous, CJ had to fight hard to be brave. Had she passed her own fears, of discovery and danger, onto her son?

"Yes, we should have," she agreed, and she pulled her hand away from the door. "We should do that..."

"Now?" CJ asked, his dark bluish-green eyes brightening with hope. "We gonna get ice cream now?"

"It's too late for ice cream tonight," she said. "But we can get some tomorrow."

"And bring it back?"

She wasn't sure about that. She would have to pose as the legal secretary again and learn more about her father's condition. Just how fragile was his health?

Josie turned away from the door and from the nearly overwhelming urge to run inside and into her father's arms—the way she always had as a child. She had hurled herself at him, secure that he would catch her.

She'd been so confident that he would always be there for her. She had never considered that he might be the one to leave—for real, for good—that he might be the one to really die. Given how young she was when her mother died, she should have understood how fragile life was. But her father wasn't fragile. He was strong and powerful. Invincible. Or so she had always believed.

But he wasn't. And she couldn't risk causing him harm only to comfort herself. She stepped away from the door, but her arm jerked as her son kept his feet planted on the floor.

"I wanna see Grampa," he said, his voice still quiet but his tone determined. Afraid to draw attention to himself, her son had never thrown a temper tantrum. He'd never even raised his voice. But he could be very stubborn when he put his mind to something. Kind of like the grandfather he'd suddenly decided he needed to meet.

"It's late," she reminded him. "He'll be sleeping and we shouldn't wake him up."

His little brow still furrowed, he stared up at her a moment as if considering her words. Then he nodded. "Yeah, you get cranky when I wake you up."

A laugh sputtered out of her lips. Anyone would get cranky if woken up at 5:00 a.m. to watch cartoons. "So we better make sure I get some sleep tonight." That meant postponing the drive back and getting a hotel. But she needed to be close to the hospital…in case her father took a turn for the worse. In case he needed her.

"And after you wake up we'll come back with ice cream?"

She hesitated before offering him a slight nod. But instead of posing as the lawyer's assistant again, she would talk to Charlotte.

Someone else had answered the woman's phone at the palace on the affluent island country of St. Pierre where Charlotte had gone to work as the princess's bodyguard after leaving the U.S. Marshals. That person had assured Josie that Charlotte would be back soon to return her call. But Josie hadn't left a message—she couldn't trust anyone but Charlotte with her life. Or her father's. She would talk to Charlotte and see what the former marshal could find out about Josie's father's condition and the attack. Then she would come back to see him.

Her son accepted her slight nod as agreement and finally moved away from the door to his grandfather's room. "Does Grampa like 'nilla ice cream or chocolate or cookie dough or…"

The kid was an ice-cream connoisseur, his list of flavors long and impressive. And Josie's stomach nearly growled with either hunger or nerves.

She interrupted him to ask, "Do you want to press the elevator button?"

His brow furrowing in concentration, he rose up on tiptoe and reached for the up arrow.

"No," she said. But it was too late, he'd already pressed it. "We need the down arrow." Before she could touch it, a hand wrapped around her wrist.

Her skin tingled and her pulse leaped in reaction. And she didn't need to lift her head to know who had touched her. Even after more than three years, she recognized his touch. But she lifted her head and gazed up at him, at his thick black hair that was given to curl, at his deep, turquoise-green eyes that could hold such passion. Now they held utter shock and confusion.

This was the man who'd killed her, or who would have killed her had the U.S. marshal and one of her security guards not diffused the bomb that had been set inside the so-called *safe* house. They had set it off later to stage her death.

Since he had wanted her dead so badly, he was not going to be happy to find her alive and unharmed—if he recognized her now. She needed for him *not* to recognize her, as she wasn't likely to survive his next murder attempt. Not when she was unprotected.

If only she'd listened to that inner voice…

The risk had been too great. Not just to her life but to what would become of her son once she was gone.

Would her little boy's father take him or kill him? Either way, the child was as doomed as she was.

Chapter Two

For more than three years, her memory had haunted Brendan—her image always in his mind. This woman didn't look like her, but she had immediately drawn his attention when he'd stepped out of the stairwell at the end of the hall. Her body was fuller and softer than Josie's thin frame had been. And her chin-length blond bob had nothing in common with Josie's long red hair. Yet something about her—the way she tilted her jaw, the sparkle in her eyes as she gazed down at the child—reminded him of her.

Then she'd spoken to the boy, and her soft voice had hit him like a blow to the stomach. While he might not have recognized her body or face, he could not mistake that voice as anyone's but hers. Her voice had haunted him, too.

Before he could recover, he turned his attention to the child and reeled from another blow. With his curly red hair and bright green eyes, the child was more recognizable than the woman. Except for that shock of bright hair, he looked exactly like the few childhood photos of Brendan that his stepmother hadn't managed to *accidentally* destroy.

He didn't even remember closing the distance between them, didn't remember reaching for her. But now he held her, his hand wrapped tightly around her delicate wrist.

She lifted her face to him, and he saw it now in the almond shape and silvery-green color of her eyes. What he didn't recognize was the fear that widened those eyes and stole the color from her face.

"Josie…?"

She shook her head in denial.

She must have had some cosmetic work done, because her appearance was different. Her cheekbones weren't as sharp, her chin not as pointy, her nose not as perfectly straight. This plastic surgeon had done the opposite of what was usually required; he'd made her perfect features imperfect—made her look less movie-star gorgeous and more natural.

Why would she have gone to such extremes to change her identity? With him, her effort was wasted. He would know her anywhere, just from the way his body reacted—tensing and tingling with attraction. And anger. But she was already afraid of him and he didn't want to scare the child, too, so he restrained his rage over her cruel deception.

"You're Josie Jessup."

She shook her head again and spoke, but this time her voice was little more than a raspy whisper. "You're mistaken. That's not my name."

The raspy whisper did nothing to disguise her voice, since it was how he best remembered her. A raspy whisper in his ear as they'd made love, his body thrusting into hers, hers arching to take him deep. Her nails digging into his shoulders and back as she'd screamed his name.

That was why he'd let her fool him once, why he'd

let her distract him when he had needed to be focused and careful. She had seduced and manipulated him with all her loving lies. She'd only wanted to get close to him so she could get a damn story. She hadn't realized how dangerous getting close to him really was. No matter what she'd learned, she didn't know the truth about him. And if he had anything to say about it, she never would. He wouldn't let her make a fool of him twice.

"If you're not Josie Jessup, what the—" He swallowed a curse for the child's sake. "What are you doing here?"

"We were gonna see my grampa," the little boy answered for her, "but we didn't wanna wake him up."

She was the same damn liar she had always been, but at least she hadn't corrupted the boy.

His son...

JOSIE RESISTED THE urge to press her palm over CJ's mouth. It was already too late. Why was it *now* that her usually shy son chose to speak to a stranger? And, moreover, to speak the truth? But her little boy was unfailingly honest, no matter the fact that his mother couldn't be. Especially now.

"But we got out on the wrong floor," she said. "This isn't where your grandfather's room is."

CJ shook his head. "No, we watched the numbers lighting up in the el'vator. You said number six. I know my numbers."

Now she cursed herself for working with the three-year-old so much that he knew all his numbers and letters. "Well, it's the wrong room."

"You said number—"

"Shh, sweetheart, you're tired and must not remember correctly," she said, hoping that her son picked up the warning and the fear in her voice now. "We need to leave. It's late. We need to get you to bed."

But those strong masculine fingers were still wrapped tight around her wrist. "You're not going anywhere."

"You have no right to keep me," she said.

With his free hand, he gestured toward CJ. "He gives me the right. I have a lot of rights you've apparently denied me."

"I—I don't know what you're talking about." Why the hell would she have told the man who'd tried to kill her that she was pregnant with his baby? If his attempts had been successful, he would have killed them both.

"You know exactly what I'm talking about, Josie."

CJ tugged on her hand and whispered loudly, "Mommy, why does the man keep calling you that?"

Now he supported her lie—too late. "I don't know, honey," she said. "He has me mixed up with someone else he must have known."

"No," Brendan said. "I never really knew Josie Jessup at all."

No. He hadn't. Or he would have realized that she was too smart to have ever really trusted him. If only she'd been too smart to fall for him...

But the man was as charming as he was powerful. And when he'd touched her, when he'd kissed her, she had been unable to resist that charm.

"Then it's no wonder that you've mistaken me for her," Josie said, "since you didn't really know her very well."

She furrowed her brow and acted as if a thought had just occurred to her. "Josie Jessup? Isn't that the daughter of the media mogul? I thought she died several years ago."

"That was obviously what she wanted everyone to believe—that she was dead," he said. "Or was it just me?"

She shrugged. "I wouldn't know." *You. Just you.* But unfortunately, for him to accept the lie, everyone else had had to believe it, too. "I am not her. She must really be gone."

And if she'd had any sense, she would have stayed gone. Well away from her father and this man.

"Why are *you* here?" she asked. "Are you visiting someone?"

Or knowing all this time that she wasn't really dead, had he set a trap for her? Was he the one who had attacked her father? According to the reports from all her father's media outlets, there was no suspect yet in his assault. But she had one now.

She needed to call Charlotte. But the phone was in her purse, and she had locked her purse in her vehicle so that if anyone was to recognize her, they wouldn't be able to find her new identity.

"It doesn't matter why I'm here—just that I am," he said, dodging her question as he had so many other questions she had asked him during the months they'd been together. "And so are you."

"Not anymore. We're leaving," she said, as much to CJ as to Brendan. As if on cue, the elevator ground to a stop, and the doors slid open. She moved to step into the car, but her wrist was clutched so tightly she couldn't move.

"That one's going up," Brendan pointed out.

"As I said, we got off on the wrong floor." She tugged hard on her wrist, but his grip didn't ease. She didn't want to scream and alarm her already trembling son, so through gritted teeth she said, "Let go of me."

But he stepped closer. He was so damn big, all broad muscles and tension. There were other bulges beneath the jacket of his dark tailored suit—weapons. He had always carried guns. He'd told her it was because of the dangerous people who resented his inheriting his father's businesses.

But she'd wondered then if he'd been armed for protection or intimidation. She was intimidated, so intimidated that she cared less about scaring her son than she did about protecting him. So she screamed.

HER SCREAM STARTLED Brendan and pierced the quiet of the hospital corridor. But he didn't release her until her son—*their* son—launched himself at Brendan. His tiny feet kicked at Brendan's shins and his tiny fists flailed, striking Brendan's thighs and hips.

"Leggo my mommy! Leggo my mommy!"

The boy's reaction and fear startled Brendan into stepping back. Josie's wrist slipped from his grasp. She used her freed hand to catch their son's flailing fists and tug him close to her.

Before Brandon could reach for her again, three men dressed in hospital scrubs rushed up from the room they'd been loitering near down the hall. Brendan had noted their presence but had been too distracted to realize that they were watching him.

Damn! He had been trained to constantly be aware of his surroundings and everyone in them. Only Josie had ever made him forget his training to trust no one.

"What's going on?" one of the men asked.

"This man accosted me and my son," Josie replied, spewing more lies. "He tried to grab me."

Brendan struggled to control his anger. The boy—his boy—was already frightened of him. He couldn't add to that fear by telling the truth. So he stepped back again in order to appear nonthreatening, when all he wanted to do was threaten.

"We'll escort you to your car, ma'am," another of the men offered as he guided her and the child into the waiting elevator.

"Don't let her leave," Brendan advised. Because if she left, he had no doubt that he would never see her and his son again. This time she would stay gone. He moved forward, reaching for those elevator doors before they could shut on Josie and their son.

But strong hands closed around his arms, dragging him back, while another man joined Josie inside the elevator. Just as the doors slid shut, Brendan noticed the telltale bulge of a weapon beneath the man's scrubs. He carried a gun at the small of his back.

Brendan shrugged off the grasp of the man who held him. Then he whirled around to face him. But now he faced down the barrel of his gun. Why were he and at least one of the other men armed? They weren't hospital security, and he doubted like hell that they were orderlies.

Who were they? And more important, who had sent them?

The guy warned Brendan, "Don't be a hero, man."

He laughed incredulously at the idea of anyone considering *him* a hero. "Do you know who I am?"

"I don't care who the hell you are," the guy replied, as he cocked the gun, "and neither will this bullet."

Four years ago Brendan's father had learned that it didn't matter who he was, either. When he'd been shot in the alley behind O'Hannigan's early one morning, that bullet had made him just as dead as anyone else who got shot. Even knowing the dangerous life his father had led, his murder had surprised Brendan.

As the old man had believed himself invincible, so had Brendan. Or maybe he just remembered being fifteen, running away from the strong, ruthless man and never looking back.

But Dennis O'Hannigan's death had brought Brendan back to Chicago and to the life he'd sworn he'd never live. Most people thought he'd come home to claim his inheritance. Even now he couldn't imagine why the old man had left everything to him.

They hadn't spoken in more than fifteen years, even though his father had known where Brendan was and what he'd been doing. No one had ever been able to hide from Dennis O'Hannigan—not his friends or his family and certainly not his enemies.

Which one had ended the old man's life?

Brendan had really returned to claim justice. No matter how ruthless his father had been, he deserved to have his murder solved, his killer punished.

Some people thought Brendan had committed the murder—out of vengeance and greed. He had certainly had reasons for wanting revenge. His father had been as cruel a father and husband as he'd been a crime boss.

And as a crime boss, the man had acquired a fortune—a destiny and a legacy that he'd left to his only blood relative. Because, since his father's death, Brendan was the only O'Hannigan left in the family. Or so he'd thought until he'd met his son tonight.

He couldn't lose the boy before he even got to know him. No matter how many people thought of him as a villain, he would have to figure out a way to be the hero.

He had to save his son.

And Josie.

Four years ago she must have realized that she was in danger—that must have been why she'd staged her own death. Had she realized yet that those men in the elevator with her were not orderlies or interns but dangerous gunmen? Had she realized that she was in as much or more danger now than she'd been in before?

Chapter Three

Fear gripped Josie. She was more scared now than she'd been when Brendan wouldn't let go of her. Maybe her pulse raced and her heart hammered just in reaction to his discovering her. Or maybe it was because she wasn't entirely certain she had really gotten away from him…even as the doors slid closed between them.

"Thank you," she told the men. "I really appreciate your helping me and my son to safety."

"Was that man threatening you?" one of them asked.

She nodded. More threatening than they could possibly understand. Brendan O'Hannigan could take even more from her now than just her life. He could take away her son.

"H-he's a b-bad man," CJ stammered. The little boy trembled with fear and the aftereffects of his physical defense of his mother.

"Are you okay?" she asked him, concerned that he'd gotten hurt when he'd flung himself at Brendan. She couldn't believe her timid son had summoned that much courage and anger. And she hated that she'd been so careless with their safety that she'd put him in such a dangerous predicament. Dropping to her knees in front of her son, she inspected him to see if he had been harmed.

His little face was flushed nearly as bright red as his tousled curls. His eyes glistened with tears he was fighting hard not to shed. He blinked furiously and bit his bottom lip. Even at three, he was too proud to cry in front of strangers. He nodded.

Her heart clutched in her chest, aching with love and pride. "You were so brave." She wound her arms tightly around him and lifted him up as she stood again. Maybe a good parent would have admonished him for physically launching himself at a stranger. But it was so hard for him to be courageous that she had to praise his efforts. "Thank you for protecting Mommy."

She hadn't been able to shake Brendan's strong grip. But CJ's attack had caught the mobster off guard so that he'd released her and stepped back. She released a shuddery breath of relief that he hadn't hurt her son.

CJ wrapped his pudgy little legs around her waist and clung to her, his slight body trembling against her. "The bad man is gone?"

"He's gone."

But for how long? Had he just taken the stairs to meet the elevator when it stopped? CJ had pushed the up arrow, so the car was going to the roof. She doubted Brendan would waste his time going up. Instead he would have more time to get down to the lobby and lay in wait for her and CJ to leave for the parking garage.

And if he followed her there, she would have no protection against him. Unlike him, she carried no weapons. Just a can of mace and that was inside her purse, which she had locked in her vehicle.

But these men had promised to see her safely to her car. Surely they would protect her against Brendan...

But who would protect her from them?

The thought slipped unbidden into her mind, making her realize why her pulse hadn't slowed. She didn't feel safe yet.

Not with them.

Balancing CJ on her hip and holding him with just one arm, she reached for the panel of buttons. But one of the men stepped in front of it, blocking her from the lobby or the emergency call button. Then the other man stepped closer to her, trapping her and CJ between them.

She clutched her son more closely to her chest and glanced up at the illuminated numbers above the doors. They were heading toward the roof. Why hadn't they pushed other buttons to send the car back down? These men would have no patients to treat up there. But then, just because they wore scrubs didn't mean that they actually worked at the hospital.

When Charlotte had relocated her more than three years ago, she'd taught Josie to trust no one but her. And her own instincts. She should have heeded that warning before she'd stepped inside the elevator with these men. She should have heeded that warning before she'd driven back to Chicago.

"My son and I need to leave," she said, wishing now that she had never left her safe little home in Michigan. But she'd been so worried about her father that she'd listened to her heart instead of her head.

"That's the plan, Miss Jessup," the one standing in front of the elevator panel replied. "To get you out of here."

Somehow she suspected he wasn't talking about just getting her out of the hospital. And, like Brendan, he had easily recognized her.

She should have heeded Charlotte's other advice all those years ago to have more plastic surgery. But Josie had stopped when she'd struggled to recognize her own face in the mirror. She hadn't wanted to forget who she was. But maybe she should have taken that risk. It was definitely safer than the risk she'd taken in coming to see her father.

She feared that risk was going to wind up costing her everything.

"COME ON, GUY, just walk away," the pseudo-orderly advised Brendan.

"You don't want to shoot me," Brendan warned, stepping closer to the man instead of walking away. That had always been his problem. Once he got out of trouble, the way he had when he'd run away nearly twenty years ago, he turned around and headed right back into it—even deeper than before.

The other man shrugged. "Doesn't matter to me. The security cameras are not functioning up here."

Brendan suspected that had been intentional. While he had been completely shocked to see Josie, these men had been expecting her. They had actually been waiting for her…with disabled security cameras and weapons.

So Stanley Jessup's assault hadn't been such a random act of violence. It was the trap that had been used to draw Josie out of hiding.

Was he the only one who hadn't known that she was really alive?

"And Jessup, who's heavily drugged, is the only patient in a room near here. So by the time someone responds to the sound of the shot," the man brazenly bragged, "I'll be gone. We planned our escape route."

Brendan needed to plan his, too. But he didn't intend to escape danger. He planned to confront it head-on and eliminate the threat.

"In fact," the man continued, his ruddy face contorting with a smirk, "it would be better to kill you than leave you behind as a potential witness." He lifted the gun, so there was no way the bullet would miss. Then he cocked the trigger.

Brendan had a gun, too, holstered under his arm. And another at his back. And one strapped to his ankle. But before he could pull any of them, he would have a bullet in his head. So instead of fighting with a weapon, he used his words.

"I'm Brendan O'Hannigan," he said, "and that's why you don't want to shoot me."

First the man snorted derisively as if the name meant nothing to him. Then he repeated it, "O'Hannigan," as if trying to place where he'd heard it before. Then his eyes widened and his jaw dropped open as recognition struck him with the same force as if Brendan had swung his fist at him. "Oh, shit."

That was how people usually reacted when they learned his identity—except for Josie. She had acted as if she'd known nothing of his family or their dubious family business. And she had gotten close to him, with her impromptu visits to the tavern and her persistent flirting, before he'd realized that she had been doing just that: acting.

She had known exactly who he was or she would have never sought him out. She'd been after a scoop for her father's media outlets. Even after all those other stories she'd brought to him, she'd still been trying to prove herself to *Daddy*.

Brendan had devoted himself to just the opposite, trying to prove himself as unlike his father as possible.

Until the old man had died, drawing Brendan back into a life that he had been unable to run far enough away from when he was a kid.

"Yeah, if you shoot me, you better hope the police find you before any of my family does," Brendan warned the man. But it was a bluff.

He really had no idea what his "family" would do or if they would even care. He was the only one who cared about his father's murder—enough to risk everything for justice. Hell, his "family," given the way they'd resented his return and his inheritance, would probably be relieved if he died, especially if they knew the truth about him.

The man stepped back and lifted his gun so that the barrel pointed toward the ceiling, waving it around as if there were a white flag of surrender tied to the end of it. "I don't want any trouble—any of *your* kind of trouble."

Brendan didn't want that kind of trouble, either. But it was too late. He was in too deep now—so deep that he hadn't been able to get out even after he'd thought Josie had been killed. But then her death had made him even more determined to pursue justice.

"If you didn't want trouble," Brendan said, "then you shouldn't have messed with my son and his mother." Now he swung his fist into the man's face.

The guy fell back, but before he went down, Brendan snapped the gun from his grasp and turned it on him. There was no greater power play than turning a man's own gun on him. His father had taught him that, starting his lessons when Brendan was only a few years older than his son was now.

"What the hell do you want with her?" he demanded.

"I just got paid to do a job, man," the man in scrubs said, cringing away from the barrel pointed in his face.

"What's the job?"

The man opened his mouth but hesitated before speaking, until Brendan cocked the trigger. Then he blurted out, "To kill Josie Jessup!"

"Damn it!" he cursed at having his suspicions confirmed.

He had only just discovered that she was alive and that she'd given birth to his son. He didn't want to lose the boy before he'd gotten the chance to claim him. And he didn't want Josie to die again. He glanced back at the elevator, at the numbers above the doors that indicated it had stopped—on the top floor.

"You're not going to make it," the man advised. "You're not going to be able to save her."

Brendan cursed again because the guy was probably right. But still he had to try. He turned the gun and swung the handle at the man's head.

One down. Two to go...

THE WIND ON the roof was cold, whipping through Josie's light jacket and jeans. She slipped the side of her unzipped jacket over CJ's back to shield him from the cold bite of the breeze. He snuggled against her, his face pressed into her neck. Her skin was damp from the quiet tears he surreptitiously shed. He must have felt the fear and panic that clutched at her, and he trembled with it while she tensely held herself together.

She had to do something. She had to make certain these men didn't hurt her son. But since she hadn't reached Charlotte, earlier, the former U.S. marshal couldn't come to her rescue as she had last time. Josie had only herself—and the instincts she'd previously ignored—to help her now.

The two men were huddled together just a few feet away from them, between her and CJ and the elevator. There was no way to reach it without going through them. And with the bulges of weapons at their backs, she didn't dare try to go through them. Nor did she want to risk turning her back on them to run, for fear that they would shoot. And since they were on the roof, where could she go? How far could she run without falling over the side?

One of the men spoke into a cell phone about the change in plans: *CJ.*

While they had somehow discovered that she was really alive, they must not have been aware that she was pregnant when she'd gone into hiding.

Despite the fact that he'd lowered his voice, it carried on the wind, bringing the horrifying words to her.

"…never agreed to do a kid."

"…someone else knows she's alive and hassled her in the hall."

Because Brendan wasn't any happier she was alive than these men apparently were. Of course he hadn't seemed as eager to rectify that as they were.

"Okay, I understand," said the man holding the phone before he clicked it off and slid it back into his pocket. Then he turned to his co-conspirator and nodded. "We have to eliminate them both."

A shudder of fear and revulsion rippled through Josie. Thankfully CJ wouldn't understand what they meant by "eliminate." But eventually he would figure it out, when he stared down the barrel of a gun.

"I don't know what you're getting paid to do this," she addressed the men as they turned toward her. "But

I have money. Lots of money. I can pay you more than you're getting now."

The man who'd been on the phone chuckled bitterly. "We were warned you might make that offer. But you forfeited your access to that money when you faked your death, lady."

They were right. Josie Jessup's bank accounts and trust fund had closed when she'd *died.* And JJ Brandt's salary from the community college was barely enough to cover her rent, utilities and groceries. She had nothing in her savings account to offer them.

"My father would pay you," she said, "whatever you ask." But first they would have to prove to him that she was really alive. She hadn't dared step inside his room. What would happen if gunmen burst inside with her? The shock would surely bring on another heart attack—maybe a fatal one.

The men shared a glance, obviously debating her offer. But then one of them shook his head. "This is about more than money, lady."

"What is it about?" she asked.

As far she knew, Brendan was the only one with any reason to want her dead. If these men worked for him, they wouldn't have held him back from boarding the elevator with her. If they worked for him, they wouldn't have dared to touch him at all. She still couldn't believe that she had dared to touch him, that she'd dared to go near him even to pursue her story. The police had been unable to determine who had killed his father, the legendary crime boss, so she had vowed to find out if there was any truth to the rumors that Dennis O'Hannigan's runaway son had killed him out of revenge and greed.

She had found something else entirely. More than the story, she had been attracted to the man—the complex man who had been grieving the death of his estranged father while trying to take over his illicit empire. She had never found evidence proving Brendan was the killer, but he must have been worried that she'd discovered something. Why else would he have tried to kill her?

Just because he'd learned she'd been lying to him about what she really was? Maybe. He'd been furious with her—furious enough to want revenge. But if he wasn't behind this attempt to eliminate her, had he been behind that bomb planted more than three years ago?

Could she have been wrong about him?

"I have a right to know," she prodded, wanting the truth. That was her problem—she always wanted the truth. It was what had made her such a great reporter before she'd been forced to give it all up to save her life. But since it was probably her last chance to learn it, she wanted this truth more than she'd ever wanted any other. If not Brendan, who wanted her dead?

"It doesn't matter what it's about," one of the men replied.

She suspected he had no idea, either, that he was just doing what he had been paid to do.

"It's not going to change the outcome for you and your son," the fake orderly continued as he reached behind him and drew out his gun.

What about her father? Had he only been attacked to lure her out of hiding? Was he safe now?

If only her son was safe, too...

She covered the side of CJ's cold, damp face with her hand so that he wouldn't see the weapon. Then she turned, putting her body between the boy and the men. Her body wouldn't be enough to protect her son, though. Nothing could protect him now. "Please..."

But if the men wouldn't respond to bribes, they
would have no use for begging, either. So she just
closed her eyes and prayed as the first shot rang out.

Chapter Four

Was he too late?

As the elevator doors slid open, a shot rang out. But the bullet ricocheted off the back of the car near his head. Both men faced *him* with their guns raised. Maybe this had nothing to do with Josie.

Maybe the woman wasn't even really her and the boy not really even his son. Maybe it had all been an elaborate trap to lure him here—to his death. Plenty of people wanted him dead. That was why he usually had backup within gunshot range. But he hadn't wanted anyone to be aware of his visit to the bedside of a man he didn't really know but with whom he'd thought he'd shared a tragedy: Josie's death.

So nobody had known he was coming here. These men weren't after him, because the suspects he knew wouldn't have gone to such extremes to take him out; they wouldn't have had to. Whenever they dared to try to take him out, as they had his father, they knew where to find him—at O'Hannigan's. Inside the family tavern was where Josie had found him. He'd thought the little rich girl had just wandered into the wrong place with the wrong clientele, and he'd rescued her before any of his rough customers could accost her.

Just as he had intended to rescue her now. But both times he was the one who wound up needing to be rescued. Maybe he should have had backup even for this uncomfortable visit. With the elevator doors wide open, Brendan was a damn sitting duck, more so even than the woman and the boy. They might be able to escape. Seeing the fear on their faces, pale and stark in the light spilling out of the elevator, it was clear that they were in real danger and they knew it.

"Run!" he yelled at them.

She sprinted away, either in reaction to his command or in fear of him as well as the armed men. With her and the kid out of the line of fire, he raised the gun he'd taken off their co-conspirator.

But the men had divided their attention now. Standing back-to-back, one fired at him while the other turned his gun toward Josie.

The boy clutched tightly in her arms, she ran, disappearing into the shadows before any bullets struck her. But maybe running wasn't a good thing, given that the farther away she went, the thicker the shadows grew. The light from the elevator illuminated only a small circle of the rooftop around the open doors. The farther she ran, the harder it would be for her to see where the roof ended and the black abyss twenty stories above the ground began.

He ducked back into the elevator and flattened himself against the panel beside the doors. He could have closed those doors to protect himself. But then he couldn't protect Josie and the child. *His son...*

These men weren't just trying to kill the woman who was supposed to already be dead. They were trying to kill a helpless child.

An O'Hannigan.

His father would be turning over in his grave.

Despite his occasional violent behavior toward them, Dennis O'Hannigan had never really wanted his family harmed—at least not by anyone but him. Brendan didn't want his family harmed at all. He kept one finger on the button to hold open the doors. Then he leaned out and aimed the gun. And squeezed the trigger.

His shots drew all the attention to him. Bullets pinged off the brass handrail and shattered the smoky glass of the elevator car. The glass splintered and ricocheted like the bullets, biting into his skin like a swarm of bees.

His finger jerked off the button, and the doors began to close. But he couldn't leave Josie and the child alone up here with no protection. Despite the other man's warning, he had to play the hero. But it had been nearly four years since he'd been anything but the villain.

Had he gotten rusty? Would he be able to protect them? Or had his arrival put them in even more danger?

"THEY'RE ALL BAD men," CJ said, his voice high and squeaky with fear and panic. "They're bad! Bad!"

He was too young to have learned just how evil some people were. As his mother, Josie was supposed to protect him, but she'd endangered his life and his innocence. She had to do her best to keep her little boy a little boy until he had the time to grow into a man.

"Shh…" Josie cautioned him. "We need to be very quiet."

"So they don't find us?"

"First we have to find a hiding place." Which wouldn't be easy in a darkness so enveloping she could barely see the child she held tightly against her.

She had been able to see the shots—those brief flashes of gunpowder. She'd run from those flashes, desperate to keep her son safe. But now those shots were redirected toward Brendan, and running wouldn't keep CJ safe since she couldn't see where she was going. She moved quickly but carefully, testing her footing before she stepped forward.

"Are they shooting real bullets?" he asked.

To preserve that innocence she was afraid he was losing, she could have lied. But that lie could risk his life.

"They're real," she replied, aware that they'd come all too close to her and CJ. "That's why we need to find a place to hide until the police come."

Someone must have heard the shots and reported them by now. Help had to be on the way. Hopefully it would arrive in time to save her and her son. But what about Brendan? He had stepped into the middle of an attempted murder—a double homicide, actually. And he hadn't done it accidentally. He had tracked her to the roof, maybe to kill her himself. But perhaps he'd be the one to lose his life, since the men were now entirely focused on him.

She shuddered, the thought chilling her nearly as much as the cold wind that whipped around the unprotected rooftop.

"Let's go back there, Mommy," CJ said, lifting his hand, which caught her attention only because she felt the movement more than saw it.

"Where?" she asked.

"Behind those big metal things."

She peered in the direction he was pointing and finally noted the glint of some stray starlight off steel vents, probably exhaust pipes for the hospital's heating or cooling system. If only they could escape inside them…

But she could barely move around them, let alone find a way inside them. The openings were too high above the rooftop, towering over her. As she tried to squeeze around them, her hip struck the metal. She winced and swallowed a groan of pain. And hoped the men hadn't heard the telltale metallic clink.

"Shh, Mommy," CJ cautioned her. "We don't want the bad men to hear us."

"No, we don't," she agreed.

"They might find our hiding place."

"I'm not sure we can hide here," she whispered. She couldn't wedge them both between the massive pipes. The metal caught at her clothes and scraped her arms. "We can't fit."

"Let me try," he suggested. Before she could agree, he wriggled down from her arms and squeezed through the small space.

She reached through the blackness, trying to clutch at him, trying to pull him back. What if he'd fallen right off the building?

She had no idea how much space was on the other side of the pipes. A tiny ledge? None?

A scream burned in her throat, but she was too scared to utter it—too horrified that in trying to protect her son she may have lost him forever.

But then chubby fingers caught hers. He tugged on her hand. "Come on, Mommy. There's room."

"You're not at the edge of the roof?" she asked, worried that he might be in more danger where he was.

"Nooo," he murmured, his voice sounding as if he'd turned away from her. "There's a little wall right behind me."

"Don't go over that wall," she advised. It was probably the edge of the roof, a small ledge to separate the rooftop from the ground far below. A curious little boy might want to figure out what was on the other side of that wall.

"Okay, Mommy," he murmured again, his voice still muffled. Was he trying to peer over the side?

She needed to get to him, needed to protect him, from the men and from himself. She turned sideways and pushed herself against the space where CJ had so effortlessly disappeared. But her breasts and hips—curves she'd barely had until her pregnancy with him—caught. She sucked in her stomach, but it made no difference. She couldn't suck in her breasts or hips. "I can't fit."

CJ tugged harder on her hand. "C'mon, Mommy, it's a good hiding place."

"No, honey," she corrected him, her pulse tripping with fear that he'd go over the wall, "you need to come back out. We'll find another one."

But then she heard it. She tilted her head and listened harder. And still it was all she heard: silence. The shooting had stopped.

What did that mean?

Was Brendan dead? Were the men? Whoever had survived would be searching for her next—for her and her son. The silence broke, shattered by the scrape of a shoe against the asphalt roofing.

She sucked in a breath now—of fear. But it didn't make it any easier for her to squeeze through the small space. And maybe pulling CJ out wasn't the best idea, not when he was safe from the men.

She dropped his fingers. "You stay here," she said. "In the best hiding place."

"I wanna hide with you."

"I'll find a bigger hiding place," she said. "You need to stay here and play statue for me."

She had played the game as a kid when she'd pretended to be a statue, completely still and silent. On those mornings that CJ had woken her up at five, she'd taught him to play statue so she could sleep just a little longer. Now acting lifeless was perhaps the only way for CJ to stay alive.

The footfalls grew louder as someone drew closer. She had to get out of here, had to distract whoever it was from CJ's hiding place. But first she had to utter one more warning. "Don't come out for anyone but me."

Her son was such a good boy. So smart and so obedient. She didn't have to worry that anyone else would lure him out of hiding. She just had to make sure that she stayed alive, so that he would come out when it was safe. So she drew in a deep breath and headed off, moving as fast as she dared in the darkness. She glanced back, but night had swallowed those metal vent pipes and had swallowed her son. Would she be able to find him again, even if she eluded whoever had survived the earlier gun battle?

She would worry about finding him after she found a hiding spot for herself. But it was so dark she could barely see where she was going. So she wasn't surprised when she collided with a wall.

But this wasn't a short brick wall like the one CJ had found behind the pipes. This wall was broad and muscular and warm. Her hands tingled in reaction to the chest she touched, her palms pressed against the lapels of a suit. The other men had been wearing scrubs, which would have been scratchy and flat.

And she wouldn't have reacted this way to them. Her skin wouldn't tingle; her pulse wouldn't leap. And she wouldn't feel something very much like relief that he was alive. No matter what threat he posed to her, she hadn't wanted him dead.

"Brendan...?"

It was her. Despite her physical transformation, he'd recognized her. But now he had not even a fraction of a doubt. That voice in the darkness...

Her touch...

He recognized all that about her, too.

But more importantly, *she* had recognized *him*. If she was truly a stranger that he had mistaken for his former lover and betrayer, she wouldn't know his name. Or, if by some chance, she had just recognized him as the son of a notorious mobster, she wouldn't have been comfortable and familiar enough to call him by his first name.

"Yes, Josie, it's me," he assured her.

She shuddered and her hands began to tremble against his chest. "You—you," she stammered. "You're..."

He was shaking a little himself in reaction to what had nearly happened. Adrenaline and fear coursed through him, pumping his blood fast and hard through his veins. "You know who I am. You just said my name," he pointed out. "And I damn well know who you are. So let's cut the bullshit. We don't have time for it. We need to get the hell out of here!"

She expelled a ragged sigh of resignation, as if she had finally given up trying to deny her true identity. Her palms patted his chest as if checking for bullet holes. "You didn't get shot?"

"No." But he suspected he had come uncomfortably close. If either of the gunmen, who were probably hired assassins, had been a better shot than he was, Josie would be in an entirely different situation right now.

As if she sensed that, she asked, "And those men?"

Brendan flinched with a pang of regret. But he had had no choice. If he hadn't shot the men, they would have killed him. And then they would have found Josie and the boy and killed them, too.

"They're not a threat. But the guy I left on the floor by your father's room could be."

Her breath audibly caught in a gasp of fear. "You left him there? He could hurt my father."

The assailant was in no condition to hurt anyone. Unless he'd regained consciousness...

"I don't think your father is their target," Brendan pointed out.

"They hurt him already," she said, reminding him of the reason the media mogul was in the hospital in the first place. Because he'd been attacked.

"That must have been just to lure you out of hiding." Someone had gone to a lot of trouble to track her down, and that someone was obviously very determined to do what Brendan had thought had been done almost four years ago. Kill Josie Jessup. If only he had had more time to interrogate the man downstairs, to find out who had hired him.

"They have no reason to hurt your father now," Brendan assured her before adding the obvious. "It's you they're after."

"And my son," she said, her voice cracking with emotion. "They were going to hurt him, too."

"Where is he?" he asked. His eyes had adjusted

to the darkness enough to see her before him now. "Where's my son?"

She shuddered again. "He's not your son."

"Stop," he impatiently advised her. "Just stop with the lies." She'd told him too many four years ago. "You need to get the boy and we need to get the hell out of here."

Because the bad men weren't the only threat.

Sirens wailed in the distance. Maybe just an ambulance on its way to the emergency room. Or maybe police cars on their way to secure a crime scene. He couldn't risk the latter. He couldn't be brought in for questioning or, worse, arrested. The local police wouldn't care that it had been self-defense; they were determined to arrest him for something. Anything. That was why Brendan had used the other fake orderly's gun. No bullets could be traced back to him. He'd wiped his prints off the weapon and left it on the roof.

"I'm not leaving with you," she said. "And neither is *my* son."

"You're in danger," he needlessly pointed out. "And you've put him in danger."

She sucked in a breath, either offended or feeling guilty. "And leaving with you would put us both in even more danger."

Now he drew in a sharp breath of pure offense. "If I wanted you gone, Josie, I could have just let those men shoot you."

"But they weren't going to shoot just me."

He flinched again at the thought of his child in so much danger. Reaching out, he grasped her shoulders. "Where is my son?" he repeated, resisting the urge to shake the truth out of her. "Someone wants you both dead. You can't let him out of your sight." And he couldn't let either of them out of his.

"I—I…"

"I won't hurt you," he assured her. "And I sure as hell won't hurt him."

Her head jerked in a sharp nod as if she believed him. He felt the motion more than saw it as her silky hair brushed his chin. She stepped back and turned around and then around again in a complete circle, as if trying to remember where she'd been.

"Where did you hide him?" he asked, hoping like hell that she had hidden him and hadn't just lost him.

"It was behind some exhaust pipes," she said. "I couldn't fit but he squeezed behind them. I—I just don't remember where they were."

"What's his name?"

She hesitated a moment before replying, as if his knowing his name would make the boy more real for Brendan. "CJ."

Maybe she was right—knowing the boy's name did make him more real to Brendan. His heart pounded and his pulse raced as he reeled from all the sudden realizations. He had a son. He was a father. He was continuing the "family" of which *he* had never wanted to be part.

"CJ," he repeated, then raised his voice and shouted, "CJ!"

"Shh." Josie cautioned him.

"He might not hear me if I don't yell," he pointed out. And Brendan needed to see his boy, to assure himself that his child was real and that he was all right.

"He won't come out if he hears *you*," she explained. "He thinks you're a bad man."

Brendan flinched. It didn't matter that everyone else thought so; he didn't want his son to believe the lie, too.

"Is that what you told him?" he asked. It must have been what she'd believed all these years, because no matter how determined a reporter she'd been, she hadn't learned the truth about him.

"It's what you showed him," she said, "when you grabbed me by the elevator."

Dread and regret clenched his stomach muscles. His own son was afraid of him. How would he ever get close to the boy, ever form a relationship with him, if the kid feared him?

He flashed back so many years ago to his own heart pounding hard with fear as he cowered from his father, from the boom of his harsh voice and the sting of his big hand. Brendan hadn't just feared Dennis O'Hannigan. He'd been terrified of the man. But then so had everyone else.

"I'll be quiet," he whispered his promise. "You find him."

She called for the boy, her voice rising higher with panic each time she said his name. "CJ? CJ?" Then she sucked in a breath and her voice was steadier as she yelled, in a mother's no-nonsense tone, what must have been his full name, "Charles Jesse Brandt!"

Brandt? The boy's last name should have been O'Hannigan. But maybe it was better that it wasn't. Being an O'Hannigan carried with it so many dangers.

But then danger had found the boy no matter what his mother called him. CJ didn't respond to that maternal command only the rare child dared to disobey. Brendan certainly never would have disobeyed.

Panic clutched at his chest as worst-case scenarios began to play out in his mind. He had seen so many horrible things in his life that the possibilities kept coming. Had the man from the sixth floor somehow joined them on the roof without Brendan noticing? Had he found the boy already?

Another scenario played through his head, of Josie lying to him again. Still. Had she hidden the child and told him not to come out for Brendan? She'd hidden his son from him for three years—a few more minutes weren't going to bother her.

"Where is he?" he asked, shoving his hands in his pockets so that he wouldn't reach for her again. He had already frightened her, which was probably why she'd hidden their son from him.

She shook her head. "I don't know." The panic was in her voice, too.

Brendan almost preferred to think that she was lying to him and knew where the boy was, having made certain he was safe.

Her hand slapped against a metal pipe. "I thought he was behind here. CJ! CJ!"

"Then why isn't he coming out?" Brendan had stayed quiet and now kept his voice to a whisper despite the panic clutching at him.

"No, it can't be…" she murmured, her voice cracking with fear and dread.

"What?" He demanded to know the thought that occurred to her, that had her trembling now with fear.

"He's at the edge of the roof," she said. "He told me there was a short wall behind him. I—I told him not to go over it…"

Because there would have been nothing but the ground, twenty stories below, on the other side. If the boy was still on the roof with them, he would answer his mother. Even if he heard Brendan, he would come out to protect her, as he did before.

Oh, God!

Had Brendan lost his son only moments after finally finding him?

Chapter Five

Tears stung Josie's eyes, blinding her even more than the darkness. And sobs clogged her throat, choking her. She had been trying to protect her son, but she'd put him in more danger. She clawed at the pipes, trying to force them apart, trying to force her way back to where her son had been last.

"CJ! CJ!" she cried, her voice cracking with fear she could no longer contain.

She hadn't made sacrifices only to protect her father; she had made them to protect her baby, too. If she hadn't learned she was pregnant, she wouldn't have agreed to let her father hire bodyguards after the first attempt on her life—a cut brake line. And if she hadn't realized that no one could keep them truly safe, she wouldn't have agreed to fake her death and disappear.

Everything she'd done, she'd done for her son. Maybe that was why she'd brought him to see her father—not just so the two could finally meet, but so that her father would understand why she'd hurt him so badly. As a parent himself, he would have to understand and forgive her.

"CJ…" The tears overtook her now.

"Shh," a deep voice murmured, and a strong hand grasped her shoulder.

But the man didn't offer comfort.

"Shh," he said again, as a command. And his hand squeezed. "Listen."

Since Brendan was alive, she had just assumed that the men who'd wanted to kill her and CJ were not. But maybe he had just scared them off. And now they had returned. Or maybe that other gunman, the one he'd left near her father's room, had joined them on the roof.

She sucked in a breath, trying to calm herself. But if her child was truly gone, there would be no calming her—not even if the men had come back for them. They would need their guns—to defend themselves from her attack. This was their fault because they'd forced her to hide her son to protect him. But it wasn't their fault that she hadn't hidden him in a safe spot.

That was all on her.

"Shh," Brendan said again.

And she managed to control her sobs. But she heard their echo—coming softly from behind the metal pipes.

"CJ?" He wasn't gone. But why hadn't he come out? "Are you hurt?"

Perhaps there were more dangers behind the pipes than just that short wall separating him from a big fall. Maybe the pipes were hot. Or sharp.

"Listen," Brendan advised again.

The sobs were soft but strong and steady, not broken with pain, not weak with sickness. He was scared. Her little boy was too scared to come out, even for his mother.

"Tell him I'm not going to hurt him," Brendan said, his voice low but gruff. "Or you."

She nearly snorted in derision of his claim. When

he'd realized she had been working on a story about his father's murder, he'd been furious with her. Too furious to let her explain that even though the story was why she'd sought him out, she had really fallen in love with him.

Despite his difficult life, losing his mother, running away at fifteen, he'd seemed such a charming, loving man that she'd thought he might have fallen for her, too. But then his anger had showed another side of his personality, one dangerously similar to his merciless and vengeful father.

As if he'd heard the snort she'd suppressed, he insisted, "I'm not going to hurt either of you."

"Did you hear him, CJ?" she asked. "You don't have to be afraid." Then she drew in another breath to brace herself to lie to her son. "Mr. O'Hannigan is not a bad man."

She had actually been foolish enough to believe that once, to think that he was not necessarily his father's son. She'd thought that given all the years he'd spent away from the old man, he might have grown up differently. Honorably. That was why she'd fallen for him.

But when he'd learned she had actually been working on a story...

He hadn't been her charming lover. He had been cold and furious. But he hadn't been *only* furious. If he'd cut her brake line, he'd been vengeful, too. But she hadn't really meant anything to him then; she had been only a lover who'd betrayed him. Now he knew she was the mother of his child.

"He saved us from the bad men, CJ. The bad men are gone now." She turned back toward Brendan. He was just a dark shadow to her, but she discerned that his head jerked in a sharp nod.

She pushed her hand between the pipes, but no pudgy fingers caught hers. "CJ, you can come out now. It's safe."

She wasn't sure about that, but her son would be safer with her than standing just a short wall away from a long fall.

"It is safe." Brendan spoke now, his voice a low growl for her ears only. "But it may not stay that way. We need to get out of here before more *bad* men show up."

She shivered, either over his warning or his warm breath blowing in her ear and along her neck. Memories rushed back, of his breath on her neck before his lips touched her skin, skimming down her throat. His tongue flicking over her pulse before his mouth moved farther down her body...

Her pulse pounded faster, and she trembled. Then she forced the memories back, relegating them to where they belonged as she'd done so many times before. If she hadn't been able to keep the past in the past, she wouldn't have survived the past four years.

"CJ, why won't you come out?" she asked.

The boy sniffed hard, sucking up his tears and his snot. Josie flinched but resisted the urge to admonish him and was grateful she had done so when he finally spoke. "Cuz I—I was bad."

"No," Josie began, but another, deeper voice overwhelmed hers.

"No, son," Brendan said.

Josie gasped at his brazenness in addressing her child as his. Technically, biologically, it was true. But CJ didn't know that. And she never wanted him to learn the truth of his parentage. She never wanted him to know that he was one of *those* O'Hannigans.

"You weren't bad," Brendan continued. "You were very brave to protect your mother. You're a very good kid."

The boy sniffled again and released a shuddery breath.

"Now you have to be brave again," Brendan said. "And come out. There might be more bad men and we have to leave before they can be mean to your mother."

"You—you were mean to Mommy," CJ said. Her son was too smart to be as easily fooled by Brendan's charm as she had been. And as if compelled to protect her again, the little boy wriggled out from behind the pipes. But instead of confronting Brendan as he had inside the hospital, he ducked behind Josie's legs.

Brendan dropped to his haunches as if trying to meet the child's eyes even though it was so dark. "I shouldn't have been mean to her," he said. "And I'm sorry that I was. I thought she was someone else." His soft tone hardened. "Someone who lied to me, tricked me and then stole from me."

Josie shuddered at his implacable tone. He had saved her from the gunmen, but he hadn't forgotten her betrayal. Over the years it had apparently even been exaggerated in his mind, because she had never stolen anything from him. Judging by the anger he barely controlled, it seemed as if he would never forgive her.

"I don't like it when people lie to me," Brendan said. "But I would never hurt anyone."

"Who's lying now?" she murmured.

"Unless I had to in order to protect someone else," he clarified. "I will protect you and your mommy."

"I will p-tect Mommy," CJ said, obviously unwilling to share her with anyone else. But then, he'd never

had to before. He had been the most important person—the only person, really—in her life since the day
he was born.

Josie turned and lifted him in her arms. And she finally understood why he'd been so reluctant to come
out of his hiding place. He was embarrassed, because
his jeans were wet. Her little boy, who'd never had an
accident since being potty-trained almost a year ago,
had been so scared that he'd had one now. She clutched
him close and whispered in his ear. "It's okay."

Brendan must have taken her words as acceptance.
He slipped his arm around her shoulders. Despite the
warmth of his body, she shivered in reaction to his
closeness. Then he ushered her and CJ toward the elevator. He must have jammed the doors open, because it
waited for them, light spilling from it onto the rooftop.

As she noticed that the armed men were gone, fear
clutched at her. Brendan must not have injured them
badly enough to stop them. They could be lurking in
the shadows, ready to fire again. She covered CJ's face
with her hand and leaned into Brendan, grateful for his
size and his strength.

But then as they crossed the roof to the open doors,
she noticed blood spattered across the asphalt and then
smeared in two thick trails. Brendan had dragged away
the bodies. Maybe he'd done it to spare their son from
seeing death. Or maybe he'd done it to hide the evidence of the crime.

It hadn't actually been a crime though. It had been
self-defense. And to protect her and their son. If she
believed him...

But could she believe him? No matter what his motives were this time, the man was a killer. She didn't
need to see the actual bodies to know that the men were

dead. Her instincts were telling her that she shouldn't trust him. And she damn well shouldn't trust him with their son.

BRENDAN HELD HIS son. For the first time. But instead of a fragile infant, the boy was wriggly and surprisingly strong as he struggled in his grasp. He had taken him from Josie's arms, knowing that was the only way to keep her from running. She cared more about their son's safety than her own.

Maybe she really wasn't the woman he'd once known. Josie Jessup had been a spoiled princess, obviously uncaring of whom she hurt with her exposés and her actions. She had never run a story on Brendan though—she'd just run.

Brendan wouldn't let that happen again. So he held his son even though she reached for him, her arms outstretched. And the boy wriggled, trying to escape Brendan's grasp.

"Come on," he said to both of them. "We need to move quickly."

"I—I can run fast," CJ assured him.

Not fast enough to outrun bullets. Brendan couldn't be certain that the guy from the sixth floor hadn't regained consciousness and set up an ambush somewhere. He couldn't risk going through the hospital, so he pressed the garage express button on the elevator panel. It wouldn't stop on any other floors now. It would take them directly from the roof to the parking level in the basement.

"I'm sure you can run fast," Brendan said. "But we all have to stay together from now on to make sure we stay safe from the bad men."

But the little boy stopped struggling and stared up

at him, his blue-green eyes narrowed as if he was trying to see inside Brendan—to see if he was a bad man,
too. He hoped like hell the kid couldn't really see inside his soul.

It was a dark, dark place. It had been even darker
when he'd thought Josie had been murdered. He had
thought that she'd been killed because of him—because
she'd gotten too close, because she'd discovered something that he should have.

From the other stories she'd done, he knew she was
a good reporter. Too good. So good that she could have
made enemies of her own, though.

At first he hadn't thought this attack on her had anything to do with him. After all, he hadn't even known
she was alive. And he'd certainly had no idea he had
a child.

But maybe one of *his* enemies had discovered she
was alive. She stared up at him with the same intensity
of their son, her eyes just a lighter, smokier green. No
matter how much her appearance had been altered and
what she'd claimed before, she was definitely Josie Jessup. And whoever had discovered she was really alive
knew what Brendan hadn't realized until he heard of
her death—that he'd fallen for her. Despite her lies.
Despite her betrayal.

He had fallen in love with her, with her energy and
her quick wit and her passion. And he'd spent more
than three years mourning her. Someone might have
wanted to make certain that his mourning never ended.

Josie shook her head, rejecting his protection. "I
think we'll be safer on our own."

She didn't trust him. Given his reputation, or at least
the reputation of his family, he didn't necessarily blame
her. But then she should have known him better. Dur-

ing those short months they'd spent together before her "death," he had let her get close. He may not have told her the truth about himself, but he'd shown her that he wasn't the man others thought he was. He wasn't his father.

He wasn't cruel and indifferent. "If I'd left you alone on the roof…"

She and CJ would already be dead. She shuddered in revulsion at the horrible thought. She could not deny that Brendan O'Hannigan had saved their lives. But she was too scared to thank him and too smart to trust him.

Despite her inner voice warning her to be careful, she had thought only of her father when she'd risked coming to the hospital. She hadn't considered that after spending more than three years in hiding someone might still want to kill her. She hadn't considered that someone could have learned that she was still alive. "I was caught off guard."

Brendan stared down at the boy he held in his arms. "I can relate."

He had seemed shocked, not only to find her alive but also to realize that he was a father. Given that they had exactly the same eyes and facial features, Brendan had instantly recognized the child as his. There had been no point for her to continue denying what it wouldn't require a DNA test to prove.

"Are you usually on guard?" he asked her.

"Yes." But when she'd learned of the assault on her father, she had dropped her guard. And it had nearly cost her everything. She couldn't take any more risks. And trusting Brendan would be the greatest risk of all. "I won't make that mistake again."

"No," he said, as if he agreed with her. Or supported her. But then he added, "I won't let you."

And she tensed. She lifted her arms again and clasped her hands on her son's shoulders. After nearly losing him on the rooftop, she should have held him so tightly that he would never get away. But he'd started wriggling in the elevator, and she'd loosened her grip just enough that Brendan had been able to easily pluck him from her.

A chill chased down her spine as she worried that he would take her son from her just that easily. And permanently.

Josie's stomach rose as the elevator descended to the basement. Panic filled her throat, choking her. Then the bell dinged, signaling that they had reached their destination. They had gone from one extreme to another, one danger to another.

"We'll take my car," Brendan said as the doors slowly began to slide open.

We. He didn't intend to take her son and leave her alone, or as he'd left the men on the rooftop. Dead. But she and her son couldn't leave with him, either. She shook her head.

"We don't have time to argue right now," he said, his deep voice gruff with impatience. "We need to get out of here."

"Do you have a car seat?" she asked. She had posed the question to thwart him, thinking she already knew the answer. But she didn't. As closely as she followed the news, she hadn't heard or read anything about Brendan O'Hannigan's personal life. Only about his business. Or his *alleged* business.

He'd kept his personal life far more private than his professional one. But she had been gone for more than three years. He could have met someone else. Could even have had another child, one he'd known about, one with whom he lived.

He clenched his jaw and shook his head.

"CJ is too little to ride without a car seat."

"I'm not little!" her son heartily protested, as he twisted even more forcefully in Brendan's grasp. Her hands slipped from his squirming shoulders. "I'm big!"

If CJ had been struggling like that in her arms, she would have lost him, and just as the doors opened fully. And he might have run off to hide again.

But Brendan held him firmly, but not so tightly that he hurt the boy. With his low pain threshold, her son would have been squealing if he'd felt the least bit of discomfort.

"You are big," Josie assured him. "But the law says you're not big enough to ride without your car seat."

Arching a brow, she turned toward Brendan. "You don't want to break the law, do you?"

A muscle twitched along his clenched jaw. He shook his head but then clarified, "I don't want to risk CJ's safety."

But she had no illusions that if not for their son, he would have no qualms about breaking the law. She had no illusions about Brendan O'Hannigan anymore.

But she once had. She'd begun to believe that his inheriting his father's legacy had forced him into a life he wouldn't have chosen, one he'd actually run from when he was a kid. She'd thought he was better than that life, that he was a good man.

What a fool she'd been.

"Where's your car?" he asked as he carried their son from the elevator.

She hurried after them, glancing at the cement pillars, looking at the signs.

"What letter, Mommy?" CJ asked. He'd been sleeping when she'd parked their small SUV, so he didn't know. She could lie and he wouldn't contradict her as he had earlier.

But lying about the parking level would only delay the inevitable. She wasn't going to get CJ away from his father without a struggle, one that might hurt her son. Or at least scare him. And the little boy had already been frightened enough to last him a lifetime.

"A," she replied.

CJ pointed a finger at the sign. "That's this one."

"What kind of car?" Brendan asked.

"A—a white Ford Escape," she murmured.

"And the plate?"

She shook her head and pointed toward where the rear bumper protruded beyond two bigger sport utility vehicles parked on either side of it. "It's right there."

Because CJ had been sleeping, she'd made certain to park close to the elevators so she wouldn't have far to carry him. As he said, he was a big boy—at least big enough that carrying him too far or for too long strained her arms and her back.

She shoved her hand in her jeans pocket to retrieve the keys. She'd locked her purse inside the vehicle to protect her new identity just in case anyone recognized her inside the hospital. She was grateful she'd taken the precaution. But if she'd had her cell phone and her can of mace, maybe she wouldn't have needed Brendan to come to her rescue.

Lifting the key fob, she pressed the unlock button. The lights flashed and the horn beeped. But then another sound drowned out that beep as gunshots rang out. The echo made it impossible to tell from which direction the shots were coming.

But she didn't need to know where they were coming from to know where they were aimed—at her. Bullets whizzed past her head, stirring her hair.

A strong hand clasped her shoulder, pushing her down so forcefully that she dropped to the ground. Her knees struck the cement so hard that she involuntarily cried out in pain.

A cry echoed hers—CJ's. He hadn't fallen; he was still clasped tightly in Brendan's arms. But one of those flying bullets could have struck him.

Now she couldn't cry. She couldn't move. She could only stay on the ground, frozen with terror and dread that she had failed her son once again.

Chapter Six

Vivid curses reverberated inside Brendan's head, echoing the cries of the woman and the child. Those cries had to be of fear—just fear. He'd made certain that they wouldn't be hit, keeping them low as the shots rang out. If only he'd had backup waiting…

But just as he had taken on the gunmen inside the hospital, he also had to confront this one alone—while trying to protect people he hadn't even known were alive until tonight. So he didn't utter those curses echoing inside his head, not only because of his son but also because he didn't have time.

He'd taken the gun off the guy he'd left alive. But that didn't mean the man hadn't had another one on him, as Brendan always did. Or maybe if he'd come down to ambush them in the garage he'd retrieved a weapon from his vehicle.

Where the hell were the shots coming from? Since they ricocheted off the cement floor and ceiling and pillars, he couldn't tell. So he couldn't fire back—even if he'd had a free hand to grab one of his concealed weapons.

His hands were full, one clasping his son tightly to his chest while his other wrapped around Josie's arm.

He lifted her from the ground and tugged her toward the car she'd unlocked. Thankfully, it was next to two bigger SUVs that provided some cover as he ushered them between the vehicles.

"Do you still have the keys?" he asked.

Josie stared at him wide-eyed, as if too scared to comprehend what he was saying, or maybe the loud gunshots echoing throughout the parking structure had deafened her. Or she was just in shock.

Brendan leaned closer to her, his lips nearly brushing her ear as her hair tickled his cheek. Then he spoke louder. "Keys?"

She glanced down at her hand. A ring of keys dangled from her trembling fingers.

He released her arm to grab the keys from her. Then, with the keys jamming into his palm, he pulled open the back door and thrust her inside the vehicle.

"Stay low," he said, handing their son to her. As he slammed the door shut behind them, a bullet hit the rear bumper. The other vehicles offered no protection if the shooter was behind them now.

Brendan let a curse slip out of his lips. Then he quickly pulled open the driver's door. As he slid behind the steering wheel, he glanced into the rearview mirror. He couldn't see anyone in the backseat. Josie had taken his advice and stayed low.

But he noticed someone else. A dark shadow moved between cars parked on the other side of the garage, rushing toward Josie's SUV. In the dim lighting, he couldn't see the guy's face, couldn't tell if this was the supposed orderly from the sixth floor. He couldn't risk the guy getting close enough for Brendan to recognize him.

He shoved the keys in the ignition. As soon as

the motor turned over, he reversed. He would have slammed into the cars behind them, would have tried to crush the shooter. But Josie and the boy were not buckled in, so he couldn't risk their being tossed around the vehicle.

And Brendan couldn't risk the gunman getting close enough to take more shots. If these guys were all hired professionals, they were bound to get an accurate shot. So he shifted into Drive and pressed his foot down on the accelerator. If only he could reach for one of his weapons and shoot back at the shadow running after them…

But he needed both hands on the wheel, needed to carefully careen around the sharp curves so he didn't hit a concrete pillar, or fling Josie and his son out a window. He had to make sure that he didn't kill them while he tried so desperately to save them.

Josie didn't know what would kill them first: the gunshots or a car accident. Since Brendan was driving so fast, he must have outdistanced the gunman so no bullets could fly through the back window and strike CJ. She quickly strapped him into his booster seat. As short as he was, his head was still beneath the headrest.

"Stay down," Brendan warned her from the front seat as he swerved around more sharp corners and headed up toward the street level and the exit. "There could be more—"

Hired killers? That was probably what he'd intended to say before stopping himself for their son's sake, not wanting to scare the boy.

"Bad men?" she asked. She hadn't expected any of them or she never would have brought her son to the hospital. She wouldn't have put him at risk. How the hell had someone found out she was alive?

He had acted surprised. Had he really not known until tonight?

She had so many questions, but asking Brendan would have been a waste of time. He had never told her anything she'd wanted to know before. And she wasn't certain that he would actually have any answers this time. If he really hadn't known she was alive, he would have no idea who was trying to kill her.

She needed to talk to Charlotte.

Leaning forward, she reached under the driver's seat and tugged out the purse she'd stashed there earlier. She hadn't left only her identification inside but also her cell phones. Her personal phone and that special cell used only to call her handler. But Josie couldn't make that confidential call, not with Brendan in the vehicle.

"What are you doing?" he asked, with a quick glance in the rearview mirror. He probably couldn't see her, but he'd felt it when she'd reached under his seat. Was the man aware of everything going on around him? Given his life and his enemies, he probably had to be—or *he* wouldn't be alive still.

"Getting my purse," she said.

"Do you have a weapon in it?" he asked.

"Why?" Did he want her to use it or was he worried that she would? She reached inside the bag and wrapped her fingers around the can of mace. But even if he wasn't driving so fast, she couldn't have risked spraying it and hurting her son.

His gaze went to the rearview mirror again. "Never mind. I think we lost him," he said. But he didn't stop at the guard shack for the parking garage. Instead he crashed the SUV right through the gate.

CJ cried, and Josie turned to him with concern. But his cry was actually a squeal as his teal-blue eyes twinkled with excitement. What had happened to her timid son?

She leaned over the console between the seats. "Be careful."

"Are you all right?" he asked. "And CJ?"

"We're both fine. But is the car all right?" she asked. One of the headlamps wobbled, bouncing the beam of light around the street. "I need to be able to drive it home."

But first she had to get rid of Brendan.

"You can't go home," he told her. "The gunman was coming up behind the vehicle. He could have gotten your plate and pulled up your registration online. He could already know where you live."

She didn't know what would be worse: the gunman knowing where she lived or Brendan knowing. But she wouldn't need to worry about either scenario. Charlotte had made certain of that. "The vehicle isn't registered to me."

JJ Brandt was only one of the identities the U.S. marshal had set up for her. In case one of those identities was compromised, she could assume a new one. But for nearly four years, she had never come close to being recognized. Until tonight, when no one had been fooled by her new appearance or her new name.

Thanks to Brendan's interference, JJ Brandt hadn't died tonight. Literally. But she would have to die figuratively since Brendan might have learned that name. And she would have to assume one of the other identities.

But she couldn't do anything until she figured out how to get rid of him. Maybe she needed to ask him how to do that. He was the one around whom people tended to disappear.

First her.

But according to the articles she'd read, there had been others. Some members of his "family" and some of his business rivals had disappeared over the past four years. No bodies had been found, so no charges had been brought against him. But the speculation was that he was responsible for those disappearances.

She'd believed he was responsible for hers, too, blaming him for those attempts on her life that had driven her into hiding. Since he'd saved her on the roof and again in the garage, she wanted to believe she'd been wrong about him.

But what if she'd been right? Then she'd gotten into a vehicle with a killer. Was she about to go away for good?

THE FARTHER THEY traveled from the hospital, the quieter it was. No gunshots. No sirens. He'd made certain to drive away from the emergency entrance so that he wouldn't cross paths with ambulances or, worse yet, police cars. It wasn't quiet only outside, but it was eerily silent inside the vehicle, too.

Brendan glanced at the rearview mirror, his gaze going first to his son. He still couldn't believe he had a child; he was a *father*.

The boy slept, his red curls matted against the side pad of his booster seat. Drool trickled from the corner of his slightly open mouth. How had he fallen asleep so easily after so much excitement?

Adrenaline still coursed through Brendan's veins, making his pulse race and his heart pound. But maybe it wasn't just because of the gunfire and the discovery that Josie was alive and had given birth to his baby.

Maybe it was because of her. She was so close to

him that he could feel the warmth of her body. Or maybe that was just the heat of his own attraction to her. She didn't look exactly the same, but she made him feel the same. Just as before, she *made* him feel when he didn't want to feel anymore.

She leaned over the console, her shoulder brushing against his as she studied the route he was taking. Did she recognize it? She'd taken it several times over those few months they had gone out. But then that was nearly four years ago.

Four years in which she'd been living another life and apparently not alone. And not with only their son, either.

"This isn't your vehicle?" Brendan asked, unable to hold back the question any longer. It had been nagging at him since she'd said the plate wasn't registered to her.

"What?" she asked.

"You borrowed it from someone else?" Or had she taken it from a driveway they shared? Was she living with someone? A boyfriend? A husband?

And what would that man be to CJ? His *uncle?* Stepfather? Or did he just have CJ call him *Daddy?*

Had another man claimed Brendan's son as his?

"Borrowed what?" she asked, her voice sounding distracted as if she were as weary as their son. Or maybe she was wary. Fearful of telling him too much about her new life for fear that he would track her down.

"This vehicle. You borrowed it?" Maybe that was the real reason she had worried about him wrecking it—it would make someone else angry with her.

"No," she said. "It's mine."

Had someone given it to her? Gifted her a vehicle? It might have seemed extravagant to the man. But to

Stanley Jessup's daughter? She was able to buy herself a fleet of luxury vehicles on her weekly allowance.

"But it's not registered to your name?" he asked. "To your address?"

"No, it's not," she said. And her guard was back up.

His jealousy was gone. The vehicle wasn't a gift; it was registered under someone else's name and address to protect her, to prevent someone running her plates and finding where she and her son were living.

"You do usually have your guard up," he observed. "You are very careful."

"Until tonight," she murmured regretfully. "I never should have come here."

"No," he agreed. "Not if you wanted to stay in hiding."

"I *have* to stay in hiding."

"Why?" he asked.

She gasped. "I think, after tonight, it would be quite obvious why I had to…" Her voice cracked, but she cleared her throat and added, "Disappear."

Brendan nodded in sudden realization of where she had been for almost four years. "You've been in witness protection."

Her silence gave him the answer that he should have come to long ago. He was painfully familiar with witness protection. But he couldn't tell her that. Her identity might have changed, but he suspected at heart she was still a reporter. He couldn't tell her anything without the risk of it showing up in one of her father's papers or on one of his news programs.

So he kept asking the questions. "Why were you put in witness protection?"

What had she seen? What did she know? Maybe

she'd learned, in those few short months, more than he'd realized. More than he had learned in four years.

"What did you witness?" he asked.

She shrugged and her shoulder bumped against his. "Nothing that I was aware of. Nothing I could testify about."

"Then why would the marshals put you in *witness* protection?"

Her breath shuddered out, caressing his cheek. "Because someone tried to kill me."

"Was it like tonight?" he asked.

She snorted derisively. "You don't know?"

So she assumed he would know how someone had tried to kill her. But he didn't. "You were shot at back then?"

"No," she said. "The attempts were more subtle than that. A cut brake line on my car." She had driven a little sports car—too fast and too recklessly. He remembered the report of her accident. At the time he had figured her driving had caused it. She was lucky that the accident hadn't killed her. "And then there was the explosion."

"That was subtle," he scoffed. The explosion had destroyed the house she'd been staying in, as well as her "remains," so that she'd only been identifiable by DNA. "It wasn't just a ploy the marshals used to put you into witness protection?"

She shook her head and now her hair brushed his cheek. His skin tingled and heated in reaction to her maddening closeness. He should have told her to sit back and buckle up next to their son. Or pulled her over the console into the passenger's seat.

But she was closer where she was, so he said nothing.

"No," Josie replied. "Someone found the supposedly *safe* house where I was staying after the cut brake line and set the bomb to try again to kill me."

No wonder she'd gone into protection again. Faking her death might have been the only way to keep her alive. But he might have come up with another way… if she'd told him about the attempts.

But they hadn't been talking then. He'd been too furious with her when he'd discovered that she'd been duping him—only getting close for a damn exposé for her father's media organizations. Once Brendan had figured out her pen name, he'd found the stories she'd done. No one had been safe around her, not even her classmates when she'd been at boarding school and later at college.

None of her friends had been safe from her, either. Maybe that was why she'd had few when they'd met. Maybe that was why it had been so easy for her to leave everyone behind.

Including him.

Except her father. That was why she'd come to the hospital after he'd been assaulted. Perhaps they hadn't actually severed contact, as she had with Brendan— never even letting him know he'd become a father.

She probably didn't know the identity of her would-be killer or she wouldn't have had to stay in hiding all this time. But he asked anyway. "Who do you think was trying to kill you?"

She answered without hesitation and with complete certainty, "You."

Chapter Seven

Maybe Josie was as tired as her son was. Why else would she have made such an admission? Moreover, why else would she have let him drive her here—of all places?

She should have recognized the route, since her gaze had never left the road as he'd driven them away from the hospital. She had driven here so many times over those months when they had been seeing each other. She'd preferred going to his place, hoping that she would find something or overhear something the police didn't know that could have led her to a break in his father's murder investigation.

And she hadn't wanted him to find anything at her apartment that would have revealed that she was so much more than just the empty-headed heiress so many others had thought she was. Things like her journalism awards or her diploma or the scrapbook of articles she'd published under her pseudonym.

But it didn't matter that he had never found any of those things. Somehow he'd learned the truth about who she was anyway. And after the ferocious fight they'd had, the attempts on her life had begun.

"How could you think I would have tried to kill

you?" he asked, his voice a rasp in the eerie silence of the vehicle. Even CJ wasn't making any sounds as he slept so deeply and quietly.

Brendan had pulled the SUV through the wrought-iron gates of the O'Hannigan estate, but they had yet to open the car doors. They remained sealed in that tomblike silence he'd finally broken with his question.

"How could I *not* think it was you?" she asked, keeping her voice to a low whisper so that she didn't wake her son. He didn't need to know that tonight wasn't the first time a bad man had tried to hurt his mommy. Even the authorities had suspected Brendan O'Hannigan was responsible. That was why they'd offered her protection—to keep her alive to testify against him once they found evidence that he'd been behind the attempts. "Who else would want me dead?"

He turned toward her, and since she still leaned over the console, he was close. His face was just a breath away from hers. And his eyes—the same rare blue-green as her son's—were narrowed, his brow furrowed with confusion as he stared at her. "Why would *I* want you dead?"

"I lied to you. I tricked you," she said, although she doubted he needed any reminders. And given how angry he'd been with her, she shouldn't have reminded him, shouldn't have brought back all his rage and vengeance. He might forget that she was the mother of his son. Of course he had earlier mentioned those things to their son. He'd included stealing, too, although she'd stolen nothing from him but perhaps his trust.

Despite how angry he'd been, Brendan literally shrugged off her offenses, as if they were of no consequence to him. His broad shoulder rubbed against hers, making her skin tingle even beneath her sweater and jacket. "I've been lied to and tricked before," he said.

She doubted that many people would have been brave enough to take on Dennis O'Hannigan's son— the man that many people claimed was a chip off the block of evil. She still couldn't believe that she had summoned the courage. But then she'd been a different woman four years ago. She'd been an adrenaline junkie who had gotten high on the rush of getting the story. The more information she had discovered the more excited she had become. She hadn't been only brave—she'd been fearless.

Then she had become a mother, and she had learned what fear was. Now she was always afraid, afraid that her son would get sick or hurt or scared. Or that whoever had tried to kill her would track them down and hurt him.

And tonight that fear, her deepest, darkest fear, had been realized. She shuddered, chilled by the thought. But the air had grown cold inside the car now that Brendan had shut off the engine. His heavily muscled body was close and warm, but the look on his ridiculously handsome face was cold. Even colder than the air.

"And," he continued, "I never killed any of those people."

With a flash of that old fearlessness, she scoffed, "Never?" All the articles about Brendan O'Hannigan alleged otherwise. "That's not what I've heard."

"You, of all people, should know better than to believe everything you hear or read," he advised her.

Growing up the daughter of a media magnate, she'd heard the press disparaged more than she'd heard fairy tales. Fairy tales. What was a bigger lie than a fairy tale? Than a promise of happily-ever-after?

"If it's coming from a credible source, which all of my father's news outlets are, then you should believe the story," she said.

He snorted. "What makes a source *credible?*"

As the daughter of a newsman, she'd grown up instinctively knowing what a good source was. "An insider. Someone close to the story."

"An eyewitness?" He was the one scoffing now.

She doubted anyone had witnessed him committing any crime and lived to testify. She shivered again and glanced at their son. She shouldn't have put his life in the hands of a killer. But the gunman in the garage had given her no choice. Neither had Brendan.

"Even grand juries rarely issue an indictment on eyewitness testimony," he pointed out, as if familiar with the legal process. "They need evidence to bring charges."

Had he personally been brought before a grand jury? Or was he just familiar with the process from all the times district attorneys had tried to indict his father? But she knew better than to ask the questions that naturally came to her. He had never answered any of her questions before.

But he kept asking his own inquiries. "Is there any evidence that I'm a—" Brendan glanced beyond her, into the backseat where their son slept peacefully, angelically "—a bad man?"

She hadn't been able to find anything that might have proven his guilt. She'd looked hard for that evidence—not just for her story but also for herself. She'd wanted a reason not to give in to her attraction to him, a reason not to fall for him.

But when, as a journalist, she hadn't been able to come up with any cold, hard facts, she'd let herself, as a woman, fall in love with an incredibly charming and smart man. And then he'd learned the truth about her.

What was the truth about him?

BRENDAN WAITED, but she didn't answer him. Could she really believe that he was a killer? Could she really believe that he had tried to kill *her?*

Sure, he had been furious because she'd deceived him. But he'd only been so angry because he'd let himself fall for her. He'd let himself believe that she might have fallen for him, too, when she'd actually only been using him.

He wasn't the only one she'd used. There were the friends in boarding school she'd used as inside sources to get dirt on their famous parents. Then there was the Peterson kid in college with a violence and drug problem that the school had been willing to overlook to keep their star athlete. She'd used her friendship with the kid to blow the lid off that, too. Hell, her story had probably started all the subsequent exposés on college athletic programs. It had also caused the kid to kill himself.

"You really think that I'm the only one who might want you dead?" Josie Jessup had been many things but never naive.

She gasped as if shocked by his question. Or maybe offended. How the hell did she think he felt with her believing he was a killer?

He was tempted, as he'd been four years ago, to tell her the truth. But then he'd found out she was really a reporter after a story, and as mad as he'd been, he'd also been relieved that he hadn't told her anything that could have blown his assignment.

Hell, it wasn't just an assignment. It was a mission. Of justice.

She didn't care about that, though. She cared only about exposés and Pulitzers and ratings. And her father's approval.

But then maybe his mission of justice was all about his father, too. About finally getting his approval— postmortem.

"Who else would want me dead?" she asked.

"Whoever else might have found out that you wrote all those stories under the byline Jess Ley." It was a play on the name of her father, Stanley Jessup. Some people thought the old man had written the stories himself.

But Brendan had been with her the night the story on her college friend had won a national press award. And he'd seen the pride and guilt flash across her face. And, finally, he'd stopped playing a fool and really checked her out, and all his fears had been confirmed.

She sucked in a breath and that same odd mixture of pride and guilt flashed across her face. "I don't even know how you found out...."

"You gave yourself away," he said. "And anyone close to you—close to those stories—would have figured out you'd written them, too."

She shook her head in denial, and her silky hair skimmed along her jaw and across his cheek. No matter how much she'd changed her appearance, she was still beautiful, still appealing.

He wanted to touch her hair. To touch her face...

But he doubted she would welcome the hands of the man she thought was her would-be killer. "If I wanted you dead, I wouldn't have helped you tonight," he pointed out.

She glanced back at their sleeping son. "You did it for him. You know what it's like to grow up without a mother."

So did she. That was something that had connected them, something they'd had in common in lives that had been so disparate. They'd understood each other intimately—emotionally and physically.

He shook his head, trying to throw off those memories and the connection with her that had him wanting her despite her lies and subterfuge.

"That was sloppy tonight and dangerous," he said, dispassionately critiquing the would-be assassins, "trying to carry off a hit in a hospital."

His father and his enemies would have been indicted long ago if they had operated their businesses as sloppily. Whoever had hired the assassins had not gotten their money's worth.

Neither had the U.S. Marshals. Like the local authorities, they must have been so desperate to pin something on him that they'd taken her word that he was behind the attempts on her life. They'd put her into protection and worried about finding evidence later. Like her, they had never come up with any. No reason to charge him.

If only they knew the truth...

But the people who knew it had been kept to a minimum—to protect his life and the lives of those around him. So it might not have been his fault that someone had tried to kill Josie, yet he felt responsible.

JOSIE REALIZED THAT he was right. Even if he hadn't been with her tonight, in the line of fire on the roof and in the garage, it was possible that he had nothing to do with the attempts on her life.

Brendan O'Hannigan was never sloppy.

If he was, there would have been evidence against him and charges brought before a grand jury that would have elicited an indictment. No. Brendan O'Hannigan was anything but sloppy. He was usually ruthlessly controlled—except in bed. With her caresses and her kisses, she had made him lose control.

And that one day that had her shivering in remembrance, she'd made him lose his temper. The media hadn't been wrong about her being spoiled. Her father had never so much as raised his voice to her. So Brendan's cold fury had frightened her.

If only it had killed her attraction to him, as he had tried to kill her. Not tonight, though. She believed he hadn't been behind the attempt at the hospital.

If he'd wanted her gone, he would have brought her someplace private. Someplace remote. Where no one could witness what he did to her.

Someplace like the O'Hannigan estate.

"You're cold," he said. As close as they were he must have felt her shiver. And the windows were also steaming up on the inside and beginning to ice on the outside. It was a cold spring, the temperature dropping low at night.

And it was late.

Too late?

"Let's go inside," he said.

It would be too late for her if she went inside the mansion with him. She still clutched her purse, her hand inside and still wrapped around her cell phone—the special one she used only to call Charlotte. But she released her grip on it.

It wouldn't help her against the immediate threat he posed. She didn't even know where Charlotte was, let alone if she could reach her in time to help.

"I'll get CJ," he offered as he opened the driver's door. But she hurried out the back door, stepping between him and their sleeping son.

"No," she said.

"He's getting cold out here."

Brendan tried to reach around her, but she pushed him back with her body, pressing it up against his. Her pulse leaped in reaction to his closeness.

"You can't bring him inside," she said, "not until you make sure it's safe."

He gestured toward the high wrought-iron fence encircling the estate. "The place is a fortress."

"You don't live here alone," she said.

"You really shouldn't believe everything you read," he said.

So obviously if there had been something in the news about a live-in girlfriend, it hadn't been from a credible source. Despite her fear of him, she felt a flash of relief.

"You don't take care of this place yourself," she pointed out. "You have live-in staff."

He nodded in agreement and leaned closer, trying to reach around her. "And I know and trust every one of them."

She clicked her tongue against her teeth in admonishment. "You should know that you can't trust anyone."

He stared at her and gave a sharp nod of agreement before stepping back. "You're right."

She held in a sigh of relief, especially as he continued to stare at her. Then he reached inside the open driver's door and pulled out the keys. Obviously she was the one he did not trust—not to drive off without him. He knew her too well.

"I'll check it out." He slid the keys into his suit pocket. "And come back for you."

With a soft click, she closed the back door. "I'll go with you."

As they headed up the brick walk toward the front door, she reached inside her bag for the can of mace. She would spray it at him and retrieve the keys while he was coughing and sputtering.

She could get away from him. She could protect her son and herself.

"Remember the first time you walked up this path with me?" Brendan asked, his deep voice a warm rasp in the cold.

She shivered as a tingle of attraction chased up her spine. Their fingers had been entwined that night. They had been holding hands since dinner at a candlelit restaurant.

"I teased you about playing the gentleman," he reminisced. "And you said that you were no gentleman because you just wanted to get me alone."

Her face heated as she remembered what a brazen flirt she'd been. But she'd acted that way only with him. And it hadn't been just for the story. It had been for the way his gorgeous eyes had twinkled with excitement and attraction. And it had been for the rush of her pulse.

Brendan chuckled but his voice was as cold as the night air. "You really just wanted to get inside."

That wasn't the situation tonight. Inside his house, with its thick brick walls and leaded-glass windows to hold in her screams, was the last place Josie wanted to be. Maybe he hadn't been a bad man four years ago, but he'd only just begun taking over his father's business then. Now that business was his. And he'd been leaving his own legacy of missing bodies.

"You just wanted to search my stuff," he angrily continued, "see what secrets you could find to shout out to the rest of the world through one of your father's publications."

"You're so bitter over my misleading you," she remarked. "Can't you see why I would think you're the one who wants me dead?"

He sighed and dragged out a ring of keys from his pants pocket. She recognized them because she'd tried so often to get them away from him—so she could make copies, so she could come and go at will in his house, business and offices.

"If you would realize why I am so bitter," he said, "you would also understand why the last thing I want is for you to be gone."

He turned away from the door and stared down at her, as he had that first night he'd brought her home with him. His pupils had swallowed the blue-green irises then, as they did now. "I wanted you with me that night…and all the nights that followed."

There was that charm that had given her hope that he was really a good man. That charm had distracted and disarmed her before.

But she hadn't had CJ to worry about and protect then. So now she kept her hand wrapped tightly around the can of mace. And when he lowered his head toward hers, she started to pull it from her purse.

But then his lips touched hers, brushing softly across them. And her breath caught as passion knocked her down as forcefully as he had earlier in the parking garage.

He had saved her tonight. He had saved her and her son. And reminding herself of that allowed her to kiss him back. For just a moment though…

Because he pulled away and turned back toward the door. And she did what she should have done as he'd lowered his head—she pulled out the can of mace and lifted it toward him.

Then she smelled it. The odor lay heavy on the cold air, drifting beneath the door of the house. She dragged in a deep breath to double-check.

Maybe she was just imagining it, as she had so often the past four years, waking in the middle of the night shaking with fear. She had to check the stove and the furnace and the water heater.

And though she never found a leak, she never squelched those fears. That this time no one would notice the bomb before it exploded.

This time the fire wouldn't eat an empty house. It would eat hers, with her and CJ trapped inside. But this wasn't her house.

It was Brendan's, and he was sliding his key into the lock. Would it be the lock clicking or the turning of the knob that would ignite the explosion?

She dropped the damn can and reached for him, screaming as her nightmare became a fiery reality.

Chapter Eight

Flames illuminated the night, licking high into the black sky. The boy was screaming. Despite the ringing in his ears, Brendan could hear him, and his heart clutched with sympathy for the toddler's fear.

He could hear the fire trucks, too, their sirens whining in the distance. Ambulances and police cars probably followed or led them—he couldn't tell the difference between the sirens.

Despite the slight shaking in his legs, he pressed harder on the accelerator, widening the distance between Josie's little white SUV and the fiery remains of the mansion where he'd grown up.

It had never been home, though. That was why he'd run away when he was fifteen and why he'd intended never to return. If not for feeling that he owed his father justice, he would have never come back.

"Are—are you sure you want to leave?" Josie stammered, wincing as if her own voice hurt her ears. She was in the front seat but leaning into the back this time, her hand squeezing one of their son's flailing fists. She'd been murmuring softly to the boy, trying to calm him down since they'd jumped back into the vehicle and taken off.

The poor kid had been through so much tonight, it was no wonder he'd gotten hysterical, especially over how violently he'd been awakened from his nap.

"Are you sure?" Josie prodded Brendan for an answer, as she always had.

He replied, this time with complete honesty, "I have no reason to stay."

"But your staff…"

Wouldn't have survived that explosion. Nothing would have. If he hadn't noticed the smell before he'd turned that key, if Josie hadn't clutched his arms…

They would have been right next to the house when a staff member inside, who must have noticed the key rattling in the door, had opened it for them and unknowing set off the bomb. Instead he and Josie had been running for the SUV, for their son, when the bomb exploded. The force of it had knocked them to the ground and rocked her vehicle.

"Are you all right?" he asked again.

She'd jumped right up and continued to run, not stopping until she'd reached their screaming son. The explosion had not only awakened but terrified him. Or maybe he felt the fear that had her trembling uncontrollably.

She jerked her chin in an impatient nod. "Yes, I—I'm okay."

"Maybe we should have stayed," he admitted. But his first instinct had been to get the hell away in case the bomber had hung around to finish the job if the explosion hadn't killed them.

While Brendan wished he could soothe his son's fears, his first priority was to keep the boy and his mother safe. And healthy. "We should have you checked out."

She shook her head. "Nobody can see me, in case they recognize me like you did. And those other men…" She shuddered, probably as she remembered the ordeal those men had put her and CJ through. "We can't go back to the hospital anyway."

"There are urgent-care facilities that are open all night," he reminded her. Maybe her new location wasn't near a big city and she'd forgotten the amenities and conveniences of one.

She shook her head. "But someone there might realize we were at this explosion…" The smell of smoke had permeated the car and probably her hair. "And they might call the police," she said. "Or the media."

He nearly grinned at the irony of her wanting to avoid the press.

"And it's not necessary," she said, dismissing his concerns. "I'm okay."

He glanced toward the backseat. CJ's screams had subsided to hiccups and sniffles. Brendan's heart ached with the boy's pain and fear. "What about our son?"

"He's scared," Josie explained. And from the way she kept trembling, the little boy wasn't the only one.

"It's okay," she assured the child, and perhaps she was assuring herself, too. "We're getting far away from the fire."

Not so far that the glow of the fire wasn't still visible in the rearview mirror, along with the billows of black smoke darkening the sky even more.

"It won't hurt us," she said. "It won't hurt us.…"

"We're going someplace very safe," Brendan said, "where no bad men can find us."

He shouldn't have brought them back to the mansion. But the place was usually like a fortress, so he hadn't thought any outside threats would be able to get to them. He hadn't realized that the greatest danger was already inside those gates. Hell, inside those brick walls. Had one of his men—one of the O'Hannigan family—set the bomb?

He'd been trying to convince her that he'd had nothing to do with the attempts on her life, years ago or recently. And personally, he hadn't. But that didn't mean he still wasn't responsible...because of who he was.

As if she'd been reading his mind, she softly remarked, "No place, with you, is going to be safe for us."

But he wasn't only the head of a mob organization. He had another life, but, regrettably, that one was probably even more dangerous.

"WHERE ARE WE?" she asked, pitching her voice to a low whisper—and not just because CJ slept peacefully now in his father's arms, but also because the big brick building was eerily silent.

There had been other vehicles inside the fenced and gated parking lot when they'd arrived. But few lights had glowed in the windows of what looked like an apartment complex. Of course everyone could have been sleeping. But when Brendan had entered a special code to open the doors, the lobby inside looked more commercial than residential.

Was this an office building?

He'd also needed a code to open the elevator doors and a key to turn it on. Fortunately, he'd retrieved his keys from the lock at the mansion...just before the house had exploded.

Her ears had finally stopped ringing. Still, she heard nothing but their footsteps on the terrazzo as they walked down the hallway of the floor on which he'd stopped the elevator. He'd been doing everything with one hand, his arms wrapped tight around their sleeping son.

At the hospital she'd suspected that Brendan had held their son so that she wouldn't try to escape with him. Now he held him almost reverently, as if he was scared that he'd nearly lost him in the explosion.

If he had parked closer to the house…

She shuddered to think what could have happened to her son.

"It'll be warmer inside," Brendan assured her, obviously misinterpreting her shudder as a shiver.

She actually was cold. The building wasn't especially well heated.

"Inside what? Where are we?" she asked, repeating her earlier question. When he'd told her to grab her overnight bag, which she had slung over her shoulder along with her purse, she'd thought he was bringing them to a hotel. But this building was nothing like any hotel at which she'd ever stayed, as Josie Jessup or as JJ Brandt.

"This is my apartment," he said as he stopped outside a tall metal door.

"Apartment? But you had the mansion…" And this building was farther from the city than the house had been, farther from the businesses rumored to be owned or run by the O'Hannigan family. But maybe that was why he'd wanted it—to be able to get away from all the responsibilities he'd inherited.

"I already had this place before I inherited the house from my father," he explained as he shoved the key into the lock.

She wanted to grab her son and run. But she recognized she could just be having a panic attack, like the ones the nightmares brought on when they awakened her in a cold sweat. And those panic attacks, when she ran around checking the house for gas leaks, scared CJ so much that she would rather spare him having to deal with her hysteria tonight.

So she just grabbed Brendan's hand, stilling it before he could turn the key. "We can't stay here!"

Panic rushed up on her, and she dragged in a deep breath to control it and to check the air for that telltale odor. She smelled smoke on them, but it was undoubtedly from the earlier explosion. "Someone could remember you lived here and find us."

"No. It's safe here," he said. "There's no bomb."

"Bu—"

Rejecting her statement before he even heard it, he shook his head. "Nobody knows where I was living before I showed up at my father's funeral."

Some had suspected he hadn't even been alive; they'd thought that instead of running away, he might have been murdered, like they believed his mother was. Some had refused to believe that he was his father's son, despite his having his father's eyes. The same eyes that her son had.

His stepmother had still demanded a DNA test before she had stopped fighting for control of her dead husband's estate. She hadn't stopped slinging the accusations though. She had obviously been the source of so many of the stories about him, such as the one that Brendan had killed his father for vengeance and money. She had even talked to Josie back then to warn her away from a dangerous man.

Given the battle with his stepmother and the constant media attention, Josie could understand that Brendan would need a quiet place to get away from it all.

And it might have occurred to someone else that he would need such a place.

"But they can find out." Somehow, someone had found out she was alive.

"They didn't," he assured her. "It's safe." And despite her nails digging into the back of his hand, he turned the key.

She held her breath, but nothing happened. Then he turned the knob. And still nothing happened, even as the door opened slightly. She expelled a shaky sigh, but she was still tense, still scared.

Perhaps to reassure her even more, he added, "My name's not on the lease."

Just as her name was not on the title of her vehicle or the deed to her house...

Did Brendan O'Hannigan have other identities as well? But why? What was he hiding?

All those years ago she had suspected plenty and she had dug deep, but had found nothing. *She* had never found this place. Back then she would have been elated if he'd brought her here, since he was more likely to keep his secrets in a clandestine location. But when he pushed the door all the way open and stepped back for her to enter, she hesitated.

There was no gas. No bomb. No fire. Nothing to stop her from stepping inside but her own instincts.

"You lost your can of mace," he said. "You can't spray me in the face like you intended."

She gasped in surprise that he'd realized her intentions back at the mansion. "Why didn't you take it from me?"

He shrugged. "By the time I noticed you held it, I was distracted."

He must have smelled the gas, too.

"And then you were saving me instead of hurting me," he reminded her with a smile. "If you were really afraid of me, if you really wanted me gone from your life, you could have just let me blow up."

She glanced down at the child he held so tenderly in his arms. "I—I couldn't do that."

No matter how much she might fear him, she didn't hate him. She didn't want him dead.

"Why?" he asked, his eyes intense as he stared at her over the child in his arms.

"I—I…"

Her purse vibrated, the cell phone inside silently ringing.

"You lost the mace but you didn't lose your phone," he remarked. "You can answer it."

She fumbled inside and pulled out the phone. *That* phone, so it had to be Charlotte. Earlier Josie had wanted desperately to talk to the former marshal. But now she hesitated, as she paused outside his secret place.

"You need to talk to your handler," Brendan advised. "Tell him—"

"Her," she automatically corrected him. But she didn't add that technically she no longer had a handler. When the marshals had failed to find any evidence of his involvement in the attempts on her life, they'd determined they no longer needed to protect her. "Her name is Charlotte Green." Despite neither of them really being associated with the marshals any longer, the woman continued to protect Josie—if only from afar.

"Tell her that you're safe," he said. And as if to give her privacy, he carried their son across the threshold and inside the apartment.

Josie followed him with her gaze but not her body. She hesitated just inside the doorway, but finally she clicked the talk button on the phone. "Charlotte?"

"JJ, I've been so worried about you!" the other woman exclaimed.

That made two of them. But Josie hadn't been worried about just herself. She watched Brendan lay their child on a wide, low sofa. It was a darker shade of gray than the walls and cement floor. But the whole place was monochromatic, which was just different shades of drab to her.

Despite what he'd said, the space didn't look much like an apartment and nothing like a home. As if worried that the boy would roll off the couch and strike the floor, Brendan laid down pillows next to him. He might have just discovered that he was a father, but he had good paternal instincts. He was a natural protector.

And no matter what she'd read or suspected about him, Josie had actually always felt safe with him. Protected. Despite thinking that she should have feared him or at least not trusted him, she'd struggled to come up with a specific reason why. She had no proof that he'd ever tried to hurt her.

Or anyone else.

Maybe all those stories about him had only been stories—told by a bitter woman who'd been disinherited by a heartless and unpitying man.

"JJ?" the female voice emanated from her phone as Charlotte prodded her for a reply.

"I'm okay," she assured the former marshal and current friend.

"And CJ?" Charlotte asked after the boy who'd been named for her.

She had been in the delivery room, holding Josie's

hand, offering her support and encouragement. She hadn't just relocated Josie and left her. Even after she'd left the U.S. Marshals, she had remained her friend.

But the past six months Charlotte hadn't called or emailed, hadn't checked in with Josie at all, almost as if she'd forgotten about her.

"Is CJ okay?" Charlotte asked again, her voice cracking with concern for her godson.

"He had a scare," Josie replied, "but he's safe." While she wasn't entirely sure how safe she really was with him, she had no doubt that Brendan would protect his son.

The other woman cursed. "They found you? That was part of the reason I haven't been calling."

Betrayal struck Josie with all the force of one of the bullets fired at her that evening. "You knew someone was looking for me?"

If Josie had had any idea, she wouldn't have risked bringing CJ to meet his grandfather. Maybe Josie had trusted the wrong person all these years....

"I only just found that out a few weeks ago," Charlotte explained. "Before that I had been unreachable for six months."

"Unreachable?" Her journalistic instincts told her there was more to the story, and Josie wanted to know all of it. "Why were you unreachable?"

"Because I was kidnapped."

She gasped. "Kidnapped?"

"Yes," Charlotte replied, and the phone rattled as if she'd shuddered. "I was kidnapped and held in a place you know about. You mentioned it to Gabby."

"Serenity House?" It was the private psychiatric hospital where Josie's former student had been killed pursuing the story she'd suggested to him. She had known there were suspicious things happening there. She just hadn't imagined how dangerous a place it was. Guilt churned in her stomach; maybe Brendan had had a good reason for being so angry with her. Her stories, even the ones she hadn't personally covered, always caused problems—sometimes even costing lives.

"I'm fine now," Charlotte assured her. "And so is Gabby."

"Was she there, too?" Princess Gabriella St. Pierre was Charlotte's sister and Josie's friend. Josie had gotten to know her over the years through emails and phone calls.

"No, but she was in danger, too," Charlotte replied.

And Josie felt even guiltier for doubting her friend. "No wonder I haven't heard from either of you." They'd been busy, as she had just been, trying to stay alive.

"We think we've found all the threats to our lives," Charlotte said. "But in the process, we found a threat to yours. My former partner—"

Josie shuddered as she remembered the creepy gray-haired guy who had called himself Trigger. Because Josie hadn't felt safe around him, Charlotte had made certain that he wasn't aware of where she had been relocated.

"He was trying to find out where you are."

She hadn't liked or trusted the older marshal, and apparently her instincts had been right. "Why?"

Charlotte paused a moment before replying, "I think someone paid him to learn your whereabouts."

"Who? Did he tell you?"

"No, Whit was forced to kill him to protect Aaron."

Whit and his friend Aaron had once protected Josie. They were the private bodyguards her father had hired after the accident caused by the cut brake lines. But then Whit had discovered the bomb and involved the marshals. He had helped Charlotte stage Josie's death and relocate her. But no one had wanted to put Aaron in the position of lying to her grieving father, so he'd been left thinking he had failed a client. He and Whit had dissolved their security business and their friendship and had gone their separate ways until Charlotte had brought them back together to protect the king of St. Pierre.

"I would have called and warned you immediately," the former marshal said, "but I didn't want to risk my phone being tapped and leading them right to you."

So something must have happened for her to risk it. "Why have you called now?"

"I saw the news about your father," Charlotte said, her voice soft with sympathy. She hadn't understood how close Josie had been to her father, but she'd commiserated with her having to hurt him when she'd faked her death. "I wanted to warn you that it's obviously a ploy to bring you out of hiding."

"Obviously," Josie agreed.

Charlotte gasped. "You went?"

"It was a trap," Josie said, stating the obvious. "But we're fine now." Or so she hoped. "But please check on my dad." The man who had fired at them in the garage was probably the one Brendan had left alive on the sixth floor. He could have gone back to her father's room. "Make sure my dad is okay. Make sure he's safe."

"I already followed up with the hospital," she said. "He's recovering. He'll be fine. And I think he'll stay fine as long as you stay away from him."

Pain clutched Josie's heart. But she couldn't argue

with her friend. She never should have risked going
to the hospital.

"You're in extreme danger," Charlotte warned her.
"Whoever's after you won't stop now that they know
you're alive."

They wouldn't stop until she was dead for real.

"You have no idea who it could be?" Josie asked.
She'd never wanted the facts more than she did now.

"It has to be someone with money," Charlotte said,
"to pay off a U.S. marshal."

Josie shivered. It wasn't any warmer in Brendan's
apartment than it was in the hall. But even if it had
been, her blood still would have run cold. "And hire
several assassins."

Charlotte gasped. "Several?"

"At least three," she replied. "More if you count
whoever set the bomb."

"Bomb!" Charlotte's voice cracked on the excla-
mation.

"We're fine," Josie reminded her. "But whoever's
after me must have deep pockets."

"It's probably O'Hannigan," Charlotte suggested.
And she'd no sooner uttered his name than the phone
was snapped from Josie's hand.

Brendan had it now, pressed to his ear, as the former U.S. marshal named him as suspect number one.
Charlotte hadn't been wrong about anything else. She
probably wasn't wrong about this, either.

Chapter Nine

"If you hurt her, I will track you down—"

He chuckled at the marshal's vitriolic threat. And *he* had been accused of getting too personally involved in his job.

Of course, this time he had. But then no one else had been able to take on the assignment. Maybe that was why his father had left him everything. Because Dennis O'Hannigan had known that if anyone ever dared to murder him, Brendan would be the only person capable of bringing his killer to justice.

He couldn't share any of this with Josie though, not with the risk that she would go public with the information. Risk? Hell, certainty. It would be the story of her career. So he stepped inside his den and closed the door behind him, leaving her standing over their sleeping son.

"I'll be easy to find," he assured the marshal. "And I suspect that if anyone gets hurt in my involvement with Josie, it'll be me." Just like last time. And he began to explain to her why he couldn't trust the journalist but why she could trust him.

Of course the marshal was no fool and asked for names and numbers to verify his story. Her thorough-

ness gave him comfort that she'd been the one protecting Josie all these years. But then she made an
admission of her own—that she was no longer on the
job.

"What the hell!" he cursed, wishing now that he'd
checked her out before he'd told her what so few other
people knew. "I thought you had clearance—"

"I do. Through my current security detail, I still
have all my clearances and contacts," she assured him.
"But as you know, that doesn't mean I couldn't be corrupted like so many others have been."

She was obviously suggesting that he may have
been.

"Call those numbers," he urged her.

"I will," she promised. "I will also keep protecting
Josie. I can't trust anyone else. That's why I insisted
she stay in hiding even after the marshals deemed she
wasn't really a witness and withdrew their protection.
I had to make certain she stayed safe."

"Why?" he wondered. Then he realized why she'd
threatened him, why she cared so much: Josie had become her friend. Hell, the *C* of CJ's name, for Charles,
was probably for her.

But her answer surprised him when she replied,
"Because of you."

"Because of me?"

"You're part of a powerful family," she reminded
him needlessly. "You have unlimited resources of both
money and manpower. Josie said several gunmen came
after her tonight and someone had set a bomb."

"And those gunmen were shooting at me, too," he
said. "And the bomb was set at *my* house."

She sucked in an audible breath of shock.

"I would *never* hurt her," Brendan promised. "I can't

believe she thought that I would." After everything they'd shared...

He hadn't given her a declaration of his feelings, but he had shown her over and over how he felt. Despite his tough assignment, he'd let her distract him. Of course his superiors had authorized it, saying his having a relationship helped establish his cover—that he would have been more suspicious had he remained on his own.

But hell, he'd been on his own most of his life. He was used to that.

"I protected her and CJ tonight," he said. "Hell, I would have died for her—for them." He had wound up having to kill for them instead.

Silence followed his vehement declaration. It lasted so long that he thought he might have lost the connection. Maybe the marshal had hung up on him.

Then she finally spoke again. "I think I know why you wouldn't hurt her, and it has nothing to do with what you've just told me and everything to do with what you *haven't* told me."

Maybe the cell connection was bad, because the woman seemed to make no sense. "What?"

"You love her."

He'd thought so. Once. But then he'd learned the truth about her and why she'd tried so hard to get close to him. "I can't love someone I can't trust."

She laughed now. "I thought that once, too."

"But you fell anyway?"

"No," she said. "My husband did—once Aaron understood my reasons for keeping things from him. He realized that I was only doing my job. Josie will understand when you tell her the truth."

"I can't trust her with the truth," he said.

Charlotte's sigh rattled the phone. "Then you won't be able to make her trust you, either."

"Tell her that she can," Brendan implored her. "She trusts you."

"For a good reason," Charlotte said. "I tell her the truth. And I need to call these people you've given me numbers for and check out your story. Once I do, I'll call Josie back, but I'm not sure she'll take my word without proof. She's been afraid of you for a long time."

Brendan's heart clutched at the thought of the woman he'd once loved living in fear of him, thinking that he would kill her if he found out she was still alive. Maybe he was more like his old man than he'd realized. He clicked off the cell phone and opened the door to his den, half expecting to find Josie listening outside.

But the apartment was eerily silent. Charlotte was right. He couldn't make Josie trust him. And now he didn't have the chance because she'd taken their son and run.

Josie wasn't as strong as Brendan. She couldn't carry her son, her purse and the backpack with their overnight clothes and toys, and struggle with the special locks and security panels. So she had awakened CJ for an impromptu game of hide-and-seek.

But she hoped Brendan never found them.

CJ was too tired to play though. The poor child had had such a traumatic day that he was physically and emotionally exhausted. He leaned heavily against Josie's legs, nearly knocking her over as she stood near the elevator panel.

She realized that even if she had picked up the code Brendan had punched in, she didn't have the key to work the elevator. He had shoved it back into his pocket.

So she abandoned the elevator and searched for the door to a stairwell. But they were all tall metal doors that looked the same. They could have been apartments. If this place were really an apartment complex...

Its austereness had Josie imagining what Serenity House must have been like. It had her feeling the horror that Charlotte must have felt when she'd been held hostage for six months.

Did Brendan intend to keep her here that long? Longer?

She kept pressing on doors but none of them opened. All were locked to keep her out. Or to keep other people inside?

"Mommy, I wanna go to bed," CJ whined.

"I know, sweetheart." Josie was exhausted, too. She wished she were under the covers of her soft bed and that this whole night had been a horrible nightmare.

But the smoke smell clung to her clothes and hair, proving that it hadn't been a dream. It had happened— every horrible moment of it had been real. She lifted the sleepy child in her arms. For once he didn't protest being carried but laid his head on her shoulder.

"I'm scared, Mommy."

"I know." *Me, too.* But she couldn't make that admission to him. She had to stay strong for them both.

"I wanna go home!"

Me, too. Finally one of the doors opened, and she nearly pitched forward, down the stairs. She'd found the stairwell. Her feet struck each step with an echoing thud as she hurried down. Her arms ached from the weight of the child she carried, and her legs began to tremble in exhaustion.

A crack of metal echoed through the stairwell as a door opened with such force it must have slammed against the wall. Then footsteps, heavier than hers, rang out as someone ran down the steps above her. She quickened her pace. But with CJ in her arms, she couldn't go too fast and risk tumbling down the stairs with him.

Finally she reached the bottom and pushed open the door to the lobby. There was no desk. No security. Nothing but the door with its security lock. She pressed against the outside doors, but they wouldn't open.

Footsteps crossed the lobby behind her. With a sigh of resignation, she turned to face Brendan.

"ARE YOU GOING to stop running from me now?" he asked as she stepped from his den and rejoined him and CJ in the living room. He hated seeing that look on her face, the one he'd seen at the hospital and again in the lobby—that mixture of fear and dread swirling in her smoky-green eyes.

Because of his last name, a lot of people looked at him with fear and he'd learned to not let it bother him. But he didn't want her or their son looking at him that way.

While she'd been on the phone with the former marshal, he had made progress with CJ. Before she'd made her call, she'd given the boy a bath and changed him into his pajamas for bed. So Brendan had told the child a bedside story that his mother used to tell him. The story had lulled the boy to sleep in his arms.

Of course the kid had been totally exhausted, too. But even as tired as he'd been, CJ had kept fighting to keep his eyes open and watchful of Brendan. If a three-year-old couldn't trust him, he probably had no hope of getting a woman, who'd actually witnessed him losing his temper, to trust him.

He eased CJ from his arms onto the couch and then stood up to face the boy's mother. His son's mother. She'd been carrying his baby when she'd disappeared. If only she could have trusted him then...

Obviously still distrustful, Josie narrowed her eyes with suspicion. "What did you tell Charlotte?"

He expelled a quick breath of relief. He hadn't known if he could trust the former U.S. marshal to keep his secrets. Out of professional courtesy she should have. But then, obviously, there wasn't always any communication or respect between the different agencies. And she was no longer with the marshals.

Unable to suppress a slight grin, he innocently asked, "What do you mean?"

She moved her hand, beckoning him inside the den with her so that they wouldn't awaken the child. At this point, Brendan wasn't sure anything—even another explosion—could wake the exhausted boy. But he stepped away from the couch and joined her.

She closed the door behind her and leaned against it with her hands wrapped around the handle, as if she might need to make a quick getaway. After her last attempt, she should have realized she wouldn't easily escape this complex.

He should have brought her and his son here immediately. But since she'd already been in witness protection, he'd worried that she might recognize a "safe" house and question, as she questioned everything, why he had access to one.

"You know what I mean," she said, her voice sharp

with impatience. "What did you say to make Charlotte Green trust you?"

The truth. But that wasn't something with which he could trust Stanley Jessup's daughter. He shrugged as if he wasn't sure. "What I told her doesn't really matter. I think it would take a lot more to make you trust me than her."

"True." She nodded in agreement. "Because I know you better than Charlotte does."

Images flashed through his mind, of how she knew him. She knew how to kiss him and touch him to make him lose control. She knew how to make love with him so that he forgot all his responsibilities and worries, so that he thought only of her. And even during all the years she was gone, he'd thought of her. He'd mourned her.

He stepped closer so that she pressed her back against the door. He only had to lean in a few more inches to close the distance between them, to press his body against hers, to show her that she still got to him, that he still wanted her.

His voice was husky with desire when he challenged, "Do you?"

Her pupils darkened as she stared up at him and her voice was husky as she replied, "You know I do."

Were those images of their entwined naked bodies running through her mind, too? Was she remembering how it felt when he was inside her, as close as two people could get?

She cleared her throat and emphatically added, "I know you."

"No." He shook his head. "If you did, you would have known I wasn't the one who tried to kill you three years ago."

"But you were so angry with me...."

"I was," he agreed. "You were lying to me and tricking me."

"But I didn't steal from you." She defended herself from what he'd told their son earlier.

She had stolen from him; she just didn't know it. She'd stolen his heart.

But he just shrugged. "My trust…"

"I guess that went both ways," she said.

"You never trusted me," he pointed out. "Or you would have known you wouldn't find the story you were after, that I'm not the man my father was."

She leaned wearily against the door, as if she were much older than she was. "I never found the story," she agreed. "And I gave up so much for it."

She had given up the only life she'd known. Her home. Her family. Brendan could relate to that loss.

Then a small smile curved her lips and she added, "But I got the most important thing in my life."

"Our son?"

She nodded. "That's why I have to be careful who I trust. It's why I have to leave here."

"You're safe here," he assured her. Only people who knew what he really was knew about this place. Until tonight, when he'd taken her here.

She shook her head. "Not here. CJ and I need to go home. We've been safe there. I know I can keep him safe."

He appreciated that she was a protective mother. "You don't have to do that alone anymore."

"I haven't," she said. "I had Charlotte. She was even in the delivery room with me."

That was why Josie had named their son after the U.S. marshal.

"She's too far away to help you now," he pointed out. "That's why she told you to—" he stepped closer and touched her face, tipping her chin up so she would meet his gaze "—let me."

She stared up at him, her eyes wide as if she were searching. For what?

Goodness? Honor?

He wasn't certain she would find them no matter how hard she looked. In his quest for justice for his father, he had had to bury deep any signs of human decency—at least when he was handling business. When he'd been with her, he'd let down his guard. He'd been himself even though he hadn't told her who he was.

"What would I have to say to you," he asked, "to make you trust me?"

"Whatever you told Charlotte," she said. "Tell me what you told her."

He shook his head. "I can't trust you with that information."

She jerked her chin from his hand as if unable to bear his touch any longer. "But you expect me to trust *you*—not with just my life, but CJ's, too."

She had a point. But he'd worked so long, given up so much.

If only she hadn't lied to him…

He flinched over her disdainful tone. "Why would I be more untrustworthy than anyone else?"

"Like you don't know why," she said.

"Because of who I am?"

"Because of *what* you are."

Charlotte had definitely not told her anything that he had shared with the former U.S. marshal.

"What am I?"

"I never got my story about you," she said, "because

you never answered my questions. But I need you to answer at least one if you expect me to stay here."

He nodded in agreement. "I'll answer one," he replied. "But how do you know I'll tell you the truth?"

"Swear on your mother's grave."

He wouldn't need to tell her the truth then, because his mother wasn't dead. Like everyone else, he had believed she'd been murdered when he was just a kid. But she was actually the first person he'd known who'd entered witness protection. The marshals hadn't let her take him along, forcing her to leave a child behind with a man many had considered a psychopath as well as her killer.

If Brendan hadn't run away when he was fifteen, he might have never learned the truth about either of his parents.

"Do you swear?" she prodded him. "Will you answer me honestly?"

"Yes," he agreed, and hoped like hell he wouldn't have to lie to her. But no matter what he'd promised her, he couldn't tell her what he really was. "What do you want to know?"

"Before tonight, before those men on the roof—" she shuddered as though remembering the blood and the gunshots "—have you killed anyone else?"

He had promised her the truth, so he answered truthfully. "Yes."

Chapter Ten

He was a killer. Maybe she should have believed everything she had heard and read about him—even the unsubstantiated stories.

"But just like tonight, it was in self-defense," he explained, his deep voice vibrating with earnestness and regret, as though killing hadn't been easy for him. "I have only killed when there's been no other option, when it's been that person's life or mine, or the life of an innocent person." He flinched as if reliving some of those moments. "Like you or our son."

"You've been in these life-and-death situations before tonight," she said.

He nodded.

"How many times?" she asked. "Twice? Three times?"

"I agreed to answer only one question," he reminded her.

She swallowed hard, choking on the panic she felt just thinking of all the times he'd been in danger, all the times he could have died. "And you were trying to say I was responsible for what happened tonight. And for the attempts on my life years ago. You're the one leading the dangerous life."

He stepped back from her and sighed. "You're right."

She appealed to him. "So you need to let us leave, to let me go home."

"I can't do that."

"How can you expect to keep me and CJ safe when you're always fighting for your own life?" she asked.

He stripped off his suit jacket. Despite the crazy night they'd had, it was barely wrinkled, but he carelessly dropped it on the floor. And in doing so, he revealed the holsters strapped across his broad shoulders, a gun under each heavily muscled arm. She'd already known about the concealed weapons; she'd already seen all of his guns. Then he reached up and pulled one of those guns from its holster and pointed it toward her.

She gasped and stepped back, but she was already against the door and had no place else to go. Unless she opened the door, but then her son might see that the man he didn't even realize yet was his father was holding a gun on his mother.

"What—what are you doing?" she stammered. "I—I thought you wanted me to trust you."

"That's why I'm giving you this gun," he said. The handle, not the barrel, was pointed toward her. "Take it."

She shook her head. "No."

"Don't you know how to shoot one?"

"Charlotte taught me." The marshal had taken her to the shooting range over and over again until Josie had gotten good at it. "She tried to give me one, too. But I didn't want it."

"You don't like guns?"

Until tonight, when they'd been shooting at her, Josie hadn't had any particular aversion to firearms. "I don't want one in the same house with CJ."

"You can lock it up," Brendan said, "to make sure he doesn't get to it."

"So if I take this gun, you'll let us leave?" she asked, reaching for it. The metal was cold to the touch and heavy across her palms. She identified the safety, grateful it was engaged.

He shook his head. "Until we find out who's trying to kill you, I can't let you or our son out of my sight."

"Then why give me this?"

"So you'll trust me," he said. "If I wanted to hurt you, I wouldn't give you a gun to protect yourself."

She expelled a ragged sigh, letting all her doubts and fears of Brendan go with the breath from her lungs. A bad man wouldn't have given her the means to defend herself from him. Had she been wrong about him all these years?

Had she kept him from his son for no reason?

Guilt descended on her, bowing her shoulders with the heavy burden of it she already carried. For her student, and for that other young man's death she'd inadvertently caused. She hadn't needed Brendan to remind her that there were other people with reason to want to hurt her, as she'd hurt them. She hadn't meant to.

She'd only been after the truth. But sometimes the truth caused more pain than letting secrets remain secret. If only she'd understood that sooner...

"Are you okay?" he asked, his deep voice full of concern.

How could he care about her—after everything she'd thought of him, everything she'd taken from him? He had been right that she'd stolen from him. She had taken away the first three years of his son's life.

Her hands trembled so much that she quickly slid the

gun into her purse so that she wouldn't drop it. "I—I'm fine," she said. "I'm just overwhelmed."

"You're exhausted," he said.

And he was touching her again, his hands on her shoulders. He led her toward the couch. Like the one in the living room, it was wide and low, and as she sank onto the edge of it, it felt nearly as comfortable as a mattress.

Her purse dropped to the floor next to the couch, but she let it go. She didn't need the gun. She didn't need to protect herself from Brendan, at least not physically. But emotionally she was at risk of falling for him all over again.

"You can lie down here," he said. "And I'll keep an eye on CJ."

"He's out cold," she said. Her son wouldn't awaken again before morning. But regrettably that was only a few hours off.

Brendan shook his head. "I can't sleep anyway."

"I can't sleep, either." She reached up and grabbed his hand, tugging him down beside her.

He turned toward her, his eyes intense as he stared at her. The pupils dilated, and his chest—his massively muscled chest—heaved as he drew in an unsteady breath. "Josie..."

"You gave me a gun," she murmured, unbelievably moved by his gesture.

"Most women would prefer flowers or jewelry."

The woman she'd once been would have, but that woman had died nearly four years ago. The woman she was now preferred the gun, preferred that he'd given her the means to protect herself...even from him.

"I'm not most women," she said.

"No," he agreed. "Most women I would have been able to put from my mind. But I never stopped thinking about you—" he reached for her now, touching her chin and then sliding his fingers up her cheek "—never stopped wanting you."

Then his mouth was on hers as he kissed her deeply, his tongue sliding between her lips. She moaned as passion consumed her, heating her skin and her blood.

Her fingers trembled, and she fumbled with the buttons on his shirt. She needed him. After tonight she needed to feel the way he had always made her feel— *alive.*

He caught her fingers as if to stop her. Josie opened her eyes and gasped in protest. But then he replaced her hands with his. He stripped off his holsters and then his shirt, baring his chest for her greedy gaze.

He was beautiful, the kind of masculine perfection that defied reality. That weakened a woman's knees and her resolve. Josie leaned forward and kissed his chest, skimming her lips across the muscles.

Soft hair tickled her skin.

His fingers clenched in her hair, and he gently pulled her back. Then his hands were on her, pulling her sweater over her head and stripping off her bra.

"You're beautiful," he said, his voice gruff.

She wasn't the woman she'd once been, emotionally or physically. She'd worried that he wouldn't look at her as he once had—his face flushed with desire, his nostrils flaring as he breathed hard and fast. But he was looking at her that way now.

"You're even more beautiful," he murmured, "than you once were."

She didn't know whether to be offended, so she

laughed. "Then the marshals didn't get their money's worth from the plastic surgeon."

"It's not an external thing," he said. "You have a beauty that comes from within now."

"It's happiness," she admitted.

"Despite all you had to give up?" His hands skimmed along her jaw again. "Even your face?"

"I have my son," she said, "our son…"

"Our son," he said.

"I'm sorry I didn't tell you I was pregnant," she said, "that I didn't tell you when he was born."

"You didn't trust me," he said. "You thought I wanted to kill you."

"I was wrong." She knew that now. She didn't know everything. He was keeping other things from her— things that he'd shared with Charlotte but wouldn't tell her. But maybe it was better that she didn't know. Maybe the secrets kept her safer than the gun.

He kissed her again, as he had before. Deeply. Passionately. His chest rubbed against her breasts, drawing her nipples to tight points.

She moaned again and skimmed her hands over his back, pressing him closer to her. As she ran her palms down his spine, she hit something hard near his waistband. Something cold and hard.

Another gun.

How many did he have on him?

He stood up and took off that weapon, as well as another on his ankle. Then his belt and pants came off next.

And Josie gasped as desire rushed over her. She had never wanted anyone the way she'd wanted Brendan. Because she'd known she never would, she hadn't gotten involved with anyone else the past four years. She'd focused on being a mother and a teacher and had tried to forget she was a woman.

She remembered now. Her hands trembling, she unclasped her jeans and skimmed them off along with her simple cotton panties. Brendan reached between them and stroked his fingers over her red curls.

Her breath caught. And she clutched his shoulders as her legs trembled.

"You haven't changed completely," he murmured.

He continued to stroke her until she came, holding tight to him so that she didn't crumple to the floor. But then he laid her down on the couch. And he made love to her with his mouth, too, his fingers stroking over her breasts, teasing her nipples until she completely shattered, overcome with ecstasy. But there was more.

She pulled him up her body, stroking her hands and mouth over all his hard, rippling muscles...until his control snapped. And he thrust inside her, filling the emptiness with which she'd lived the past four years.

Their mouths made love like their bodies, tongues tangling, lips skimming, as he thrust deep and deeper. She arched to take all of him. A pressure wound tightly inside her, stretching her, making her ache. She gasped for breath as her heart pounded and her pulse raced.

Then Brendan reached between them; his fingers stroked through those curls and his thumb pressed against that special nub. And she came. So she wouldn't scream, she kissed him more deeply as pleasure pulsed through her.

He groaned deeply into her mouth as his body tensed and he joined her in ecstasy. Pleasure shook his body, just as hers still trembled with aftershocks. But even once their bodies relaxed, he didn't let her go. He wrapped his arms tightly around her, holding her close to his madly pounding heart.

And she felt safe. Protected. For the first time in nearly four years.

FOR THE FIRST time in nearly four years, Brendan didn't feel so alone. Josie had had their son; he had had no one. No one he dared get close to. No one he dared to trust.

Part of that had been her fault. After her subterfuge, he'd been careful to let no other woman get to him. But he suspected that even if he hadn't been careful, no other woman could have gotten to him.

Only Josie...

Maybe Charlotte Green was right. Maybe he did love Josie. And maybe he should trust her. He hadn't noticed any articles she'd written showing up in her father's papers. Maybe she'd stepped away from the media world. Not that her articles had been sensationalized. They had been brutally honest, stripping the subject bare. That was why he would have recognized anything she'd written—her style was distinctive.

But maybe becoming a mother had changed her priorities. Maybe she cared more about keeping CJ hidden than exposing others.

He stroked his fingers over her shoulder and down her bare back. "Your skin is so soft." He'd thought it was because of fancy spa treatments she would have had as American princess Josie Jessup. But with the new lifestyle the marshals would have set up for her, she wouldn't have been able to go to expensive spas.

She would have had to live modestly and quietly, or else she would have been found before now. Because someone was looking for her.

Why?

To get to him?

She was his only weakness. Hurting her would draw him out, and maybe make him careless enough for someone to get the jump on him.

Had she had to give up everything—her home, family and career—because of him? Then she deserved to know the truth.

"Josie…"

"Hmm…" she murmured sleepily.

He looked down at her face and found her eyes closed, her lashes lying on the dark circles beneath. And her body was limp in his arms, relaxed. He couldn't wake her. After everything she'd been through that night, she needed to rest and recuperate. Because their ordeal wasn't over yet. It wouldn't be over until he discovered who was trying to kill her.

But they were safe now, here, wrapped in each other's arms, so he closed his eyes.

He didn't know how long he'd been asleep when the alarm sounded. No, the piercing whistle was not from a clock but from the security panel in the den.

"What!" Josie exclaimed as she jerked awake in his arms. "What is that?"

"Security has been breached," he said, already reaching for his clothes and his weapons.

There were other apartments inside the building, other witnesses or suspects or agents the intruder could have been after. But Brendan knew the alarm was for them—the danger coming for them.…

He had just one question for her. "How well do you know how to shoot?"

Chapter Eleven

While she'd held the gun when he'd handed it to her, the weight of it was still unfamiliar in her hands. Before tonight she hadn't held one in years, let alone fired one. And when she had fired one, it had only been at targets—not people.

Could she pull the trigger on a person?

"Mommy, the 'larm clock is too loud," CJ protested with his tiny hands tightly pressed against his ears.

Brendan scooped him up and headed toward the apartment door. "Grab your stuff," he told her over his shoulder. He carried the boy with one arm while he clutched a gun in his other hand.

"Sh-shouldn't we stay here?" she asked. "And just lock the door?"

His turquoise eyes intense, he shook his head. "We don't know if the breach was someone getting inside or *putting* something inside."

A bomb.

Josie gasped and hurried toward the door. But she slammed into Brendan's back as he abruptly stopped.

"We have to be very quiet," he warned them.

"CJ, you have to play statue," she told their son. "No matter what happens, you have to be quiet."

"Like on the roof?"

Not like that. She wouldn't dare leave her little boy alone in the dark again. "Well…"

"We're all staying together," Brendan said, "and we're staying quiet."

She released a shaky sigh.

"Mommy, shh," the little boy warned her.

A corner of Brendan's mouth lifted in a slight grin. Then he slowly opened the door. He nodded at her before stepping into the hall. It was clear. He wouldn't have brought their son into the line of fire.

But they needed to get out of the building. Fast.

She breathed deep, checking for the telltale odor of gas. But she smelled nothing but Brendan; the scent of his skin clung to hers. While they'd been making love, someone had gotten inside the building.

What if that person had gotten inside the apartment? He or they could have grabbed CJ before his parents had had a chance to reach him.

Her heart ached with a twinge of guilt more powerful than any she'd felt before. And she'd felt plenty guilty over the years.

She followed after Brendan, watching as he juggled the boy and his gun. "If we're taking the elevator…"

He would need to give her the code to punch into the security panel. But he shook his head and pushed open the door to the stairwell.

Of course they wouldn't want to be in the elevator. If the building exploded, they would be trapped. But wouldn't they be trapped inside the stairwell, too? If the gunmen were heading up, they would meet them on the way down—and CJ would be caught in the crossfire.

Brendan didn't hesitate though. He hurried down the first flight and then the second.

"Brendan…"

Over his father's shoulder, their little boy pressed a finger to his lips, warning her again to be quiet.

They had stopped, but their footsteps echoed. Then she realized it wasn't their footsteps that were echoing. It was someone else's—on their way up, as she'd feared. But Brendan continued to go down.

"No," she whispered frantically. "They're coming!"

He stopped on the next landing and pushed open the door to the hall. "Run," he told her.

"To the elevator?" They could take it now. The men wouldn't have come inside if they'd set a bomb.

"No," he said. "Door at the end of the hall. Go through it." He pushed her ahead of him and turned back as the door to the stairwell opened. But he kept his back toward that door, his body between their son and whoever might exit the stairwell. Before anyone emerged, he fired and kept firing as he ran behind Josie.

She pushed through that door he'd pointed at and burst onto a landing with such force that she nearly careened over the railing of the fire escape. Brendan, CJ clutched tight against his chest, exited behind her.

He momentarily holstered his gun, even though the men had to be right behind him, and he grabbed up a pipe that lay on the landing and slid it through the handle, jamming the door shut.

How had he known the pipe was there? Had he planned such an escape before?

The door rattled as another body struck it.

"Go," he told her. "Run!"

She nearly stumbled as she hurried down the dimly illuminated metal steps. But gunfire rang out again— shots fired against that jammed door.

Brendan, still holding their son, who was softly sobbing, rushed down the stairs behind her. The shots, the urgency, the danger had her trembling so uncontrollably that she slipped, her feet flying from beneath her.

She would have fallen, would have hit each metal step on the long way to the ground. But a strong hand caught her arm, holding her up while she regained her footing.

When they neared the bottom of the fire escape, the gun was back in his hand, the light from the parking lot lamps glinting off the metal.

She hadn't lost the gun she'd carried. She hadn't used it, either, and wasn't even sure that she could. But then she heard a car door open and a gun cock.

And she knew that someone had a clear shot at them. So she slid off the safety and turned with the gun braced in both hands. But before she could squeeze the trigger, a shot rang out and she heard a windshield shatter.

"Come on," Brendan urged her. "Your car's over here. Hurry."

"But—"

There was a shooter in the lot. Or had Brendan already shot him? The gun was in his free hand while his other hand clasped their son to his chest.

"Do you have the keys?" he asked.

She pulled them out of her purse and clicked the key fob. Lights flashed on the SUV, guiding them to it and also revealing it to the gunmen as they erupted from the lobby of the building.

This time she squeezed the trigger, shooting at the men pointing guns at her son and the man she loved. The weapon kicked back, straining her wrist.

"Get in!" Brendan yelled as he put their boy into the backseat. "Buckle him up!"

She dropped the gun into her bag and jumped into the passenger's seat. As she leaned over the console and buckled up their son, Brendan was already careening out of the lot.

"Stay down!" he yelled at her, just as more shots rang out. Bullets pinged and tires squealed.

And their son continued to play statue, staying silent in the backseat. "You're so brave," she praised him, reaching back to touch his face.

His chin quivered and she felt moisture on her fingers—probably his tears. But he had his eyes squeezed tightly shut, trying not to cry. She pulled back her hand and studied what was smeared across her fingers. It wasn't tears. It was something red and sticky. Blood.

"Brendan! He's hurt!" she exclaimed, fear and dread clutching her heart in a tight vise. "Get to the hospital! Call the police!"

"No," HE CORRECTED her as blood trickled down his temple. "CJ wasn't hit." He'd made damn certain of that.

"Th-there's blood on his face," she said, her voice shaking with fear and anger.

Brendan tipped the rearview mirror and studied their son in the backseat. The little boy scrubbed at his face and held up a hand sticky with blood. "It's not mine, Mommy. It came off…" His son didn't know what to call him, didn't know who he was to him.

"Your daddy," Brendan answered the boy. "I'm your daddy."

Josie gasped, probably at his audacity for telling their child who he was. But then she was reaching across the console and touching his head. "Where are you hit?"

"Daddy?" CJ asked.

Brendan's head pounded. He wanted to pull off the road, wanted to explain to his son who he was, wanted to let Josie touch him. But he had to tip the mirror back up and check the road behind them. Had anyone followed them?

He'd thought he'd been vigilant on his way from the estate to the complex, that he hadn't been followed. Had he missed a tail?

With blood trickling into his eyes, he was more likely to miss one now, so he asked Josie, "Do you see anything?"

Her fingers stroked through his hair. "No. Where were you hit?"

He shook his head, and the pain radiated, making him wince. "I wasn't hit," he replied, lifting his fingers to his left temple. "I was grazed. It's just a scratch." A scratch that stung like a son of a bitch, but he ignored the pain and focused on the road. "Is there anyone behind us?"

"What?" She must have realized what he was referring to, because she turned around and peered out the rear window. "I don't see any other lights."

The roads were deserted this early in the morning. He passed only a garbage truck going the other direction. No one was behind him. No one had been behind him earlier, either. He blinked back the trickle of blood and remarked, "I was not followed to the complex."

"So how did they find us?" she asked.

"Daddy?" CJ repeated from the backseat, interrupting them. "You're my daddy?"

Josie sucked in an audible breath as if just noticing

that Brendan had told their son who he was. He waited to see if she would deny it now, if she would call him a liar for claiming his child. If she did, he would call her on the lie. After his close call with that bullet, he wanted his son to know who he was…before it was too late. Before he never got the chance to tell him.

Josie turned toward the backseat and offered their son a shaky smile. "Yes, sweetheart, he's your daddy."

"I—I thought he was a bad man."

Josie shook her head. "No, sweetheart, he's a good man. A hero. He keeps saving us from the bad men."

Was she saying that for the boy's sake? To make CJ feel better? Safer? Or did she believe it? Had she finally really come to trust Brendan, even though he hadn't told her the truth?

"My daddy…" the little boy murmured, as if he were falling back to sleep. Given that his slumber kept getting violently interrupted, it was no wonder that the little boy was still tired.

"Well, we know who I am," Brendan said. A hero? Did she really see him that way? "What about who's after us?"

She kept staring into the backseat as if watching her son to make sure that the blood really wasn't his. Or that the news of his parentage hadn't affected him.

"Whoever it is," he said, "appears to want us both dead."

"They're gone," she murmured. Apparently she'd been watching the back window instead. "We're safe now."

"We should have been safe where we were," he replied. It was a damn *safe* house.

"We need to go home," she murmured, sounding as dazed as their son. But she wasn't just tired; she was probably in shock. She'd fired her gun at people. If that had been the first time, she was probably having an emotional reaction. She was trembling and probably not just because the car had yet to warm up. "We need to go home," she repeated.

She wasn't talking about his home. Neither the mansion where he'd grown up nor the apartment where he'd spent much of his adult life was safe. But she couldn't be talking about her place, either.

Maybe her father's? But if the news reports were correct, he'd been attacked in the parking garage of his condominium complex.

"We can't," he said. "It's not safe at your dad's, either."

"We have to go home," she said, her voice rising slightly now, as if with hysteria. "To what CJ and I call home, where we've been living."

"Don't you get it?" he asked. "The only one who could have tracked down where we were was your *friend*."

She leaned forward and peered into his face as if worried that the bullet had impaired his thinking. "Friend?"

"The former marshal," he said. "She must have traced the call to where we were staying. She sent those people." It couldn't have been anyone else. Damn! Why had he trusted the woman?

Josie sucked in an audible breath of shock. "Charlotte? You think Charlotte is behind the attempts on my life?"

"No." He knew she considered the woman a friend, at one point maybe her only friend. And she had to be devastated. But she also had to know the truth. "But she must have sold out to whoever wants you dead."

Josie chuckled. Maybe she'd given over completely to hysteria and shock. "You think Charlotte Green sold out?"

He nodded, and his head pounded again. "It had to be her. You can't trust her."

"She told me to trust you," she reminded him. "So now you're saying that I shouldn't?"

"No, no," he said. "You should trust me but not her. Remember what you told our son—I'm not a bad man. I've saved you."

Something jammed into his ribs, and he glanced down. She held the gun he'd given her, not just on him but nearly in him as she pushed the barrel into his side. After the night she'd had, he could understand her losing it. But was she irrational enough to pull the trigger?

Had she slid off the safety? If he hit a bump in the road, she might squeeze the trigger. She might shoot him and then he might crash the SUV and take them all out.

He hadn't realized that he might need to protect Josie from herself.

HE WAS LOOKING at her nervously, as if he worried that she'd lost her mind. Maybe she had.

Could she do it? Could she pull the trigger? If she had to… If killing Brendan was necessary to save her life or CJ's.

But she believed what she'd told their son. He was a hero—at least he had been their hero—time and time again the past night. Moreover, she believed in him.

She had the safety on the gun, in case there were any bullets left in it. She hoped like hell there were none. But with Brendan looking as nervous as he was, he obviously thought there could be.

And he thought she could fire the gun.

Good. That was the only way she was going to co-
erce him to take her where she wanted to go. Where
she needed to go. Home.

"We're doing things my way now," she said. Since
the shoot-out at the hospital, he had brought her from
one place to another and neither had been safe.

"You're not going to pull the trigger," he said.
"You're not a killer."

She flinched, hoping that was true. She'd fired the
gun back at the complex. Had she hit anyone?

She shot back at him with a smart remark. "Guess
that makes one of us."

"Then why pull the gun on me if you don't intend
to use it?" he asked, his body pressed slightly against
the barrel of her gun as if he were beginning to relax.
Had he realized that she hadn't gone crazy? That she
was just determined?

"I don't want to use it," she admitted, "but I will if
you don't take me where I want to go."

"It's too dangerous," he protested. "Since Charlotte
gave up our safe house, she sure as hell gave up the
place where she relocated you."

"Why?" she asked.

"I told you—for money."

She laughed again. "Do you have any idea who
Charlotte Green is?"

He glanced at her with that look again, as if he
thought she belonged in a place like Serenity House.
"A former U.S. marshal."

"Her father is king of a wealthy island country near
Greece," she shared. The last thing Charlotte needed
was money. "She's a princess."

"What?" He definitely thought she was crazy now.

"She's Princess Gabriella St. Pierre's sister," she explained. "They're royal heiresses." Of course Charlotte had spent most of her life unaware that she was royalty. Only upon her mother's death had she learned the woman had been the king's mistress and herself his illegitimate heir.

"So are you."

She snorted over the miniscule amount of royal blood running in her veins. Her mother had been a descendent of European royalty, but she'd given up her title to marry Josie's father. "Not anymore," she reminded him. "I gave up that life."

And she shouldn't have risked coming back to it, not even to see her father, because her arrival had only put him in more danger. God, she hoped he was safe. She had asked Charlotte to check on him, to protect him. What if Brendan was actually right about her?

No, that wasn't possible. Charlotte would never betray her.

"I have a *new* home," she said. "And we're going there. It might be the only safe place we have left to go."

"Or it could be a trap," he said. "They could be waiting for us there."

"Charlotte wouldn't have given us up," she said. "She's CJ's godmother. My friend. She wouldn't have given us up."

She barked out directions, and he followed them. She suspected it wasn't because of the gun she pressed into his side but because he had no place else to take her. He'd tried the O'Hannigan mansion and what had probably been some type of safe house. Why had no other tenants come out into the halls when the alarm had sounded? Why had it only been them and the gunmen?

"What if you're wrong about her?" he asked. "What if she's not really who you think she is?"

Then Charlotte wouldn't be the only one she'd misjudged. Brendan O'Hannigan wasn't who she'd thought he was, either. She had been wrong about him for so long. What if she was wrong about Charlotte, too? What if the marshal had been compromised?

She wouldn't have sold out Josie for money, but she might have sold her out if there was a threat against someone she loved, such as her sister. Or Aaron…

The closer they got to her home, the more scared Josie became that Brendan might be right. They could be walking right into the killer's trap.

Chapter Twelve

Brendan could have taken the gun away from her at any time. He could have snapped it out of her hand more easily than he had taken the weapon off the faux orderly who'd grabbed him on the sixth floor. But he hadn't wanted to hurt her. She had already been hurt enough. And if he was right, she was about to be hurt a hell of a lot more.

He intimately knew how painful it was to be betrayed by someone you loved. As a friend, as a lifeline to her old life, she had loved Charlotte Green. And he'd been fool enough to trust the woman with the truth about himself.

But he'd wanted her to convince Josie to trust him. Now Josie held a gun on him, forcing him to bring her back to a trap. Should he trust her?

Was she part of it? Was this all a ploy to take him down? If not for the boy, he might have suspected her involvement in a murder plot against him. But she loved her son. She wouldn't knowingly endanger him.

As he drove north, light from the rising sun streamed through her window, washing her face devoid of all color. Her eyes were stark, wide with fear, in her pale face.

"Are you sure you want to risk it?" he asked.

"You're trying to make me doubt myself," she said. "Trying to make me doubt Charlotte."

"Yes," he admitted.

She looked at him, her eyes filling with sadness and pity. "You don't trust anyone, do you?"

"I shouldn't have," he said. "But I trusted you."

She pulled the gun slightly away from his side. "You gave me this gun."

"The one you're holding on me."

"I wouldn't really shoot you," she assured him, and with a sigh, she dropped the gun back into her purse.

"I know."

"Then why did you come here?" She sat up straighter as they passed a sign announcing the town limits of Sand Haven, Michigan. Another sign stood beyond that, a billboard prompting someone named Michael to rest in peace.

Josie flinched as she read the sign.

"Do you know Michael?" he asked.

She jerked her chin in a sharp nod. "I knew him."

"I'm sorry." Had her recent loss explained why she'd been so desperate to see her father that she'd risked her safety and CJ's?

She hadn't been in contact with her father, as he'd initially expected. The man, who'd looked so sad and old at her funeral, had believed she was dead just as Brendan had.

"You hadn't seen your dad until—" he glanced at the sun rising high in the sky "—last night?"

"I didn't see him last night, either," she said.

"But you were on the right floor," he said, remembering the lie she'd told him.

She bit her lip and blinked hard, as if fighting tears,

before replying, "The assault brought on a heart attack. I didn't want his seeing me to bring on another one."

"So he has no idea that you're really alive?"

She shook her head. "I thought it would be better if he didn't know. I thought he'd be safer."

"You and your father were close," he said. "It must have been hard to leave him."

"Harder to deceive him," she said.

But she'd had no problem deceiving him when she'd been trying to get her story. But then she hadn't loved him.

He drew in a deep breath and focused on the road. She'd given him directions right to her door. Giving her the gun had made her trust him. But she had placed her trust in someone she shouldn't have.

"Let me go in first," he suggested as he drove past the small white bungalow where she lived now. "Let me make sure that it's not a trap."

She shuddered as if she remembered the bomb set at his house. There had been very little left of the brick Tudor; it wouldn't take a very big bomb to totally decimate her modest little home.

He turned the corner and pulled the SUV over to the curb on the next street. After shifting into Park, he reached for the door handle, but she clutched his arm.

Her voice cracking, she said, "I don't want you to go alone."

"You can't go with me," he said. "You have to protect our son."

"If you can't?" She shook her head. "It's not a trap. It can't be a trap." She had been on her own so long that she was desperately hanging on to her trust for the one person who'd been there for her.

He forced a reassuring smile for her sake. "Then I'll be right back."

She stared at him, her eyes wide with uncertainty. She wanted to believe him as much as she wanted to believe that Charlotte hadn't betrayed her.

"I'll be back." He leaned across the console and clasped her face in his hands, tipping her mouth up for his kiss. He lingered over her lips, caressing them slowly and thoroughly. "Wait here for me."

She opened her mouth again, but she made no protest. He opened the driver's door and then opened the backseat door. She turned and looked over the console as he leaned in and pressed a kiss against his son's mussed red curls. The boy never stirred from his slumber.

"Thank you," he said. "Thank you for telling him that I'm his father."

"You told him."

"But you didn't contradict me," he said. "He would have believed what you told him over whatever I told him." Because he loved and trusted his mother. Brendan was a stranger to him. And if he was right about the trap, he may forever remain a stranger to him.

The little boy might grow up never knowing his father.

BRENDAN HAD BEEN gone too long. Longer than he needed to check out the house and make sure it was as safe as she was hoping it was.

But what if it wasn't?

The keys dangled from the ignition. He hadn't taken them this time, because he wasn't sure he'd be coming back. Josie's heart rate quickened, pounding faster with each second that passed.

She needed to go to her house. Needed to check on him.

Or perhaps she should call Charlotte for backup. But he wouldn't need backup unless Charlotte had betrayed them. Panic and dread clutched her heart. Not Charlotte. Not her friend, her son's godmother.

Charlotte couldn't have revealed Josie's new location, not even to protect someone else. But maybe someone had found out anyway. Josie needed to learn the truth.

She wriggled out of the passenger's seat, over the console and behind the steering wheel. Then she turned the keys in the ignition.

CJ murmured as the engine started. He was waking up. She couldn't leave him in the car and she couldn't bring him with her—in case Brendan was right about her house being a trap now.

So she brought her son where she brought him every morning, where she would have brought him that morning if she hadn't taken a leave from work. She drove him to day care. It was only a few blocks from her house, at the home of a retired elementary schoolteacher.

Mrs. Mallory watched CJ and two other preschool children. The sixty-something woman opened the door as Josie carried him up the walk. And the smile on her face became tight with concern the closer Josie came.

"Are you all right?" the older woman anxiously asked.

How awful did she look?

A glance in the mirror by the door revealed dark circles beneath her eyes, and her hair was tangled and mussed, looking as though she'd not pulled a comb through it in days. She probably hadn't.

"I'm fine," Josie assured her. "I'm just in a hurry."

Mrs. Mallory reached out for the sleepy child. "I wasn't even expecting you. I thought you were taking some time off." As she cradled the boy in one arm, she squeezed Josie's shoulder with her other hand. "You really should. Let this whole tragic situation with Michael die down."

"So people are blaming me?"

Mrs. Mallory bit her lip and nodded. "It's not your fault, though, honey. That boy wanted to be a reporter since he wasn't much older than CJ here."

"But I suggested the story...."

"But you didn't pull the trigger," the older woman pointed out. "People are blaming the wrong person and they'll realize that soon enough. Just give them some time. Or take some for yourself."

She had no time to lose—not if Brendan had walked into a trap. "Even though you weren't planning on it, would you mind watching him for a little while?"

"'Course not," the older woman assured her, and she cuddled him close in her arms. She was wearing one of the velour tracksuits that CJ loved snuggling into. "I was just starting to miss him."

CJ lifted his head from Mrs. Mallory's shoulder as if just realizing where he was. "Daddy? Where's my daddy?"

Mrs. Mallory's eyes widened with shock. The boy had never mentioned him before. Of course, before last night he hadn't even known he had a father. Or a grandfather.

"You have to stay here with Mrs. M," Josie told him, leaning forward to press a kiss against his freckled cheek, "and be a good boy, okay?"

His bottom lip began to quiver and his eyes grew

damp with tears he fought back with quick blinks. "What if the bad men come here?"

"Bad men?" Mrs. Mallory asked, her brow wrinkling with confusion and uneasiness.

Josie shrugged off the question. "He must have had a bad dream."

If only that had been all it was...

Just a bad dream.

The little boy vehemently shook his head. "The bad men were real and had guns. They were shootin' at us and then there was a big bang!"

Josie shook her head, too, trying to quiet the boy's fears and Mrs. Mallory's. "It must have been quite the dream," she said, "and his imagination is so vivid."

Mrs. Mallory glanced from the boy to Josie and back. "He does have quite the imagination," she agreed, his story, although true, too fanciful for the older woman to believe. "He's a very creative boy. Did you watch a scary movie with him last night—something that brought on such a horrible dream?"

"No," Josie replied. She touched her little boy's trembling chin. "You have no reason to be afraid," she told him. "You're perfectly safe here."

Not buying her assurances in the least, CJ shook his head and wriggled out of Mrs. Mallory's arms. "I need my daddy to p'tect me."

Brendan had gone from bad man to hero for his son. He needed to know that; hopefully he was alive for her to share that news with him. She needed to get to her house. If it had blown up, she would have heard the explosion—or at least the fire trucks.

He had to be okay....

Josie knelt in front of her son and met his gaze. "I

am going to go get your daddy," she promised, "and he will come back here with me to get you, okay?"

"I can get Daddy, too," he said, throwing his arms around her neck to cling to her.

Her heart broke, but she forced herself to tug him off and stand up. He used to cling to her like this every morning when she'd first started bringing him to Mrs. Mallory, but today was the first time he'd had a reason for his fears. Not only because of the night he'd had, but also because she might not be able to come back— if she walked into the same trap his father might have. But then his godmother would take him....

Charlotte. She wouldn't have endangered them. Brendan must have had another reason for not returning to the SUV. Maybe that injury to his head was more severe than he'd led her to believe.

"No, honey," she said, and it physically hurt her, tightened her stomach into knots, to deny his fervent request. The timid boy asked her for so little that she hated telling him no. "I have to talk to Daddy alone first, and then we'll come get you."

Mrs. Mallory had always helped Josie escape before when her son was determined to cling. But now the older woman just stood in the foyer, her jaw hanging open in shock. As Josie stared at her, she pulled herself together. But curiosity obviously overwhelmed her. "His—his father? You've never mentioned him before."

With good reason. She had thought he wanted her dead. "We haven't been in contact in years," she honestly replied.

"But he's here?"

She nodded. "At my house."

Or so she hoped. Maybe he'd come back to where

he'd parked the SUV and found her gone. What would he think? That she'd tricked him again?

Hopefully she wasn't the one who'd been tricked. Hopefully he wasn't right about Charlotte.

"I—I have to go," she said. It had been too long. Now that she'd stood up, CJ was clinging to her legs.

Finally Mrs. Mallory stepped in and pried the sniffling child off her.

"I'll be back," she promised her son.

"With Daddy?"

She hoped so. But when she parked in the alley behind her house moments later, her hope waned. She hadn't seen him walking along the street. And while the house wasn't in pieces or on fire, it looked deserted.

She opened the driver's door and stepped out into the eerie quiet. Her neighbors would have already left for work, their kids for school. Josie was rarely home this time of day during the week. Maybe that was why it felt so strange to walk up to her own back door.

The glass in the window of the door was shattered. Of course, since Brendan had left her keys in the car, he would have had to break in to gain entrance. She was surprised he would have done it with such force, though, since the wooden panes were broken and the glass shattered as if it had exploded.

She sucked in a breath of fear. But she smelled no telltale odor of gas or smoke. The glass may have exploded, but a bomb had not.

Could a gunshot have broken the window?

If so, her neighbors would have called the police. There would have been officers at her home, crime scene tape blocking it off from the street. But there was nothing but a light breeze blowing through her broken window and rattling the blind inside.

The blind was broken, like the panes and the glass. Had Brendan slammed his fist through it? Or had someone else?

Gathering all her courage, she opened that door and stepped inside the small back porch. Glass crunched beneath her feet, crushed between the soles of her shoes and the slate floor. As she passed the washer and dryer on her way to the kitchen, she noticed a brick and crumpled paper sitting atop the washer.

Someone had thrown a brick through her window? Brendan?

Or was he the one who'd found it and picked it up? She suspected the latter, since there had obviously been a note secured to the brick with a rubber band. The broken band lay beside the brick and the crumpled paper.

She picked up the note and shivered with fear as she read the words: *You should have been the one who died.*

Oh, God. She was too late. Brendan had walked into a trap meant for her.

Chapter Thirteen

The scream startled Brendan, chilling his blood. He'd lost all sense of time and place. How long ago had he left Josie and their son? Had someone found them?

He'd left them alone and defenseless but for the gun he'd given Josie. Had she even had any bullets left?

He reached for the weapon at his back, pulling the gun from under his jacket. Then he crept up the stairs from the room he'd found in the basement, the one that had answered all the questions he'd had about ever trusting Josie Jessup.

The old steps creaked beneath his weight, giving away his presence. A shadow stood at the top of the stairwell, blocking Brendan's escape. The dim bulb swinging overhead glinted off the metal of the gun the shadow held, the barrel pointed at Brendan. He lifted his gun and aimed. But then he noticed the hair and the figure. "Josie!"

"Brendan? You're alive!" She launched herself at him, nearly knocking him off the stairs. "I thought you were dead!"

He caught himself against the brick wall at his back. "Now you know how it feels," he murmured. Despite his bitterness, his arms closed around her, holding her against him.

Her heart pounded madly. "I was so worried about you. You didn't come back to the car and then I found that note."

"You thought that note referred to me?"

She nodded.

"As you can see, I'm alive," he said. "So who does it refer to?"

She gasped as that guilt flashed across her face again.

And he remembered the sign. "Michael?"

"Yes," she miserably replied. "Some people blame me for his death."

"Did you kill him?"

She gasped again in shock and outrage. "No. I would never…"

"It's not a good feeling to have people thinking you're a killer," he remarked.

Her brow furrowed with confusion as he set her away from him. "Where have you been all this time?" she asked. As he turned and headed back down the steps, she followed him. "You've been down here?" Then as she realized exactly where he'd been, she ran ahead of him and tried blocking the doorway to her den.

Bookshelves lined knotty pine walls. But it wasn't there he'd found what he'd spent the past four years looking for.

"You broke into my filing cabinet!" she said.

He could have lied and blamed it on whoever had thrown the brick through her window. But that person would have had no interest in what he'd discovered. So he just shrugged.

"You had no right!" she said, as she hurried over to where he'd spread the files across her desk.

"I think I have more right to those records than you do," he pointed out. "They're all about me."

She trembled as she shoved the papers back into folders. "But you shouldn't have seen them."

"That's what you were working on when we were together," he said, his gut aching as it had when he'd found the folders. If the drawer hadn't been locked, he probably wouldn't have bothered to jimmy it open. But he'd wanted to know all her secrets so that he might figure out who was trying to kill her. "You thought I killed my own father? That's the story you were after when you came after me."

She released a shuddery sigh. "That was a lifetime ago."

"But you're still a reporter."

She shook her head. "No."

"You teach journalism," he said, gesturing toward a framed award that sat among the books on the shelves of the den. She had given up so much of her old life, except for that. No matter where she was or what she was calling herself, she was still a journalist.

"I teach," she said, her tone rueful, "because I can't *do*."

"Because you can't give it up." Not for him. Not even for their son.

"I had to give up everything," she said. "My home. My family."

Family.

"Where's CJ?" he asked, glancing around the shadows. She'd been alone on the stairs. Where had she stashed their child this time?

"He's at his sitter's," she said. "He's safe."

"Are you sure?" He never should have let the boy out of his sight.

"I can trust the people here."

Skeptical, he snorted. "She wouldn't have thrown the brick?"

"Absolutely not," she said. "It must have been one of my other students. Or one of Michael's friends."

"What happened to Michael?"

Sadness dimmed her eyes and filled them with tears. "He was killed pursuing a story."

He touched his fingers to the scratch on his temple. It didn't sting anymore; it throbbed, the intensity of it increasing with his confusion and frustration. "How could you be responsible for that?"

Her eyes glistened with moisture. "It was a story I suggested that he cover." She blinked back the tears. "But that brick—that has nothing to do with what happened in Chicago. Nobody here knows who I really am. Nobody here would have tried to kill me."

"Just scare you," he said. But the brick and the note were nothing in comparison to gunfire and explosions. "You should be scared," he said. He reached out and jerked one of the folders from her hand. "This story could have gotten *you* killed."

She sucked in a quivering breath. "It almost did. It is why someone tried to kill me four years ago."

"Someone," he agreed. And now he knew who. "But not me."

She gestured toward those folders. "But you see why I suspected you. All the people I talked to named you as your father's killer."

People he should have been able to trust—men who'd worked with his father since they were kids selling drugs for Brendan's grandfather. And his step-

mother. When his father had first married her, she had
pretended to care about her husband's motherless son.
But when Brendan had returned to claim the inheritance Margaret O'Hannigan thought should have been
hers, she'd stopped pretending.

Josie continued, "In all the conversations I overheard while hanging out with you at O'Hannigan's,
only one suspect was ever named in his murder."

"Me." Did she still suspect him?

"I was wrong," she admitted, but then defended herself. "But I didn't know you very well then. You were
so secretive and you never answered my questions."

She didn't know him very well now, either. But it
was obvious she couldn't stop being a journalist, so
he couldn't trust her with the truth. He couldn't tell
her who he really was, but he could tell her something
about himself.

"We wanted the same thing, you know," he told her.

"We did?" she asked, the skepticism all hers now.

"I didn't want an award-winning exposé," he clarified. "But I wanted the truth."

She nodded. "That's why I never printed anything.
I had no confirmation. No proof. I could have written
an exposé. But I wanted the truth."

And that was the one thing that set her apart from
the other reporters who'd done stories about him over
the past four years. She wouldn't print the unsubstantiated rumors other journalists would. She'd wanted
proof. She just hadn't recognized it when she'd found it.

"I want to know who killed him, too," he said. "I
came back to that *life* because I wanted justice for my
father." After years of trying to bring the man to justice, it was ironic that Brendan had spent the past four

years trying to get justice for his father—for his cold-blooded murder.

"You spent a lot of time reading through everything," she said, staring down at the desk he'd messed up. "Did you find anything I missed?"

Because he didn't want to lie outright to her, he replied, "You weren't the only one who must have gone through those papers. If there'd been something in there, one of the marshals would have found it."

"Nobody else has ever seen this stuff," she admitted.

The pounding in his head increased. If anyone familiar with his father's murder case had looked at her records, they would have figured it out. They would have recognized that one of her sources knew too much about the murder scene, things that only the killer would have known. She never would have had to go into hiding, never would have had to keep his child from him. "Why the hell not?"

She lifted her chin with pride. "My dad taught me young to respect the code."

"What code?"

"The journalist code," she said. "A true journalist *never* reveals a source."

Ignoring the pain, he shook his head with disgust. "After the attempts on your life, I think Stanley Jessup would have understood."

She chuckled. "You don't know my dad."

"No," he said, "you never introduced me. I was your dirty little secret."

"He would have been mad," she admitted. "He wouldn't have wanted me anywhere near you, given your reputation."

"Good," Brendan said. He'd worried that the man had put her up to it, to getting close to him for a story.

"And if he cared that much for your safety, he would have understood you breaking the code."

She nodded. "Probably. But I didn't think so back then. Back then, I figured he would have been happier for me to die than reveal a source."

"Josie!" He reached for her, to offer assurance. He knew what it was like to feel like a disappointment to one's father. But when his arms closed around her, he wanted to offer more than sympathy. He wanted her... as he always did.

"But I realized that he wouldn't have cared about the code. He would have cared only about keeping me safe when I had CJ," she said. "CJ!"

She said his name with guilt and alarm, as if something bad had happened to their child.

"What? What about CJ?"

PULLING HIM OFF her, leaving him, had killed her earlier. She hated disappointing her child. So she'd kept her promise and had brought Brendan with her to pick up their son.

And for the entire day they had acted like a normal family. CJ had proudly showed Brendan all his toys and books, which the rumored mob boss had patiently played with and read to the three-year-old boy. Brendan had also looked through all the photos of their son, seeing in pictures every milestone that had been stolen from him.

Through no fault of his own. It was her fault for not trusting him. But she'd felt then that he had been keeping secrets from her. And she had imagined the worst.

As Brendan, with CJ sitting on his lap, continued to flip through the photo albums, she felt every emotion that flickered across his handsome face, the loss, the regret and the awe. He loved their son.

Could he ever love her?

Or had her lies and mistrust destroyed whatever he might have been able to feel for her? If only she'd known then what that damn story would wind up costing her...

The only man she would ever love.

He glanced up and caught her watching them, and his beautiful eyes darkened. With anger? Was he mad at her?

She couldn't blame him. She was mad at herself for all that she had denied him and her son. So today she'd tried making it up to them. She'd made all CJ's favorite foods, played all his favorite games, and she'd pretended that last night had never happened.

The gunfire. The explosion.

She was actually almost able to forget those. It was making love with Brendan that wouldn't leave her mind. She could almost feel his lips on hers, his hands on her body.

Feel him inside her...

She shivered.

"Why don't you take a shower," he said. "Warm up."

God, did she still look like hell?

"It's getting late," she said. "CJ should go to bed, too." The little boy had already had his bath. Brendan had helped give it to him. His rolled-up shirtsleeves were still damp from playing with the ducks and boats in the tub.

"I'll put him to bed," Brendan offered, as if he didn't want to waste a minute of the time he had with his son.

She had longed to clean up, so she agreed with a silent nod. But knowing that her little boy had to be tired, she leaned down to press a kiss to his forehead. "Good night, sweetheart."

Over the red curls of their son, she met Brendan's gaze. His eyes were dark, but not with anger. At least not anger she felt was directed at her. But he was intense, on edge.

As if he were biding his time...

To leave? Was his desire to tuck CJ in so that he could say goodbye?

THE HOUSE WAS small, but it had two bathrooms. So while she was soaking in the tub in the one off her bedroom, he'd used the small shower in the hall bathroom. But when he pushed open the steamed-up door, she was standing there—wrapped in a towel, waiting for him.

His pulse quickened, and his body hardened with desire. Her gaze flicked down him and then up again, her pupils wide with longing.

"Guess I should have locked the door," he remarked even as he reached for her. He slid his fingers between her breasts, pulling loose the ends of the towel she'd tucked in her cleavage, and then he dragged the towel off her damp body. He pulled the thick terry cloth across his own wet skin as she squeaked in protest.

"Hey!"

"Oh, I thought you'd meant to bring me a towel, like a good hostess." All day she'd played the perfect host, making sure that he and CJ had everything they'd needed. As if she'd felt guilty for keeping them apart.

Was that why she was here now? Out of guilt?

He wanted her, but not that way. God, he wanted her though. She was so damn beautiful, her silky skin flushed from her bath, her curves so full and soft.

He curled his hands into fists so that he wouldn't

reach for her. He had to know first. "Why are you here?"

"Why are you?" she asked. "I figured when I got out of my bath that I would find you gone."

He'd thought about it. But he'd had trouble getting CJ to keep his eyes closed. Every time he'd thought he could leave the little boy's bedside, CJ had dragged his lids up again and asked for Daddy.

Brendan's heart clutched with emotion: love like he'd never known. He'd felt a responsibility to his father to find his killer. But the responsibility he felt to CJ was far greater, because the kid needed and deserved him more. Brendan had to keep the little boy safe—even if he had to give up his own life.

"Why would you think that I would be gone?" he asked. Had becoming a mother given her new instincts? Psychic powers?

"I can feel it," she said. "Your anxiousness. Your edginess."

"You make me anxious," he said. "Edgy…"

She sucked in a shaky breath. And despite the warmth of the steamy shower, her nipples peaked, as if pouting for his touch. He wanted to oblige.

"You make me anxious," she said, "that you're going to sneak out."

"Why would I do that?"

"Because you learned something from going through my files earlier," she said, and her eyes narrowed with suspicion.

"Are you ever not suspicious of me?" he asked, even though this time he couldn't deny that she had reason to be. She'd nearly lost her life, several times, because of him. He wouldn't let her put herself in danger again.

She had so much more to lose now than she'd been forced to give up before.

"I wouldn't be," she replied, "if I ever felt like you were being completely honest with me. But there are always these secrets between us."

"You've kept secrets, too," he reminded her. "One of them is sleeping in the other room."

As if remembering that their son was close, she grabbed a towel from the rack behind her and wrapped it around her naked body.

He sighed his disappointment and hooked the towel he'd stolen from her around his waist. He'd wanted to make love with her again. He'd needed to make love with her again…before he left her.

But she opened the door first as if unable to bear the heat of the bathroom any longer. He followed her down the hall to her bedroom. Like the rest of the house, she'd decorated it warmly. The kitchen was sunny-yellow, the living room orange and her bedroom was a deep red. Like the passion that always burned between them.

"The difference between us," she said, "is that I don't have any more secrets."

He closed the door behind his back before crossing the room and grabbing her towel again. "No, no more secrets."

"You can't say the same," she accused him.

"I know how you feel," he said. "How you taste…"

And he leaned down to kiss her lips. Hers clung to his. And her fingers skimmed over his chest. She wanted him, too.

He slid his mouth across her cheek and down her neck to her shoulder. She shivered in reaction and moaned his name. "Your skin is so warm," he murmured. "So silky."

He skimmed his palms down her back, along the curve of her spine to the rounded swells of her butt. She'd been sexy before, but thin with sharp curves. Now she was more rounded. Soft and so damn sexy that just touching her tried his control.

He had to taste her, too. He gently pushed her down onto the bed. He kissed his way down her body, from her shoulder, over the curve of her breasts. He sucked a taut nipple between his lips and teased it with the tip of his tongue.

She squirmed beneath him, touching him everywhere she could reach. His back. His butt...

He swallowed a groan as the tension built inside him. Another part of him other than his head throbbed and ached, rubbing against her and begging for release.

But he denied his own pleasure to prolong hers. He moved from her breasts, over the soft curve of her stomach to that apex of curls. He teased with his tongue, sliding it in and out of her.

She clutched at his back and then his hair. She arched and wriggled and moaned. And then she came—shattering with ecstasy.

While she was still wet and pulsing, he thrust inside her. And her inner muscles clutched at him, pulling him deeper. She wrapped her legs and arms around him and met each of his thrusts.

Their mouths mated, their kisses frantic, lips clinging, tongue sliding over tongue. He didn't even need to touch her before she shattered again. He thrust once more and joined her in madness—unable to breathe, unable to think...

He could only feel. Pleasure. And love.

He loved her. That was why he had to make certain she would never be in danger again because of him. If he had to give up his life for hers and their son's, he would do it willingly.

Chapter Fourteen

Her body ached. Not from the explosion or even from running from gunmen. Her body ached from making love. Josie smiled and rolled over, reaching across the bed. The sheets were still warm, tangled and scented with their lovemaking. He'd made love to her again and again until she'd fallen into an exhausted slumber.

And she realized why when she jerked awake to an empty bed. An empty room. He'd left her. She didn't need to search her house to confirm that he was gone. But she pulled on a robe and checked CJ's room before she looked through the rest of the house.

Her son slept peacefully, the streetlamp casting light through his bedroom window. It made his red curls glow like fire, reminding her of the explosion.

And she hurried up her search, running through the house before reaching out over the basement stairwell to jerk down the pull chain on the dangling bulb. It swung out over the steps, the light dancing around her as she hurried down to her den. He wasn't there and neither were her folders.

He had found something in them. What?

What had she had?

Notes she'd taken from the conversations she'd overheard in the bar and from informal interviews she'd done with other members of the O'Hannigan family. News clippings from other reporters who'd covered the story. Sloppily. They hadn't dug nearly as deep as she had. A copy of the case file from his father's murder, which she'd bought off a cop on the force. Brendan wasn't wrong that many people had a price. They could be bought.

But not Charlotte.

Too bad the former U.S. marshal wasn't close enough to help her now. Maybe Josie wasn't close enough, either—to stop Brendan from doing what she was afraid he was about to do: either confront or kill his father's murderer.

"But who? Who is it?" she murmured to herself.

She'd gone through the folders so many times that she pretty much had the contents memorized. Brendan had figured it out; so could she. But she couldn't let him keep his head start on her. She had to catch up with him.

No doubt he had taken her SUV. But she had another car parked in the garage off the alley, a rattletrap Volkswagen convertible. It wasn't pretty, but mechanically it should be sound enough to get her back to Chicago. She had bought the car from a student desperate to sell it for money to buy textbooks.

She had never had to struggle for cash as her community college students did. Her father had given her everything she'd ever wanted.

Brendan's father had not done the same for him. In fact, if rumors could ever be believed, Dennis O'Hannigan had taken away the one thing—the one person—who had mattered most to Brendan: his mother.

Why would he want to avenge the man's death? Why would he care enough to get justice for him?

Was it a code? Like the one her father had taught her. She shrugged off her concerns for now. She had to wake CJ and take him over to Mrs. Mallory's.

The little boy murmured in protest as she lifted him from his bed. "C'mon, sweetheart," she said. "I need to take you to Mrs. M's."

He shook his head. "I don't wanna go. Gotta p'tect you like Daddy said."

She tensed. "Daddy told you to protect me?"

"Uh-huh," CJ murmured. "He's gonna get rid of a bad person and then he'll come home to us."

The words her sleepy son uttered had everything falling into place for Josie. Brendan may not have trusted her enough to tell her the truth. But he had inadvertently told their son.

BRENDAN WASN'T SURE who he could trust, especially now that he knew who'd killed his father. But he knew that Josie had at least one person she could trust— besides himself.

Charlotte Green's outraged gasp rattled the phone. "You thought I might have given up her location?"

He pressed his fingers to that scratch on his head. If the bullet hadn't just grazed him…

No, he wouldn't let himself think about what might have happened to Josie and his son. She'd had the gun though—she would have defended herself and their child.

He glanced around the inside of the surveillance van, which was filled with equipment and people— people he wasn't sure he should have trusted despite their federal clearances. If U.S. marshals could be bought, so could FBI agents. He lowered his voice. "After gunmen tracked us down at my safe house and tried to kill us…"

"I didn't even know where you were when you called me, and if I had," she said, her voice chilly with offended pride, "I sure as well wouldn't have sent gunmen after you and Josie and my godson."

He still wasn't so sure about that. But, he realized, she hadn't told anyone where she'd relocated Josie. Why keep that secret and reveal anything else?

"You must have been followed," she said.

He'd thought about that but rejected the notion. "No. Nobody followed us that night."

"Maybe another night then," she suggested. "Someone must have figured out where you would take her."

The only people who knew about the safe house were fellow FBI agents. He glanced around the van, wondering if one of them had betrayed him, if one of them had been bought like Charlotte's former partner had been bought and like he'd thought she might have been. "You didn't trace the call?"

"No."

He snorted in derision. "I thought you were being honest with me. That's why I trusted you."

More than he trusted the crew he'd handpicked. The other men messed with the equipment, setting up mikes and cameras, and he watched them—checking to see if anyone had pulled out a phone as he had. But then if they were tipping off someone, they could have made that call already, before they'd joined him.

"But you must have a GPS on that phone you gave her," he continued, calling her on her lie. "You must have some way to keep tabs on her."

She chuckled. "Okay, maybe I do."

That was why he'd left Josie the phone. "That's what I thought."

"Until recently she was easy to track," Charlotte said. "She was at home or the college."

"Teaching journalism," he remarked. "That's why you kept my secret from her. You realized that I had reason to be cautious with her. That no matter how much you changed her appearance or her identity, she was still a reporter."

"A teacher," Charlotte corrected him.

He snorted again. "Of journalism." And she'd still had the inclination to seek out dangerous stories. For her, there was no story more dangerous than this one. He had to make certain she was far away from him.

"Use your GPS," he ordered, "and tell me where she is now." Hopefully still at home, asleep in the bed he'd struggled to leave. He had wanted to hold her all night; he'd wanted to hold her forever.

Some strange noise emanated from the phone.

"Charlotte?"

"She's on the move."

"But I took her car." She must have borrowed a neighbor's or maybe Mrs. Mallory's. Hopefully, she'd left their son with his babysitter.

"The Volkswagen, too?"

"I didn't know she had another." As modestly as she'd been living in that small, outdated house, he hadn't considered she'd had the extra money for another car.

Charlotte sighed. "I'm surprised that clunker was up to the trip."

"Trip?"

"She's in Chicago."

"Damn it," he cursed at her. "I could have used you

here. I'm surprised you didn't come to help protect her. She thinks you're her friend."

"I am."

"You're also a princess. What is it? Couldn't spare the time from waving at adoring crowds?"

"I'm also pregnant," she said, and there was that sound again. "And currently in labor...since last night. Or I would have come. I would have sent someone I trusted, but they refused to leave me."

Brendan flinched at his insensitivity.

"So like you asked me to, I trusted you," she said. "I thought if anyone would keep Josie safe, it would be the man who loves her."

"I'm trying," he said. And the best way to do that was to remove the threat against her.

He glanced at the monitors flanking one side of the surveillance van. One of the cameras caught a vehicle careening down the street, right toward the estate they were watching on the outskirts of Chicago.

For all the rust holes, he couldn't tell what color the vehicle was. "Her second car," he said. "Is it an old convertible Cabriolet?" Even though the top was currently up, it looked so frayed that there were probably holes in it, too.

"Yes," Charlotte said.

"I have to go," he said, clicking off the cell. But it wasn't just the call he had to abort. He had to stop the whole operation.

"Block the driveway!" he yelled at one of the men wearing a headset. That agent could communicate with the agents outside the van. But he only stared blankly at Brendan, as if unable to comprehend what he was saying. "Stop the car," he explained. "Don't let her get to the house."

"From the way you're acting, I'm guessing that's the reporter you dated," another of the agents inside the van addressed Brendan. He must have been eavesdropping on his conversation with Charlotte. Or he'd tapped into it. "The one you just discovered was put into witness protection and that she had the evidence all this time?"

This agent was Brendan's superior in ranking, and even though he had worked with him for years—four years on this assignment alone—he didn't know him well enough to know about his character.

Could he be trusted?

Could any of them, inside the van or out?

His blood chilled in his veins, and he shook his head, disgusted with himself for giving away Josie's identity so easily. All of his fellow agents had been well aware of how he'd felt about Josie Jessup.

"It isn't?" the agent asked.

"No, it's her," he admitted. "And that's why we have to stop her." Before she confronted face-to-face the person who'd tried to kill her.

The supervising agent shook his head, stopping the man with the headset from making the call to stop her. So Brendan took it upon himself and reached for the handle of the van's sliding door. But strong hands caught him, holding him back and pinning his arms behind him.

Damn it.

He should have followed his instincts to trust no one. He should have done it alone. But he'd wanted to go through the right channels—had wanted true justice, not vigilante justice. But maybe with people as powerful as these, with people who could buy off police officers and federal agents, the only justice was vigilante.

He was going to kill her.

Josie had to stop him—had to stop Brendan from doing something he would live to regret. Taking justice into his own hands would take away the chance for him to have a real relationship with his son.

And her?

She didn't expect him to forgive her for thinking he was a killer. She didn't expect him to trust her, especially after she'd come here. But she had to stop him.

She hadn't seen her white SUV along the street or along the long driveway leading up to the house. But that didn't mean he hadn't exchanged it for one of those she had seen. The house, a brick Tudor, looked eerily similar to Brendan's, just on a smaller scale. Like a model of the original O'Hannigan home.

Brendan had to be here. Unless it was already done....

Was she was too late? Had he already taken his justice and left?

The gates stood open, making it easy for her to drive through and pull her Volkswagen up to the house. But she hadn't even put it in Park before someone was pulling open her door and dragging her from behind the steering wheel. She had no time to reach inside her bag and pull out the gun.

Strong hands held tightly to her arms, shoving her up the brick walk to the front door. It stood open, a woman standing in the doorway as if she'd been expecting her.

Yet she acted puzzled, her brow furrowed as if she was trying to place Josie. Of course, Josie didn't look the same as she had when she'd informally interviewed Margaret O'Hannigan four years ago. Back then the woman had believed Josie was just her stepson's girlfriend. And since they'd only met a few times, it was no wonder she wouldn't as easily see through Josie's disguise as Brendan had.

But Margaret must have realized she'd given herself up during one of their conversations. That was why Margaret had tried to kill Josie.

While Josie had changed much over the past few years, this woman hadn't changed at all. She was still beautiful—her face smooth of wrinkles and ageless. Her hair was rich and dark and devoid of any hint of gray despite the fact that she had to be well into her fifties. She was still trim and tiny. Her beauty and fragile build might have been what had fooled Josie into excluding her as a suspect in her husband's murder.

But now she detected a strength and viciousness about the woman as she stared at Josie, her dark eyes cold and emotionless. "Who the hell are you?" she demanded.

"Josie Jessup," she replied honestly. There was no point clinging to an identity that had already been blown.

"Josie Jessup? I thought you were dead," the woman remarked.

Josie had thought the same of her. That Brendan might have killed her by now.

"Are you responsible for this?" Margaret asked, gesturing toward the open gates and the dark house. An alarm sounded from within, an insistent beeping that must have driven her to the door. "Did you disable the security system, forcing open the gates and unlocking the doors?"

Brendan must have. He was here then. Somewhere. Josie wasn't too late.

"Search her car," Margaret ordered the man who'd held her arms.

Josie stumbled forward as he released her. But the woman didn't step back, didn't allow Josie inside her house.

"I wouldn't know how to disable a security system," Josie assured her. "I am no criminal mastermind."

"No, you're a reporter," Margaret said. "That was why you were always asking all those questions."

"And you were always eager to answer them," Josie reminded her. Too eager, since she hadn't realized she'd given herself away. But then neither had Josie. She still wasn't sure exactly what it was in those folders that had convinced Brendan of the woman's guilt. "You were eager to point the blame at your stepson."

"A man shouldn't benefit from a murder he committed," she said, stubbornly clinging to her lies.

"Brendan didn't kill his father," Josie said, defending the man she loved.

Margaret smiled, but her eyes remained cold. "You weren't so convinced back then. You suspected him just like everyone else."

"And just like everyone else, I was wrong," Josie admitted. "But you knew that."

The woman tensed and stepped out from the doorway. She held a gun in her hand.

For protection? Because of the security breach? Or because someone had tipped her off that either Brendan or Josie was coming to confront her?

"How would I know something that the authorities did not?" Margaret asked, but a small smile lifted her thin lips. "They all believed Brendan responsible, as well."

"But they could never find proof."

"Because he was clever."

"Because he was innocent."

The woman laughed. "You loved him."

It wasn't a question, so Josie didn't reply. Or deny what was probably pathetically obvious to everyone but Brendan.

"That's a pity," the woman commiserated. "It's not easy to love an O'Hannigan. At least you don't need to worry about that anymore."

"I don't?" Josie asked.

"Brendan is dead."

Pain clutched her heart, hurting her as much as if the woman had fired a bullet into her heart. He'd already been here. And gone.

"You didn't know?" Margaret asked. "Some journalist you are. How did you miss the reports?"

Had his death already made the news? The Volkswagen had no radio—just a hole in the dash where one had once been. The kid who'd sold her the auto had been willing to part with his car but not his sound system.

Margaret sighed regretfully. "And it was such a beautiful estate. I'd hoped to return there one day."

"The house?"

"It blew up…with Brendan inside." Margaret shook her head. "Such a loss." With a nasty smile, she clarified, "The house, not Brendan."

The explosion. She was talking about the explosion. Brendan wasn't dead. Relief eased the horrible tightness in Josie's chest, but the sigh she uttered was of disgust with the woman. "How can you be so…"

"Practical?" Margaret asked. "It's so much better than being a romantic fool."

Josie hadn't been a fool for being romantic; she'd been a fool for doubting Brendan. Then. And maybe now.

If he'd intended to kill his stepmother, wouldn't he have already been here? Where was he?

"You're better off," Margaret assured her. "You were stupid to fall for him."

"You didn't love your husband?" Josie asked. That would explain how she'd killed him in cold blood.

She chuckled. "My mama always told me that it was easier to love a rich man than a poor man. My mama had never met Dennis O'Hannigan." She shuddered but her grip stayed steady on the gun. "You were lucky to get away from his son."

"Brendan is—was—" she corrected herself. It was smarter to let the woman think the explosion she'd ordered had worked. "He was nothing like his father."

"You don't believe that or you wouldn't have gone into hiding," Margaret remarked. "You even changed your hair and your face. You must have really been afraid of him."

She had spent almost four years being afraid of the wrong person.

"Were you afraid of his father?" Josie asked.

Margaret shrugged her delicate shoulders. "A person would have been crazy to *not* be afraid of Dennis."

Dennis wasn't the only O'Hannigan capable of inspiring fear. Neither was Brendan.

Despite her small stature, Margaret O'Hannigan was an intimidating woman.

So Josie should have held her tongue. She should have stopped asking her questions. But maybe Brendan was right—maybe she wasn't capable of *not* being a journalist. Because she had to know…

Even if the question cost her everything, she had to ask, "Is that why you killed him?"

Chapter Fifteen

Brendan fought against the men holding him. He shoved back with his body and his head. He knocked the back of his skull against one man's nose, dropping him to the floor while the other stumbled into the equipment. Then he whipped a gun from his holster and whirled to confront his attackers.

Men he had hoped he could trust: fellow FBI agents.

"I should have known," he berated himself. "I should have known the leak was inside the Bureau. I should have known there was no one I could trust."

Special Agent Martinez, the man supervising the assignment, calmly stared down the barrel of Brendan's gun. "I've heard about this happening to agents like you, ones who've been undercover more than they've been out. Ones who get so paranoid of the lives they're living that they lose their grasp on reality. On sanity. You're losing it, O'Hannigan."

"No, we're losing *her,*" Brendan said, as one of the monitors showed Josie walking inside the house with a killer. Margaret O'Hannigan held a gun, too, pointed at the woman he loved.

"We've got the house wired," Martinez reminded him. "We're going to hear everything that they say."

"But the plan was for *me* to get her to talk," he said and lowered the gun to his side. He wasn't going to use it. Yet...

Martinez nodded in agreement. "But once she sees you're alive, you wouldn't get anything out of her."

"Neither will Josie," he argued.

"Josie Jessup is a reporter." Martinez was the one who'd confirmed Brendan's suspicions about it, who'd tracked her back to the stories written under the pseudonym of Jess Ley. "A damn good one. She fooled you four years ago."

And allowing himself to be deceived and distracted had nearly gotten Brendan thrown off the case. But because he'd inherited his father's business, he had been the only one capable of getting inside the organization and taking it apart, as the FBI had been trying to do for years.

"She won't fool Margaret." Because Margaret had fooled them all for years. Even his father.

Martinez shook his head. "She's Stanley Jessup's daughter. She has a way of making people talk. She knows what buttons to push, what questions to ask."

That was what Brendan was afraid of—that she'd push the wrong buttons. "If Margaret admits anything to her, it's only because she intends to kill her."

"Then we'll go in," Martinez assured him. "The evidence you found got us the federal warrants for the surveillance. But there isn't enough for an arrest. We need a confession. You were the one who pointed that out."

And he'd intended to get the confession himself. He hadn't intended to use Josie—to put her in danger. Their son needed his mother; Brendan needed her, too.

On the surveillance monitors, one of Margaret's

bodyguards walked into the house, something swing-ing from the hand that wasn't holding a gun.

"We won't get there fast enough to save her," Bren-dan said, as foreboding and dread clutched his heart. The van was parked outside the gates. Even though they were open, thanks to the security system being dismantled, they were still too far down the driveway.

"There are guys closer," Martinez reminded him.

But were they guys he could trust? Could he really trust anyone?

SHE SHOULD HAVE trusted Brendan. Just because he'd discovered the identity of his father's killer didn't mean he was going to avenge the man's death.

But she'd thought the worst of him again. And she'd worried that CJ would lose his father before he ever got a chance to really know him. Now a gun was pointed at her, and the risk was greater that CJ would lose his mother. At least he had his godmother; Charlotte would take him. She would protect him as Josie had failed to do.

With the lights off and the draperies pulled, it was dark inside the house—nearly as dark as if night had fallen already. Except a little sliver of sunlight sneaked through a crack in the drapes and glinted off the metal of Margaret O'Hannigan's gun.

She looked much more comfortable holding a weapon than Josie was. Maybe she should reach for hers. Her purse was on the hardwood floor next to where Margaret had pushed her down onto the couch. Even the inside of the home was a replica of Dennis O'Hanningan's.

"Are you insinuating that I killed my husband? What

the hell are you talking about?" the older woman demanded to know.

"The truth." A concept that Josie suspected Margaret O'Hannigan was not all that familiar with. "And I'm not insinuating. I'm flat-out saying that you're the one. You killed Brendan's father."

"How dare you accuse me of killing my husband!" she exclaimed, clearly offended, probably not because Josie thought her capable of murder but because she hadn't gotten away with it.

Hell, she would still probably get away with it. Josie glanced down at her bag again. She needed to grab her gun, needed to defend herself. But then it was no longer just the two of them.

Heavy footsteps echoed on the hardwood flooring. "There was nothing in her car," the man who had dragged Josie from the Volkswagen informed his boss as he joined them inside the house. "But this."

Josie turned to see CJ's booster seat dangling from his hand.

"You have a child?" Margaret asked.

She could have lied, claimed she'd borrowed a friend's car. But she was curious. Would Margaret spare her because she was a mother? "Why does it matter that I have a son?"

"How old is he?" Margaret asked.

"Three." Too young to lose his mother, especially as she'd been the only parent he'd ever known until a day ago.

Margaret shook her head. "No. No. No…"

"It's okay," Josie said. "You can let me go. I don't really know anything. I have no proof that you killed Dennis O'Hannigan."

The man glanced from her to Margaret and back.

Had he not worked for her back then? Had he not realized his employer was a killer?

Maybe he would protect her from the madwoman.

"You have something far worse," Margaret said. "You have Brendan O'Hannigan's son."

"Wh-what?"

"The last time I saw you, I suspected you were pregnant," Margaret admitted. "You were—" her mouth twisted into a derisive smirk "—glowing."

Josie hadn't even known she was pregnant then. She hadn't known until after her big fight with Brendan, until after she'd had the car accident when her brakes had given out and she'd been taken to the hospital. That was when she'd learned she carried his child.

"You—you don't know that my son is Brendan's," Josie pointed out.

"All I'll have to do is see a picture," she said. She pointed toward Josie's purse and ordered her employee, "Go through that."

He upended the contents of the bag, the gun dropping with a thud to the floor.

"You should have used that while you had the chance," Margaret said. "I didn't waste my chance."

"Are you talking about now?" Josie wondered. "Or when you shot your husband in the alley behind O'Hannigan's?" She suspected this woman was cold-blooded enough to have done it personally.

The man handed over Josie's wallet to his boss. The picture portfolio hung out of it, the series of photos a six-month progression of CJ from infancy to his birthday a couple of months ago. Usually people smiled when they saw the curly-haired boy. But his step-grandmother glowered.

"Damn it," Margaret cursed. "Damn those O'Hannigan eyes."

Josie could not deny her son's paternity. "Why do you care that Brendan has—had—a son?"

"Because I am not about to have another damn O'Hannigan heir come out of the woodwork again and claim what is rightfully mine," she replied angrily. "I worked damn hard for it. I earned it."

"So you didn't kill your husband because you were afraid of him. You killed him because you wanted his fortune," Josie mused aloud.

The woman's eyes glittered with rage and her face— once so beautiful—contorted into an ugly mask. "He was going to divorce me," she said, outraged at even the memory. "After all those years of putting up with his abuse, he was going to leave me. Claimed he never loved me."

"You never loved him, either," Josie pointed out.

"That was why it felt so damn good to pull the trigger," she admitted gleefully. "To see that look of surprise on his face as I shot him right in the chest. He had no idea who he was married to—had no idea that I could be as ruthless as he was. And that I was that good a shot."

So she had fired the gun herself. And apparently she'd taken great pleasure from it. Josie had no hope of this callous killer sparing her life.

Margaret chuckled wryly. "The coroner said the bullet hit him right in the heart. I was surprised because I didn't figure he had one."

"Then why did you marry him?"

"For the same reason I killed him—for the money," she freely admitted.

She stepped closer and pointed the barrel right at

Josie's head. "So your kid is damn well not going to come forward and claim it from me now."

Margaret thought Brendan was dead—that CJ was the only threat to her inheriting now. But if Brendan had really died, the estate would go to his heirs, not his stepmother. Then Josie remembered that Dennis O'Hannigan had had a codicil in his will that only an O'Hannigan would hold deed to the estate. Before Brendan had accepted his inheritance, he'd had to sign a document promising to leave it only to an O'Hannigan. Margaret must have thought she was the only one left.

"He's only three years old," Josie reminded her. "He's not going to take anything away from you."

"I didn't think Brendan would, either. After he ran away I thought he was never coming back." She sighed. "I thought his dad had made sure he could never come back, the same way that he had made sure Brendan's mother could never come back."

"You thought Dennis had killed him?"

"He should have," Margaret said. The woman wasn't just greedy; she was pure evil. "Then I wouldn't have had that nasty surprise."

She was going to have another one when she learned that once again Brendan wasn't dead. But if he wasn't... where was he? Shouldn't he have been here before now?

Could someone else have hurt him? Or maybe the authorities had brought him in for questioning about the explosion and the shootings at the hospital....

Maybe if she bided her time...

But Margaret pressed the gun to Josie's temple as if ready to squeeze the trigger. The burly guard flinched as if he could feel Josie's pain. "Now you are going to tell me where you've left your brat so we can make sure I don't get another nasty surprise."

"He doesn't need your money," Josie pointed out. "He's a Jessup. My father has more money than CJ will ever be able to spend."

"CJ?"

Josie bit her tongue, appalled that she'd given away her son's name. Not that his first name alone would lead the woman to him.

"So where is CJ?"

"Someplace where you can't get to him," Josie assured herself more than the boy's step-grandmother. He was safe now, and Brendan would make certain he stayed that way. No matter what happened to her.

"You'll tell me," Margaret said as she slid her finger onto the trigger.

Uncaring that the barrel was pressed to her temple, Josie shook her head. "You might as well shoot me now, because I will never let you get to my son."

The trigger cocked, and Josie closed her eyes, waiting for it. Would it hurt? Or would it be over so quickly she wouldn't even realize it?

The gun barrel jerked back so abruptly that Josie's head jerked forward, too. "Help me persuade her," Margaret ordered her guard.

And Josie's head snapped again as the man slapped her. Her cheek stung and her eyes watered as pain overwhelmed her.

"Where is he?" Margaret asked.

Josie shook her head.

And the man slapped her again.

A cry slipped from her mouth as her lip cracked from the blow. Blood trickled from the stinging wound.

"I'm never going to tell you where my son is," she vowed. "I don't care how many times you hit me."

"I care."

Josie looked up to see Brendan saunter into the living room as nonchalantly as if he were just joining them for drinks. But instead of bringing a bottle of wine, he'd brought a gun—which he pointed directly at Margaret. Probably because she had whirled toward him with her weapon.

But her guard had pulled his gun, and he pressed the barrel to Josie's head. Brendan may have intended to rescue her, but Josie had a horrible feeling that they were about to make their son an orphan.

She should have thought it out before she'd chased after Brendan. She had been concerned about CJ losing his father, but now he might lose both his parents.

"I THOUGHT YOU were dead," Margaret said, slinging her words at him like an accusation.

"You keep making that mistake," Brendan said. "Guess that's just been wishful thinking on your part."

"I thought the explosion killed you."

"You were behind that?"

"I wanted you dead," she admitted, without actually claiming responsibility.

But she'd already confessed to enough to go away for a long time. Martinez had been right about Josie making her talk. Now that Josie had gotten what they'd wanted, he needed to get her to safety.

"I've wanted you dead for a long time," Margaret continued. "This time I'll personally make sure you're gone. You've disrupted my plans for the last time." She cocked her gun at him now. "Then we'll retrieve your son."

She gestured at Josie as if they were co-conspirators. Had she not heard anything Josie had said to her? Josie would die before she would give up her son's location. That was what a mother should be like. CJ was one lucky boy. And Brendan would make sure they were reunited soon.

But Margaret was not done. She was confessing to crimes she had yet to commit. Crimes that Brendan would make damn certain she never got the chance to commit. "And when I get rid of that kid, I'll be making damn sure there will be no more O'Hannigans."

"You're the one who'll be going away forever," Brendan warned her as he cocked his gun. But if he shot her, would the guy holding Josie surrender or kill her?

Chapter Sixteen

"Don't kill her," Josie implored Brendan. Maybe she had been right to be concerned that he would take matters into his own hands. But why had he taken so long to show up here? Where had he been?

Brendan narrowed his eyes as if he were still thinking about pulling the trigger, about taking a life. He could even excuse it as he had the others—that he'd done it to save another.

"Josie, I have to," he said, as if he'd been given no choice.

She had been thrilled to see him, thrilled that he might protect her from this madwoman. But she didn't want him becoming her—becoming a killer.

"You told me you wanted justice," she reminded him. "Not vengeance."

"He's a killer," Margaret said, spit flying from her mouth with disgust. "All O'Hannigans are killers. That's why it's best to get rid of the boy, too. Or he'll grow up just like Brendan has."

"Brendan isn't a killer," Josie told her—and him. "He came back for justice. He figured out you killed his father."

"How?" the woman arrogantly scoffed. "No one else has figured it out in four years."

"She did," Brendan said. "And she has evidence."

"What evidence?" Josie asked. He had to be bluffing or at least exaggerating the evidentiary value of what he'd found. She'd gone through those folders so many times but hadn't figured out what he'd discerned so quickly.

Margaret snorted. "Evidence. It doesn't matter. It's never going to get to court. I will never be arrested."

That was Josie's concern, too. And then Brendan's name would never be cleared.

"I already brought the evidence to the district attorney," Brendan said, answering one of Josie's questions.

Now she knew where he'd been. He had gone through the right channels for justice.

"The arrest warrant should have been issued by now," Brendan continued. But he was looking at her henchman instead of Margaret, as if warning him. Or trying to use his bluff to scare him off. "Do you want to go to jail with her?"

"I had nothing to do with her killing your dad," the man said. "I didn't even work for her then."

"But you're working for her now," Brendan said. "You've assaulted a woman and threatened the life of a child. I think those charges will put you away for a while, too, especially if you're already on parole for other crimes."

The man's face flushed with color. He shook his head, but not in denial of his criminal record. Instead he pulled the gun away from Josie and murmured, "I'm sorry."

"Don't let him get to you," Margaret said. "He's bluffing. He's just bluffing."

The man shook his head again, obviously unwilling to risk it. It wasn't as if they were playing poker for money. They were playing for prison.

"Where are you going?" Margaret screamed after him as he headed for the door. "How dare you desert me!"

The man was lucky that she was having a standoff with Brendan or she probably would have fired a bullet into his back. She was that furious.

"You should just give it up," Josie told her. "You have no help now."

Margaret glared. "Neither does he."

"He has me," Josie said.

"Not for long," Margaret said. "He's going to lose you just like you're going to lose that brat of yours."

"You just shut the hell up," Josie warned the woman, her temper fraying from the threats and insults directed at CJ. "Don't ever talk about my son."

Margaret chuckled, so Josie struck her. She'd hoped to knock the gun from the petite woman's hand. But the older lady was surprisingly strong. She held on to her gun and swung it toward Josie, pressing it into her heart—which was exactly what her insults and threats had been hitting.

"You get involved with a killer, sooner or later you're going to wind up dead," the woman said. "Too bad for you it's going to be sooner."

Wasn't it already later—since Margaret had first tried to kill her four years ago? But Josie kept that question to herself.

"YOU'RE THE KILLER," Brendan corrected Margaret. So she would have no compunction pulling the trigger and killing Josie. It was what she'd intended to do from the moment she'd forced her inside the house. That was why she'd confessed to her—because she planned to make sure Josie could never testify against her.

"If you had really turned over proof to the district attorney, the police would be here already," Margaret said. "You have nothing."

"You confessed to Josie."

"Just now," she said. "And she'll never live to testify against me."

"No," he said, "you confessed to her four years ago."

Margaret laughed. "She doesn't even know what evidence you had. I think she damn well would have known had I confessed to her."

"You weren't confessing," Brendan admitted. "You were trying to convince her of my guilt. You told her that it must have been someone he trusted since my father had never pulled his gun."

Josie gasped. "And all the other reports—except for the official police report—claimed he'd been killed with his own gun."

Since Dennis O'Hannigan was legendary for turning a person's weapon on them, it had been the height of irony that he'd had his own gun turned on him.

Brendan shook his head. "But all his guns were in their holsters." He'd learned from his father to have more than one backup weapon. "Only the killer would know that he hadn't pulled any of them, that he'd trusted his killer."

Margaret snorted. "Trusted? Hell, no. Underestimated is what he'd done. He thought I was too weak and helpless to be a threat."

"And he would have considered me a threat," Brendan said, because his father had known what his son had become. What he really was.

So why had he left him the business?

"You underestimated me, too," she accused Brendan. "You never considered me a threat, either."

He hadn't realized just how dangerous she was—until she'd turned her gun on the woman he loved. "It's over, Margaret."

"On that flimsy evidence?" she asked, nearly as incredulous as the district attorney had been.

"No, on the confession that the FBI has recorded."

She glanced at Josie as if checking her for a wire.

"When your security system was hacked, the house was bugged. Every intercom in the place turned on like a mike."

She glanced around at the intercom by the door and another on the desk behind her.

"You're under arrest for the murder of Dennis O'Hannigan," he said, "and the attempted murders of Josie Jessup and—"

The woman raised her eyebrows and scoffed. "You're arresting me? On what authority?"

"FBI," he said. "I'm an FBI agent."

Josie's eyes widened with surprise. He'd hoped that she might have figured it out, that she would have realized he was not a bad man.

"You are not," Margaret said. "You're bluffing again, treating me like a fool just like your father did."

With his free hand he pulled out his credentials, which he hadn't been able to carry for the past four years, and flashed his shield at her. "No. Game over."

She stubbornly shook her head and threatened, "I am going to pull the trigger."

"Then so will I," he replied. And he was bluffing now.

"You won't risk her life." Margaret knowingly called

him on his lie. "I saw how you were when she disappeared four years ago. You were as devastated as you were when your mother disappeared."

He couldn't deny the truth—not anymore.

"So you're going to step back and let me leave with her," Margaret said.

"And what do you think you're going to do?" Brendan asked. "Talk her into taking you to our son?"

Margaret's gaze darted between him and Josie. That had been her plan—all part of her deranged plan.

"She'll never do that," Brendan said. "You won't be able to kill all the O'Hannigans. And even if you thought you did, you still wouldn't be the last one." He chuckled now at how incredibly flawed the woman's plan was. "You're actually not even a real O'Hannigan."

Anger tightened her lips into a thin line. "I married your father."

"But it wasn't legal," he informed her.

She glared at him. "I have the license to prove it, since you're all about evidence."

"It wasn't legal because he was still married," he explained.

"What?" she gasped.

"My mother isn't dead."

"Yes, she is," Margaret frantically insisted. "Your father killed her. Everyone knows that."

"He'd beaten her...." Which Brendan had witnessed; he'd been only eleven years old and helpless to protect her. "He sent her to the hospital, but she didn't die. She went into witness protection."

But still she wouldn't testify against him. Not because she had still loved the man but because she'd loved Brendan. And to protect him, she had struck a bargain with the devil.

Maybe he would have to do the same to protect Josie.

"You're lying," Margaret said. She was distracted now, more focused on him than Josie.

He shook his head, keeping her attention on him while he tried to ignore Special Agent Martinez speaking through his earpiece. Brendan was calling the shots now. And he wouldn't do that until Josie was out of the line of fire.

"Where do you think I ran away to when I was fifteen?" he asked. Thank God he hadn't wound up living on the streets, which he'd been desperate enough to do. He'd found a place to go. A home.

"I didn't think you really ran away," Margaret said. "I know you tried, that you stole one of your father's cars. But that car was returned that same night—without you. And you were never seen again."

As he relived that night, his heart flipped with the fear he'd felt when his father's men had driven him off the road and into the ditch. At fifteen he hadn't had enough experience behind the wheel to be able to outmaneuver them. And when they'd jerked him from behind the wheel and left him alone with his father, he'd thought he was dead, that he'd be going to see his mother in heaven.

His father had sent him to her with a bus ticket and a slip of paper with an address on it. His mother had been relocated to New York, where she had built a life fostering runaway kids. And somehow, either using money or threats, Dennis had found out exactly what had happened to his wife and where she was. Brendan had used that bus ticket to reunite with her and become one of those kids. And in exchange for getting her son back, his mother had agreed to never testify against Dennis O'Hannigan.

"My mom will actually be here soon," he said with a glance at Josie. "But the other agents will be here before her."

That was the cue, sent through his headset, to make all hell break loose.

Chapter Seventeen

Josie was reeling from all the answers she'd just received to questions she hadn't even known to ask. Was it true? Was any of it true?

Brendan had flashed the badge, but she hadn't had a chance to read it. Was it *his* name on it? Was he really an FBI agent? And what about his mother being alive all these years in witness protection?

It all seemed so unrealistic that it almost had to be real. And it explained so much.

She heard the footsteps then. And so did Margaret. Before the woman could react and pull the trigger, Josie shoved her back and then dropped to the floor as shots rang out.

The house exploded. There was no bomb, but the effects were the same. Glass shattered. Footsteps pounded. Voices shouted. And shots were fired.

She wasn't sure she would feel if any bullets struck her. She was numb with shock. She'd thought she had fooled and deceived Brendan four years ago. But she had been the fool. In her search for what she'd thought was the truth, she had fallen for the lies. This woman's lies. The other news reports about him.

He could have set her straight, but he had chosen instead to keep his secrets. And to let her go…

A hand clutched her hair, pulling her head up as a barrel pressed again to her temple. How many times could a gun be held to her head before it was fired? Either on purpose or accidentally?

Josie worried that her luck was about to run out.

"Let her go!" Brendan shouted the order. And cocked his gun.

Another shot rang out, along with a soft click, and Josie flinched, waiting for the pain to explode in her head. But then Margaret dropped to the floor beside her, blood spurting from her shoulder. Her eyes wide open with shock, she stared into Josie's face. Then she began to curse, calling Josie every vulgar name as agents jerked her to her feet.

Then there were hands on Josie's arms, hands that shook a little as they helped her up. Her legs wobbled and she pitched slightly forward, falling into a broad chest. Strong arms closed around her, holding her steady.

"Are you all right?" Brendan asked, his deep voice gruff with emotion.

She wasn't sure. "How—how did she not shoot me… when she got shot?"

"She'd already fired all her bullets," he replied.

She realized the soft click she'd heard had been from the empty cartridge. "Did you know?"

"I counted."

How? In the chaos of the raid, how had he kept track of it all? But then she remembered that he was a professional. She was the amateur, the one who hadn't belonged in his world four years ago and certainly didn't belong there now.

She belonged with her son. She should have never left him.

Exhausted, she laid her head on his chest. His heart beat as frantically as hers, both feeling the aftereffects of adrenaline and fear. At least Josie had been afraid.

She wasn't sure how Brendan felt about anything. She hadn't even known who he really was.

PARAMEDICS HAD PUT her in the back of an ambulance, but she had refused to lie down on the stretcher. She sat up on it, her legs dangling over the side. She wasn't a small woman, yet there was something childlike about her now, Brendan thought. She looked...lost.

"Is she okay?" he asked the paramedic who'd stepped out of the ambulance to talk quietly to him.

"Except for some bruises, she's physically all right," the paramedic assured him. "But she does appear to be in shock."

Was that because she'd been held and threatened by a crazy woman? Or because she had finally learned the truth about him?

"It looks like you were hit," the paramedic remarked, reaching up toward Brendan's head. He hadn't been hit, but not for lack of trying on his stepmother's part. As lousy a shot as she was, she must have been very close to his father to have killed him.

Too close for his father to have seen how dangerous the woman really was. His father had been so smart and careful when it came to business. Why had he'd been so sloppy and careless when it had come to pleasure?

Four years ago, when Brendan had found out his lover was really a reporter after a story, he'd thought he had been careless, too. And his carelessness had nearly gotten Josie killed.

"I'm fine," he told the paramedic. "That's not even recent." Two nights ago seemed like a lifetime ago. But then it had been a different life, one that Brendan didn't need to live anymore. He'd found the justice for which he'd started searching four years ago.

As he watched an agent load a bandaged and hand-cuffed Margaret into the back of a federal car, he knew he had justice. But he held up a hand to halt the car. Her wounded shoulder had already been treated, so she'd been medically cleared to be booked. But he didn't want them booking her yet, not before he knew all the charges against her.

"It's not scabbed over yet," the young woman persisted, as she continued to inspect the scratch on Brendan's head.

"I'm fine. But maybe you should double check the suspect," he suggested. After the paramedic left, he turned back toward the ambulance and found Josie staring at him.

She had lost that stunned look of shock. Her brow was furrowed, her eyes dark, and she looked mad. She had every right to be angry—furious, even. "I'm sorry," he said.

"Are you sorry that you saved my life?" she asked. "Or are you sorry that you lied to me?"

"I never lied."

She nodded her head sharply in agreement. "You didn't have to. You just let me make all my wrong assumptions and you never bothered to correct me. Is that why you're sorry?"

"I'm sorry," he said, "because I never should have gotten involved with you—not when I had just started the most dangerous assignment of my career." But he'd been sloppy and careless. He'd let his attraction to her overcome his common sense.

Special Agent Martinez had urged him to go for it, that having a girlfriend gave Brendan a better cover and made him look more like his dad. That it might have roused suspicions if he'd turned down such a beautiful woman. But Brendan couldn't blame Martinez. It hadn't been an order, more so a suggestion. Brendan hadn't had to listen to him.

It was all his fault—everything Josie had been through, everything she'd lost. She hadn't died, but she'd still lost her home, her family, her career. If only he'd stayed away from her...

If only he'd resisted his attraction to her...

But he'd never felt anything as powerful.

"You thought I was going to blow your cover," she said. "That's why you didn't tell me what was going on. You didn't trust that I wouldn't go public with the story."

"I know you, Josie. You can't stop being a reporter," he reminded her. "Even after they relocated you, you were ferreting out stories."

"But if you had asked me not to print anything, I would have held off," she said. "I wouldn't have put your life in danger."

No. He was the one who'd put her life in danger. And he understood that she would probably never be able to forgive him, especially if her father didn't make it.

"But you didn't trust me," she said.

"You didn't trust me, either," he said, "or you wouldn't have raced here to make sure I didn't kill Margaret for vigilante justice. You still suspected that I might be a killer."

"I didn't know who you really are," she said.

She hadn't known what he really did for a living, but she should have known what kind of person he was. Since she hadn't, there was no way that she could love him.

"How did you figure out where I had gone?" he asked. "You had all that information for years, but you never put it together. And then I took everything to present to the district attorney. So how did you realize it was Margaret?"

"CJ told me."

He laughed at her ridiculous claim. "CJ? How did he figure it out?"

"*You* told him," she said, "when you told him that you were going to get rid of the bad person so he'd be safe."

He hadn't even known if the little boy was truly awake when he'd told him goodbye. It was wanting to make sure that goodbye wasn't permanent that had had Brendan going through the proper channels for the arrest warrant.

"You said bad *person*," she said, "not bad man, like we'd been telling him the shooters and the bomber was. Since Margaret was the only female I'd talked to about your father's murder, it had to be her."

He glanced to that car where his stepmother sat and waited for him. He needed to question her. But he dreaded leaving Josie after he had nearly lost her. He couldn't even blink without horrible images replaying in his mind—the burly man slapping her so hard her neck snapped and then the gun pressed to her temple...

Josie shivered as she followed his gaze. "I need to get home to CJ. I need to make sure he's safe."

"You don't need to go home," he said. "He should be here very soon."

Her brow furrowed. "How? Is Charlotte bringing him?"

"Charlotte couldn't come." He wondered if the former U.S. marshal had had her baby yet. "So I sent someone else to get him from Mrs. Mallory's."

She clutched his arm with a shaking hand. "You shouldn't have trusted anyone else, not with our son.

"I sent the only person I trust," he said.

She shivered again as if his words had chilled her. He didn't mean to hurt her feelings, but he hadn't been able to trust her—any more than she had been able to trust him.

The arrival of another vehicle, a minivan, drew their attention to the driveway. He smiled as an older woman jumped out of the driver's seat and pulled open the sliding door to the back. A redheaded little boy raised his arms and encircled the woman's neck as she lifted him from his booster seat.

"Looks like CJ likes his grandma," he murmured.

Josie gasped. "That's your mother? She really is alive?"

The dark, curly-haired woman was small, like Margaret, but she had so much energy and vibrancy. She would never be mistaken for fragile. She was the strongest woman he had ever known...until he'd witnessed Josie's fearlessness over and over again. She would have taken a bullet in the brain before she would have ever led Margaret to their son.

Almost too choked with emotion over seeing his mom and son together, Brendan only nodded. Then he cleared his throat and added, "My dangerous assignment is over now." And given what he now knew he had to lose, he didn't intend to ever go undercover again. "So I'd like to have a relationship with my son."

"Of course," she immediately agreed. "I'm glad he's met your mother. She sounds like an amazing woman. She gave up so much for you."

Just as Josie would have for their son. For him, Brendan's mother had given up justice for all the pain his father had put her through.

He nodded. "She is."

Josie smiled as the little boy giggled in his grandmother's arms as she tickled him. "I would like CJ to meet my father now—if you think it's safe."

"It's all over now," Brendan assured her. "Margaret knows that. Anyone who worked for her knows that now." The burly guard was sitting in the back of another car. Agents had apprehended him as he'd hightailed it out of the house. "It will be safe."

She bit her bottom lip and sighed. "For us. I'm not sure how safe it'll be for my father though. I don't want to risk giving him another heart attack. It's bad enough that he was attacked to draw me out of hiding."

And that was probably his fault, too—Margaret's wanting to make sure no other O'Hannigan heirs stood in the way of her greed. He needed to interview the crazy woman and find out who she'd been working with—who she'd bought.

"I'm sorry," he said again. He couldn't apologize enough for the danger in which he'd put Josie and their son.

BRENDAN WANTED A relationship with his son but not her. Would he never trust her? Would he never forgive her for deceiving him?

He had deceived her, too. Of course he'd had his reasons. And his orders. He couldn't tell her the truth and risk her blowing his cover.

Now she understood why he'd been so angry with her when he'd realized she had initially sought him out for an exposé. It hadn't been just a matter of pride. It had been a matter of life and death.

After all the times she'd been shot at and nearly blown up, she understood how dangerous his life was. That was why he'd kept apologizing to her.

He'd said he was sorry, but he'd never said what she'd wanted to hear. That he loved her.

She sighed.

"Everything all right, miss?" the driver asked.

She glanced into the back of the government Suburban where CJ's booster seat had been buckled. Her son was safe and happy. Of course he hadn't wanted to leave his daddy or his grandma, but he'd agreed when she'd explained he was going to meet his grandpa.

"Yes, I just hope that my dad is better." That he would be strong enough to handle the surprise of seeing her alive and well.

The older man nodded. She hadn't noticed him during all the turmoil earlier in Margaret's house. He didn't have a scratch on his bald head or a wrinkle in his dark suit. Maybe he hadn't been part of the rescue. Maybe he'd been in the van that they'd passed as they'd left the estate.

"Thank you for driving me to the hospital, Agent…"

"Marshal," he replied. "I'm a U.S. marshal."

"Did Charlotte send you?" she asked. Brendan had told her why her friend had been unable to come to her aid herself; she was having a baby. She hadn't even known Charlotte was pregnant. It had to be Aaron Timmer's baby. Josie had realized her friend was falling for her former bodyguard shortly after he'd been hired to work palace security, too. Had they married? She'd

been so preoccupied with her own life lately that she
hadn't gotten the specifics of what Charlotte and Princess Gabriella had endured.

"Charlotte?" the man repeated the name.

"Charlotte Green," Josie explained. "She was the
marshal who relocated me in the program."

The man nodded. "Yes, she didn't tell anyone else
where she'd placed you. Not even her partner."

Josie shuddered as she thought of the man who
would have killed to learn her whereabouts. He must
have been working for Margaret O'Hannigan. But then
why had the woman thought she was dead?

"It's a shame that Trigger was killed."

"In self-defense." Josie defended her former bodyguard. Whit was the one who'd found the bomb in
the safe house and called the marshals. Everything
had moved so quickly after that—Josie had moved so
quickly.

"He was a friend."

Josie shivered now and glanced back at CJ to make
sure he was all right. "Trigger was a friend of yours?"

"Yes, a close friend. We used to work together," he
said. "But then things happened in my life. I took a
leave from work and lost Trigger as my partner with
the Marshals. We also lost touch for a while...until recently. Then we reconnected."

"You had talked to him recently?" she asked.

"Right before he died..."

"Do you know who he was working for?" Josie
asked. It might help the district attorney's case against
Margaret to have a witness who could corroborate that
she'd hired the hit on her.

"He wasn't working for anyone," the man replied.
"He was doing a favor for a friend."

God, no...

She realized that this man was the friend for whom Trigger had been doing the favor. This man was the one who'd wanted her location, and from the nerves tightening her stomach into knots, she suspected he had not wanted her found in order to wish her well. She glanced down at her bag lying on the floor at her feet. Could she reach inside without his noticing? She didn't have the gun anymore. It had been left at the crime scene back at Margaret O'Hannigan's house. But if she could get to her phone...

She couldn't call Charlotte, but she could call Brendan. He would come; he would save her and their son as he had so many times over the past few days.

She should have trusted him four years ago. If she had showed him the information she'd compiled, they would have figured out together that it was Margaret who had killed his father. But apprehending Margaret earlier wouldn't have kept Josie safe.

"You were the friend?" she asked, as she leaned down and reached for her purse.

"If you're looking for this," he remarked as he lifted a cell phone from under his thigh, "don't bother." The driver's window lowered, and he tossed out the phone. "That way Charlotte Green's little GPS device won't be able to track you down."

He must have taken the phone from her purse while she'd been buckling CJ into his seat in the back. She was so tired that she hadn't even been aware of what the man was doing. She had barely been aware of him.

"Who are you?" she asked, her heart beating fast with panic and dread.

"You don't recognize me?"

She was afraid to look directly at him. A hostage

was never supposed to look at her kidnapper. If she couldn't identify him, he might let her live.

But as her blood chilled, she realized this wasn't a kidnapper. Unlike Margaret O'Hannigan, this person wasn't interested in money. He had an entirely different agenda.

"I—I don't know," she replied, but she was staring down at her purse, wondering what might have been left inside that she could use as a weapon. "I've been away for so many years."

"You're the one who looks different," he said. "But I know the doctor Charlotte Green sends witnesses to, so I got him to show me your files. I knew what you'd look like. I recognized you in the parking garage."

"That—that was you?" she asked.

He nodded his head. "And the other so-called orderly was at O'Hannigan's place, setting up the backup plan."

She glanced again at CJ and whispered, "The bomb?"

"But you were just so quick," he murmured regretfully. "Too quick."

"And Brendan's apartment?"

"I have a friend with the Bureau, one who knew that your little mob friend is really an agent, so he knew where his safe house is."

The guy had gotten to another marshal and an agent. Which agent? Were Brendan and his mother safe?

"Is—is this agent going to hurt Brendan?"

He chuckled. "He thinks O'Hannigan walks on water. He didn't realize why I was asking about the guy."

"He'll put it together now," she warned him. "Since the bomb and the shooting."

The man shook his head. "No. No one would ever consider me capable of what I've done and what I'm about to do."

"Because you're a U.S. marshal?"

"Because I'm a good marshal," he said, "and I've always been a good man."

Then maybe he would change his mind. Maybe he wouldn't shoot her and her son....

"But you and your father changed all that," he said. "That's why you have to pay. You and your father took everything from me, everything that mattered. So now I'm going to do that to your father. I'm going to take away what matters most to him. Again."

So even four years ago, this man had been the one—the one who'd cut her brakes and set up the bomb. All of it had been because of him.

"Mr. Peterson," she murmured as recognition dawned. How had she not remembered that Donny Peterson's father was a U.S. marshal? Her former college classmate had brought it up enough, using it as a threat against whoever challenged him. She hadn't heeded that threat, though; she'd continued to pursue the story that had led to Donny's destruction. So all of it had been because of *her*.

Neither of the bombs or the shootings at the hospital and the apartment complex had had anything to do with Brendan's job, his family or his relationship with her.

It was all her fault and she was about to pay for that with her life. But Brendan, who'd had nothing to do with it, would pay, too—when he lost his son.

"Now you know who I am."

If only she'd realized it earlier...

If only she and CJ hadn't gotten inside the SUV with him.

"I understand why you're upset," she assured him, hoping to reason with him. "But you should be upset with me. Not with my son. Not with my father."

"You fed him the information, but he wrote the damn story." He snorted derisively. "Jess Ley."

"I'm Jess Ley," she corrected him. "I wrote the story."

He sucked in a breath as if she'd struck him. He hadn't known. "But if your father hadn't printed it and broadcast it everywhere…"

His son might still be alive.

"That was my fault," she said.

She alone had caused this man's pain—as she was about to cause Brendan's. Because this man must have originally planned to take her from her father in his quest for an eye for an eye. Now he would also take her son from her.

Chapter Eighteen

"I think you should have gone with them to the hospital," his mother chastised Brendan.

While other agents slapped him on the back to express their approval, his mother leaned against her minivan with her arms crossed. Her brown eyes, which were usually so warm and crinkled at the corners with a smile, were dark and narrowed with disapproval.

"I have to talk to Margaret," he said.

"Why?" she asked with a glance at the car in which her husband's killer sat. "She confessed, right?"

"To killing my father," Brendan said.

"Isn't that all you need?" she asked. "It's not like there's any mystery as to why."

He shook his head. "No, she explained that, too. Dad was going to divorce her and leave her with nothing. She wanted it all. That must be why she wanted to hurt Josie and my son, why she wanted to kill them, too—to make sure there were no more O'Hannigans."

"Your father's damn codicil," she remarked.

He grinned as his mother and stepmother glared at each other through the back window of the police car. "She didn't know about you."

His mother shrugged. "Doesn't matter. I'm not an O'Hannigan anymore."

No. She'd dropped her married name when the marshals had moved her. To the runaways she'd fostered, she'd been just Roma. Perhaps they'd all known the Jones surname was an alias.

"She thought you were dead," Brendan remarked as he opened the back door to the police car.

"What the hell is it with you people?" Margaret asked. "Is anyone really dead?" She turned her glare on Brendan. "First you come back from the dead and show up to claim what was mine. And then your nosy girlfriend comes back from the dead with a kid. And now her..." She curled her thin lips in disgust.

He'd been so scared that Josie had been alone with a suspected killer that he hadn't been paying much attention to the conversation coming through the mike. But now he remembered Margaret's surprise that Josie wasn't dead. He'd thought it was because she'd incorrectly assumed Josie had been killed with him from the bomb set at his house, but he realized now that she'd never admitted to planting it.

But why? When she had confessed to murder, why would she bother denying attempted murder?

"You didn't know Josie was alive?" he asked.

She shrugged. "I didn't care whether she was or not until she showed up here with pictures of your damn kid in her purse and all those damn questions of hers. How could you have not realized she was a reporter?"

Especially given who her father was. Brendan had been a fool to not realize it. But then he hadn't been thinking clearly. He never did around her.

He had just let Josie walk off with their son before

he'd confirmed that she was safe. Hell, he'd told her she was—that Margaret wouldn't be a threat anymore. But had Margaret ever been the threat to Josie?

"You didn't know Josie was in witness relocation?"

"I didn't know that anybody was in witness relocation," the woman replied. A calculating look came over her face. "But perhaps I should talk to the marshals, let them know what I know about your father's business and his associates."

Despite foreboding clutching his stomach muscles into tight knots, he managed a short chuckle. "I gave them everything there was to know." Along with the men who'd disappeared—either into prisons or the program.

"You have nothing to offer anyone anymore, Margaret," he said as he slammed the door. Then he pounded on the roof, giving the go-ahead for the driver to pull away and take her to jail. He couldn't hear her as the car drove off, but he could read her lips and realized she was cursing him.

But he was already cursing himself. "Where did Josie go?" he asked his mother.

"To see her father," she said, as if he were being stupid again. "You and I should have gone along. I could have talked to her father and prepared him for seeing his daughter again after he spent the past four years believing she was dead."

"Yeah, because you prepared *me* so well," he said. He nearly hadn't gone to the address his father had given him. But after he'd gotten off the bus, he'd been scared and hungry and cold. So he'd gone to the house and knocked on the door. And when she'd opened it, he'd passed out. Later he'd blamed the hunger and the cold, but it was probably because he'd thought he'd seen a ghost.

It had taken him years to live down the razzing from Roma's other runaways.

"You're right," he said. "I should have gone with her."

"Do you know which hospital?"

He nodded. He knew the hospital well. He just didn't know how she'd gotten there. "What vehicle did she take?"

Roma shook her head. "She got a ride in a black SUV."

"With whom?"

"A marshal, I think. The guy had his badge on a chain around his neck." That was how the men who'd taken her into the program had worn theirs, or so she'd told him when she'd explained how she had disappeared. "He offered to drive her and CJ to see her father."

How had the man known that her father was in the hospital? And why had a marshal walked into the middle of an FBI investigation? The two agencies worked together, but usually not willingly and not without withholding more information than they shared.

Brendan had become an FBI agent instead of a marshal because he'd resented the marshals for not letting his mother take him along—for making him mourn her for years, as he'd mourned Josie.

He had a bad feeling that he might be mourning her again. And CJ, too, if he didn't find her. Charlotte wouldn't have sent another marshal; she had trusted Brendan to keep Josie and their son safe.

And he had a horrible feeling, as his heart ached with the force of its frantic pounding, that he had failed.

"Why—why did you bring us here?" Josie asked as she rode up in the hospital elevator with her son and a madman.

Before Donald Peterson could reply, CJ answered, "We came to see Grampa." He'd even pushed the button to the sixth floor. "We shoulda brought Gramma."

No. Brendan was already going to lose one person he loved—if Josie didn't think of something to at least save their son. She didn't want him to lose his mother, too.

She looked up at their captor. "We should have left him with his grandmother," she said. "And his father. He isn't part of this."

"He's your son," Peterson said. "Your father's grandson. He's very much a part of this."

She shook her head. "He's a three-year-old child. He has nothing to do with any of this."

The elevator lurched to a halt on the sixth floor, nearly making her stomach lurch, too, with nerves and fear. With a gun shoved in the middle of her back, the U.S. marshal pushed her out the open doors. She held tight to CJ's hand.

He kept digging the gun deeper, pushing her down the hall toward her father's room. A man waited outside. He was dressed like an orderly, as he'd been dressed the night he'd held Brendan back from getting on the elevator with her and CJ. She'd been grateful for his intervention then.

He wasn't going to intervene tonight—just as his partners in crime had refused to be swayed from the U.S. marshal's nefarious plan. But still she had to try. "Please," she said, "you don't want to be part of this."

"He's already part of it," Peterson replied. "Even

before he set the bomb, he was already wanted for other crimes."

She understood now. "You tracked them down on their outstanding warrants but you worked out a deal for not bringing them in."

Peterson chuckled. "You can't stop asking questions, can't stop trying to ferret out all the information you can."

She shuddered, remembering that Brendan had accused her of the same thing. No wonder he hadn't been able to trust her.

"But you and your father won't be able to broadcast this story," he said.

"You're not going to get away," she warned him.

"I know. But it's better this way—better to see his face and yours than have someone else take the pleasure for me." He pushed the barrel deeper into her back and ordered, "Open the door."

"I—I think someone should warn him first," she said. "Let him know that I'm alive so that he doesn't have another heart attack."

"It was unfortunate that he had the first one," Peterson agreed. "He was only supposed to be hurt, not killed." He glanced at the orderly as he said that, as if the man had not followed orders. "But the doctors have put him on medication to regulate his heart. He's probably stronger now than he was when he thought you died four years ago. That didn't kill him."

His mouth tightened. "It would be easier to die," he said, "than to lose a child and have to live."

He wasn't worried about getting away anymore, because he had obviously decided to end his life, too.

"I'm sorry," she murmured.

"Not yet," he replied, "but you will be." He pushed her through the door to her father's room.

"Stop shoving my mommy!" CJ yelled at him. "You're a bad man!"

"What—what's going on?" asked the gray-haired man in the room. He was sitting up as if he'd been about to get out of bed. He was bruised, but he wasn't broken. "Who are you all? Are you in the right room?"

"Yes," CJ replied. "This is my grampa's room number. Are you my grampa?"

Stanley Jessup looked at his grandson through narrowed eyes. Then he lifted his gaze and looked at Josie. At first he didn't recognize her; his brow furrowed as if he tried to place her, though.

"You don't know your own daughter?" the U.S. marshal berated him. "I would know my son anywhere. No matter what he may have done to his face, I would recognize his soul. That's how I knew he couldn't have done the things that article and those news reports said." He raised the gun and pointed it at Josie's head. "The things—the lies—your friend told you, claiming that my Donny had tried to hurt her."

"Donald Peterson," her father murmured. He recognized her attempted killer but not his own daughter.

"Your son told me, too," Josie said. "He had once been my friend, too."

"Until you betrayed him."

"Until he tried to rape my roommate," she said. If not for her coming to her father with the article, he might have gotten away with it—just as he'd gotten away with his drug use—but the athletic director hadn't wanted to lose their star player from the football team. So they'd tried paying off the girl. When she'd refused money, they'd expelled her and labeled her crazy.

So just as she had done with Margaret O'Hannigan today, Josie had gotten Donny Peterson to confess.

"Josie…" Her father whispered her name, as if unable to believe it. Then he looked down at the little boy, who stared up at him in puzzlement.

Poor CJ had been through so much the past few days. He'd met so many people and had been in so much danger, he had to be thoroughly confused and exhausted. He whispered, too, to his grandfather, "He's a bad man, Grampa."

"Your mama and grandpa are the bad ones," Donald Peterson insisted. "My Donny was a star, and they couldn't handle it. They had to bring him down, had to destroy him."

After the confession and the subsequent charges, Donny Peterson had killed himself, shortly before the trial was to begin, shortly before Josie's brakes were cut. Why hadn't she considered that those attempts might have been because of Donny? Why had she automatically thought the worst of Brendan? Maybe because she'd already been feeling guilty and hadn't wanted to admit to how much to blame she'd been.

"And that is why I'm going to destroy them," Donald continued.

"You're a bad man," CJ said again, and he kicked the man in the shin.

Josie tried to grab her son before the man could strike back. But he was already swinging and his hand struck Josie's cheek, sending her stumbling back onto her father's bed. Stanley Jessup caught her shoulders and then pulled her and his grandson close, as if his arms alone could protect them.

CJ wriggled in their grasp as he tried to break free to fight some more. "My daddy told me to p'tect you," he reminded Josie. "I have to p'tect my mommy until my daddy gets here."

Donald Peterson shook his head. "Your daddy's not coming, son."

"My daddy's a hero," CJ said. "He'll be here. He always saves us."

"It is a daddy's job to protect his kids," Donald agreed, his voice cracking with emotion. "But your daddy's busy arresting some bad people."

"You're bad."

"And he's too far away to get here to help you."

Tears began to streak down CJ's face, and his shoulders shook as fear overcame him. He'd been so brave for her—so brave for his father. But now he was scared.

And Josie could offer him no words of comfort. As Donald Peterson had stated, there was no way that Brendan could reach them in time to save them.

They had to figure out a way to save themselves. Her father shifted on his bed and pressed something cold and metallic against Josie's hip. A gun. Had he had it under his pillow?

After the assault, she couldn't blame him for wanting to be prepared if his attacker tried again. But Donald's gun barrel was trained on CJ. And she knew—to make her father and her feel the loss he felt—he would shoot her son first. Could she grab the gun, aim and fire before he killed her little boy?

THE CAMERAS HAD still been running inside the van, and they'd caught the plate on the black SUV that had driven off with Brendan's son and the woman he loved. The vehicle had a GPS that had led them right to its location in the parking garage of the hospital.

When they'd arrived, Brendan hadn't gone down to

check it out. He already knew where they were. So he ducked under the whirling FBI helicopter blades and ran across the roof where just a few nights ago he'd nearly been shot. Once he was inside the elevator, he pushed the button for the sixth floor.

It seemed to take forever to get where he needed to be.

His mom was right. He should have taken Josie here. He never should have let her and CJ out of his sight. And if he wasn't already too late, he never would.

Finally the elevator stopped and the doors slowly opened. He had barely stepped from the car when a shot or two rang out. He fired back. And his aim was better.

The pseudo-orderly dropped to the floor, clutching his bleeding arm. His gun dropped, too. Brendan kicked it aside as he hurried past the man. The orderly wasn't the one who'd driven off with his family. He wasn't the one with the grudge against Josie.

That man was already inside and he had nothing to lose. Running the plate had tied it to the marshal to whom the vehicle had been assigned, and a simple Google search on the helicopter ride had revealed the rest of Donald Peterson's tragic story. There was no point in calling out, no point in trying to negotiate with him. The only thing he wanted was Josie dead—as dead as his son.

So Brendan kicked open the door, sending it flying back against the wall. He had his gun raised, ready to fire, but his finger froze on the trigger.

The man holding a gun was not the marshal but the patient. The marshal lay on the floor, blood pooling beneath his shoulder. His eyes were closed, tears trickling from their corners. But his pain wasn't physical.

It was a pain Brendan had nearly felt himself. Of loss and helplessness…

"See, I knew my daddy would make it," CJ said, his voice high with excitement and a trace of hysteria. "I knew he would save us."

Brendan glanced down at the floor again, checking for the man's weapon. But Josie held it. He looked back at his son. "Doesn't look like you needed saving at all. Your mommy and grandpa had it all under control."

Stanley Jessup shook his head. "If you hadn't distracted him with the shooting outside the door, I never would have been able to…" He shuddered. While the man was a damn good marksman, he wasn't comfortable with having shot a person.

"Are you okay, Daddy?" Josie asked.

He grabbed her, pulling her into his arms. "I am now. A couple of nights ago I heard a scream and then a female voice, and I recognized it. But I didn't dare hope. I thought it was the painkillers. I couldn't let myself believe. Couldn't let myself hope… You're alive…"

"I'm so sorry!" she exclaimed, her body shaking with sobs. "I'm so sorry."

It was a poignant moment, but one that was short-lived as police officers and hospital security burst into the room. It was nearly an hour later before the men had been arrested and the explanations made.

Finally Stanley Jessup could have a moment alone with his daughter and grandson, so Brendan stepped outside and pulled the door closed behind him. He walked over to his mother, who had insisted on coming along in the helicopter with him and the other agents.

"I'm going to get some coffee and food," Roma said. "I'm sure my grandson is hungry. He's had a long day." She rose on tiptoe and pressed a kiss to Brendan's cheek. "So has my son."

"It's not over yet," he said.

Her brow furrowed slightly. "Isn't it all over? All the bad people arrested?"

"There's still something I need to do," Brendan said. For him it wasn't all over. It was just beginning.

She nodded as if she understood. She probably did; his mother had always known what was in his heart.

Josie didn't, but he intended to tell her.

After patting his cheek with her palm, his mother headed down the hall and disappeared into the elevator, leaving him alone. He had spent so much of his life alone—those years before he'd joined his mother in witness protection. Then all the years he'd gone undercover—deep undercover—for the Bureau. He'd been young when he'd started working for the FBI, since his last name had given him an easy entrance to any criminal organization the Bureau had wanted to investigate. And take down.

He had taken down several of the most violent gangs and dangerous alliances. But none of them had realized he was the one responsible.

If the truth about him came out now, his family could be in danger of retaliation—revenge like that the marshal had wanted against the Jessups because of the loss of his son.

Pain clutched Brendan's heart as he thought of how close he had come to losing his son. CJ had told him how he'd tried to "p'tect" his mommy as he'd promised. The brave little three-year-old had kicked the man with the gun.

He shuddered at what could have happened had Josie

obviously not taken the blow meant for their boy. She'd had a fresh mark on her face.

As she stepped out of her father's room and joined him in the hall, he studied her face. The red mark was already darkening. He found himself reaching up and touching her cheek as he murmured, "I should have kicked him, too."

She flinched. "I used to worry that CJ was too timid," she said, "but now I worry that he might be too brave."

"Are you surprised?" he asked. "You've always been fearless."

"Careless," she corrected him. "I didn't care about the consequences. I didn't realize what could happen to me."

He'd thought that was because she'd been spoiled, that she'd been her father's princess and believed he would never let anything happen to her. Now Brendan realized that she'd cared more about others than herself.

"You're the brave one," she said. "You've put yourself in danger to protect others. To protect me. Thank you."

He shook his head. He didn't want her gratitude. He wanted her love.

"I thought you might have left with the others," she said, glancing around the empty hall. "With your mom…"

"She's still here," he said. "She's getting food and coming back up." The woman had made a life of feeding hungry kids—food and love.

"I'm glad she's coming back," she said. "CJ has been asking about her. He wants his grampa to meet his gramma. I think he thinks they should be married like other kids' grandparents are."

A millionaire and a mobster's widow? Brendan chuckled.

"I'm really glad that you're still here," she said.

His heart warmed, filling with hope. Did she have the same feelings he had?

"I owe you an apology," Josie said. "It was all my fault—all of it. And my mistakes cost you three years with your son." Her voice cracked. "And I am so sorry...."

He closed his arms around her and pulled her against his chest—against his heart. She trembled, probably with exhaustion and shock. She had been through so much. She clutched at his back and laid her head on his shoulder.

"My father knew who you were," she remarked. "What you were. From his sources within the FBI, he knew you were an agent. If I'd told him what story I was working on when the attempts started on my life, he would have told me to drop it—that there was no way you could be responsible. I should have known...."

"He knew?" Brendan had really underestimated the media mogul in resources and respect. He could be trusted with the truth, so Brendan should have trusted his daughter, too.

"He's a powerful man with a lot of connections," she said, "but still he didn't know that I wasn't dead. I hate that I did that to him. I hate what I did to you. I understand why you can't trust me."

"Josie..."

She leaned back and pressed her fingers over his lips. "It's okay," she said. "I understand now that sometimes it's better to leave secrets secret. There will be no stories about you or your mother in any Jessup publications or broadcasts. And there will never be another story by me."

"Never?"

Tears glistened in her smoky-green eyes, and she shook her head. "I should have never…"

"Revealed the truth?" he asked.

"Look what the consequences were," she reminded him with a shudder.

"Yes," he agreed, and finally he looked at the full picture, at what she'd really done. "You got justice for your friend—the girl that kid assaulted. If you hadn't written that article, it never would have happened. And I know from experience that it's damn hard to move on if you never get justice."

"That's why you went after all those crime organizations," she said, "to get justice for what your dad did to your mom."

"She gave up her justice for me," he said.

"So you got it for her and for so many others."

He shook his head. "No, Margaret got it for her. Go figure. But *you* helped your friend when no one else would. You can't blame yourself for what the boy did. And neither should his father."

"He needs someone to blame," she said.

Just as the people in her new town had blamed her for her student's death. Someone always needed someone else to blame.

"And so did I," she added. "I shouldn't have blamed you."

"You shouldn't have," he agreed. "Because I would have never hurt you, then or now." He dragged in a deep breath to say what he'd waited around to tell her, what he'd waited four years to tell her. "Because I love you, Josie."

"You love me?" She asked the question as if it had never occurred to her, as if she had never dared to hope. Until now. Her eyes widened with hope and revealed her own feelings.

"Yes," he said, "I love your passion and your intelligence and—"

She stretched up his body and pressed a kiss to his lips. "I didn't think you'd ever be able to trust me, much less love me."

"I don't just love you," he said. "I want to spend my life with you and CJ. No more undercover. I'll find a safer way to get justice for others, like maybe helping you with stories."

She smiled. "That might be more dangerous than your old job."

"We'll keep each other safe," he promised. "Will you become my wife?"

"It will thrill CJ if his parents are together, if every day is like that day at my house," she said.

That had been such a good day—a day Brendan had never wanted to end. His heart beat fast with hope. She was going to say yes....

"But as much as I love our son, I won't marry you for his sake," she said. "And you wouldn't want me to."

He wasn't so sure about that. But before he could argue with her, she was speaking again.

"I will marry you," she assured him, "because I love you with all my heart. Because even when I was stupid enough to think you were a bad man, I couldn't stop loving you. And I never will."

"Never," he agreed. And he covered her mouth with his, sealing their engagement with a kiss since he had yet to buy a ring. But it was no simple kiss. With them, it never was. Passion ignited and the kiss deepened.

If not for the dinging of the elevator, they might have forgotten where they were. His mother stepped through the open doors, her eyes glinting with amusement as if she'd caught him making out on the porch swing.

"We're getting married, Mom," he said.

"Of course," she said, as if there had never been any question in her mind. "Now, open the door for me." She juggled a tray of plates and coffee cups and a sippy cup.

He opened the door to his son, who threw his arms around Brendan's legs. "Daddy! Daddy, you're still here."

"I'm never leaving," he promised his son.

"Gramma!" the little boy exclaimed, and he pulled away from Brendan to follow her to his grandfather's bedside.

With a happy sigh, Josie warned him, "We're never going to have a moment alone."

"Our honeymoon," he said. "We'll spend our honeymoon alone."

Epilogue

"We're alone," Brendan said as he carried Josie over the threshold of their private suite.

Since his arms were full with her and her overflowing gown, she swung the door closed behind them. It shut with a click, locking them in together. "Yes, we're finally alone.…"

And she didn't want to waste a minute of their wedding night, so she wriggled in his arms, the way their independent son did because he thought himself too big to be carried. As she slid down Brendan's body, he groaned as if in pain.

"Was I too heavy?" she asked.

He shook his head. "No, you're perfect—absolutely perfect." He lifted his fingers to her hair, which was piled in red ringlets atop her head. "You looked like a princess coming down the aisle of the ballroom."

"Well, technically…" She was. It had made her an anomaly growing up, so she'd often downplayed her mother's royal heritage. When she'd married Stanley Jessup, her mother had given up her title anyway. But here it was no big deal. Josie was only one of three princesses in the palace on St. Pierre Island. Four, actually, counting Charlotte Green-Timmer's new daughter.

Charlotte and Aaron had married shortly before their daughter's premature birth.

There was a prince, too—Gabriella and Whit Howell's baby boy. The princess had fallen in love with and married her father's other royal bodyguard. There were so many babies…

So much love. But she'd felt the most coming from her husband as he'd waited for her father to lead her down the aisle to him. In his tuxedo, the same midnight-black as his hair, he looked every bit the prince. Or a king.

And standing at his side, in a miniature replica of his father's tuxedo, had stood their son—both ring bearer, with the satin pillow in his hand, and best little man.

"It was the most perfect day," she said. A day she had thought would never come—not four years ago when she'd had to die, all those times she nearly had died, and during the three months it had taken to plan the wedding.

"As hard as you and my mom worked on it," he said, "it was guaranteed to be perfect."

She blinked back tears at the fun she'd had planning the wedding with Roma. "Your mother is amazing."

"She's your mother, too, now," he reminded her.

And the tears trickled out. "I feel that way." That she truly had a mother now. "And my dad loves you like a son." He couldn't have been prouder than to have his daughter marry a hero like FBI Agent Brendan O'Hannigan.

"I'm glad," Brendan said. "But right now I don't want to talk about your dad or my mom." He stepped closer to her, as if closing in on a suspect. "I don't want to talk at all."

Her tears quickly dried as she smiled in anticipation. "Oh, what would you rather do?"

"Get you the hell out of this dress," he said as he stared down at the yards of white lace and satin.

With its sweetheart neckline, long sleeves and flowing train, it was a gown fit for a princess—or so his mother had convinced her. Josie was glad, though, because she had wanted something special for this special day. A gown that she could one day pass down to a daughter.

"Your mom told the seamstress to put in a zipper," she told him. "She said her son was too impatient for buttons."

He grinned and reached for the tab. The zipper gave a metallic sigh as he released it, and the weight of the fabric pulled down the gown. She stood before her husband in nothing but a white lace bra and panties.

"You're the one wearing too many clothes now," she complained and reached for his bow tie.

He shrugged off his jacket, and for once he wore no holsters beneath it. He carried no guns. When their honeymoon was over, he would, but as a supervising agent, he wouldn't often have occasion to use them. He wasn't going undercover anymore—except with her.

She pulled back the blankets on the bed as he quickly discarded the rest of his clothes. "In a hurry?" she teased.

"I don't know how much time we'll have before CJ shows up," he admitted.

"His grandparents promised to keep him busy for the next couple of days," she reminded him. "And he's more fascinated with the royal babies right now than he is with us."

Brendan grinned and reached for her.

"He wants one, you know," Josie warned.

Brendan kissed her softly, tenderly, and admitted in a whisper, "So do I."

She regretted all that her unfounded suspicions had cost him—seeing her pregnant, feeling their son kick, seeing him born, holding him as a sweet-smelling infant...

But she would make it up to him with more babies—and with all her love. She tugged her naked husband down onto the bed with her. "Then we better get busy..."

Building their family and their lives together.

* * * * *

A sneaky peek at next month...

INTRIGUE...

BREATHTAKING ROMANTIC SUSPENSE

My wish list for next month's titles...

In stores from 21st June 2013:

❑ Carrie's Protector — Rebecca York

& For the Baby's Sake — Beverly Long

❑ Outlaw Lawman — Delores Fossen

& The Smoky Mountain Mist — Paula Graves

❑ Triggered — Elle James

& Fearless — HelenKay Dimon

Romantic Suspense

❑ The Colton Ransom — Marie Ferrarella

Available at WHSmith, Tesco, Asda, Eason, Amazon and Apple

Just can't wait?

Join the Mills & Boon Book Club

Want to read more **Intrigue** books?
We're offering you **2 more** absolutely **FREE!**

We'll also treat you to these fabulous extras:

- Exclusive offers and much more!

- FREE home delivery

- FREE books and gifts with our special rewards scheme

Get your free books now!

**visit www.millsandboon.co.uk/bookclub
or call Customer Relations on 020 8288 2888**